Sign up for our newsletter to hear
about new and upcoming releases.

www.ylva-publishing.com

OTHER BOOKS BY SHAYLYNN ROSE

The Tales of Y'Myran

Banshee's Honor
(Book One)

Banshee's Vengeance
(Book Two)

BANSHEE'S VENGEANCE

SHAYLYNN ROSE

DEDICATION

To all the writers whose worlds inspired me to dream of my own lands—thank you.

For Cie. I miss you, my friend.

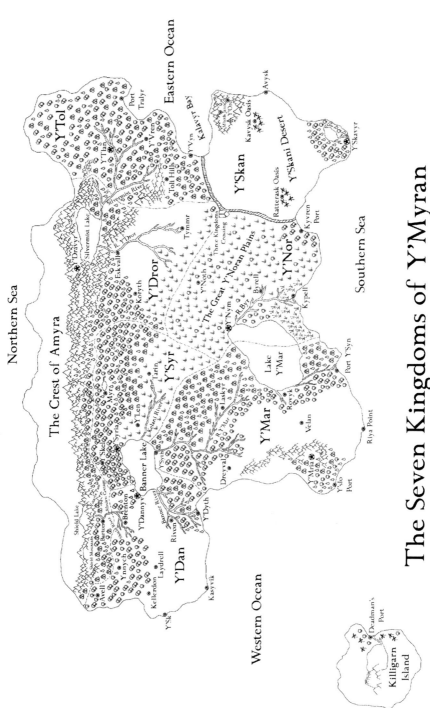

CHAPTER ONE

Stardancer Kyrian cursed and slid off her saddle.

"Trouble?" Azhani called as she turned to glance back.

"He's taken a stone in his shoe. Again."

Dismounting, Azhani quickly joined her. "Padreg did warn you he'd need new ones soon."

"Aye, I know. But where was I to find a blacksmith in the middle of the Y'Syran plain?" Kyrian coaxed Arun to lift his leg so she could pop the culprit—a pebble the size of a child's thumb—out from between the shoe and the horse's hoof.

"Well, we're not far from Y'Syria, though night is falling." Azhani patted Arun's flank soothingly. "Why don't we find a place to camp? You can poultice that hoof, and in the morning, we'll walk the rest of the way."

"You can accept the delay?"

Azhani shrugged. "I'm not so eager to meet my fate that I'll murder a good horse just to race to the hangman's noose."

"That is not funny, Azhani. Not even a little!" Kyrian straightened and glared at her. "You are not going to die!"

"So you say, but we both know Queen Lyssera isn't going to welcome her sister's murderer with open arms—even if I am innocent of the crime. She wouldn't know that."

"That's why we're going to tell her," Kyrian said acerbically. "And why you should have asked Padreg and Elisira to come with us. Twain's grace, Azhani, Elisira lived in Ydannoch! If anyone had any inkling of the truth, she did!"

Azhani sighed heavily. "Aye, she did. Padreg said she was…that she likely witnessed something, but I couldn't ask her to speak for me, not when doing so might tar her from the same pot of guilt that has already been poured upon me. No. If Lyssera wants me to hang, then so be it. She will either hear me because she is willing to grant me the honor of speaking for myself, or she will not. There is no other way."

"You are so damned stubborn!" Kyrian said in frustration. "I swear, if you let them kill you, I will *find* a way to save you, you silly warrior!" Taking Arun's reins, she pointed to an area off the side of the road. "There's a clearing over this way. I saw it earlier. Be useful—go find some wood for a fire."

It was an uncomfortably quiet camp. Azhani stared morosely into her bowl of stew and tried not to drown in guilt. Ever since parting from Padreg and Elisira, she and Kyrian had spent almost every night of their journey to Y'Syria arguing about what she was planning to do. *Oh Ylera, I wish you were here. You'd know how to fix this, how to help me make her understand why I must do this alone.*

She desperately wanted to say something to break this box of angry quiet and bring back the laughter and joy they shared in winter, but it seemed a near-impossible task. After scraping the last of the stew from her bowl, she stood and walked to a nearby stream to rinse it. The water was snow-melt and painfully cold, but she plunged her hands into it, accepting the ache as penance.

Moonlight made the water glitter, but something shone even brighter under the rippling current. Curious, she grabbed for it and came back with a strange, battered old coin. Octagonal, gold, and smaller than her thumbnail, it bore an unfamiliar device on one side and a sigil she did not recognize on the other. For a long while, she stood there studying it, trying to puzzle out its origin. Unable to do so, she returned to the fireside and thrust it at Kyrian. "Ever seen one of these?"

Kyrian looked up from mending her velvet robes. Putting aside the fabric, she took the coin and considered it with a frown. "No...but I know it. This is Alyrran. These coins are very, very rare," she said. "Y—A friend once told me that Queen Lyssera has a small collection of them."

"Alyrran?" Azhani replied as she settled on her log seat.

"An ancient, powerful people. They're long gone now, but before the Firstlanders—humans—came to this land, they were the ones who ruled it. I don't know much; the records of their lives and deeds are few. You might learn more in Y'Skan, for it is said their magicks are what destroyed the land in that kingdom."

"I've heard a little about them, but was never interested enough to pursue further knowledge," Azhani said with a casual shrug. "It's enough that you recognized the coin. Keep it. Maybe it'll bring some luck."

"Then you should have it," Kyrian said softly. "For you are the one who needs it."

"I don't need luck," she replied. "I have you."

Grimacing, Kyrian shook her head. "Damn it, Azhi! How can I stay mad at you when you say things like that?"

She chuckled. "I would hope you wouldn't, especially since I am glad you are here, my friend."

"Oh, Azhi," Kyrian murmured as she moved to sit beside her and rested her head on Azhani's shoulder. "I don't want us to be fighting."

"Neither do I, but I must do what I must, and I know it bothers you."

"It does, but you are right—you have made your choice. All I can do is support you."

"Thank you."

A new silence wrapped around them then, but this time, it was calm, warm, and full of promise. Azhani only hoped that it would not revert when Kyrian learned of her true plans, for there were things that had to be done, paths that only she could walk.

But I swear I will not forget you are behind me, my friend. I only hope you will wait for me to find you when I have need.

Y'Syria rose before them, climbing out of the horizon and spreading its branches until all that was visible was the tree-dwellings of Kyrian's ancestors. Even though they were still most of a day's travel away, she could see where ground-bound homes hugged the great oak and aspen trunks while above, bridges of rope and vine linked one great tree to another.

"Twain's grace," she whispered, clutching Arun's reins and gaping in shock. "It seems so massive."

"Have you not been to the city?" Azhani seemed surprised.

Kyrian smiled. "Infrequently. I've traveled, but mostly in Y'Dan. Once to Y'Dror and once to Y'Mar, but rarely have I visited Queen Lyssera's court."

"It is a beautiful sight, I suppose. Ylera spoke often of how dear it was to her. I guess… I guess it just hurts to look at it too closely. We might have lived here, once my service to Y'Dan ended." The depth of sadness in Azhani's voice made Kyrian want to grab her and drag her off into the forest where they would never again look upon anything that could cause her such pain.

If Ylera had actually married you. Though she knew Ylera had been a good person, Kyrian found it hard to believe she could divorce herself from the bigotry of her elven peers. *I believe that she loved you, but she was a creature of her court, and the elves of Y'Syr don't take kindly to Y'Dani interlopers.* Even Kyrian had suffered the snide remarks and ugly scowls of her companions growing up, though her human parent was not known to be Y'Dani. Just the implication of such was enough to tarnish her in the eyes of some.

Still, it did no good to say these things to Azhani. Instead, she touched her arm and said, "Tell me about it. The city, I mean. You must have many stories."

Azhani gave her an odd look, then laughed briefly. "You are so fond of stories, and yet you rarely tell your own. Why is that?"

"Because yours are far more interesting, of course," she said with a winsome smile. "Unless you think learning how to set a broken bone or which herbs to mix to fight a pregnant woman's nausea are as fascinating as tales of intrigue and heroism?"

"Well, they're certainly more useful than hearing about skulking in shadows and shoving three feet of steel into someone's belly for looking at you cross-eyed!"

"Something I'm sure you've never done." Kyrian began walking toward the city. "You're too damned honorable to kill someone for spite."

"You'd think so," Azhani said. "But you've never met his honor, the great and mighty Lord Flagan Vildefleur."

"Who in Twain's name is that?"

"Was," Azhani replied dryly. "Most definitely was."

"Oh, now you must tell me!" Kyrian elbowed Azhani eagerly. "Please?"

Azhani made a face, but merriment sparkled in her eyes. "Very well. It was…oh, about ten years back. My father and I were in Y'Syria on Thodan's business, and I was frequenting a rather seedy little dive on the waterfront. I'd gone there to search for some information that would tell us which of the elven lords was sneaking across the border to break into the homes of the wealthy and steal their valuables. You see, one of the bastards was not only thieving but raping the servants of the households."

Kyrian gasped in shock. "Goddess! But why?"

Azhani shook her head. "Why do Y'Danis and Y'Syrans ever fight like cats and dogs? It was a habit, a terrible, ugly habit, and the humans weren't guiltless, for there was plenty of trouble on the Y'Dani side of the border, as well. Cattle rustling, for one—and more than a few elves found themselves waking up in Y'Skan on the wrong side of a slaver's whip."

"How did peace ever happen with all that stacked against it?" Kyrian whispered sadly. Ylera was a fine, fine speaker, but even she would be hard-pressed to soothe the frayed tempers of families who'd lost loved ones to such tragedy.

"Patience, a lot of gold, and Thodan's sheer force of will. And the work Father and I did finding the perpetrators and bringing them to justice." There was fierce pride in Azhani's words. "Lord Flagan was one of them. Young, stupid, and full of his own self-importance."

"I know the Vildefleur name—they're perfumers, right? Elisira has a bottle with that name on it." Smiling, Kyrian closed her eyes at the memory of the sweet, light fragrance.

"Aye, but Flagan was a younger son of a younger son—and no heir to the fortunes of his better relatives. So he, along with others who shared his idleness, worked up the brilliant plan to raid Y'Dan to fill their pockets. As long as the two kingdoms were content to cordially loathe each other, he could get away with it." Azhani stopped to kick several stones from their path. "But once the idea of peace started spreading, his activities needed to be stopped. Or rather," she added, giving Kyrian a nasty smile, "I needed to find out who he was, first, then stop him. Permanently."

"And did you?"

"Yes. We fought a duel. He lost."

"That simple?"

"No," she said, shaking her head. "It's never that simple."

"Then tell me."

"Are you sure? It's ugly."

"It's important."

"All right."

They started walking again, and slowly, Azhani told her tale. "I paid a lot of good gold to get his name. When I found him, he was drunk, half naked, and making free with one of the pot boys out behind the Blue Dove. I didn't give him much chance to spin pretty lies. The pot boy ran off as I drew my blade."

Kyrian found herself filled with rage. Though Azhani had used gentle words, she knew what was being implied. "He was…was…with a child!"

"Aye. It was the last time," Azhani said darkly. "We dueled—or rather, I ran him through while telling him I was challenging him to a duel. No one bothered to report my haste."

"Goddess," she said softly. "Did the attacks stop?"

"Immediately. I left Flagan's head sitting on the doorstep of another of the other culprit's houses."

"I can't believe you'd do something like that!"

"I did. My king ordered it of me." Azhani looked out across Banner Lake. "Those girls and boys, they were broken by what he did to them. They needed vengeance. I gave it to them."

Kyrian swallowed heavily. "You… I can't say you did the right thing, but you did the *just* thing, and that, in this case, was right."

Azhani looked at her. "Now perhaps you can see why I do what I must. What is right and what is just aren't always the same, but justice is closer to honor in Astariu's eyes."

Kyrian could not argue that, not with a woman who had taken the mark of the goddess' warrior. "What happened to the boy?" she asked then, hoping something good had come of that night.

Now Azhani smiled. "Eskyn grew up. Got strong—put on a lot of muscle working on the docks. Last I heard, he was making extra coin as a wrestler at the Blue Dove. He's given me a lot of good tips over the years."

"I hope you'll introduce me," Kyrian said as they started down the road that would lead them to the city gates long before the sun set.

"If you'd like."

"I would. Will I meet anyone else you know?"

"Of course…so long as they don't throw us to the guard the moment they see us."

Kyrian grimaced. "Is that something I should worry about?"

Solemnly, Azhani replied, "Probably, but we'll cross that bridge if we must. For now, just pray to the Twain my old friend Tellyn Jarelle still likes me enough to give us shelter."

"Old friend? Is this going to be another story?"

Azhani laughed. "Maybe for another time. How about we find a place to sit and enjoy a bit of cold stew, hm? It might be the last meal we get for a while."

CHAPTER TWO

Leaning forward, Arris glared down at a grubby, cowering lad who was panting heavily and clutching a mud-and-snow caked cap. "You're certain of this, boy?" he demanded.

Winter's grip still choked the lowlands of Y'Dan, and the messenger had run himself near to death. Quavering before the Granite Throne, he stammered, "Y-yes, Your M-majesty. The mayor of Ynnych hisself gimme th'message. R-rimerbeasts hunt!"

At the boy's fearful outburst, the court gallery erupted in a cloud of panicked gasps.

"What?"

"That's impossible!"

Seizing the opportunity presented, Porthyros leaned close to the throne and whispered, "And here, my liege, would be yet one more example of the treachery of Azhani Rhu'len. For did she not lead the last battle against our ancient foes? Did your beloved and esteemed father not command her to 'rid the lands of the beasts for the season'?"

Jerking as if prodded in the privates by a very sharp implement, Arris shot to his feet. "Here, people of Y'Dan! Here is more proof of the incompetence of that most despicable of women, the harridan and whore herself, Azhani Rhu'len!" He paced, nearly foaming at the mouth as he spat, "I know some of you felt my actions harsh, but now, can you not see the wisdom of your wise and beneficent king?"

There was no one among the gathered nobles who did not appear utterly shocked.

Voice pitched to carry to the king's ears alone, Porthyros murmured, "We must discover the truth of the messenger's words, so that Y'Dan can be protected from this horrible menace." Again, Arris jerked slightly, though no one but Porthyros noticed. *I must lower his dosage. He is growing ill. Perhaps I shall blend in a pinch or two of vortrix chitin.*

"Scouts will be sent at once to verify the boy's tale! No one in Y'Dan shall suffer for that traitorous bitch's failure!" Spinning on his heel, Arris marched out of the grand hall.

Quickly, Porthyros followed. "Ably spoken, my king!"

"Yes, I was particularly good, wasn't I?" he said, puffing out his chest in pride. "And now, it's time to send for Captain Niemeth, that he may inform me of his plans to defend my kingdom."

Porthyros bowed deeply, pleased with how these events were turning out. "Of course, my king."

Without further conversation, Arris headed for his chambers and Porthyros sought out a page. Once the boy was sent him to find the captain, Porthyros then scurried off to his rooms to look for his next set of instructions.

The note he found in its hidden cubbyhole was simple, the script plain, stating only,

"Direct the boy to a winter campaign. I will visit on the morrow."

After burning the note, he made a fresh pot of the king's tea, adding in just a pinch of the vortrix chitin and tasting it to be sure it hadn't changed the flavor. Arris, having had many years' experience with the brew, could notice the subtlest of differences. Sometimes, this was fine, as he would ascribe it to too much honey, but some additives were bitter or tart, and Arris liked neither. The vortrix, however, only sweetened the tea, so Porthryos added a touch less honey than usual and took himself to the king's chambers. There, he found him standing with Captain Niemeth in front of a table covered in maps of the kingdom.

Rubbing his chin thoughtfully, Arris tugged on his short, manicured beard and frowned as he eyed the maps. "Ah, you're here, 'Thyro. Good. The captain was just about to tell me what he knows."

"I made you some tea, Your Highness," Porthyros said quietly, offering him a cup.

Arris took it and sipped the brew, but focused his attention on Niemeth.

Clearing his throat, Niemeth straightened. "Well, we all know the traditional cycle of a beast season, my king. Once the demons are spotted, we send men into the hills to search the caves. It could be weeks before we know anything for certain."

Excitedly, Arris asked, "And if rimerbeasts be present?"

"Then I pray we shall drive them from our land, as we have always done before," Niemeth said proudly.

"Of course we will! Y'Dan is mine!" Arris snarled. "By Ecarthus, I'll see them rooted from every glen and dale, cave and hollow."

Porthyros shivered. *Perhaps we pushed too hard—if he's so determined to destroy them, he may do something we cannot control!* Still, he had his orders. Softly, he said, "My king, perhaps it would be the better part of wisdom to be sure we have the supplies to begin a winter campaign?"

After draining his cup, Arris set it aside and began to pace the chamber restlessly. "You are absolutely right, Master Porthyros. Captain, I order you to outfit my armies with the finest supplies—when it comes to war, I must have all I require to defeat the foul creatures!"

"Of course, my king. Have you any further orders?" Niemeth asked respectfully.

Porthyros studied the captain, wondering again if it had been wise to leave someone who had been vocally in support of Azhani Rhu'len in such a position of command. And yet he seemed to be quite loyal to Arris—so much so that the king was becoming very reliant upon the man for his wise counsel regarding martial matters. Thus far, Porthyros had not been commanded to change this, so he allowed Niemeth to live. *But if I must slip a dagger between his ribs or poison his nightly wine cup, I will, for the good of the plan and the gold in my purse!*

Arris grinned. "Yes. I wish you to find me a decent sword master—that last barbarian couldn't be bothered to make me into the hero I know I'm destined to be! All he wanted me to do was scrub floors and wash windows. Pfagh! I am a king, not a scullery boy!"

Bowing, Niemeth replied, "Of course, Your Majesty. I'll see to immediately."

"Thank you, Captain." As the man turned to leave, Arris smiled. "Oh, and Captain, please remind your men that my laws extend to *everyone* in my kingdom, even the relatives of my soldiers."

Porthyros nearly laughed aloud at the look on Niemeth's face. It was no secret that under Thodan's rule, the men and women who served his banner received honor and special treatment. Nor was it uncommon for their families to accrue some of that honor to themselves, using it to further their place in

Y'Dani society. Not so anymore, not when they were doing their best to purge Y'Dan of all nonhumans. Porthyros himself was unsure why Ecarthus disliked the elves, dwarves, and halfbreeds—despising morgedraal most of all, ordering that any of the desert-born people be fed to his fires on sight—but he was not about to argue the point.

"Yes, Your Majesty," Niemeth said. This time, his reply was taut and tinged with a hint of hatred, as Porthyros expected, since the captain's half-elven wife had been one of those who had fled Y'Dan, taking their children with her. Bowing once again, Niemeth quickly exited the room.

After he'd gone, Arris prowled around the table, picking up his empty teacup and absently stroking it. "I will be a part of the cave expeditions. Y'Dan must see its king doing his part to defend them from evil. My people must know that I am the one chosen to lead them to their grand destiny. They must understand that the Twain are lies constructed to hide us from the glory of Ecarthus, our one true god!" He grinned gleefully. "And how better to do that than to be the instrument of his glory myself!"

Arris' words nearly caused Porthyros to choke. Letting the boy play at being hero was one thing—actually allowing him to put himself in harm's way before they were done with him was inconceivable. Calmly, he took Arris' cup and filled it again. "What a thoroughly splendid idea, my king—for a scullery boy." After stirring a sizable portion of honey into it, he presented the drink to Arris and said, "Digging around in dirty caves is a task for a servant, not a king. A king leads armies, not spelunking expeditions. Your people need you to rule them, not clean up after them."

Eyes narrowing, Arris said, "You are right. I am their king. Thank you for reminding me. I will not have the gossiping nags of the court mocking me and telling all and sundry that I am no better than a common kitchen drudge!"

"Winter, my king." Porthyros kept his voice soft and compelling, using the same tone he had always employed when coaxing Arris to come to heel. "That will be the time of your great glory." *For by then, we won't need you, you useless, sniveling, brat—though I may keep you around to amuse myself. There are so many things I've yet to try with you.* Porthyros' feelings for Arris had always been deeply mixed. On the one hand, he felt a great affection for him, for never had anyone been able to practice the apothecary's art upon another as he had on Arris, but on the other, he loathed the boy for his simple-minded need for affection and praise. "For if the rimerbeasts truly be rising, then winter is when heroes will be called to ride forth and lead your army to blessed glory!"

"Yes! Yes, winter!" Arris eagerly drained a second cup of krile-laced tea.

"And I have the best of tidings for you, my king, for I have had word that Lord Oswyne has returned and will seek you out for yet another game of chess tomorrow."

"Has he? He will? How wonderful!" Arris replied happily. "I know I'll beat him this time!" Yawning, he rubbed his eyes. "You think he'll tell me more about Ecarthus? I do so wish to be a proper servant to Him."

Smiling, Porthyros said, "Almost certainly, Your Majesty. After all, it is by your grace and wisdom that Lord Oswyne has given Ecarthus the temple that was prophesied so very long ago."

"Ah, yes. The great temple." Arris let out a wistful sigh. "I am so pleased to attend services that do not bore me with pablum and pageantry, as the worship of that useless pair of upstarts that call themselves the Twain once did!"

Ah, but you have only seen what we want you to, my king. No sacrifice services for you yet, not until we know your bloodlust is as strong as ours. Porthyros nearly laughed aloud, but kept himself serene, saying only, "As I said, my king, your wisdom knows no bounds. I am certain that Lord Oswyne will be quite pleased to know that you have become filled with such warm feeling for his god." *Feelings which I, of course, have taught you to hold. Ah, Arris, you are my greatest creation. More my son than Thodan's, for certain! Look upon him, Ecarthus, and see how I have served you—reward me, oh yes, reward me!* The pleasure with which Porthyros eyed his future once Ecarthus was freed could only be described as orgasmic.

Coins spilled from Kasyrin's hands, filling his minion's lap. "I am beyond pleased with your efforts, Porthyros."

Standing in the prelate's office of the newly formed Temple of Ecarthus in Y'Dannyv, Kasyrin Darkchilde looked down at the other man and smiled. "Tomorrow, I will bring a most wondrous gift for our would-be hero of a king. See that it occupies as much of his time as possible, but do not tamper with it yourself, for I will not be responsible for the consequences." The enchantments he'd placed on the game board and pieces were contrived to snare Arris in a variety of spells, including those that would build upon the krile poisoning to make him even more Kasyrin's creature—and push him right toward certain doom, for soon, they would have little need for a puppet.

Once Ecarthus is free, Y'Dan—and all of Y'Myran—will tremble before us!

Bowing his head, Porthyros murmured, "Yes, Master. I will do as you command."

Kasyrin poured a few more coins into the man's lap. "Excellent. Now, is there any news of Rhu'len's bitch of a daughter?"

He shook his head. "Nay, Master, but my spies may have been hampered by the weather." Though spring's thaw had come to the mountains, winter had given the kingdom a parting gift of several inches of fresh snow on the lowlands.

Dismissively, Kasyrin said, "No matter. She will be found and sent screaming to the lowest pits of Hell soon enough. For now, return to Arris. See to it that he learns all this new weapons instructor has to teach—I need him to be inspiring enough that thousands will flock to his banner to die for his glory."

Gathering his gold, Porthyros said, "It will be done as you command, Master," and bowed his way out of the room.

The moment he was certain the sniveling cretin was gone, Kasyrin stepped from the office and into a small antechamber, triggering a complex lock that none but the most skilled of thieves could open without a key, of which there was only one—his. This was a room he had built himself, transforming what had been an acolyte's bedchamber into his private place of worship. The walls had been scrubbed down to stone, then consecrated in his own blood. Carving the protection circle in the center of the chamber had cost him more magick than he usually liked to spare, but now he was glad of the effort. Not even a master mage trained in one of the grand Y'Skani schools would detect what rested here, hidden away from everyone but himself. At the center of the chamber sat a small obsidian obelisk. The glowing artifact was his masterwork, and deep in the bowels of his soul, he sensed Ecarthus' pride in this place.

Stepping into the circle, Kasyrin shed his clothes and felt the runes inscribed on his body burn to life. Power drained out of him and activated the protective magicks in the room. He began to chant, the words seeming to echo as they tore open his mind, allowing Ecarthus to possess him.

Kasyrin's lips moved, but the voice coming from them was like nothing heard in Y'Myran. It boomed hollowly, making his ears ring. ::**Thou hast become a worthy vessel, my toy.**:: Ecarthus' pleasure was so strong that Kasyrin could hardly bear the demon's fervid joy. Every word struck him like a drover's whip, opening wounds that covered his body from neck to knee. ::**My** children shall breed soon, for they are well fed. Each passing day sees the barrier between the lands of the mortals and my prison become thinner. I take great pleasure in harvesting the power of thy sweet offerings. It serves me well, for I have begun to forge the key that will unlock the gates that bar my return to thy world. Soon I will come and lay my love upon the land like a lash.::

Kasyrin's strength was beginning to wane, for Ecarthus' touch was powerful and painful. Often the demon did not care what condition he left his toy in, but today, much to Kasyrin's relief, he chose to withdraw early.

::Find the child of Rhu'len,:: he commanded sternly. ::Only her death will insure that I will be truly free. Give her soul to me, and thy reward will make what thou hast now seem as but petty stones from a pauper's pocket. And remember, my Darkchilde, thy vengeance is my vengeance—the screams of the Scion of DaCoure shall offer us pleasure for eons!::

With that, he was gone.

Several hours later, Kasyrin crawled out of the antechamber, his body riven with bloody gashes, his muscles weakened from the torturous pleasures Ecarthus had visited upon him. Panting heavily, he lay upon the warm wooden floor, waiting for the power twisting about him to settle. Eventually, he dragged himself onto the desk chair. From a drawer he removed a small vial and drank from it, the bitter, sharply scented fluid restoring much of his vigor. Fresh robes waited for him, no doubt left by one of the acolytes.

Dressing, he considered his every option, making plans faster than a shuttle could fly across a weaver's loom. Over the years, he'd placed trusted operatives in major homes and courts all over Y'Myran. With the magickal abilities Ecarthus granted him, he would be able to swiftly set those plans in motion. He took a series of scroll tubes from the desk, laid them out one by one, and then studied them. Each was marked by a special sigil. After examining them for cracks and tampering, he opened them and read the messages contained within before replying and sending them off.

No other gift could be so wondrous as this, for who else could boast of near-instant communication with their spies? All they had to do was read his instructions, burn the messages, and send their replies, and none would be the wiser. Many of Ecarthus' magicks had been remarkable beyond compare—

things Kasyrin found himself likening to legendary objects created by the mythical Alyrr themselves. However, this device of seemingly simple cantrips had changed everything for him, and he would never dismiss its significance.

A scream echoed faintly from outside the room and he smiled. The sacrifices were becoming much more frequent. His handpicked cadre of priests were growing steadily as those dissatisfied with the shackles the virtuous Twain placed upon the dark desires of the human soul came flocking to Ecarthus' banner. Every death reaped rewards of gold, lust, or luxury for them to share, inciting further greed. Knowing they could earn even greater rewards, his priests had become very creative when extracting the blood-soaked power from their victims.

Never before had Kasyrin been in the company of so many who were dedicated to the art of torture. It gave him great pleasure to know that not far away from where he was now, someone was carving tiny strips of flesh from the body of one sacrifice while others burned, whipped, beat, and strangled their offerings.

There must be more—more death, more torture, more suffering if Ecarthus is to be freed! Soon the temple would open its doors to everyone. Once within, they would find dark halls stained with sigils and runes meant to stir fear while carefully crafted incense filled the air with narcotic smoke. Those who entered Ecarthus' temple would be infested with visions of horror upon horror, making them scream out their prayers, begging to be released from Ecarthus' loving embrace.

A draught of drugged wine would erase all but a sense of vague pleasure from their minds, and the more they visited the temple, the more they would crave its environs, for the smoke was disastrously addictive. Both smoke and wine had been a gift to him from Porthyros, and for that alone, he would see to it that the man had command of whatever he desired when victory was finally assured.

Kasyrin was pleased with how things were progressing. By the end of spring, his little "presents" to each of the kingdoms should be arriving just where they would do the most good. The bearers of these gifts knew little of what they carried, only that the reliquaries were to be entombed at the center of each kingdom. These talismans had cost quite a bit of magick to create, but inside they bore the seeds of doom for Y'Myran. By winter's next calling, Y'Dan would stand alone against a hoard of his master's beloved children that waited high in the mountains.

So much death would come, it would be as an ocean of blood descending on the land, and Kasyrin would ride its tides of power, harnessing it to free Ecarthus from his long imprisonment. He was close. All that was left was to see to his latest efforts to destroy the Cabal. If he could get Y'Dan completely under his control, he could access the kingdom's archives to discover his old enemy Istaffryn's true identity. After that, he would drag him from his beloved shadows and unveil him for all to see—then take everything the bastard ever held dear.

Then and only then would he consider killing him. First, though, he must suffer, just as Kasyrin had. It was, after all, only fair.

Revenge was within his grasp. Nothing could be allowed to take it now.

A horrified scream echoed through the temple, and he smiled in euphoric sympathy, drawn into memory. From the very first time since Ecarthus had come, pain had become Kasyrin's chosen pleasure and reward, for from pain had come power, and he was extremely fond of power. The screams faded. After enjoying a cup of restorative wine, he headed out to the temple. Today Kasyrin's underlings would have the privilege of watching their master lead the next ceremony.

Nervously looking over his shoulder, Hardag the fruit seller loaded the last of his belongings onto a cart. Over the winter, he and his wife had sold what they could, and now all they had was what would fit on a small, fast wagon that he hoped would get them to Y'Syr before week's end.

Just down the street sat the still-smoking ruins temple of the Twain. It had burned to the ground two nights ago and no one had bothered to see if there were any priests left inside. Nothing else around it had burned, either; not even a single blade of grass was scorched. Terrified, no one spoke of it, not even Hardag himself, for to speak out was to draw attention, and the last thing he wanted was the gaze of Ecarthus' black-robed priests falling on his house.

Sooner or later someone—a friend hoping to avoid a similar fate, an enemy seeking to gain prominence—would recall that Hardag's great-grandsire had been half-elven, and then those black robed bastards would come and drag him and his wife away.

Nelia was pregnant. She'd shared the news with him over winter solstice. It should have been a time of great celebration. Instead, he'd spent the night huddled in a ball before his secret shrine to Astariu, sobbing, begging her for help. The next night, and every night after, he dreamed of going east, to Y'Syr, home of his great-grandsire's people and their queen, and begging her to let them take shelter in their lands.

Fear now drove his hands to move faster, his fingers shaking as he tied down the last package. There, across the way, was that a black robe? Were those priests? He ducked to avoid notice. He was just a simple merchant heading out to a provincial market. That was his story. It wasn't wise to invite scrutiny, to announce that he was leaving, for then he would have to pay the departure tax and he and Nelia needed that money now more than ever.

Maybe I should go south instead? Maybe Ysradan hasn't gone mad like Arris. No. No, my dreams said east. We must go east, to Y'Syr.

Across the way, the robed men moved on, and he let out a sigh of relief. It was time, they must go. There would be no more chances. He only prayed that the Twain had not forsaken the whole of Y'Myran as they had Y'Dan.

CHAPTER THREE

EVER SINCE ELISIRA HAD SO boldly defied him, Derkus Glinholt was a changed man. His power in Arris' court dwindled until he was little more than a wraith summoned to do his master's bidding. Today, though, he had come to lay himself before the Granite Throne and beg for a chance at redemption. Today, he had received word of his errant daughter's whereabouts.

"Please, my glorious liege, I do humbly beg of you, lend me but a score of men and I shall lead them into the wilds of Y'Nor and fetch my ungrateful child and that scoundrel she ran off with! I'll drag them both back here to face your wrath!"

Arris, however, was not listening. From the corner of his eye, Derkus watched as the young king stared in mute fascination at an object that had become the marvel of the court. A gift from the merchant Kesryn Oswyne, it was an enchanted chess board and it, like all other toys sent by the proud popinjay that often graced the king's right hand, was now a favorite.

It was clear why Arris was so consumed by the game, for unlike a set of simple ivory and dark wood, this board's pieces were gloriously carved gems that moved themselves as though controlled by the hands of invisible players. One could play alone or with an opponent by means of issuing various commands, though Arris rarely bothered with living antagonists, preferring to pit his skills against those of the spirit Derkus assumed was trapped within the cursed thing.

When his plea got no response from the king, Derkus turned to First Adviser Porthryos Omal, who merely said, "As you can see, our king has much on his mind, Councilor. I am certain, however, that he will take your offer under advisement. For now, be content with the knowledge that King Padreg has not defiled her pure Y'Dani soul by marrying her."

Sourly, Derkus replied, "Yes, it is such a comfort that he has only stolen her body."

Much as he was loyal to his king, this new faith, this Ecarthan religion that had supplanted his beloved Twain, left a bitter taste in Derkus' mouth. Many times, in the secrecy of his own bed, he had lain awake silently praying that someone would come and end Arris' foolishness before High King Ysradan took notice of the goings-on north of his borders and decided to put a stop to it himself. Derkus had a strong feeling that any who had stood on Arris' side against Azhani Rhu'len would not fare well under the high king's chastisement.

Frowning, Porthyros stared at Derkus for a long, long time. Sweat began to pool in the small of his back and fear made him shake. It was certain death to irritate Porthyros, for those that annoyed him soon found themselves faced with the blades and fires of the Ecarthan priests.

"Go now, Lord Glinholt, and tend to your duties. Word will be sent if there is any news." With a dismissive flick of his fingers, Porthyros looked away, the arrogant sneer on his face so filled with cruelty that for just one heartbeat Derkus actually considered leaping up and punching him.

Instead, he slunk away, retreating from the throne and bowing, mumbling, "May you walk before the lash of His love."

With Councilor Derkus' departure, open court was finished for the day. As the guards ushered the courtiers from the chamber, Porthyros signaled a man in elaborate black and gold robes who was nearly lost in the shadows at the back of the room. The man nodded, and once everyone had gone, made his way to the throne.

Arris still watched the game unfold. Had his master not warned him against tampering with the chess board, Porthyros had to admit he might have been temped to try a game, for it was a marvel to behold. The pieces had been carved to resemble Arris and his armies on one side of the board and on the other, there were rimerbeasts, led by a queen whose face bore a near perfect likeness to Azhani Rhu'len.

"King takes pawn," Arris murmured. The king piece glowed, drew its sword, and then marched across the board to the last rimerbeast pawn and skewered it. "I'm going to do that," he said, smiling gleefully. "I'm going to kill them all. One by one, they will die, until there are no more threats to my people." Absently, he drained his mug and shoved it at Porthyros to refill.

On the board, a rimerbeast knight moved toward one of Arris' pawns and slew it. Arris merely smiled, and Porthyros could hardly understand why until he sent his king over to destroy the knight. Laughing softly, Arris said, "And once I'm done with them, I'm coming for you." The queen, the only remaining rimerbeast token, stood alone. Her stone features were drawn in a mask of terror as she faced Arris' king.

Porthyros cleared his throat. "My king, High Priest Lundovar has come."

Instantly, Arris turned away from the game and stood to greet the priest. "Lundovar, it is good to have you with us again," he said warmly. "Have you come to regale me with more stories of how I was chosen to be Ecarthus' first king? I am pleased to be able to serve him so well." The grin that lit his face when he embraced the urbane priest was almost painfully bright.

For his part, Porthyros could barely stand being in the same room as Lundovar, for the man was overly fond of certain expensive perfumes that aggravated Porthyros' delicate sense of smell and made it difficult for him to practice his arts as an apothecary.

"I am here, my king, only to report on the progress of our great temple, but of course, I will be happy to offer Ecarthus' praises and blessings once more." Lundovar's eerily soft voice made Porthyros' skin crawl.

"Please, please tell us how the project fares," Arris replied expansively. "And of course I will take your blessings! I shall need them all if I am to make my enemies cower before my might!" He turned and grinned boyishly at Porthyros. "And get that bitch Azhani to come crawling back to me, begging me to make her my slave!"

Porthyros refrained from groaning, but only just. If Arris' fixation on the Rhu'len woman had returned, he would have to see about upping his krile dosage again. The last thing they needed was for Arris to suddenly decide to go off hunting for her.

Lundovar, however, was as educated on their master's desires as Porthryos and neatly distracted the king by laying a series of elaborate, and likely fake, blessings upon him, then giving him—and therefore Porthyros—a thorough report on the temple. By the time he was done, Arris was drowsy from his tea and more than pliable enough for Porthyros to control. Once Lundovar left, Porthyros set to the task of having Arris sign several new decrees into law. Taxes to fill the temple's coffers, new crimes to fill the city jail—and eventually feed Ecarthus' never ending hunger. *Master Darkchilde will surely be pleased today!*

Toward afternoon, the krile wore off and Arris perked up, allowing Porthyros to send him to meet with his new sword master. It was a little strange to watch as Arris, who had always been clumsy, was transformed into a competent swordsman. Somehow he had developed an ability to focus on his lessons that was almost preternatural. Porthyros suspected it had something to do with the chess board, but could not bring himself to ask Master Darkchilde about it. He had a feeling he wouldn't like the answer. That board was uncanny enough as it was.

Some things aren't worth knowing.

After treating them to the best that spring had to offer, Y'Syr turned around and slapped Azhani and Kyrian with a vengeance. They were still some distance from Y'Syria's gates when heavy, cold rains suddenly drenched the land. After two candlemarks of suffering through it, Azhani called a halt when Kyrian found an abandoned barn that would suffice as shelter. Though the roof was only partially intact, there was an area that they could huddle in to stay dry, if not very warm.

As she wrung out her robes, Kyrian sighed and hoped they would have a fire soon. "Good old soggy Y'Syr. I did not miss this part of my homeland."

"I've campaigned in worse than this," Azhani muttered while she took out a bag of supplies. After emptying it, she unlaced the heavy leather and used it to create a lean-to to block off a portion of their shelter. Shortly, she had a small fire going.

"You know, I didn't think you'd get a fire started without Devon around to light it," Kyrian said after warming her hands over the flames. "I'm impressed."

Azhani smirked. "If you can't make fire in everything from a monsoon to a blizzard, then you're not much of a warleader, are you?"

"Good thing we've got a warleader with us, then," she said with a cheeky smile.

"Hmph. What's for dinner?" Azhani replied sourly.

Investigating their supplies, Kyrian made a face. "You have your choice of soggy bread, smashed fruit, and whatever this green, fuzzy thing is." Delicately, she lifted something shaped a bit like a wedge of cheese from the bag and held it out to her. "Or dried beef. We ate the last of our stew this morning, remember? You thought we'd be in Y'Syria by now."

"Damn. All right. You stay here. I'll be back." Azhani grabbed her bow and ducked out into the rain.

Frowning, Kyrian watched her go. "Right, fine, if she's going to fetch us something for the pot, I'd best try to have something to add to it."

While Azhani was gone, Kyrian mixed the bread and fruit together, added honey and nuts to it, and then set the resultant gooey mess in a covered pot near the fire. She found a few potatoes at the bottom of a sack, sliced them up into a pot of water, and set it on the fire. After that, she got out their bedrolls and made a place for them to sleep.

By the time Azhani returned with a single rabbit, already cleaned and ready for the stew pot, there was a cozy little camp awaiting her. "Very nice," she said with an approving smile.

"Thank you." Taking the rabbit, Kyrian added it to the pot with some herbs and a bit of wine, leeks, and chopped mushrooms. "Shouldn't be too long before we have something edible."

"Good." Azhani pulled off her armor and put it by the fire to dry.

"So, once we get to Y'Syria, what then?"

Azhani regarded her for a moment, then shrugged. "We seek sanctuary with Tellyn Jarelle until we have had a chance to gauge the queen's mood."

"I could go and petition her alone, you know," Kyrian said. "It is my right as stardancer."

"No!" she snapped, turning and glaring at her so intently that Kyrian felt the hairs on the back of her neck rise in fear. "I will present myself to Lyssera on my own terms. She must know that I come to her of my own free will."

"Damn you and your stubborn pride," Kyrian muttered. Crossing her arms, she returned Azhani's glare. "I won't let you leave me out of this, Azhi. We face it together!"

Tension formed around Azhani's jaw as she pressed her lips together. "Fine. But on *my* terms."

"Of course. But just remember—I didn't save your life so you could throw it away for some stupid act of self-sacrifice," Kyrian replied quietly.

Lowering her head, Azhani sighed. "I know." Hesitantly, she reached out and put her hand on Kyrian's arm. "Trust me to be chary of your gift, my friend. I'll not throw it away needlessly."

"That's all I can ask," Kyrian whispered, trying to ignore the faint tingle that formed in the pit of her stomach at Azhani's touch.

Though they stood wide open, the heavy oak and gilded steel gates of Y'Syria had never seemed so foreboding. Flags bearing the arms of all the Y'Syran noble houses within the city snapped and fluttered in the wind while guards stood at the ready, watching as travelers made their way along the road. A dark flag of mourning flew just below the Kelani banner. Kyrian stared at it for a moment, then resolutely focused on following Azhani. Long shadows cast by the setting sun danced along the walls as Azhani and Kyrian slipped through on the heels of an Y'Skani caravan. It had taken the better part of a day just to slog through the rain to get here and now, exhausted and soaked through, all Kyrian wanted was a warm fire and a hot meal.

To the west, lake birds flew in formation, performing their sunset ballet of feeding, filling their bellies while looking for a place to roost. Banner Lake shimmered, its glassy surface seeming to trap the fires of doom, though it was merely an illusion made by nature. The city itself ringed the shore of the lake, a glorious web of massively tall trees all linked by ancient bridges, some connecting the treetops themselves.

Looking up, Kyrian shaded her eyes and gaped at the command of magick her ancestors must have had to create such pure magnificence.

"Haven't been here in a while, have you?" Azhani asked softly.

"Not for a very long time, and when I last came, I was too young to care about anything beyond my next meal." Kyrian shook her head slowly. "Y'Len is nothing like this. I'd forgotten what it was like. Y-No one ever talked about it much at the temple," she murmured, completely at a loss for words.

Azhani chuckled softly. "This is definitely not my first time, though I still remember the first. Never quite ceases to leave me feeling…" Letting out a slow, contented breath, Azhani looked around and smiled briefly. "I like it here. The only place I've ever felt more comfortable was the cottage. I might have enjoyed visiting, with Ylera. Had she invited me."

Instinctively, Kyrian reached out to put her hand on Azhani's arm. "You know she would have. You were to marry her, right?"

"Yes. It's hard to be here, now, without her. But not as hard as it would have been had we been here together." Briefly, Azhani closed her eyes. Kyrian wondered if the pain was too great for words. "Maybe it's for the best," she finally said. "I don't see her everywhere here. Just memories of working with my father, with Thodan, and with Lyssera. Nothing of Ylera exists in this place for me."

Oh, but it does for me, my friend. Goddess, no wonder Ylera always thought Y'Len was such a boring backwater. We had nothing like this there, nothing at all! Kyrian just couldn't believe what she was seeing. Homes, businesses—they all seemed to blend together. An entire second city of buildings existed at the base of the trees, though had there not been people obviously going in and out of them, Kyrian might well have assumed them to be some kind of shrubbery. The structures were simply far too natural-seeming in appearance to stand out. It was the same everywhere she looked. Even the docks echoed their surroundings, being constructed in sinuous, fish-like shapes.

To Kyrian, the city was an impossible maze, but Azhani seemed to have no trouble at all navigating the streets and even through some of the lower bridges between the trees, stopping only when they reached a mighty aspen. Here, they found a shop that bore an apothecary's sign. Tiny magelights illuminated the path and continued up the side of the tree, tracing out the shape of the inhabitant's home. The air was rich with the scents of fresh herbs and Kyrian grinned, knowing there must be a garden near. Dismounting, they tied the horses to a hitch and approached the shop.

A single knock brought an elven boy with a mop of curly black hair and a dusting of freckles over his long, narrow nose. He stood in the doorway staring at them a moment before saying, "Yes? May I help you?"

"I am here to see Tellyn Jarelle," Azhani replied.

The boy rolled his eyes as if this were a most impossible request. "She's busy. Come back tomorrow." The door closed on them.

Azhani glanced at Kyrian, who shrugged and knocked again.

Once again, the door was opened. This time, the boy took one look at them, scowled, and said, "I told you, she's busy. Go away."

Before he could slam the door, Azhani shoved her foot against the frame and grabbed his arm. "Get your mistress now. I won't ask again."

At the boy's squeak of pain, Kyrian softly said, "Azhi, we can come back."

Azhani glared at her. "You're welcome to find an inn."

The sharp tone stung. Stepping back, she was just about to give up when someone yelled, "Gyp? What is it boy? Shut the damned door! You're letting out all the warm air."

"Visitors, Mistress," Gyp replied, a touch of fear in his voice. "They won't go away like ye told me t'say."

"Well, if they're so damned intent on interrupting an old woman's work, let them in," she called irritably. "Just stop letting out all the heat! My bones can't take the cold!"

Gyp looked up at Azhani, smiled sourly and jerked his arm free. "Be welcome to Mistress Tellyn's house, my lady."

Smirking, Azhani strode in as if her entry had been a foregone conclusion. Kyrian crept in behind her. As she passed Gyp, she murmured, "Sorry to disturb you."

"Ye best be tellin' that t'her," he said, nodding in the direction of an elderly woman who was busily scrubbing a vat full of clothing.

Kyrian nodded, but it was Azhani who said, "I am very sorry to call on you right now, old friend, but I thought perhaps the welcome I received here would be a touch less *pointed*." She touched the hilt of her sword for emphasis.

Looking up from her chore, the old woman merely stared at them. Finally, she shook her head. "Azhani Rhu'len. Astarus' balls, you always did have more courage than sense! Come, come, have a seat by the fire. My home is your haven—as it has always been."

Well, this didn't start off half as badly as I feared. Kyrian looked around the herbalist's shop, taking in the racks of dried herbs, vials and jars of unguents, balms, and curatives. Most she recognized, but there were several preparations she either did not know or only half recognized from descriptions in ancient Firstlander texts. *Goddess, she has everything here, even a pill press!*

"Come, let us repair to a more comfortable space," Tellyn said, leading them to a sitting room. Here, there was a wood stove that put out very welcome heat. Opening the grate, she added a log to the fire and then warmed her hands at it, saying, "So you've finally come to Y'Syria after all that mess in Y'Dan." She sighed sadly. "Have you seen the queen?"

That Tellyn didn't sound accusatory or even terribly angry with Azhani made Kyrian wonder if her countrymen weren't as convinced by Arris' tales of deception and treachery as everyone else seemed to be. If so, it might mean a slightly easier road for Azhani to follow now that she was here.

Azhani shook her head. "No. I wanted to ask a favor of you, first."

Clearly surprised, Tellyn said, "A favor? You might be welcome here, Azhani, but I won't hide you from the guards if they come seeking your head. I am loyal to my queen."

"I would never ask you to betray your honor, Tellyn," she said. Gesturing to Kyrian, she added, "This is Stardancer Kyrian. She is a friend. We need a safe place to stay until I've seen Lyssera."

As soon as Tellyn looked at her, Kyrian knew she was being measured—but against what, she could not know. Feeling nervous, she nonetheless offered the herbalist a warm smile. "Thank you for welcoming us to your home on such a chilly night."

"You would always be welcome here, Beloved One," Tellyn replied, bowing respectfully, though moving clearly pained her.

Hurrying to her side, Kyrian put her hand on her back. "No, you need not be so formal, Mistress. Please, call me Kyrian. Let me help you sit."

"No, no, I'm fine, really. Once you've had a sore back for a few hundred years, you forget it exists," she said, her gruff manner returning. Shuffling over to a tray, she poured herself a draught of some fiery orange liquid, drank it, and said, "You may stay. Take that room there." She pointed to a door that had been stained berry purple. "I have customers six days of the week. On the seventh, I clean." Glaring at both of them, she added, "I don't wear mystical robes, I don't make love potions, I don't give deals to handsome men, and I absolutely cannot stand the stench of rotting food." Now she looked to Gyp, who shuffled his feet ruefully. "Which is why Gyp is not allowed near the laundry. Boy can't be bothered to scrub properly."

This room, unlike the shop area where Tellyn had been doing her laundry, was filled with an absolute jumble of things—more jars, chairs, tables, shelves containing books, curios, and even a few soot-stained paintings and tapestries hung from the walls.

Wryly, Azhani said, "I think I agree more with Gyp. I'd rather not go through all the bother, even though I do." Then, she smiled. "Come Kyrian, we should unpack. I'll move the horses to a stable afterward."

"You might want to collect us some supper as well, for I had planned on a light meal," Tellyn said calmly. "I doubt you'll be wanting to sup on dry toast and tea. Oh, and fetch us a bottle or two of good wine. It's been a while since Gyp and I have entertained company. We should celebrate. Gyp! Find my warmer slippers. These are all wet and I need to finish the washing."

Shaking her head, Azhani chuckled as the boy grabbed a fresh pair of slippers from a basket near the door. "Is there anything else I should get?"

"Well, since you're offering, here." Tellyn shoved a scroll and a sack of coins at her. "I was going to send Gyp with this tomorrow, but if you run, you can get it all tonight. And hurry! I'll be needing some of that first thing in the morning!"

"If you're doing the shopping, then that means I'll be helping with the laundry," Kyrian said with an amiable chuckle.

"Tellyn, you haven't changed a bit," Azhani replied fondly. Patting the elven boy on his shoulder, she said, "Gyp, you're with me. I've a feeling you're going to be very handy."

When Gyp looked over at Tellyn for confirmation, she nodded and waved him off. "Yes, yes, go! You need the exercise."

Swiftly, he ducked outside, leaving Kyrian to say, "Be careful out there, Azhi. I know you want to see the queen, but it's best if you don't do so in irons."

Azhani nodded. "I know. I plan to keep my head low and let the boy do most of the talking. It shouldn't take long. Don't let Tellyn run you ragged," she said softly. "She's more capable than she lets others see."

"She's an herbalist, Azhani. Her knowledge makes her one of the deadliest people in all of Y'Myran—and also one of the safest, since I doubt she wants to poison herself," Kyrian said. "And she's earned my respect because she has the good sense to be your friend."

"Or the lunacy," she said, winking at her. Gyp returned wearing a hooded cape and carrying a large pack. "Ah, there's my porter now. We'll be back."

Kyrian chuckled ruefully as they exited the shop. "Just let me see to our gear, Mistress Jarelle, and then I'll help with that laundry."

"Oh, take your time, take your time. The old have nothing but time," Tellyn said as she stirred the laundry pot.

Three days passed—days in which Azhani calmly asked Kyrian to wait for her at the shop while she "discovered the lay of the terrain", whatever that meant. She never spoke of what she learned, which made it all the more frustrating for Kyrian, who only wanted to help. It was Tellyn who managed to discover that none of the Cabal operatives in the city had heard of a contract being offered for a stardancer, leaving them to speculate that Kyrian had been taken for pleasure, rather than monetary gain.

Learning this brought back all the confusion Kyrian had felt when she'd first awakened, so many weeks ago, in Azhani's arms. She remembered Arun's swaying gait, the pounding headache, the rush of fear and relief and then, upon learning her rescuer's identity, the tumbler's dance of emotions that started her on the path that led here, to Y'Syria.

Damn you, Azhani Rhu'len! Irritation sizzled through Kyrian as she looked down at the note in her hands once more. *I thought we had agreed we were doing this together!*

Although the text itself was plain enough—

Kyrian, I pray you'll understand. The wrath that falls upon my shoulders is not yours to bear. Azhani

—the meaning behind it, the lack of faith, trust, and above all, courage Azhani showed by leaving such a thing behind rather than speaking to Kyrian directly was so deeply wounding, Kyrian wondered if she'd made a mistake about the other woman.

Are we truly friends, then? Has anything I've said or done been more to her than a simple cobblestone on her road to vengeance? Kyrian fought not to cry.

Heartsick, she stuffed the note into a pouch and tried to forget anything but the work at hand. Sadly, poor Gyp ended up feeling the sharp side of her tongue for much of the day.

Twelve candlemarks passed, and then a full day—making this the fourth they'd been in the city and, aside from the brief note, the first without word from Azhani. At breakfast, Kyrian sat and stared at her food, lacking an appetite and beset by the beasts of rage and utter frustration.

Leaving the table with her meal uneaten, she stomped back into the room and immediately tore the note to shreds, tossing each piece into the fire and watching it burn. It offered little satisfaction and when it was over, she wanted to take it all back and cherish the script, just in case it was the last thing she had of Azhani's.

"How could she do this?" she whispered, scrubbing at tears that scorched her cheeks. "How could she treat my friendship like a joke?"

Later, as she was helping Tellyn prepare an unguent, she blurted, "I should go find her!"

"No, child, you should not. That one has a head like a mule," Tellyn said dourly.

Driving the pestle into the herbs in her mortar, Kyrian replied, "I can pull a mule to water."

"Aye. But you cannot make 'er drink—or like the journey. Be content to know that Azhani is cut from stiffer cloth than you or I...and Lyssera knows this. You've got to trust in our queen, my friend, for she is not some grief-maddened half-wit ready to ignore all signs of innocence. Trust in her, for she is wise well beyond her years."

Kyrian blew out a breath in frustration and stared at the mashed herbs for a long moment. "I feel like all my promises meant nothing."

Sadly, Tellyn patted her shoulder. "I know. But she tried to spare you troubles, which tells me she cherishes your friendship above your aid. So think on that when you curse her name afore you sleep, lass."

"I'll try." She scraped out the herbs and then wiped the mortar down with a dry cloth. As she added fresh leaves to the vessel, she asked, "How did you meet her, anyway?"

Tellyn chuckled softly and touched the side of her nose. "Azhani'd not thank me for telling you this, I think, but it's a story worth the knowing. So, settle in and hear then, of a wildling child, her noble warrior father, and a series of dares that ended up with that child attempting to swim the whole of Banner Lake!"

"Oh Goddess," Kyrian muttered as she listened to the tale weave itself. Eventually, she found herself smiling, even laughing along as Tellyn told of a proud, stubborn, and brave child's struggle to prove herself to her elven peers—especially to those who claimed kinship with the Oakleaf family. As Tellyn paused to take a sip of her drink, Kyrian asked, "Why that family in particular?"

"The Oakleafs? I'm not sure, though as Azhani bears a rather striking resemblance to Kadrevan, the family patriarch, I might suspect that she be the child Ashiani was rumored to have birthed before she died," Tellyn said solemnly. Turning to pour herself a fresh cup of tea, she added, "Of course, this be little more than an old woman's speculation, and would not carry any weight with the Queen's Council."

Kyrian made a face. "Of course not. All right, what happened next?"

Tellyn chuckled. "Well then, that's when Rhu'len brought her to me, for though he was proud she were so determined to stand her ground against the bullies, the water here is terribly cold in winter. Thus, he thought it best she learn herbcraft to create the brews she would need to cure herself of any ills."

"Smart man," Kyrian said quietly. "Perhaps there's some advice in those actions—if Azhani's pride pushes her to do something stupid, it's better to stand back and be ready to catch her than to shove her aside to avoid the trouble altogether."

"I cannot find fault with such wisdom, child," Tellyn said as she stirred honey into her tea. "Not one bit."

Seated on a pile of soft carpets, surrounded by the familiar scents of grass, horse and cooking meat, Padreg Keelan sipped at his cup of dark tea and looked at his companion as if he were a few nails shy of a fully shod horse. As he was his oldest and most trusted friend, Aden had been sent on to Y'Nym, Y'Nor's largest city, while Padreg stayed out with his clan, roving the plains and introducing Elisira to the life she had agreed to share with him. It was a selfish choice, really. Perhaps he should have gone to Y'Nym instead, but he'd wanted Eli's first taste of Y'Noran life to be truth and not the pretty lies of its largest and therefor most cosmopolitan city.

Still, it wasn't the city nor its export tallies of horses and grain that had him so shocked, but rather the contents of Aden's report on the activities of the other kingdoms. Shaking his head slowly, Padreg said, "Sea monsters?" and tried to make the words make some vestige of sense, though really, how did one envision such horrific creatures as kraken, leviathans, and sirens without calling upon the fireside stories of youth? "Are you sure?" He stared at his mug and wished it was something with a bit more kick. "It's not like Ysradan to go chasing after myths."

Through the open flap of his tent, he could see his mother, Ketri, teaching Elisira how to cut and fashion a saddle the way their clan had for centuries.

It pleased him that Elisira sat and listened to his mother with a look of complete concentration on her face. The smile on Ketri's face spoke volumes, for it boded well with regard to her approval of her son's choice in mates.

"Aye, Paddy. I be certain," Aden said, drawing Padreg's attention back to the conversation at hand. "Had it from Cragus One-Eye hisself. Near a month ago, Ysradan took his best men, boarded the *Ymaric's Hammer* and headed out to hunt down giant, tentacled beasts that had already torn apart two ships bound for Killigarn Island, killing most everyone aboard."

Padreg blinked in shock. "A kraken? By Astarus' balls! Would that I had not pledged myself to Azhani's side to strike the rimerbeasts, for to hunt kraken would surely be a feat seen only once in all of history!"

"I don't know, Paddy, it seems to me that the hunting of kraken, if that is what these be, must be a simple thing, for 'tis said the bodies of the beasts now litter the shores of Y'Mar."

"What a thing! What a terrible and incredible thing! Just as rimerbeasts come out of season, now there are kraken?" It was too hard to grasp, and yet, he knew there was more. Aden had barely begun to give his report.

"Aye," Aden said darkly. "And if even a piece of the old tales of kraken are true, then it'll be a long while afore Ysradan will have the time to deal with Y'Dan."

"You're right, of course. Who is regent? Perhaps I can appeal to them for help," he said, knowing that Ysradan's son, Prince Ysrallan, was too young to hold the throne. "Would that it was Queen Dasia, but we both know that's unlikely. Last time Ysradan went charging after brigands, I hear she chased after the *Hammer* in a canoe."

Aden laughed. "Ah, that must be *korethka* at work, eh, Paddy?"

"'Tis a powerful thing, old friend. Love like that is the truest gift of the Twain. Ysradan is wise to cherish it." Soberly, he said, "So, with the high king and queen out to sea, do we then turn to Princess Syrelle?"

Wincing, Aden replied, "Nay. Ye know the high council'd sooner shit in a grass pot than look to a willowy girl for guidance. Ysradan made Count Madros his regent so his kingdom wouldn't scheme itself to pieces."

Shock piled on shock. A heavy slap of disgust made Padreg spit as he replied, "What? How could he leave that overgrown windbag cousin of his in charge?" Jumping to his feet, he began to pace irritably. "Everyone knows Pirellan doesn't tie his own boots without first consulting his astrologer, two priests, and the village idiot! How can a man like that rule a kingdom?" There was little room to truly vent his aggression, forcing him to take careful steps lest he topple the brazier in his anger. "The bloody high council won't be any help, either. Those old men care less for justice than they do gold and glory. Oh, by the hooves of my herds, Aden, the Twain have not played us easy, have they?"

"Indeed not, but there may not have been another choice. If Dasia would not stay, and Syrelle couldn't hold the council's respect, who else could Ysradan trust? Pirellan Madros might be an idiot, but at least he's Ysradan's man through and through."

Padreg sighed. "Aye. I suppose it could be much worse. He could have chosen one with a heart like Arris' and not had a kingdom to call home once he returned."

Still, it rankled him to think of the high king so far from his throne, and he knew Aden felt the same. As boys, both had spent time living in Ysradan's palace to learn the ways of nobles. They'd started as pages and worked their way up to becoming squires. The experience had given them a deep insight into a monarch's duties and taught them just how difficult it was for one man to balance so many responsibilities. It was the alliances made with others that ensured a kingdom's prosperity and success, not the glory won on battlefields. Power came from respect that was given and received. With that kind of command, a king could be capable of great things.

Sitting down again, he sighed. "All right, you've told me of Y'Mar. What news of the rest of the kingdoms? Surely they have had some inkling of the madness plaguing Y'Dan?"

"Oh aye," Aden replied. "But it seems Y'Mar be not the only kingdom to suffer the sting of strange invasion."

Padreg's stomach turned sour. "Your smile bodes ill."

"Aye, and what I have to tell will like your ears no better than it did mine, for had I not heard it from those I know to be tellers of nothing but the solid truth, I would think them madmen," Aden said quietly. "Monsters have come to Y'Myran, old friend. Monsters the like of which populate our myths and stories, whose bones rot in inns and taverns, moldering on shelves, and whose origins are known only to the sages."

Weight wrapped about Padreg's shoulders. This was responsibility coming to call. "What monsters, and where do they hunt?"

"In Y'Dror, there is a dragon—they say it crawled out of a crack right in the middle of the kingdom and flew up, breathing great torrents of fire and ashen smog, choking and burning all in its path. In Y'Nym, there's a man who was caught in the beast's breath, and Paddy, ye know me to be no coward, but I'll gladly face rimerbeasts over this thing, for his skin had been boiled from his body and he were yards from the blast!"

"Twain's grace," he whispered, unable to imagine such devastation. "Can we send aid? Has Y'Dror's king asked anything of us?"

"Stefan Payle sent two hundred of our finest horsemen to aid both men and dwarves. Much more, we cannot spare."

Nodding, he said, "And Y'Skan, what of the desert? Or Y'Tol? Surely fair Y'Tol has escaped these tragedies?"

"Sadly, the Y'Tolians face beetles the size of birds—King Naral sent word that their crops are decimated. There'll be no wine this season or the next, and little food, as well. We've heard only rumor from Y'Skan, but travelers have reported being attacked by scorpions the size of horses. Most of the nomad clans have been forced into Ratterask Oasis."

Padreg stared at the brazier and tried not to feel as though the weight of hundreds of thousands of lives were suddenly crushing his spine. "We stand alone then, we of Y'Nor, for Y'Syr will have rimerbeasts come winter. And Y'Dan has both the beasts and a madman for a king."

"Aye, but we are strong, Paddy. Our warrior's blades are sharp, our horses are fleet, and we alone of Y'Myran are ready to send aid where we can," Aden said proudly.

Bolstered by Aden's courageous words, Padreg smiled. "Aye, we are. And we will. Come, let's seek out Stefan and see to sending more of our forces out to help our brother and sister monarchs."

Just as he reached for the flap, there was a commotion outside the tent, then a shout. "Ogres! Ogres attack Y'Nym!"

CHAPTER FOUR

Somewhere, the temple time keeper struck the half-mark, telling those citizens of Y'Syria who were still wakeful that it was one and a half hours beyond the stroke of midnight's calling. Shrouded in darkness, Azhani stood outside a doorway in Oakheart Manor, the ancestral home of the elven monarchs, and silently worked up the nerve to face Ylera's twin. Regret tainted her thoughts, for she wished Kyrian were there with her to bolster her up and offer comfort. But no, this was her moment, her chance to wear every shred of blame Queen Lyssera would no doubt heap upon her.

"Time for the bitter drink," she muttered ruefully. "My sins are here to roost."

Taking a final breath, she stepped into the lantern-lit room. Though her boot steps surely made little noise on the heavily carpeted floor, the figure seated at the desk across the room stiffened, then turned to face her.

"Give me one good reason why I shouldn't call out to my guards, Oathbreaker."

Mouth dry, Azhani chose not to offer any reply in words. Instead, she knelt and set her sword at the feet of the other woman, a woman who, by this light, was more than the twin to her beloved—she was every inch the woman she had lost. Only her eyes were different. Clear, gray, and thunderous, like the sky on a stormy day, and behind them lurked anger just as dangerous as the lightning that leaped from cloud to cloud. She was Lyssera Kelani, older than Ylera by just moments. It was an accident of birth that gave her the crown and allowed her sister the chance to enter Azhani's life.

With a snort of contempt, Lyssera leaned back in her chair and ignored the blade. She regarded Azhani speculatively, the cool look on her face sending rivers of nervous sweat racing down Azhani's spine.

"You're the reason my sister is dead," she said darkly. "Though you look little like the vaunted 'Banshee of Banner Lake'. No, I'd hazard you're more likely little more than an errant crowscare looking for it's field."

Azhani winced. She knew she barely resembled the warrior Lyssera had last seen. That woman had been tall, proud, and strong. Thanks to the events of Banner Lake, she was a shadow of her former glory. Kyrian might have healed her and the winter might have given her time to regain some skill, but Arris' deeds had marked her, had riven her body as surely as they had scourged her soul. It would take more than a few months' time to put it back to rights.

Solemnly, Azhani replied, "I am whatever Your Majesty wishes."

A thin smile creased Lyssera's lips. "What I wish is for my sister's killer to be flayed alive, packed in sea salt, and shipped to the farthest Hells!" she replied icily. "But I'd settle for having you hung in the public square. That is how we punish murders here in Y'Syr—or had you forgotten the very law you saw written?"

It was hard not to flinch, but she had known this could be the outcome of her actions. "What I remember is that your justice is merciful, Your Majesty. That you, and your court, treated all who stood before it as innocent until proven guilty."

Abruptly, Lyssera sat forward. "Do you claim innocence, then?" There was a look in her eyes, a tension in the way she gripped the arms of her chair, that told Azhani more than her own life hung in the balance here. Lyssera desperately needed something from her.

It's almost like she's begging me to tell her what I can't possibly know.

"Yes. I am innocent, Your Majesty. It was not my hand that ended Ylera's life. She..." Azhani's voice broke as she rasped, "She was my very heart and soul."

The words seemed to galvanize Lyssera, for she leaped to her feet and paced in restless circles around Azhani. "You profess love, but love's no shield against murder! How does your word stand against the documents I have proving your guilt?" Stopping in front of her, Lyssera drew her dagger and pressed the tip to Azhani's throat. "Do you know what those documents tell me you did to her, Oathbreaker?"

Swallowing heavily, she replied, "I can guess."

"They say you are a traitor!" Lyssera hissed, the point of the blade kissing Azhani's skin sharply enough to draw blood. "They say that you used," she ground the word against her teeth, "my sister as a shield against the guardsmen who tried to arrest you." The blade slipped deeper into Azhani's neck as Lyssera's hand shook. "They say that you cut her throat when the guards would not back away." Tears crept down her cheeks. Suddenly, the blade slackened as she grabbed Azhani's jaw and yanked, pulling her face toward the light and driving her thumb right into the scar on her cheek. "So you'd better have a damned-good reason why I should believe a branded oathbreaker!"

Fighting urge to retaliate against the crazed woman who held her life on a dagger's point, Azhani said, "How fares relations with Y'Dan these days, my queen? Do your merchants prosper from the open trade we worked so hard to establish? Do the priests of the Twain still train gifted acolytes from Y'Dan's families? Has Arris invited you to his coronation? Did he offer to make witnesses to my corruption and treachery available for questioning at your leisure? Did he ever once give you any damned opportunity to come to Y'Dan and hunt for me yourself—or to send someone in your stead?"

Lyssera's hands dropped away as if burned.

Calm now, Azhani stood and asked, "Have any Y'Dani nobles fostered those of Y'Syr or indeed, do you house a son of Y'Dan here in Oakheart? Can gold stamped with your face buy wheat in the markets of Y'Dan? Have you seen the Writ of Behavior? Could you follow its decrees? Will you implement it here, so as to make Arris and his lackeys feel more comfortable should they visit Y'Syria? Will you then replace your stardancers with his black-robed 'doctors' or allow them to preach the faith he is spreading?"

When Lyssera flinched, Azhani knew her words had struck a nerve. Once more, she knelt, reached for her blade, and offered it to her lover's twin.

"What if I ordered you to fall on your sword?" Lyssera asked, a hint of sour amusement in her tone.

"Then you should summon a servant to mop up the mess," Azhani replied calmly. "And I do hope you're prepared to replace the rug. You can never quite get the smell of spilled guts out of fur."

Pinching the bridge of her nose, Lyssera sighed. "By the First Tree, Azhani, must you always take things so literally?"

Dropping to her knees, Lyssera pushed the sword out of her way as she reached for Azhani. "I don't want you dead. Twain's grace, I'd be a fool to turn you aside!" Desperately, she clung to her and whispered, "I know you're innocent. I know it as deeply as Oakheart's roots penetrate the rock and mud of Y'Syr. When we heard what happened, Starseeker Vashyra was able to contact Ylera's spirit. She told us everything. Arris' treachery, how she died, and even why." Cupping Azhani's face, she looked into her eyes and murmured, "Her last words were for you. She said, *'You will know me through others. You will hear my foibles and fallacies. You will think my love was lies, but it was the deepest truth*

I have ever felt. I loved you freely and without regret, Azhani Rhu'len, though I knew it to be the death of me.'"

"No…" Azhani rasped, shaking her head in disbelief as tears flooded her cheeks. "She knew she'd die if she loved me? But…how? Why…"

"All students of the goddess look into the mirror of fate," Lyssera said quietly. "What we see, we rarely speak of, but I suspect Ylera knew her fate from the moment you met."

"No," she whispered, horrified. "Why would she stay in Y'Dan if she knew she was going to die? Why didn't she say something? I could have stopped it, stopped him!" Anger dripped from her words like poison.

"Perhaps she did not know the why or the how. Perhaps she assumed the prediction meant something else—something innocuous, like sickness. When I looked into the mirror, all I saw was the crown. Others see who they will be—all stardancers see themselves in crimson, starseekers see the blue robes. What did you see when it was your turn?" Lyssera asked gently.

"A sword. Or it's shadow. It was just a flash. Enough for the tattoo to be declared mine," she said dully.

"Would you have taken it, had you known being who you are would lead to the deaths of so many?"

"No!" Azhani hesitated then, her tears drying on her face. She'd saved hundreds, maybe thousands with her skills. How many lives would be gone if she'd never picked up a blade, never taken the oaths she had? *Kyrian. Goddess—who would have been there to rescue her from the Cabal, if not me?* Feeling sick, she bowed her head and mumbled, "Yes. Yes, the sword is my fate."

"If you accept your fate, then you must also accept Ylera's," Lyssera replied sadly. "Neither of us has to like it or cherish its impact or even stop grieving for the woman we both loved. She was my sister, my beautiful twin, and with her went half of me," she said, her tears falling rapidly. "But we must not be angry with her—or the gods, for they cannot control destiny any more than we. It is by their grace alone that we know our Ylera will be waiting for us when it is our time, and that, my friend, is a tie that binds us together stronger than blood alone!"

Grief wrecked Azhani then. It savaged her chest and tore her heart to shreds as she and Lyssera wept together, both of them finding solace no other had been able to offer.

It was late—so late in fact that Lyssera knew no sleep would follow this night of revelations and ghosts. Still, there had been plenty of sleepless nights in the past and the future would likely bring more. Tonight, she gladly sacrificed comfort and rest for the peace Azhani's visit had brought, even though her heart ached over the wounds her presence opened. It was for the sake of a promise—the last one Ylera would ever claim of her—that she suffered the pain of loss and grief all over again.

Ylera's voice was still clear in her head, still struck through with emotion and need, her eyes fixed on a point Lyssera could not see as she wrapped her ghostly fingers over hers. Closing her eyes, Lyssera returned to that moment and once again saw her sister speak for the final time. *"Protect her from herself, Lyss. She's headstrong. Bold. But her heart is too tender for its own good. She needs someone who can steady her. Maybe you can be for her what I was not. And for Astariu's sake, encourage her to let that great big heart of hers love! It would break me to know she was lonely and bitter because I was selfish enough to love her first, even though I could not be the last."*

Now she and Azhani sat with the remains of a hasty meal between them. All their tales had been told, all news had been shared, and the morass of the future was waiting to be plumbed. It was a beautiful, incredible mess, and she both loved and loathed it, for from this moment forward nothing would be the same. "Will you seek to depose Arris?" she asked softly.

A log on the hearth cracked and popped as the fire ate into a pocket of sap. Azhani jumped slightly. "That was my goal, at first. The rimerbeasts are the larger threat, though. Vengeance must wait. Y'Myran's safety is paramount." As Lyssera began to nod, her respect for the former warleader growing again, Azhani leaned forward and said, "I beg of you, please, send your rangers out tomorrow! They must find the caves where the egg sacs grow, for every cave that escapes cleansing will mean the slaughter of innocents come next winter."

"Yes. The orders will be sent, you may have no fear of that, Azhani," she replied. "Once they are dealt with, however, it is my intention to aid you in deposing Arris."

"Thank you. I know the import of what you offer. I will hope we can accomplish my aims without striking the drums of war."

"We will seek redress of the high king, but if Ysradan offers you no ear, then I shall marshal our allies, which are many, and we will crush Arris into insignificance," Lyssera said grimly. "And hang all those whose treachery hid the truth of Ylera's death." She shifted in her seat. "Did you come to Oakheart alone?" Then she laughed, shaking her head bemusedly. "I should have asked that earlier—you have not left someone hidden on a branch somewhere, suffering in the cold, have you, Azhani?"

"No. I came alone, of my own free will. It had to be that way, though my companion will likely not forgive me for it," she said with regret. "She is innocent of the way of politics—as innocent as I once was, I suspect."

Thinking over those Azhani had mentioned in her tale, Lyssera tried to envision which of them would fit that description—her southern cousin Padreg or his liegemen, Elisira, the lady of the court, or Devon, the page—and could not see how any of them would be ignorant of the politics that infused their daily lives. That left only one. "The stardancer," Lyssera said, feeling assured of her guess. There had been much joy in Azhani's tone when she had spoken of Kyrian, and not all of it was because she had saved her leg. *There is feeling there, as there should be. If she is the same Kyrian Ylera spoke of in her letters from Y'Len, she is a good and gentle woman whose skills and devotion to Astariu are almost unparalleled.*

"Aye." Wryly, Azhani chuckled. "It seems you find me as easy to read as Ylera did."

"Surely not. For though I take into account the lessons I've learned in your body language from the times we've sparred, I suspect Ylera's abilities came from a much richer and more enjoyable source," Lyssera said teasingly.

Azhani blushed. "I—she—we…"

"Did you love her?" she asked intently.

"With everything of me that is mine to give," was Azhani's instantaneous reply.

"Then you have nothing to be embarrassed about, my friend," Lyssera said solemnly. "For that is all I could ask for as a sister. Love is rare and imperfect. That Ylera should have it, should recognize it and not squander it is a gift I cannot thank you enough for giving."

Azhani wiped her eyes. "I don't think I could have done anything else, Lyss. She was the fire in my soul and, Goddess, I never wanted to put her out!"

They embraced again, and Lyssera held her, knowing Azhani would see Ylera in her, knowing that for Azhani, she might well be a temptation—and indeed, there was a draw there, a shadow of intoxicating, but forbidden fruit that she might taste. Their lust, shared through grief, could be very fulfilling in the moment, but she would ever be Ylera's ghost, the face of lost love, not the joy and splendor of truth. So when Azhani pulled back, she did not stop her, but let her go, content that their paths would diverge from this moment and friendship would remain.

Masking her thoughts with a curious smile, she said, "I know of a Stardancer Kyrian, I think. Those of Y'Len say she is deeply touched by Astariu's Fire. I trust if this is she, you will bring her to meet me?"

Azhani nodded. "Aye, I suspect it is she, unless another of her name was educated within Y'Len's monastery. And if she has not decided I am everything Arris claimed, then you will meet her soon enough."

"You always were too damned honorable for your own good." Ruefully, Lyssera shook her head. "You did not need to leave her behind—I would not have treated her badly for being your ally, even had I considered you my enemy."

"But what of your court?" Azhani countered. "Would they have been so forgiving of her? Would they have seen her as impartial? As one not tainted by my actions? And would they believe me as willing to confess my sins if I had come in the company of such a powerful priestess? Or would they think she had somehow coerced me, thus making my actions not those of honor, but of duress?"

Lyssera frowned. "Sadly, I think you have learned your lesson in politics too well, my friend. Most would not act as you suggest, but there are enough hidebound idiots populating my court—nobles whose pride still stings from the drubbing Thodan and I delivered them in our peace accords—who would jump at the chance to derail any merit your surrender would buy. To that end, I shall finally take the steps to make the court fully aware of your innocence and honor. She will be free to move about Oakheart without fear. I hope you will forgive me for not doing so earlier. Until I was assured of your safety, I had no wish to arouse Arris' suspicions." She bit her lip pensively. "Perhaps a part of me also still needed to test you, as well."

"I understand."

"For now, consider Oakheart your home. You and Stardancer Kyrian are welcome under its boughs."

"Thank you. I'd like to take a few days to get acquainted with its byways and peoples before I bring Kyrian here. We both know that there will be those who refuse to accept even the dictates of the queen. I can't have Kyrian placed in danger over actions that are perceived to be mine," Azhani said.

"I cannot disagree with your choices, my friend." Standing, Lyssera went to summon a servant. "I will house you in the rooms overlooking the lake, as always. Go now, and rest, for I have much to prepare." She chuckled softly. "My court is going to receive a bit of shaking up come the morning."

Queen Lyssera stepped into her council chamber and paused, looking at the men and women seated around the vast, horseshoe-shaped table that occupied the room. At its apex stood one empty chair, hers. On the wall directly across from that chair hung a tapestry depicting Y'Syr and its surrounding kingdoms.

"Good morrow, my friends," she said as she sat and rested her hands on the table. "I do apologize for the earliness of my summons, but we have much of great import to discuss."

Four seats away, Lord Bethelsel yawned, scratched his ancient, careworn face, and grumbled, "Out with it, Lyss. I'm tired and want to crawl back to my warm bed."

"Aye. I've shipments to oversee," said Lady Zishara. Her tone was sharp—and Lyssera expected nothing less, for Zishara had a long-held reputation for having the tongue like a sword master's dagger. "And merchants screaming for their wares to pass customs sometime this month."

Other councilors made similar complaints, though a few spoke in favor of their queen, one even saying, "Oh, hush everyone. If Lyss dragged us out of bed this early, it has to be for a good reason!"

"Thank you, Sidar," she said warmly. If Zishara was poisonous and sour, it could almost be guaranteed that Sidar would be sweet and accommodating. Lyssera hoped this did not bode ill—she had little time to deal with a personal battle right now, but as both had been at odds for years, she hoped that whatever enmity tumbled between them, it would remain locked behind private doors. For now, she turned a brilliant smile on her councilors. "My lords and ladies, I come to you this morning with grave news that must be passed on to you immediately, for it is nothing less than the identity of Princess Ylera's murderer."

No one reacted except Lord Bethelsel, who simply sighed.

Lady Zishara rolled her eyes. "Lyss, I don't know what's gotten into you this morning, but we all know it was Rhu'len DaCoure's halfbreed bastard! King Arris was quite clear in that."

Nodding, Lord Bethelsel said, "Yes. That is exactly what happened. She was exiled and is likely food for the wolves."

"That is what we were told," Lyssera replied solemnly. "But we were also told there were no witnesses to interview. Her body was sent to us already prepared for interment—we could not even perform our own investigation!" Angrily, she slammed her hands down on the table. "And now, now my lords and ladies, I know why." Standing, she began to circle the room. "I was always suspicious of Arris' word of the event, mostly because I had worked closely with Azhani Rhu'len many times—we all have, in order to secure the peace Thodan and I both desired for our kingdoms." Several of the nobles in the room nodded. "Then Starseeker Vashyra came and brought to me proof that Arris' word was little more than ugly lies!" She stopped beside her chair and leaned on the table, looking each of them in the face. "My lords and ladies, Azhani Rhu'len did not kill our beloved Ylera. No, that deed falls squarely in the hands of King Arris himself!"

They all jerked as if slapped. "Can you prove this?" Lord Bethelsel asked darkly. "For that is surely an act of war, my queen."

"I will share with you the proofs I was given." She motioned to a page, who dashed outside. "And I hope you will forgive me for withholding it."

Soon after, a priestess and two acolytes stepped into the room. Clad in the blue robes of a starseeker, the priestess carried about her an air of peaceful serenity, though in truth, she was one of the kingdom's most powerful mages.

"Thank you for coming, Vashyra," Lyssera said calmly, watching as the acolytes quickly constructed a framework of brass rods. "Will you show them the crystal, please?"

Vashyra bowed. "At your command, my queen." She produced a large shard of clear quartz. "My lords and ladies, you know this to be a memory crystal, a powerful magick gifted to us by the Twain themselves." She waited for the acolytes to finish, then placed the crystal at its apex. "It is not a magick we use lightly, though all can kneel before the altar of the Twain and beg its gifting. For some, it is merely a chance to say goodbye to one who is truly dear, but for others, it is their last chance to know the truth." Carefully, she hung a series of intricately decorated charms from hooks on the framework. As the crystal began to softly hum, she said, "See then, the truth of Ylera Kelani's death."

As Starseeker Vashyra stepped away from the device, the crystal began to emit a soft glow that slowly transformed into a hazy, ghost-like image of Ylera Kelani. Beseechingly, she reached her arms out to Lyssera. *"It is all lies, Lyss. My beloved Azhani did not do the things of which she is accused. Arris tried to force me to sign a confession. I refused."* Haltingly, she told a harrowing tale of kidnap, torture, rape, and murder that left the councilors staring at the shade in utter shock.

Having heard it before was no buffer for Lyssera, and she stood weeping openly, again filled with hatred for the man who had brought such suffering to her sister. Once more she vowed to have justice for Ylera and for Azhani, whose name and honor had been wrongly sullied by Arris' machinations. "Enough! They have heard enough," she said as Ylera's story came to an end. They did not need to hear her messages of love to Azhani. Those were for her lover's ears alone, should Azhani wish to hear them.

Vashyra nodded and ended the spell that had activated the crystal. As suddenly as it had appeared, Ylera's spirit vanished. "One more time can we access the memory, my queen, then the crystal's magick will be exhausted."

"Thank you, Vashyra. I think my councilors are convinced of its veracity," Lyssera said as she looked around the room at the faces of her nobles. Each bore expressions of shock, of grief, of anger, and of rage.

"Vengeance," Lord Bethelsel bellowed, slamming his fists on the table. "We must make war on Y'Dan at once!"

"Yes, we must make the Y'Dani scum pay!" Lady Zishara snarled, her face twisting into a rictus of hate.

"No! War can't be the only answer!" Lady Sidar cried worriedly. "Surely this is a matter for the high king!"

One of the other nobles turned to her. "You know nothing, Sidar. You easterners are too damned busy picking through ruins to pay attention to the troubles we've had to endure at the hands of those people!"

"Hold!" Lyssera waited until the room fell silent once more. "There is more to be heard before any plans are made," she said, turning and walking to the door. Opening it, she motioned for someone to enter.

"My queen," Azhani said as she stepped inside. "My lords and ladies," she added, bowing to those seated at the table. "I trust I am once again welcome? That the words I wish to share with you now will be viewed as truth and not the lies of an oathbreaker?"

"Of course." Calmly, Lyssera looked around the room and waited for someone to argue. No one did.

"Good," she said. Moving into the room, she made her way over to the tapestry that covered one wall of the council chamber and looked up at the mountains representing the Crest of Amyra. "For though I desire vengeance, there is a far more pressing concern." She reached up to caress an area known for being full of caves and solemnly said, "A beast season is upon us."

The council chamber erupted in a flurry of panicked questions, all of which she, Lyssera, and Vashyra strove to answer to the best of their abilities. By lunch time, they had decided to wait until they could confirm that rimerbeasts were spawning. If such was a case, then Azhani was heralded as an invaluable resource, one to be exploited should there be an invasion.

That she was to be trusted, however…that remained to be seen. Lyssera knew her nobles well, and could recognize that a few among them still held bitter resentment against both the Y'Danis and those whose blood wasn't purely elven.

"I fear my presence will cause much strife for you, my queen," Azhani said regretfully, once the room had emptied. "Lady Zishara does not much like me—she never has."

Lyssera nodded. "Aye, but she will put up with you. It is the ones who say nothing that worry me. 'Deep run the scars of ancient wounds,' or so my father once said of those who live on the border with Y'Dan. He would never have tried what Thodan and I did, though he would have approved." She rubbed her brow. "They will learn to deal with you, Azhani. They must. Y'Syr needs you."

"And I will serve her, and you, faithfully," Azhani murmured. "For Ylera."

Nodding, Lyssera looked over at the memory crystal and blinked back tears. "For Ylera."

News, like rumor, spread on the wings of whisper and conversation. By afternoon court the whole of Oakheart knew of Azhani Rhu'len's exoneration. The why of it was up for speculation, but for many, that the queen's proclamation was proof enough of her innocence. Not even Astariu herself would convince others, but they were wise enough to keep quiet—at least until their words would not fall on deaf ears.

Azhani cared little for those who sought her out and tried to ingratiate themselves as her "steadfast friends," for hands that were offered only during fair weather were of little value. What worried her was seeing gazes shift away whenever she approached, for those were the people who might be dangerous to Kyrian. Still, by directing an innocent seeming question or two toward would-be friends, she slowly became more comfortable with the idea that Kyrian would not be harmed should she join Azhani at the castle. As court began, she took a place at Lyssera's side and listened as the queen stood to address the hall.

Spreading her arms wide, Lyssera smiled. "Good afternoon, my friends. I trust your bellies are full and your minds are ready to ponder the fate of our beloved kingdom?"

Lady Sidar stood. "We are ready, Highness."

Inclining her head toward the scholarly noblewoman, Lyssera said, "Thank you, Sidar. Our first order of business is quite simple—due the rimerbeast threat, I have retained Azhani Rhu'len's services. Please know that she has my full faith and trust."

Azhani waited for her to turn before kneeling. "I give you my sword," she said, offering her weapon to the queen hilt first, "in token of my willingness to champion your cause, Highness."

Taking it, Lyssera touched the pommel to her breast. "I accept your sword, Azhani Rhu'len, and grant you permission to walk in my shadow, armed against my enemies and those who would wish Y'Syr harm."

Solemnly, Azhani's blade was returned. She stood, sheathing it carefully before turning and bowing to the court. "My lords and ladies, I serve at the will of Lyssera, queen of Y'Syr. May Astariu guide my hand to the hearts of her enemies."

There were many stunned faces looking back at them. Azhani remained calm, knowing that they would not like what Lyssera had done. Accepting her innocence was easy, but she was still a halfbreed, and right now anyone of Y'Dani blood would find themselves in bad odor with the Y'Syran court.

Those who had been upset before now hurled questions like stones. "You're an oathbreaker! How can you serve our glorious queen?"

"Murdering bitch, how can we trust you not to stab Lyssera in the back?"

"Wasn't killing one Kelani sister enough?"

"Silence!" Queen Lyssera glared at everyone until the courtiers grew mum. "Azhani's innocence has been proven to myself and the council of nobles and that is all you need know."

Even as she wore an outward mask of calm, Azhani feared some of the agitated members of the court might act brashly. But the presence of the queen's guard—and Lyssera herself—forced them to keep their distance.

Lyssera looked around the room, pausing from time to time to stare at particular members of the court before saying, "And if our word is not enough for you, then I enjoin you to speak to Starseeker Vashyra."

With a soft chuckle, Lady Sidar said, "I think, my queen, that they would rather shout at you then have a conversation with the eminent and undoubtedly impatient mage."

"Perhaps you are right, Sidar, but she does know the truth they seek." Lyssera smiled icily. "Now, as I am certain there are more important matters pending before this court, I will ask the herald to call the afternoon session and announce the first order of business."

As the herald stepped forward, Lyssera took her seat on the throne and Azhani retreated into the shadows, keeping one ear turned toward the chatter that slowly filled the silences between petitioners. It was informative, though also frustrating, to listen to the petty natterings that fluttered about the room like half-crazed butterflies. In the space of a few candlemarks, she learned such dubiously interesting things as the fact that Lord Bethelsel was currently wooing Lady Volkirk's favorite maid while Lady Zishara was unhappy with the master of the weaver's guild and was, according to her handmaiden's page, planning to cause him a great deal of trouble at the docks the next time he brought in a shipment of spun-gold threads from Y'Tol.

Interestingly, Lady Sidar seemed one of the few who eschewed the trappings of gossip and focused instead on the reason for court, keeping her gaze fixed on the petitioners. Of course, some found this offensive. More than once, Azhani heard someone say, "That Sidar thinks she's doing the Twain's work by listening to every mud-daubed goatherd beg for coin. When is she going to learn that our true calling is to show the people of Y'Myran that we of Y'Syr are the best of all?"

Of course, there were those whose thoughts lay in Azhani's direction, one even muttering, "She's got to have some kind of hold over the queen—information she's using, perhaps, to force Lyssera into accepting her. There's no other reason for it! How could she be innocent? I don't believe it!"

"Hush, Mazrodi, unless you want Lyssera to send her new pet over here to muzzle you!" another courtier hissed. "Innocent or not, she's got the queen's ear and we don't!"

I may have the queen's ear, but my position is not secure. Still, Mazrodi's harmless. I remember him—a fifth son of a fifth son. His family is more name than power in Oakheart. If that's all I need worry about, then Kyrian's safety is almost assured.

She was troubled by guilt. Leaving Kyrian to wait at Tellyn's shop might have seemed wise in the beginning, but with all that loomed ahead, she wondered if she'd made the right decision. Had honor been satisfied? Her pardon had come of her own merit and she now held an unassailable perch at the queen's side.

I miss her. An ache that was as unfamiliar as it was troubling settled itself in her gut. *Maybe tomorrow, I can fetch her here. Lyssera did say she had some things to share with me tonight.*

Court eventually came to an end, allowing the courtiers to disperse. Azhani hurried away from the chamber and met Lyssera in a nearby hall.

"I know we must focus on the rimerbeast threat," Lyssera said quietly, taking Azhani's arm as they walked together. "But I've another task for you, as well."

"Yes?"

"My nephew—Allyndev—he will rule one day, if I do not produce heirs. Sadly, he lacks the character of a leader." Lyssera sighed. "Some may see this as a blessing, for he is not what they would choose as their king, but I know his troubles to be merely the moodiness of a lad who cares little for anything beyond his own pursuits. Thus I wish you to make him your squire, that he might learn to see past his own wants. And to impart to him a sense of martial ability, as well, for thus far he has gained none."

Azhani quirked one eyebrow upward. "Why not simply give him to one of your sword masters?"

"Because he is tainted in their eyes—by the scourge of Y'Dani blood no less," she replied unhappily. "They think him unworthy of their focus and treat him poorly when he doesn't perform better than his Y'Syran peers. And there is little I can do to discourage this, as it will only weaken his position further. Allyndev must earn their respect, and so far he has not found the desire to even try. This makes him seem lazy, for he is a dreamer and lacks the proper adherence to his training."

Having had more than a few young men and women like that under her command, Azhani simply said, "That will change—or he will find himself mucking stalls all day."

Lyssera chuckled. "Let me take you to him."

As they continued on their way, Azhani glanced over at a liveried guardsman and smiled wolfishly. "You know, I met the captain of your guard earlier. He seemed rather irritated with me. I wonder why?"

With a delighted laugh, she said, "Oh, I suspect it has something to do with the four guardsmen he recently found sleeping on the job."

"Ah, well, he shouldn't blame them too much—they had soft heads," Azhani said, the slyness of her grin belying the innocence of her tone. "I'm sure the proper headgear will fix that problem neatly."

"I trust you'll not find Allyndev's head quite as soft, though if it is, I'm sure you'll do your best to thump him in it," Lyssera said dryly. "When you are not educating the prince on martial matters, I want you to work with my guards and soldiers. Teach them all you can about rimerbeasts and how to fight them."

"All that I know will be at their immediate disposal. Now, tell me more about Allyndev," she said as they exited Oakheart and entered one of the gardens surrounding the massive tree.

With a sigh, Lyssera looked around. "What is there to tell? Allyndev is the son of my youngest sister, Alynna. His father was Y'Dani. He might have a better position here at court if Alynna were here to shield him, but she has been gone since he was a small child and I fear I am a poor substitute for a mother. Ylera tried, but she had her own duties—and destiny—to follow."

Solemnly, Azhani murmured, "With me. And then she died."

"Yes. And Allyndev has had an opportunity to ignore his own destiny, dabbling in things that one of Kelani blood would not normally find interesting. It is yet one more reason why he is out of place in court."

"Thus he is viewed as neither fish nor fowl, and ignored as useless fluff by those members of the court with whom he should be familiar." Azhani shook her head as she snorted derisively. "I really do hate politics."

"Aye, but for a prince of the blood to be so disgracefully unfit to defend the realm," Lyssera said as she stopped a moment. Placing her hand on Azhani's arm, she looked her in the eye and said, "Were it up to me, I would let him be, but I cannot risk civil war should I die childless."

Azhani nodded. "I understand, my queen."

They started walking again.

Ahead of them stood a grove of massive trees, all part of the structure of Oakheart Manor and Y'Syria itself. High above, the trunks were linked by bridges and branches that melded together, allowing citizens and visitors to traverse the distances between floors without ever having to descend to the ground. At the base of one such tree knelt a young man.

Sweat liberally stained his tunic. Dirt smudged his pants and clogged the tines of the hand rake hanging from his belt. Nearby, the fruits of his labors lay in a pile waiting to be transferred to a wheelbarrow. Seeming not to have noticed their approach, he hacked away at a dark green vine that had woven itself around the trunk and was slowly leeching the life from the wood.

If Azhani was surprised to see someone that had been described as a "dreamer" doing what was, essentially, the work of groundskeepers, she said nothing, merely studied the young man as they approached.

Just as they reached him, he let out a string of curses, then attacked the remaining bits of vine with vigor. Azhani was suitably impressed. *If he can channel that aggression into pell work, I might be able to do something with him after all.* She could easily imagine him taking a weapon to one of the rope-wrapped poles that lined the practice yards of nearly every guardhouse in Y'Myran. *I was afraid he'd be some pampered pet too frail to lift a dagger, much less a sword.*

Thoughtfully, she considered his appearance. Allyndev was tall, like herself, but light of skin—so pale, in fact, that it had reddened under the harsh glare of the sun. Thin, though not frail, the young man's frame was obviously not built for heavy arms and armor. *Leather, then, studded with steel strips and fitted to him for now. Chain later, when he's built up the wind to carry it. Short sword for close work, a bow, perhaps, and I'll train him up to the longer blades. He'll never carry a claymore, but he won't have to. And light shields should do—bucklers, I think. Though the elves do prefer the kite. I'll have to see if he can strengthen that arm up enough to use one. Might as well try to make him more palatable to those he might one day serve.* He was not unpleasant to look at, having the sort of sweetly handsome face she had come to expect on elven men, though it was tempered by the rounder features of his Y'Dani heritage—his cheeks were stubbly and she wondered if he'd yet learned to shave. He wore his blond hair long, as was fashion with the court of Oakheart.

"Good afternoon, nephew," Lyssera said, startling him into turning around to face them.

"Hello, aunt." He bowed quickly. "Is there aught you require of me?" he asked, coming closer to them. His gait was gawky, as if both of his legs had been affixed to his knees backwards. Something about him was very familiar, though. A round fullness to his face that was both human and uniquely Y'Dani, which made Azhani feel an immediate connection to the young man.

Though men and elves had shared both kingdom and gods for many generations, each side still viewed the other with a bit of wariness born of old—and in the case of the Y'Dan-Y'Syr border, recently ongoing—conflicts. Thodan and Lyssera's peace had been hard won, which was why it was so gut wrenching to know that Thodan's son was doing his best to destroy it with his new laws favoring humans.

Azhani watched Allyndev closely, making mental notes as to what she could do to help him become the man his aunt hoped he could be. *Hm. Perhaps we'd best work on his balance first, then move into more martial pursuits. I'll need to make use of the practice salle. Maybe even take him into the forest, away from judgmental eyes.*

"Yes. I wish you to meet someone," Lyssera said with a warm smile. "Someone you may find as vexing as I, but who you will also learn can be a great friend." She gestured to Azhani. "This is Azhani Rhu'len, and if Fate's hand had been kinder, she might have become your aunt."

To hear herself characterized as such caused Azhani a sharp pang of grief, but it was the truth. Had she and Ylera been able to marry as they desired, Ylera's kin would have been Azhani's. Filled now with mixed feelings as she beheld the young man, she nevertheless kept her expression neutral.

Allyndev blinked slowly. "I had heard she was here." He turned to her. "Welcome to Oakheart. I…sorrow with you. I treasured Aunt Ylera deeply."

"Thank you," she said.

Grinning proudly, Lyssera draped her arm around Allyndev's shoulders. "You are to become her student, Allyn. It's my hope she'll be able to instill in you some sense of how to defend yourself."

The look on Allyndev's face was anything but excited, but Azhani ignored it. Still filled with mixed feelings, she brusquely told him, "We'll meet in the salle at dawn. Don't be late." She started to go, wondering if he'd react to her tone at all.

With a much-put-upon sigh, Allyndev sullenly replied, "Yes, Azhani."

Lesson one. Respect everyone, regardless of station—for if you offer it, it will be returned. With hardly a flicker of motion, she was upon him, ripping the axe from his hand and pushing him out of Lyssera's grasp, pinning him to the trunk of the great tree. Pressing the edge of the blade to his throat, she growled, "Master Azhani, my prince. Queen Lyssera has named me as your instructor, and as such, I will tell you that respect offered brings its return. I may be little more than a simple retainer, but I am more than your match in the arena of weaponry. You will accord me the title of master until such time as you can walk from a battlefield beside me." She pulled the axe back, stepped away from him, and offered him the tool hilt first.

"Y-yes, Master Azhani," he stammered, managing not to drop the axe as he took it back.

The first lesson had been learned.

Two days passed. Each morning, Azhani promised herself that *this* would be the day she fetched Kyrian from the herbalist's house. By the end of the day, she'd talked herself out of it, making excuses to keep busy. First, she had to relearn every corridor and bridge of Oakheart Manor, to be certain nothing hid in the shadows that might harm her friend. Then there was Allyndev, whose needs as a student kept her busy for many candlemarks. Lyssera also bought much of Azhani's precious time, calling her into meetings for advice and education about the rimerbeasts, about Arris, and about anything else she or her council might ask.

It was after one such meeting that Azhani discovered an old friend wandering the halls of Oakheart. Kuwell Longhorn, a dwarven blacksmith and warrior with a huge sense of humor and an even greater sense of honor, had been a friend to her family for close to twenty years.

"Azhani! By the hammers of my ancestors, it's good to see you!" He embraced her, pounding her back with rough affection.

"Kuwell, old friend! I didn't expect to see you so far from your mead hall!" She kissed his bearded cheek fondly.

A look of sheer surprise crossed his craggy features. "Ye haven't heard then? Old Uldvar dragged his arse up to me door and set me to th' task o' roostin' among these elven birds!"

Chuckling in amusement, she said, "No, I hadn't heard," as they made their way over to a cluster of chairs near a fireplace and motioned for a servant to bring refreshments. "You'll have heard what happened since last we met in the Crest, then?"

"Aye. 'Tis a tale fit to make a man drown himself in ale and mead. I'd hear it again, though, if ye've a mind to tell an old man the truths which rumors make lies," he said quietly.

Over mulled wine and pheasant pie, she told him of loving—and losing— Ylera Kelani. Her tale covered every facet of the truth from serving her king, to Thodan's death, to Arris' rise to power and her own terrible fall from grace. In the end, he was holding her hand, his massive, scarred and calloused fingers engulfing hers. "Lass, ye know ye've got me at yer side. And rimerbeasts!" He spat. "I'll be to my writing desk after this, though I don't know how much Uldvar can help us—have ye heard? There be reports of a dragon harrowing tunnels and farms!"

In shock, she blurted, "No! Goddess!" Dragons had been gone from Y'Myran so long that they were myths when the Firstlanders came. "Surely it's something else?"

He shook his head. "Not accordin' to the few reports that have made their way here. Frankly, 'tis fair surprisin' I've not been called home to help battle the beastie. 'Til I'm told otherwise, ye've got the aid o' the Longhorns. I swear by Astarus' forge, we'll see that no rimerbeasts come east."

"Thank you. I'll inform Lyssera of your pledge. I'm sure it'll help for her to know that she has you at her back," she said, feeling very grateful for this chance meeting. After arranging to speak again in a few days' time, they parted.

It was now time for Allyndev's afternoon lesson. With most everyone off at court, it was quiet in the halls, allowing her the opportunity to reflect on her surroundings. There was not much about Oakheart she could not admire. The castle—indeed most of the city—was a living structure shaped from the trees by Y'Syr's greatest mages, a secretive sect of elves known only as "the gardeners".

Holding a position in elven society above that of even the most venerable of starseekers, a gardener's entire life was given to the care of the kingdom's massive trees. From a young age, those gifted with the skills of a gardener were taught to control a form of magick that allowed them to manipulate the very essence of life itself. It was an art that could be—and sadly, had been—used for great evil, thus only those with the purest of hearts and souls were allowed to join their ranks.

Azhani felt nothing but respect for the gardeners, and for young Allyndev himself, for he had wished to be among their number. Sadly, he had not been born with the gift. Otherwise his place in the Y'Syran court would have been quickly assured, for gardeners were respected and beloved no matter their familial origins. She passed a liveried guard, who offered her a sketchy half bow. Her own status had been finalized the prior evening, and now she wore a tabard that marked her as one of Lyssera's personal retainers. It gave her access to all of Oakheart Manor, a stipend, and a suite of rooms not far from the queen's study. For that, she was accorded the official title of Special Liaison to the guard and Master-at-Arms for Prince Allyndev.

Titles notwithstanding, this meant that in the event of a rimerbeast spawning, she would do as she had during previous beast seasons and lead Lyssera's army. Y'Syr had been without a warleader since Princess Alynna's untimely death, and Lyssera had yet to choose a successor. In past years, Azhani had liaised with several of the queen's lieutenants and sergeants, coordinating the efforts between the Y'Syran and Y'Dani armies in order to combat the rimerbeast threat.

Many of the Y'Syran foot soldiers—and most of the court—had been blissfully unaware that their defense had been due to her efforts. In the event that she was called to lead the armies north, Azhani expected to face anger and outrage from certain members of the court and the military. To say that this didn't bother her would be a lie, but it was among the least of her current worries.

Azhani had asked the queen why she did not just name a new warleader, but Lyssera had been adamant about keeping the position open, though she'd laughed and jokingly added, "Unless you want the job?"

While it was tempting to take up the mantle once again, it felt like putting on a cloak of honor she had not yet earned. Hastily she'd declined and changed the subject to Arris and how to deal with him over the coming months, for he was certain to learn of her whereabouts and seek to do something about it. Lyssera's answer had been pointedly simple—she would deal with Arris when the time came.

Of the other kingdoms, they had little news beyond unsubstantiated rumors of strife and trouble, but with Y'Dror dealing with a dragon and rimerbeasts spawning far out of season, Azhani was beginning to wonder if those stories might contain a grain of truth.

Prince Allyndev had learned his first lesson well—almost too well, for now his respect was heavily tinged with fear. Over time, she hoped this would ease. What else he would learn from her remained to be seen. Guilt touched her thoughts then, for he had initially greeted her with kindness and she had returned it with harsh words—words he may not have deserved had she given him time to know her. She could only attribute her actions to the maelstrom of emotion that had affected her upon their meeting. In Ylera's nephew, Azhani could see so many ghosts of her lost beloved—ghosts she saw in Lyssera, as well.

Oh, Kyrian, I need you. You would help me make sense of everything in my head. It was time and past to be honest with herself, for there were no excuses not to go back to her friend and beg her forgiveness. It was safe in Oakheart, safer than even at Tellyn Jarelle's, where there were no guardsmen to turn away those who might put a knife in Kyrian's back simply for helping Azhani Rhu'len survive. Staying away now only prolonged her friend's ire. *I'll go tonight, after Allyn's lesson.*

A page ran up to her then, and pressed a sealed message into her hand, racing off before she could say more than a hasty thanks. Opening it, she found a summons to attend Lyssera after Allyndev's lesson. For some reason, instead of being vexed, Azhani found herself relieved.

Goddess, what am I afraid of? Pausing in the hall, she stared at her reflection in a nearby mirror, noting that her eyes looked hollow and shadowed, as if she had not slept well. In truth, she had not—for when she was able to seek her bed, her nights had been filled with nightmares. Forcing herself to face the truth, she sighed and silently admitted, *I don't want her to be mad at me. Goddess, I'm a fool. I need her. She's become too important to lose. Tomorrow, I must go and apologize, and hope…hope that she isn't too vexed with me.*

"I shouldn't keep distracting you like this," Lyssera said ruefully as she welcomed Azhani into her office. "But I feel closer to her, with you here."

Solemnly, Azhani nodded. "As do I, Lyss. What did you wish to talk about?" Since she'd arrived at Oakheart, Azhani's nights had been filled with conversations. Some of them had been about war and rimerbeasts, but when it was just her and Lyssera, it had almost always focused on their one common bond: Ylera.

They each found comfort in the other's presence, though for Azhani, that comfort was bittersweet. Lyssera was a friend, but her face so closely echoed Ylera's that it made her hurt all the more for looking at it.

"Tonight, I think we should speak of Allyndev first," Lyssera replied as she gestured to the chair that was fast becoming Azhani's seat.

"All right. Where do you want to start?"

"You know he is young—by our standards still a child, though humans, of course, see him differently," Lyssera said as she sat in the chair across from Azhani's and poured them each a glass of Y'Tolian wine.

"He mentioned that he had recently passed his twentieth summer." Azhani sipped the potent wine. The last thing she needed was to wake with a muddled head.

"Aye. As you know, Alynna was our warleader, but after she died it just didn't seem right to name another in her place. I had Allyn to raise and I think part of me hoped that he would grow into the role. That somehow her prowess would have transferred to him, making him the perfect candidate to bear the Oakheart arms." Regret made Lyssera's tone wistful and touched with sadness. "That was not to be. He preferred the peaceful ways of the gardeners and honestly, I would have been overjoyed for him, were he able to wield their magicks."

"But he's no more mage gifted than I," Azhani said dryly. "And not terribly inclined to scholarship, either. In Y'Dan, he'd have been little more than a rich merchant's son, never focused, never forced to do anything but dabble in whatever delighted him."

"Exactly." Lyssera frowned and set her glass aside. "Here, however, because we prefer to pass the warleader's mantle on to one who is of the Kelani family, it was most frustrating. When he turned sixteen, the council begged me to keep the position open rather than elevate him and put lives in danger."

Considering how something like that would have made her feel, Azhani winced. "It can't have helped his self-esteem much to have his birthright withheld."

Lyssera shook her head. "It was not a pleasant day when I told him. The words he had for me were rather harsh, but perhaps deserved."

"To him they likely were," Azhani replied, then gave Lyssera a long, intent look. "But you were in the right. I know the way you elves think—you gain status from the deeds of those you influence. A sword master would care little for one whose life is short and lacking in opportunities to showcase their teacher's skill. I was lucky that Swordmaster Delaye did not think thusly about me."

"And no amount of money would entice him to stay in Oakheart, so Allyn could not benefit from his tutelage." Lyssera made a face as she refilled her wine glass. Azhani's was still half full. "But you've given me some hope, Azhi. You can prove his naysayers wrong."

Azhani inclined her head. "Perhaps. Though I must say that after you put him under my care, I spent some time with the servants. They do not have a very high opinion of him."

"No, they don't."

"Arrogant, they called him, when they were being kind."

"Aye, though my council calls him standoffish to my face," Lyssera said regretfully. "That is my failure. I let him have his way too many times when he was younger."

"Hm. Well, after hearing all that, I was certain I'd spend more time spanking him instead of training him," Azhani said dryly. "Thankfully, that has not been the case. In the main, he is merely a young man with a delicate ego, but he is also deeply uncertain of himself. In combination, this makes him difficult to teach, because he becomes filled with self-doubt if he does not immediately grasp a concept, then gets overconfident when he does."

Lyssera shook her head. "A dreadful combination in any young man, but especially in a prince of Y'Syr. We elves strive hard not to be seen as emotionless, icy wraiths—it puts us too much to mind of the mythic Alyrr."

Though Azhani knew little of the people that had ruled Y'Myran in the time before the Firstlanders, she did know the elves both feared and respected them deeply. "It is something I can train out of him, given enough time."

"Then by the Twain's grace, you shall have it," she said, lifting her glass in a toast.

They talked more of Allyn and his hoped-for future. Then Lyssera, perhaps affected by the bottle and a half of wine she had consumed, reached down beside her, pulled a harp onto her lap and played. Entranced, Azhani listened as a spell of music so familiar it made her bones ache was woven around her. After a while, Lyssera stopped playing. "How did Ylera like Y'Dani music?"

Startled from her reverie, she said, "She adored it," and then closed her eyes, trying to find the elusive sense of peace Lyssera's music had created.

"Tell me more, please."

Firelight cast golden shadows on both of them. Azhani sighed wistfully. "She...used to make me go to these recitals. Awful or artful, it mattered little to her, so long as there were many bards there to vie for her attentions."

Sorrowfully, Lyssera shook her head. "She adored music and everything to do with it. Even the poorest musician could earn coins from her if they had the courage to present themselves at court. I am not so kind. My ears cannot stand the sound of would-be minstrels savaging the greatest lays of our bards."

Lost in memories, it took Azhani some time to speak. "Thodan once begged her to stop letting the 'catgut bangers' into the castle. She promised she would, but she never did. I think it amused her to torment him a little."

Lyssera laughed, and for a brief fragment of time, Azhani was transported to when Ylera still lived and she too would throw back her head and boldly express her mirth. Through the lens of memory, she saw Lyssera as her beloved and wondered if, within her, she might find and capture what she had lost. If Lyssera could be her beloved returned.

"That, I'm afraid, was Ylera's mischievous side sneaking out to play. I, on the other hand, would have sided with Thodan from the beginning," Lyssera said with a sour frown. "And banned the untalented vagrants from the keep!"

Azhani nearly jumped, she was so startled by the sharpness of Lyssera's statement. No, no, she would not find her beloved here, not in a woman whose world was measured in terms of mastery and perfection. No matter how much she might claim Azhani's friendship, Lyssera would never see her as anything more than a dalliance and that was not who Azhani was.

My heart has felt the stamp of love too deeply to bear the press of mere lust. Though I fear my life has no place left for love, I'll not settle for anything but the equal of what I shared with Ylera. Anything less would be unfair to her memory. Whatever else Lyssera is, she is not to be my lover. And this, she realized then, was exactly what Lyssera had intended her to understand.

Wiping the tears her memories had conjured from her eyes, Azhani said, "You are far too clever, my queen."

An amused, gentle smile curved Lyssera's generous mouth. "And so I am discovered. I think I am not the only clever one in this room," she said. "Do not think me cruel, my friend. You had to see, to understand, before your heart took a path it should not."

Azhani nodded. "Yes. I know you are not Ylera, and now my heart knows it as well."

Lyssera closed her eyes. "Goddess, I do miss her. There is not a day that passes that I do not wake knowing that half of me is gone," she said softly. "I long for her presence so much! It seems as though I'll never stop needing her, wondering where she is, what she's doing, wishing she were still here, hating that she's gone. Sometimes, I feel like no one else cares beyond the fact that it's yet one more insult laid upon our people by the Y'Danis and—"

Sharply, Azhani snarled, "I miss her too! There is not a candlemark that burns that I do not wish it had been me that Arris had slain, not her." She glared at Lyssera. "Take care you do not forget that I lost the deepest part of my heart, my queen!"

Lyssera jerked back in surprise. "I know. I'm sorry—I meant no offense." Carefully, she set aside her harp. "However, you need to know that you are not the only one whose life was shattered by Arris' foul deed!" Leaping to her feet, she began to pace the room. "Do you know how we came to know of her death?"

"No—I assumed by messenger."

"Oh, aye. He sent a messenger—with a box. A plain, unadorned crate without even the barest of starseeker's spells to preserve her so we could properly prepare her for The Great Fields." Angrily, she spat, "My beautiful sister came home a stinking, rotted mess!"

Horrified, Azhani gaped at her.

"There wasn't a stardancer in Y'Syria who could tell me *how* she had died. We had to believe Arris' message of hatred and lies—but it felt so wrong, so utterly wrong! I knew my sister would never betray me, Thodan, or most importantly, our dreams of peace!"

"What changed your mind?" Azhani asked dully, the weight of Lyssera's violent outburst seeming to fuse her to the chair.

Slumping as if drained by her emotional outpouring, Lyssera murmured, "You know what."

Azhani shivered. "You mentioned…her spirit?"

"I went to Vashyra. Begged her to make a memory stone for me. We didn't think it could be done. Ylera hadn't been prepared, and she was almost gone, but Vashyra is powerful and I—I think Astariu gave us her blessing that night, for—" Grief destroyed Lyssera's ability to speak. She stood with her palms pressed to her face, shaking, her breath coming in ragged, sob-filled gasps. "S-she came. M-my sister, m-my beautiful, beautiful sister," she whispered brokenly.

Going to her, Azhani wrapped her arms around her. "Tell me," she murmured comfortingly. They'd spoken of it in fragments before—bits and pieces of a story neither of them wanted to hear, but desperately needed to tell, even though the agony of it made them both shy away from the topic.

"Oh Goddess, I can't. There was so much. She…she endured so much. And she talked. For candlemarks, she talked, telling me all she knew, all she could remember of her last few days, of loving you… Astariu's breath, she did love you so!" she said vehemently.

Azhani's throat constricted and her eyes burned. "And I loved-love her."

"I know." They separated. "I think you should hear at least some of what was said." Lyssera tugged a cloth off a nearby side table. On it was a device of rods and charms, and cradled at its apex was a crystal. "It's fragile. I'm afraid it only has strength for a final message—one I saved just for you."

"Lyss, oh no, I don't—"

It was too late, though. Lyssera was already engaging the device. Ylera appeared before them. Glorious, whole, and precious—all for her, and all Azhani could do was stare.

She was dressed in the most exquisite of silken robes. Her hair was swept back; her brow bore a circlet set with golden stones. Flowers draped her shoulders. Shaking with emotion, Azhani reached for her, but her hands slipped right through the wraith.

"Azhani," she whispered. *"Oh, my beloved. Would that you could know. Could understand the things I felt. They will tell you it was impossible, but believe them not, for all that we had was true. I was yours and you were mine, beloved."* She smiled and it was rich and beautiful. *"The Great Fields call. The path stretches before me. You have sung me home, my love, and I go, but my love stays, for it is yours, forever and always, it is yours."*

Light, brilliant and golden, suffused the stone, and, with a soft puff it turned to ashes. Ylera was gone.

Time puddled as Azhani and Lyssera stood there, clinging to each other, the nearby day candle burning into a pool of wax. A servant slipped in and replaced it, carefully not looking at either of them, though Azhani absently made note of her presence and her apparent discretion. Another day, she would find her and make an ally of her, for anyone who could move so quietly would be of immense value. For now, however, her focus was this moment, and her grief, and the loss of something so precious and vital that all she could do was mourn.

Kyrian, oh, Kyrian, I should have you here. I need you here. Oh, curse my damnable pride!

A full candlemark passed before either of them moved and by then, both were stiff. "Ah, Goddess, Azhani, if I look half as bad as you do, my maids will keel over from fright in the morning!" Lyssera said as they stepped apart and stretched wearily.

"They'll survive." Azhani smiled sardonically.

"So they shall," she replied, then chuckled in amusement. "I think I see what it is Ylera loved so much about you, my friend. She always did cherish humor when it went in concert with beauty and brains."

Azhani quirked her eyebrow upward. "Humor, my queen? I assure you, I am the least funny person Ylera would have known."

"Precisely what would have made you so amusing to her, no doubt." Lyssera resumed her seat and took her harp into her lap once more.

Azhani settled across from her and, with a shy smile, asked, "Would you play for me, my queen?"

Setting her fingers to the strings, she said, "What would you like to hear?"

"Something she loved."

Hesitantly, Lyssera picked out a tune Azhani had not heard since before Ylera's death. It was a lay of summer, a simple, strong melody that painted pictures of blue skies, gardens filled with birds, and burgeoning new life rising from the soil. There were no words to the piece, but Azhani didn't need them. Simply hearing it was enough, for its resonating notes evoked a time when Ylera lived, breathed, laughed, and loved.

It was not the same, though. Lyssera's fingers were rusty. Her harp carried a flatter tune, and she sat differently, addressed the strings with less grace, and was, in all ways, as far away from Ylera as she could be.

The music went on as Lyssera's skill returned. New songs filled the chamber. Pieces Azhani did not know, but sensed Ylera would have loved. Time passed, and little by little the band around her chest dissolved. Slowly, she took what felt like her first real breath since she had been dragged away from Ylera's body and thrown into the dungeon. For a moment, she held it, clinging to that moment, to that sharp, agonizing pain, but then she had to let it go, to exhale. She sighed, and with that breath went the grief that had been her constant, unforgotten companion. Leaning back in the chair, Azhani closed her eyes and saw again the face of her beloved.

Oh, my love. You are gone and I grieve that so deeply, but I still live. It is time to recognize that my life is not over, to take joy in that fact. I miss you, but my future still stands before me. Be happy and know that I love you, that I will always love you. One day, we will walk together in the Great Fields.

"Thank you," Azhani said quietly. "You have given me an immeasurable gift."

Lyssera stilled the harp strings. "You are welcome. I think we have both found some peace this night."

"Aye, we have," she said, wishing Kyrian was there to share it.

The next day, a message from Padreg arrived. Delivered by an exhausted courier, the heavy scroll was packed full of news about Y'Myran. Almost every rumor she'd heard in Lyssera's court was supported, and hard on the heels of Padreg's missive came couriers from the other kingdoms. The messages were all distressingly similar. In one breath, Arris' actions were condemned, but in the second, the rulers declined to offer Azhani any aid in seeking redress, claiming they were all too overwhelmed with their own woes.

King Naral of Y'Tol's letter best summed up the feeling that pervaded the scrolls spread out atop Lyssera's desk.

"Though I grieve for the loss of Princess Ylera, and it sickens me to know one of my brother monarchs is touched by the blight of madness, my forces must concentrate upon the plague that befalls my land ere I can look beyond my borders. You have, however, my support and prayers—and the hope that this horror will soon end, that Ysradan will be able to crush the imbecile before irreparable harm is done to the people of Y'Dan. Take also a small token of my greatest wishes for your success."

With the scroll had come cases of fine Y'Tolian wine. On the face of it, the gift seemed outrageously useless, but Azhani knew better.

"At least he made sure we could hire every mercenary in Three Kingdoms Crossing," she said wryly.

"Aye, and King Uldvar has provided us with the arms we'll need to coax even the most reluctant soldier to leave his warm bed when the winter snows clog the mountains," Lyssera said with a faint smile. "Though I wish I knew what to do with Queen Kalian's gift." She opened a thick roll of velvet to display a series of glass disks that had been wrapped in thin parchment.

"Oh, Lyss," Azhani whispered, shaking her head slowly. "Clearly you have not traveled far. Those are lenses meant for use in spyglasses. With them, you can view things that are a great distance away. They are worth their weight in gold and gems."

"I see. And have I the craftsmen to create this device? It seems an army might require such things."

"Aye. I know a jeweler who could craft them," Azhani replied. "Sava Kodar—do you know him?"

Lyssera nodded. "Very well. I'll have these sent over right away." After carefully wrapping the lenses, she penned a brief message to the jeweler and summoned a servant to take the lenses—and a fair amount of gold—down to the merchant's quarter of the city.

Though they'd received no word from High King Ysradan, a brief letter from his regent Pirellan Madros had arrived. In it, he politely refused to take any official action, writing that such things were "strictly within the realm of the high king's purview and out of the control of his regent."

Cursing softly, Lyssera threw the scroll aside. "I like Ysradan, but sometimes he seems to lack the grasp of what it truly means to be high king. The kingdoms need him now—he should have sent Pirellan to deal with the damned sea monsters!"

"What would he do? Bore them to death?" Azhani asked sourly. "Scare them with his shrieks of terror?"

Lyssera snorted. "Point taken. Pirellan's not the heroic type. Still, surely a better regent could have been chosen."

"But one who would easily relinquish the throne once Ysradan returned? The last thing we need is a usurper on the high throne." Azhani made a face. "I don't approve of Ysradan's choice, but I understand it."

"You are right, of course," Lyssera said ruefully. "Dragons in Y'Dror, kraken in Y'Mar, rimerbeasts, the troubles in Y'Skan and Y'Tol—it just seems too damned coincidental for this all to be mere happenstance."

Pensively, Azhani tapped Padreg's scroll against her thigh. "It is not. We face something darker than we know, but what it is, I have yet to fathom. I can only pray that we'll see ourselves through it, for even Padreg cannot help us—not with Y'Nym being overrun by ogres."

"I know," Lyssera said, then pushed a final scroll toward Azhani. "At least we have some good news."

Kuwell Longhorn had proven himself a true ally. His clan had reached out to several others that owed the ambassador favors, and from them would come a small army of dwarves who were willing to face the uncertainty of rimerbeasts over the glory of fighting a dragon. Within the next few weeks, they would be arriving, ready to take up arms in service to the crown of Y'Syr.

"It's only good news because we have so much bad to digest," Azhani replied dourly. One final artifact remained on the desk. It was a dagger. Simple, well-made and common, its blade had been completely destroyed by a rimerbeast's acidic spoor. She had taken it from an elven scout earlier that day. He hadn't wanted to surrender his blade to her, but she'd promised him that the queen herself would know he was the one who had brought back the priceless intelligence.

Then the young scout could hardly contain his glee as he'd handed the knife over, for that kind of personal glory would reflect on his family, raising their status in the court.

Lyssera prodded the dagger with the tip of a quill. A faint puff of black smoke curled through the air whenever it came into contact with the spoor. "What a frightful thing. Tell me, then, what would you do next?"

"Drink," Azhani replied, picking up a bottle of wine and pouring them both a heavy libation. "For it will be the last luxury we should afford ourselves until the beasts are again driven from the land." She raised the goblet, said a brief, silent prayer, and drained it. "Then, we rouse the army and head for the mountains. The cycle has begun, and it's best if we destroy as many of the beasts as we can while they're but sacs of caustic slop. Eventually, they'll hatch, sending scouts and egg layers out to occupy more and more caves. With each wave, the chance that innocents will die increases. Rimerbeasts eat anything in their path and they are always hungry."

Nodding, Lyssera said, "Aye. This is the same method we have followed for centuries, and I see no reason to change it now. It will take time to gather my forces from the south, but I expect you'll be heading north soon enough." She gave Azhani a considering look and narrowed her eyes. "Before you go, you'll be introducing me to your stardancer, though."

As excited as she was by the prospect of seeing Kyrian again, Azhani was equally terrified she might discover that her friend had abandoned her. Lyssera's comment came very close to a command, though, which meant she likely thought Azhani had stalled enough.

"Yes, my queen," she said quietly.

"I expect you to serve me just as you did Thodan. Y'Syr looks to you for its salvation now. You may be the banshee, but you are *my* banshee. Remember that when my soldiers balk at their orders."

Bowing, Azhani said, "I will not forget, Your Majesty. I will serve you until there's no blood left in my body and everyone who stands at my side will know it."

"Let's hope it doesn't go that far," Lyssera said dryly. "For you will have to deal with Arris once the rimerbeasts are stopped."

Malice filled Azhani's smile. "Oh, I have no intentions of dying, my queen. Not when I have three feet of steel I need to introduce to Arris' belly one inch at a time."

It was time for weapon's practice with Allyndev. Azhani traversed Oakheart's halls. Now and then, she would nod to those she passed, but mostly she was lost in her own thoughts. Absently, she noted that the route to the salle was cluttered with off-duty guards. Giving them little thought, she concerned herself with plotting out dodge-and-parry lessons the prince could easily master.

Within the salle, she found Allyndev working through the first of the exercises she had taught him to do before one-on-one practice would begin. It still amazed her that he was thought to be aloof and cold. *He is shy, yet proud—and that pride has kept him from realizing that many failures at learning a task does not make it impossible, merely difficult.*

Without any trace of arrogance, Allyndev applied himself to her teachings, and in so doing, began to show some early signs of skill. This was because Azhani had wisely tailored each lesson to improve his weakest areas first, giving him tiny boosts in his confidence. She had hopes that later, when the harder skills took longer to master, he would still feel as if he were progressing. This was how Master Delaye had taught her, and indeed how most martial skills should be learned, but Azhani knew from experience that one or two bad teachers could make any student prone to failure.

Observation of Lyssera's sword masters had shown her why Allyndev had been unable to learn anything from them. The arrogant men and women who served the queen seemed only to care about what Azhani liked to call the "theater of the sword" and not about keeping their students alive in a real battle. Six or seven fast, flashy moves might do well enough in a duel, but against an opponent whose only goal was to kill, they would be less than useless. What she was teaching Allyndev wasn't intricate or filled with flips and foolish twirls, but it would bring him home from a battlefield. Rimerbeasts wouldn't care how many times you could cartwheel around them—but they would die if you gutted them.

After almost a week of lessons, Allyndev wasn't ready for a true fight, but he was showing improvement. For whatever reason, this seemed to have drawn and audience and now, there were others tucked away in the shadows, watching him practice. Azhani hoped they would hold their peace, else she'd have to exercise her authority in a way she hoped to avoid this early in her tenure at Oakheart. Silently, she lamented the fact that no matter how well-trained Allyn became, many Y'Syrans would never offer him—or her—the respect they deserved.

Generations of peace would have to stretch out between Y'Syr and Y'Dan before those who'd spent their lives staring at the border, hating the other side, would forget their ire. Most of the nobles understood why it was so important the kingdoms be allies, but get far enough away from the halls of Oakheart and Azhani suspected that the elves living near the border would take one look at her human—and obviously Y'Dani—heritage and have a hard time not spitting at her feet. Her elven nature would earn her the same distrust in Y'Dan. Only her status as warleader had earned their respect and now, even that was gone.

Pausing at the entrance to the salle, Azhani spent some time watching Allyndev exercise, noting where he had improved as well as where he needed further instruction. He was clumsy still, but as long as he was patient, clumsiness could be trained away.

"It's really too bad he's got that damned Y'Dani blood in him," a woman standing nearby muttered to her companion. "He'd be not bad to bed, otherwise."

The young man with her grimaced. "Eh, I don't mind a hint of human in my lads. The Y'Marans, in particular, have got lovely curly hair and all those freckles…"

She snorted. "'Tis not the human I mind, but the stink of Y'Dan. Makes his face look like he got smashed with a cake platter. And them damned narrow eyes—they're creepy, if you ask me! Thank the Twain that delicious bit of muscle the Queen just hired has more than a little bit of Y'Skan in her bloodline to temper the Y'Dani blight."

Startled, Azhani started to say something to her but was arrested in her motion when Allyn missed a move and stumbled, tripping over his own two feet. She hurried over to rescue him, pulling him upright before he could face any ridicule from the gathered watchers. "Good, very good, Allyn," she said loudly. "Your cross turns are better today. Be mindful of the second phrase, though. You need to set your balance first, then step into the thrust."

Panting heavily, he nodded. "Aye, thanks, Master Azhani. Shall I begin again?"

"Please," she said, stepping off the mat to watch. The gossiping duo had left, though, so she could not address their comments about her origins. *It is of no matter*, she decided. *So my blood comes not just from Y'Dan, but Y'Skan as well. Father did say that his great-grandfather had traveled across all the kingdoms in his youth and that his great-grandmother had come from one of those kingdoms...* She did, however, agree that Allyndev was handsome, which might cause some troubles as he continued to improve. There would always be those in the court who would ignore his Y'Dani blood for the chance to crawl a little closer to the crown. If that involved seducing a pretty young man, she suspected the task would be seen as that much more pleasant.

Conversely, there would be those who wouldn't go near a young man whose father had such controversial origins that his very name was a state secret. Even Azhani did not know who he was.

In the short time she'd had to come to know Allyndev, however, Azhani had come to like the solemn young man. He felt familiar and comfortable in a court full of strangers. She hoped her lessons might help him step out of his shy world of clumsy diffidence. *Kyrian will like him, too, I think.*

Thinking of Kyrian filled Azhani with guilt. *That is, if she doesn't decide to tell me to go away and never bother seeking her company again! Damn me! I've got to stop hiding! Today must be the day I go get her!*

CHAPTER FIVE

As the temple bells rang noontide, Gyp raced into the shop. "She's coming, Mistress Tellyn! The queen is on her way!"

Tellyn glanced up from the herbs she was grinding and shared a quick smile with Kyrian. "Yes Gyp, I know. A page came to inform me of her visit this morning."

Kyrian scowled. "Why would she come here? Does she not have an apothecary in Oakheart?" It was no use wondering if the queen's visit portended anything for her. She'd had plenty of time to hope and pray that Azhani would walk through the door, and each day, she was greeted only by disappointment.

At first she'd been angry, but now all she could summon was a sick sense of hurt. *We didn't mean as much to each other as I thought.* It was a lament a jilted lover might have spoken, but Kyrian could claim no such role, only that of a spurned friend. As such she could only feel saddened by what she was losing.

Tellyn curled one shoulder into a lazy shrug. "She is the queen. Like all those in power, she is often taken by fancy. Her page informed me that she wished to purchase certain restorative teas for which I alone am known." Smiling then, she said, "However, I suspect there is a secondary reason for her coming, as the page could easily have fetched said teas. No, I believe she wishes to meet you, my young friend. After all, everyone is now aware that Azhani Rhu'len serves her, and if I know our queen, she will have learned every detail of Azhani's journey thus far." Scooping the herbs onto a sheet of parchment, she folded it into an envelope and sealed it with candle wax. Afterward, she cleaned her mortar and pestle and chose a new batch of herbs to grind. Thoughtfully, she studied Kyrian, who could hardly meet her gaze, taking more time to stare at a bunch of dried leaves than she did in looking at the person talking to her. "And it may also be that a certain mule-headed warrior has recalled that she is not merely our queen's new favorite nursemaid, but also a friend to a lonely stardancer."

Absorbing this information, Kyrian just stood there in silence. Almost two weeks had passed. All Y'Syria knew of Azhani's arrival and subsequent pardon. Most citizens gossiped about it for a few days, then moved on to the latest scandal of the court. Others would stand in the shop for candlemarks, loudly speculating about the various reasons Azhani had chosen to come to Y'Syr over heading straight for Y'Mar.

Forced to put up with it or go mad, Kyrian had chosen to barricade herself in the room she should have shared with Azhani. It was a testament to her self-control that she had not destroyed her friend's gear in a fit of pique.

That she had slept every night in one of Azhani's tunics was an admission of a far greater level of emotion than she cared to speak on, though Tellyn had tried to goad it out of her more than once. It was far too upsetting to talk about it. *She could have sent a messenger, at the very least!* Anger flared again, and once more Kyrian debated whether or not she should just take her things and go. Y'Len was nearby. There was a temple of the Twain in the city—it would be easy just to collect her stipend, a few supplies, and return home.

It was the oath of friendship she'd given that kept her rooted in Tellyn Jarelle's shop, teaching Gyp how to bind wounds and offering the occasional bit of medical advice to desperate customers. Swallowing back bitter words, Kyrian merely returned to her task and said nothing of the feelings worrying at her heart. She would stay in Y'Syria as she promised, and help Azhani any way she could—even if that help was simply filling the army's orders for wound bindings.

The source of some of her mixed feelings was no surprise, not when Lyssera was Ylera's twin. There was not a soul born in Y'Syr who was blind to the fact that their queen had been Twain gifted with her own physical mirror, so the reason why Azhani wanted to spend time with her over Kyrian was easy to deduce. *Ylera told me once that she and Lyssera were absolutely alike in so many ways. How could Azhani not want to be close to her? How could she not hope Lyssera might…want her?*

She nearly jumped out of her skin when something thumped against the front door in a heavy, rhythmic knocking. Gyp leaped to his feet and raced out of the stillroom to greet their visitors, breathlessly announcing their royal guest just moments after the door was opened.

"I present the grand and beautiful Lyssera of House Kelani," he sang out, his voice breaking just enough to make Tellyn wince. "Twain's grace to thee, my queen!"

With a sigh, Tellyn set aside her pestle. "Some hard-learned advice, stardancer. Never stuff your patient's heads with heavy-handed praise, even upon those who command respect, else they demand it of you always. Treat all equally and leave the fawning poppycock to those with no sense of honesty." Then, she took up her walking stick and limped into the foyer.

Chuckling at the sour, if apt, words, Kyrian dumped another handful of herbs into her mortar and attacked them with a vengeance.

"Mistress Tellyn." Lyssera grinned happily as she embraced the older woman. "It's been far too long."

"Peh," Tellyn said cantankerously. "If those idiots in your court would drag their heads from their posteriors, you'd have far more time to visit, Lyss."

Lyssera's warm laughter filled the room as Tellyn then turned to greet the others in her party. "You haven't changed, Mistress."

Grabbing hold of Allyndev's face, Tellyn gave him a shake. "Allyndev, by Astariu's golden breasts, boy, you're looking well! Ye've color to those half-bearded cheeks of yours! And ye look as though ye've done a something a bit more strenuous than swing a hatchet for a few candlemarks." She narrowed her eyes knowingly. "Has someone finally dragged ye away from weeding the damned garden that is Y'Syria?"

Blushing, Allyn replied, "Aye, Mistress. Master Azhani has been tutoring me. It's been a most illuminating experience." Then he grinned. "I've never felt so invigorated!"

Spotting Gyp, he released Tellyn and ran over to the younger boy. "Gyp, I've got to show you this move Master Azhani taught me! Beast's bones, but it's tough! I never thought I'd get it, but then today, it all just happened and you have to see—it's like magick!" Babbling a mile a minute, both of them hurried outside, Allyn half-drawing his sword on the way through the door.

"Mind the plants, you two, else I'll tan ye good!" Tellyn called after them in warning.

Lyssera watched them go and then chuckled. "I expect your plants are safe enough, Tellyn. Allyndev, if not Gyp, is perfectly aware of their dearness to you."

"He'd best be, for he's not too high above me that my cane won't reach his backside," Tellyn replied as she gave the third person in the room a long look.

Standing just a pace behind Lyssera, Azhani had the grace to appear nervous as she quietly asked, "Where is Kyrian?"

"It's good to know we were missed, old friend," Tellyn replied sharply. "And Stardancer Kyrian is working in the stillroom." With that, she turned to Lyssera and handed her several parchment envelopes. "I believe this is what you've come for?" At Lyssera's bemused nod, she added, "If you'd care to stay a bit, I might be persuaded to find something for us to drink while Azhani visits with her friend." There was a subtle stress on the word that made Azhani wince, but Tellyn merely smiled. "In fact, invite your men to join us. I'd rather not have them cluttering up my porch with their armor."

"Of course." Lyssera wondered if she would have to prod Azhani in the butt to get her to go into the stillroom. When the other woman didn't move, she softly said, "You'll not be tendering any apologies from here, you know. And I highly doubt Mistress Tellyn cares to wait until the beast season begins for you to remember how to be polite."

Azhani's cheeks reddened as she mumbled, "Yes, of course, Highness," before slinking off toward the stillroom door.

Once she was gone, Lyssera invited her guardsmen into the house. They marched in, stationed themselves along one wall, and stood there like mail-coated statues, faces seemingly carved from stone.

Tellyn grimaced. "Are ye sure the captain of your guard isn't whittling down a forest for the sticks he rams up their backsides?"

With a loud cackle, Lyssera replied, "Oh, Tellyn, you really wouldn't do well in court, would you?"

"Of course not," she said. "I'm too bloody honest for that gaggle of babbling geese. Now come along. I think I've got a bottle of Y'Maran fire brandy around here that'll curl your nose hairs."

"I'm not certain I'd like my nose hairs curled, but I do quite enjoy Y'Maran brandy. Please, lead the way," Lyssera said with a fond smile. "And tell me all about my city."

Tellyn sighed. "If I must. Let's start with the waterfront. I hear the rats are uglier and meaner this year."

"Oh dear. I'll be needing more of that tonic of yours then, won't I?" Lyssera replied affably.

"Of course." The door closed behind them.

Squaring her shoulders, Azhani took a deep breath, steeled herself, and opened the stillroom door. A thousand thoughts flew through her mind as it swung inward. Chief among them were, *Be honest. The lies you told will make her think all words from your tongue are poison. Best to give her facts she can discover on her own. Don't attack—she is the one wronged, not you.*

A plethora of scents filled the room. For a moment, she was transported to a world redolent of springtime pastures and mountain gardens. It was the mint that brought her back to the moment, for its crispness made her mouth water in longing for a cup of Kyrian's sweetened tea.

Words clamored on her tongue, but she could not speak. All she could do was stand there, staring at her friend's tunic-clad back and admiring the play of muscle over her shoulders and down her arms. Stalling for time, Azhani tried to think of something to say. Instead, she counted the ringlets in Kyrian's red-gold hair as it swept over the fabric of the perspiration-soaked shirt.

Suddenly, she ceased stirring whatever was in the pot and wiped her face on the back of her arm.

Swallowing quickly, Azhani moved forward. "Here, try this… it might help," she said, and offered her a skin of wine.

"Thank you." Kyrian's tone was dryer than the Y'Skani desert. Tipping her head back, she drank deeply of the wine, then returned the skin.

At least she didn't spit in my face. That's something, right? Azhani waited silently, unsure of what to say in the moment.

Licking her lips, Kyrian said, "Not bad for dungeon swill."

Inwardly, Azhani winced. *I deserved that.* Still, she did not speak.

Faint laughter from the other room echoed around them. Kyrian glanced toward the door, then fixed Azhani with a hard look before saying, "Our queen sounds rather jubilant for someone on her way to a hanging. At least she allowed you to say goodbye first." There was no anger in the words, though they struck like the sharpest of knives.

Goddess, she's…she's more than just a little upset, isn't she? It dawned on Azhani that she might have made a terrible mistake in the way she'd treated Kyrian. It must seem that she'd thrown away what the other woman had offered because of her own damnable honor. *How do I repair this? I don't want her to hate me. I don't know what I would do if…if she didn't want to know me.*

"Kyrian, I…" She tried to speak, but the words just sat there, digging claws of fear into her tongue, forcing her to stand there like a mute idiot, helplessly staring at her friend.

Kyrian crossed her arms over her chest. "Yes? Was I wrong? Have you come for another reason? Perhaps you require a tonic? Or an unguent? Surely you would not need such a thing if you were on your way to the gallows." She began to pace around the room, her cheeks growing redder the more she spoke. "Or perhaps you are here to talk? This must be one last conversation with the stupid stardancer who saved your life before you're hauled back to wherever they tie you down at night? Because otherwise, you're telling me that you weren't a prisoner. Which means the only reason you didn't come back for me was that you didn't want me around!" Venom dripped over her words like honey. "I notice your hands aren't broken—though I've had visions otherwise. For surely that's why my *friend* couldn't send me a message telling me why-why-she…she…"Tears swam in Kyrian's eyes. She looked away. "Just go, Azhani. You obviously don't want to be here, else Queen Lyssera wouldn't have had to drag you along on a trip a page could have made."

Pain the likes of which she had not felt for months stormed through Azhani's gut as she gaped at Kyrian. *No. Oh, Goddess, no…* Ice descended and with it came anger. *Fine, if she wants me gone, I'll go. To Hell with friends. I need them not!* Shivering with emotion, she took a single step backward and could go no further, not when tears, wet and glittering, suddenly streamed over Kyrian's cheeks. *No, no, no. This is wrong. This is all wrong…*

"You lied to me," Kyrian whispered harshly. "You promised that I would be at your side. That I could stand with you as a friend and you—you left me. You left me like I was nothing more than a useless pet! How could you do that?" Anguish made her voice break.

"Kyrian." Azhani shook her head, trying to deny the pain she'd caused. "Oh Kyrian, Twain's grace, I'm sorry. I'm so sorry. I never meant… I… You were with me. You were! You were in every thought. Every time something happened, I found myself wishing I could speak to you, could seek your counsel or your comfort, but…I had to face Lyssera alone. I don't know how to explain it otherwise. I had to do it." She lowered her head. "I…should have talked to you more. Should have tried to explain myself better. For that, I am truly, truly sorry."

"How can I help you when you won't even give me a chance to understand the things you want to do? I'm supposed to be your friend, Azhani. That means when you need to do something, I'm going to listen. I won't always agree, but I will listen," Kyrian said, her voice cracking with emotion.

"I did try, but you seemed so adamant about coming with me and it just felt easier to…" She grimaced. "I don't want to fight with you, Kyrian. I didn't come here for that."

"No? Then why did you come?" Kyrian retorted. "Why are you here, Azhani Rhu'len? What is it that you want so badly? To see that I've finally realized you're an oathbreaker?"

The bitter words made her flinch. "No, that is not why I came, but…if that is how you truly feel, then I'll not change your mind. Be well, Kyrian." She tossed a pouch of coin onto the table. "That should see you to Y'Len." Blinking back the sting of tears, she turned to leave.

"Azhi," Kyrian rasped.

Limbs heavy with fear, Azhani let herself look back. When she did, all she could see was the broken, lost look on Kyrian's face and knew that she had a choice. Let her pride sunder them forever, or shove it into Banner Lake and let it drown. "Oh, Kyr," she whispered, rushing to Kyrian and collapsing into her arms, holding her as much as she was held. "I came to apologize, to beg you to let me try not to be an idiot again. You are my friend, my closest ally, and truly, there is no one else I'd rather have at my side." Closing her eyes, she breathed in the earthy, sweet smell of hyssop in Kyrian's hair. "There's nothing I can say that will repair the damage I've caused, but…" She sighed heavily. "I don't regret what I did. I went to Lyssera alone for myself, Kyrian. It was pride, yes, and honor, yes, but it was also a need I felt right to the quick of me. I have no other way to say it beyond telling you that it seemed like it was the path Astariu wanted me to walk. Please, please forgive me for not being better able to say this before. Please give me a chance to mend the pain between us."

Kyrian didn't reply, just clung to her.

Softly, Azhani said, "Kyrian."

Hesitantly, Kyrian looked up at her.

"Please, come back to Oakheart with me. I need you."

The day candle flickered as they stared at one another, their hearts slowly finding a joint rhythm.

"I'm still angry with you," Kyrian said as she cracked a tiny smile.

"And you have every right to be," Azhani replied, unable to stop a blossoming smile that was the full-fledged expression of the joy spreading through her body.

"I hope your hide can take it, for I'll be working out that anger upon it every morning on the practice field," Kyrian said dryly.

"My hide is all yours—and perhaps you might even choose to aim your batons at my student's backside from time to time as well." Azhani still grinned from ear to ear.

"Ah yes. I've heard you were saddled with the prince no one wants to be king," Kyrian said as she released her and shook her head bemusedly. "You've quite a bit to tell me, I'd wager. You can start, however, by introducing me to the woman you charmed into letting you live long enough to convince her of your innocence."

Curling her arm around Kyrian's shoulder, Azhani sighed. "Well, I didn't exactly charm her so much as throw myself at her mercy…" She turned to head out to the sitting room, relating the tale of those first few, tense moments in Lyssera's study as quickly as she could.

CHAPTER SIX

As Kyrian wandered around her suite, Azhani stifled a grin. "Like it?" she asked, trying not to focus on the adorable expression on her friend's face.

"I–but–this is…it's huge, Azhi!" Kyrian blurted, waving her arms wildly. "I don't need this much space, really, it's…it's too much! I—"

"—Am grateful to the queen for her generosity?" Azhani said before Lyssera could suggest another accommodation that would put them much further away from each other than she liked.

Gaping at her, Kyrian looked from her to Lyssera and back and then nodded quickly. "Yes, of course, my queen, I didn't mean to imply that I wasn't, because this is perfect, it really is, thank you so much."

Lyssera merely smiled. "As you find this acceptable, I shall leave you to unpack and familiarize yourself with your surroundings. Unfortunately for me, court begins in half a candlemark and it would set a terrible precedent if the queen were tardy." Turning to Azhani, she added, "You, on the other hand, are released from your duties for the day, so that you might be on hand to help Stardancer Kyrian acclimate to the byways of my home." She offered Kyrian a slight bow. "You are welcome in Oakheart, Stardancer. I hope you will find it a peaceful place."

"Yes, thank you again, my queen," Kyrian replied, less nervously this time. "I am beyond astounded."

On her way toward the door, Lyssera touched Azhani's shoulder lightly. "Should I assign a guard to make sure the courtiers don't eat her alive?"

Azhani scowled. "I think, my queen, that you will find Stardancer Kyrian is of sterner stuff than your courtiers expect. In the end, it is they who might require a guardian. However, until such time as her reputation is carved in the roots of Oakheart's court, I shall watch for vipers in the dark."

"Ah, of course," Lyssera said, a quick, knowing smile curling her lips. "I look forward to spending time with you, Stardancer Kyrian. I am forever interested to hear what draws those who bear the blessings of the Twain into their service."

"And I shall be more than happy to tell you anything you wish to know, Highness," Kyrian replied calmly. "Though I suspect there are portions of my tale that would bore even the most curious of cats to sleep."

"Cats, hm?" Lyssera said, chuckling softly. "Perhaps I and my favorite feline friends will put that statement to the test some evening. Who knows, I may end up requiring you to repeat it many times, as sleep is often an elusive friend when one is burdened by the ills of a kingdom."

"If it is sleep you desire, my queen, then call upon me as you need, for as Azhani can attest, I am most practiced in the art of mixing up potent brews."

Azhani snorted. "Only if you don't mind feeling like a pole-axed bull in the morning."

Laughing, Lyssera said, "I could listen to you two all day, but alas, I must be away. Good afternoon, ladies—and may the Twain grant you a restful evening."

Once she was gone, Azhani settled into a chair near the hearth as Kyrian continued exploring the suite. Now and then, she would comment on the golden oak walls, the thick tapestries that hung from branches that grew right from those walls, or the large, sturdy glass windows that looked down on the courtyard and city below.

"I'm most partial to the rugs," Azhani said as Kyrian finally stopped to enjoy a glass of wine from a bottle that had been left on the mantle. "Helps to muffle the sound of pacing feet." She looked up at the ceiling and grimaced.

"Don't even try the curmudgeon routine with me, Azhi," Kyrian said fondly. "You love knowing every little thing that's going on around you."

Azhani laughed. "You're right, of course."

With a soft sigh, Kyrian said, "I still can't believe how much room there is in here."

Three rooms made up Kyrian's suite, a trefoil nodule consisting of a sitting area, sleeping chamber, and bathing room. Outside, a balcony wrapped around Oakheart's exterior, and was shared with a nearby suite—which just happened to be Azhani's. With a pensive look on her face, Kyrian wandered out to stare at the lake for a while, then turned and motioned for Azhani to join her.

"If it makes you feel any better, this is likely half the size of an ambassador's chambers," Azhani said quietly.

"Beast," Kyrian said, then chuckled. "It's magickal. This place, this city—it's nothing at all like anything I imagined."

Out on the lake, two ships passed each other, their bright white sails catching the wind and billowing out as they headed toward new ports.

"Y'Syria is never as one expects," Azhani murmured. Closing her eyes, she thought back to every visit she'd ever made. "Unchanging, yet forever different. It grows, lives, and moves in ways no other city in Y'Myran can. Time's hand burrows deep into the soil. Oakheart's halls still echo with the voices of those long dead, and yet just there on the harbor, you can see the ribs of new ships growing from their keels."

"Y'Len is old, but it is not of the trees. Not like it is here, anyway," Kyrian said wistfully. "There, the houses are built of brick and stone, wood and daub. There is no feeling of the hum of life, as there is here in Oakheart. I can hear it, thrumming in my chest like the echo of my heart. This place is alive and it is old, dreadfully old, yet new branches grow, new leaves ripen. The masterwork of the gardeners is truly magnificent."

Nodding, she said, "I remember Y'Len—there was hardly a stair or step in the city!"

Kyrian laughed. "Aye. Our masters said it was so we could dash around without risk of falling, but most of us found it to be nearly as troubling. Invariably our classes were at opposite ends of the temple, so that we had to run just to arrive before the bells were struck."

"Do you miss it? Do you ever think about going home?" she asked, though inwardly, she quailed, for if Kyrian wanted to leave... *Please, no, please stay. I need you.*

Glancing up at her, Kyrian smiled. "I do miss the school, and my friends. I have long thought I might go there and teach."

Ice turned her stomach hollow, but steeling herself, Azhani said, "I will escort you, when you—" The brush of Kyrian's soft fingers against her lips silenced her.

"No. I won't be going back. At least, not without you. I'm exactly where I want to be."

"But..." Stunned, Azhani gaped at her. *How can she be so sure, so willing to make such a promise when I acted like such an idiot?*

Shaking her head, Kyrian took Azhani's hand. "When are you going to accept that we are friends, Azhani Rhu'len?" Exasperation colored her tone. "And that as your friend, I have sworn to stay at your side as long as you need me?"

That…could be a very long time. Flabbergasted, Azhani grinned sheepishly. "I don't know. Frankly, I'm amazed you still want to share my company after what I did. Beast's bones, Kyr, there are many here who still believe me to be an oathbreaker! They'd sooner skewer me than spend one moment in my presence!"

"Then they are fools—more fool than you, even," she replied tersely. At Azhani's surprised look, she said, "Yes, you are a fool, but fools are allowed their mistakes, especially when those fools are your friends!" She smiled warmly. "You apologized and I expect you will try not to make such a mistake again. Now I'm telling you to cast aside your fears, for I am not leaving!"

Feeling mischievous, Azhani crooked her fingers into a claw and wiggled them. "Even if I tickle you?"

Kyrian grimaced. "Even so, but I may be forced to retaliate," she said, raising her own hooked fingers and snapping them like a crab's claw.

"Oh really?" Azhani purred, grinning broadly as she moved closer. "Perhaps I should test that threat for veracity," she said as she dropped her hand and drove her fingers into Kyrian's ribs.

With an indignant yelp, Kyrian danced away. "Ack! Azhi! Twain's grace!"

Azhani, however, didn't stop, and after a moment, Kyrian gave as good as she got, chasing Azhani around the balcony and back into the suite, both of them laughing joyfully. They played for a good long while, eventually collapsing on Kyrian's couch, breathless from the exertion.

Blowing a strand of damp hair from her face, Kyrian grinned. "Perhaps now, we should unpack my things? After all, there's still an entire castle for you to show me."

"Anything you want, friend." Azhani held out her hand.

"Oh, good. Then what I want is a bath. I stink."

"Easily done."

Kyrian's belly rumbled. "Food, too. Lots of it. Something besides oat porridge."

"Anything else, milady?" she asked subserviently, though a mischievous grin hovered on her lips.

Affecting a haughty air, Kyrian replied, "Yes, I require you to untie my boots, for I fear I am simply too weary to do so," and promptly put her feet on Azhani's lap.

Without a word, Azhani set to removing Kyrian's footwear.

Feeling distinctly out of place, Kyrian stayed close to Azhani as they wandered the halls of Oakheart Manor. Around every corner, in nooks and crannies, on walls and floors and even suspended from the ceilings were treasures from all over Y'Myran. Statues carved from the finest marble, blown glass creatures of myth and legend, and paintings by incredible artists were just some of the beautiful objects on display. All of it was absolutely breathtaking to behold.

Those same halls were also home to far too many backstabbing, gossip-whispering, toadying, shifty bureaucrats.

After passing yet another liveried individual who felt it his duty to bow and murmur, "How delightful it is to see the Twain have not forgotten to bless our lesser sisters with their gifts," Kyrian was torn between screaming aloud and retreating to the simpler world of Mistress Tellyn's apothecary shop.

It wasn't just the courtiers that got to her. The sheer mass of people crowding the halls was stunningly dense. There were pages, maids, manservants, governesses, men-at-arms, and seemingly everywhere she turned, one of the green-robed gardeners whose only task was to see to the health and well-being of Oakheart's boughs.

"It's a little overwhelming at first," Azhani said as they stepped into a blessedly empty corridor.

Wide-eyed, Kyrian nodded. "There seems to be an incredible amalgam of nobles and servants—everywhere I look, it's something different. It's like this ever-changing, amorphous dance and I'm terrified I'll trip and fall on my arse!"

"You won't," Azhani told her gently. "Because I'll be right there to catch you."

They hurried on to another section of the manor. Kyrian listened with half an ear while Azhani explained the workings of the Queen's Council, a group of nobles who had been chosen, surprisingly, by popular vote, to represent the towns and villages of Y'Syr.

Kyrian winced as they traversed a hall filled with several these councilors yelling at each other at the tops of their lungs.

"I'm telling you, Perryn, your corn fields are useless next to my pig farms!" one man said imperiously.

"You're insane! Your pigs need my corn! My farms should be first on the list when it comes time to protect them from the rimerbeasts!"

"Beast's bones, man! Your corn is nothing! What about my lumberyards!" another man wailed.

Shaking her head ruefully, Kyrian wondered how they ever got anything done if each of them was so blindly convinced their little section of the kingdom was more important than any other.

"Idiots," Azhani muttered once they passed through a door that led outside and onto a balcony that looked down into another small garden. "Thankfully, as a member of the queen's retinue, I don't have to take that hall very often. I'll show you how to access the page's throughways later. It's faster and quieter."

"Oh, thank the Twain," Kyrian said as she sunk into a nearby chair. "Else I might simply close myself in my quarters and meditate until it is time to leave."

Azhani grinned, her white teeth bright against the dusky hue of her skin. "We can't have that, Stardancer. You promised to kick my arse at practice, remember?"

Laughing, she said, "So I did. And you know, that sounds exactly like the perfect thing to do right now, if we can."

"Follow me." Affably, Azhani gestured toward a narrow, almost hidden door in the wall.

Over the next three days, Kyrian learned the swiftest routes through Oakheart's halls. As she roamed the great manor, she found herself recalling Ylera's anecdotes of her childhood home. It became increasingly difficult to withhold those stories from Azhani, especially the amusing ones. They'd pass statues missing limbs or important features, and Kyrian would have to bite her tongue or cough into her hand to hide her giggles. The worst case was when they stopped to admire a sculpture of one of Y'Syria's ancient athletes. A rather prominent piece of his anatomy was broken and had been covered with a wreath of dried flowers.

Azhani grinned at Kyrian and whistled a bit of a bawdy tune about a man with a missing rooster.

"Goddess, Azhi, you're so bad," she said in between her giggles. They faded quickly, though as they continued to ramble the halls.

Nights of listening to Ylera talk about the magnificent sprawl of a tree that had been coaxed from the ground thousands of years before the Firstlanders divided what was then Aldyran into the kingdoms of Y'Myran, overwhelmed

Kyrian's thoughts. In the evenings, she took up the task of recording those conversations, filling a journal with page after page of Ylera's words, wondering if she might someday dare to share them with Azhani.

Though the highest levels of Oakheart were reserved for the queen and her family, it was the lower halls to which Kyrian found herself most drawn. Here, those whose lives were utterly dedicated to caring for Oakheart's noble denizens dwelt. Here also was where Kyrian found other half elves, dwarves, and even a few aged morgedraal. It was a different world in the lower branches, a place of shadows that held interesting secrets, and she came to view it as almost a city hidden within the castle.

It was early in the morning. Kyrian and Azhani were on their way to the kitchens to enjoy their favorite breakfast—fruit-filled flatcakes. The scent of cooking food wafted through the halls. All around them, the jabber of conversation in five different languages blended into a polyglot of sounds that made Kyrian smile just to hear it. In one alcove, they found a group of Y'Droran dwarves dicing Y'Skani morgedraal for bags of gold and pure white sand. Another held a cluster of Y'Tolian lutenists trading merry tunes with Y'Noran bagpipers. Everywhere she turned, she caught the sound of Y'Maran docksider cant. Being in this area of Oakheart was the most beautiful thing in all the kingdoms to her, for here, there was true peace between all peoples.

All were equal in the lower halls, for what mattered was not land of birth or emblems on family crests, but the ability to do the work assigned. For Kyrian, that was simple. She was a healer and here was an entire city of people who might need her services. Indeed, she'd hardly spent more than a candlemark in the lower halls before meeting a woman who'd sliced open her hand while filleting fish.

Cleaning and healing a simple wound was the best thing Kyrian could do to earn their respect. That night she went to sleep knowing she'd found a good place.

"Do you know where you are?" Azhani asked quietly.

Kyrian nodded. "This is the Hall of Trees." She pointed to a small mosaic pressed into an alcove they had just passed. Below it was a fountain and in front of that was a bench upon which sat Prince Allyndev Kelani, Azhani's student.

Rising as they approached, he offered them a clumsy bow. "Master Azhani, have you heard? Ambassador Kuwell has just challenged Ambassador Iften to a duel!"

This was her first time meeting the prince, and Kyrian was taken aback by his glee over the prospect of such an event. Confused, she tried to spot the ambassadors he mentioned while Azhani grimaced and bit off a curse. Kyrian almost felt like doing the same, since neither person was familiar to her, though she'd heard the dwarven ambassador's name bandied about in the lower halls from time to time. The other was a mystery. Still, it never boded well to hear of a duel being called.

"What should we do?" she asked.

"Stop it," Azhani said, spinning on her heel and fighting her way through an ever-growing stream of people until they made it out to the courtyard.

Dueling was legal in Y'Syr, but Queen Lyssera preferred diplomacy to swordplay. As a Stardancer, Kyrian hoped the former could be brought to bear before the latter caused irreparable bloodshed.

"Do you think they'll kill each other?" Allyndev's eyes seemed to sparkle with delight at the prospect of violence. "Will there be a lot of blood?"

Glancing at him disapprovingly, Azhani growled, "Not if I can help it."

Quickly, she signaled one of the queen's ever-present guards and ordered him to start dispersing the gathered crowd while perhaps fifty feet away, two men circled each other.

"You dirt-grubbing mole!" an older, bearded gentleman with dark brown skin bellowed as he waved a stout cudgel over his head. "I'm going to take a strip of your flesh for every one of those fake stones you tried to pass off on me, Kuwell Longhorn!" The words dripped with pure hatred. Muscles in the man's face twitched as he sneered violently.

"Lies!" the dwarf snarled. "'Tis ye who be the thief, Iften Windstorm! Ye stole me gems and switched 'em out for bad glass. It be just like a sand-eating desert raider to try and pawn his fakes to a good, honest dwarf!" Raising his axe, he shook it at Iften threateningly and said, "Put your tail between your legs and run home to your masters, for I be about to whip ye like a dog!"

Kyrian winced. While she did not know many dwarves, she had dealt with enough of them to recognize that Kuwell Longhorn's anger was at odds with their general inclination toward joviality. With a scream of incoherent rage, Iften charged him, swinging his cudgel straight at Kuwell's head.

Acting as one, Kyrian and Azhani both leaped into the fray. Azhani snatched a shield from a stunned guardsman and deflected Iften's blow while Kyrian deftly grabbed Kuwell's arm and twisted it, stripping him of his axe.

"Stand down, Master Kuwell," she said.

Immediately, he backed off while Azhani took Iften's cudgel. "By the bones of the beast, what are you doing, Ambassadors?"

Dazedly, Iften glared at her while Kuwell sighed and drawled, "Well, we were about to have ourselves a nice little duel until ye decided to piss on my party, old friend." Indicating Iften with a nod of his head, he added, "Though he wouldn't have been much of a dance partner, seeing as how he looks near ready to kiss the cobbles."

Judging that Kuwell would not attack unprovoked, Kyrian returned the axe and then went to check on Ambassador Windstorm.

With an aggrieved sigh, Azhani said, "Trouble always finds you, doesn't it, Kuwell?"

Whatever Ambassador Longhorn said in reply was lost as Kyrian studied Ambassador Windstorm. Something was dreadfully wrong with him, though exactly what it was, she couldn't immediately discern. His eyes were wild, flecks of foam formed in the corners of his mouth, and he seemed to be sweating and shivering at the same time. Worriedly, she led him to a nearby bench and then sang herself into a trance in order to seek answers in his aura. She expected to find intoxication or even sickness, but to her stunned surprise, it was something far, far worse.

Following the trail of a black, odious shadow through the shifting colors of his aura, she tracked something so abysmally evil that she physically recoiled from him. It started in his stomach, but was fully realized and embedded in his brain. It was then that Kyrian discovered the answer.

Every one of Iften Windstorm's senses had been perforated with a rapidly spreading thread of darkness that had destroyed his ability to reason clearly. Anyone who had not spent time studying herbs with Mistress Tellyn as she would think him insane—or an addict. She, however, knew the difference.

Steeling herself for the work to come, she looked away from him and sent a soft prayer to the Twain for luck. "Azhani?"

"Yes?"

"I will need my herb bag and a flask of brandy. This man is under the influence of krile." *And if I don't act fast, he's going to die.* Softly, she began to hum, calling upon the Fire in order to stem the rush of the drug through

Iften's system. It wouldn't stop it entirely, but it would slow down its effects. What worried her was how fast it was progressing. The violent stage was almost over. Soon would come a loss of mental function, delusions, weakness, and, if not treated, death.

"Twain's grace!" Azhani cursed, and the sentiment echoed by the dwarven ambassador.

Krile, a powerful, terribly addicting narcotic, was so reviled that High King Ysradan had outlawed its use, possession, and creation in Y'Myran. Unfortunately, users existed among all levels of Y'Myrani society.

With a frown of distaste, Kuwell murmured, "I never took him for a damned krile head."

"I don't think he's a user." Kyrian lifted Iften's hand and showed it to them. "Look, his nails aren't stained. This might be a poisoning."

As Azhani knelt to study his hand, Iften giggled. "Ah, such a delight. Two pretty birds, fluttering around my head. The elves are nice, so nice, and I don't like sand anymore." Drool dribbled down his chin. "Scorpions are ugly only when they're pink."

Azhani closed her eyes briefly, then exhaled. "I'll send Allyndev to fetch what you need. Someone should contact the Y'Skani delegation to make sure they're unhurt."

"I can do that," Kuwell said solemnly. "'Tis the honorable thing, seeing as how I nearly killed the man."

"Thank you," Azhani replied after sending the prince off.

Kuwell nodded and then hurried toward the ambassadorial wing of Oakheart.

CHAPTER SEVEN

Though he'd seemed excited about the possibility of a duel on Oakheart's premises, Allyndev was still quick to fetch Kyrian's healing kit.

"Is this what you needed?"

"Yes, thank you, my prince," she replied absently, opening it to search for the right herbs. Nearby, Azhani stood watch over Ambassador Windstorm, whose silly babble had slowed to a soft mutter.

"Hurry," she said as Iften's face began to go slack.

"I'm hurrying," Kyrian muttered, crushing herbs into a paste then mixing it into the brandy, giving the bottle a quick shake afterward. "Hold him, both of you." They did so, and she gently coaxed Iften to drink the contents.

Moments later, he slumped into their arms, provoking a startled gasp from the onlookers.

"Is he dead?" someone yelled.

"No," Kyrian replied loudly. "He sleeps, though he is very ill. If you could clear the way so that we might bring him to a better place to care for him, I would appreciate that."

"Of course, Stardancer," a woman said, bowing quickly and then turning to the others. "Ye heard her, ye jackals! Back! Move it!" Her voice was like a whip, goading the others to move. Azhani scooped up the old man and carried him into the castle.

"So what happened to the ambassador?" Allyndev asked as they hurried toward the ambassadorial suite.

"Krile poisoning," Azhani replied tersely. "Find the queen. She'll want to meet in the Swan Garden."

Briefly, it seemed as though he would protest the directive, but then he nodded. "Yes, Master Azhani." Peeling away from them, he bolted in the direction of the Grand Hall.

Spying a page, Azhani pointed to him and said, "Go. Run to the kitchens. Fetch refreshments for six. Take them to the Swan Garden."

"Yes, Master Azhani," he said, then ducked into one of the near-invisible hallways the pages frequented.

"Looks like Devon's not the only page your charm works on," Kyrian said with an amused smile.

"Hush," she grumbled. "I wish it were so easy to send Allyn around. He wasn't pleased at being turned into an errand boy, that much I could see."

"He'll understand. The situation demands immediate attention. You know where we're going?"

"Yes. It's just this way." Azhani charged up a set of stairs, jogged down another hall, and then stopped at a plain-seeming door. "This is the Y'Skani delegation's quarters."

"Good." Without bothering to knock, Kyrian marched in, surprising the two guards stationed inside. She looked around, spying someone dressed as richly as the ambassador. Approaching him, she smiled politely and said, "You look important. Your ambassador is ill. Where is his room? I need to see to him."

Startled, the man dropped the scrolls he was holding. "Right through here," he said as he looked from her to Azhani and back. "What happened? Is he—"

"Krile poisoning." Hastily, she opened the indicated door. "I have neutralized it, but he will need much rest and care to recover."

Once Azhani had carried Ambassador Windstorm into his bedroom and settled him on the bed, she turned to Kyrian and said, "I have to go. Queen Lyssera will want to know what's happened. Come to the Swan Garden when you can."

"Of course. I'll be there," she replied. As Azhani headed for the door, Kyrian opened her herb bag and said, "Thankfully, I believe this was a single dose, so we shouldn't have to wean him from it."

"By the Serpent, the Twain are merciful!" he said, touching his fingers to his forehead.

The Swan Garden was the jewel in the bower of the Kelani residence. Here, generations of the royal family had spent candlemarks staring at the star-strewn sky, watched ships come to port in the harbor. On occasion, they had even enjoyed pleasurable assignations with lovers both known and mysterious.

Every bench, statue, and plant held secrets they could never divulge for upon this garden was placed a special dweomer, an enchantment so strong it had outlived its caster. Whatever was said within the Swan Garden would not be overheard by anyone standing even a foot outside its environs.

Queen Lyssera, Ambassador Longhorn, and Prince Allyndev were waiting just inside the gate when Azhani arrived.

"Any word?" Lyssera asked.

"She said he was recovering, but I know little more," she replied. "You've closed the city?"

Lyssera nodded. "For now. I can't keep it that way forever, though. It would cause a panic."

"I'm sure that's exactly what his poisoner desired," Azhani said darkly. Pacing like a caged animal, she scowled in frustration. "Kuwell, you're sure you feel fine?"

"Fit as ever, old friend," he said. "And Her Highness had it confirmed by a stardancer."

Relief tumbled over her like a load of bricks, causing her to stop and exhale slowly. "Thank the Twain. That, at least, is a blessing."

A quarter of a candlemark later, they were joined by Kyrian and the Y'Skani man from the ambassador's quarters.

Lyssera nearly pounced on Kyrian. "Ambassador Windstorm?"

"Will recover," she replied. "But he is very weak. His advanced age is cause for some concern. Krile is not a kind poison."

They all followed Lyssera to an elaborate table located almost exactly in the center of the garden.

Here was revealed the origins of the garden's name, for they were immediately surrounded by swan decorations of all shapes and sizes. Lyssera's own chair was an elaborate construction of white ash that curled around her, and cradled her in a cloak of painstakingly carved wings.

A man liveried in Kelani colors seated them, served wine, and vanished, though Azhani knew if anything was required, he could be summoned by the bell pull hanging near Lyssera's chair.

"Vice Ambassador Kirthos, I am truly sorry for what has occurred," Lyssera said once they had all taken their seats.

Dipping his head respectfully, he said, "Walker Windstorm is strong. I believe he'll be up and demanding his rights as ambassador sooner than any of us believe. In that blessed event, I would like to be able to tell him that the blackguard who committed this heinous act had danced from your nearest gibbet."

"We shall certainly do our best to see that eventuality." Anger made Lyssera's voice sharp. "I do not like to think there is one among my halls who believes it is their right to harm those who have received my blessing of peace."

"I doubt the perpetrator cares what ye feel, Queen Lyssera. This was a blatant attempt to disrupt negotiations between allies," Kuwell said irritably.

"Yes, Ambassador Longhorn, I am quite aware of this. Please, Stardancer, is there aught you can tell us?"

"Only that the ambassador woke briefly and mentioned that some of his recent meals had tasted strange," she replied. "I attempted to find a bowl or cup from which he might have supped, but your servants are quick to clean up."

With a brief glance to Vice Ambassador Kirthos, Kuwell grumbled, "Or the poisoner was."

Swiftly, Kirthos held up his hands. "Look not to me, Ambassador, for I've no desire to shoulder Walker Windstorm's burdens. I will concur that he had complained about the food, but we merely thought it to be a desert walker's inexperience with Y'Syran spices."

Lyssera snorted. "I've always heard you fire eaters thought our food far too bland for your tastes." Then she shook her head. "I just cannot fathom who would want to hurt such a harmless old man."

Flatly, Azhani said, "Any who would wish to cause chaos in your court, my queen."

Lyssera curled her hands into fists. "Yes, but which of my enemies has struck?"

"You have set Captain Evern to uncovering the poisoner?"

"Of course. But he'll not work alone." She looked at Azhani pointedly.

Understanding this to be an order, Azhani nodded. "As you command, my queen." She then turned to Kyrian. "How long until Ambassador Windstorm recovers? That may have bearing on why he was chosen."

Kyrian scowled. "A week or two. Perhaps more, if he does not rest as instructed."

"So the timing isn't exact. Hm." Thoughtfully, she pondered the schedule for the next few weeks, but could discern nothing that seemed important enough to warrant delay. *There could be a private meeting, as well—some treaty that someone doesn't want signed.* She rubbed her temples. *Goddess, I hate politics.*

"Are we sure he didn't just snort it for pleasure?" Kuwell asked with a sour grunt. "It's a bit of an odd poison to use, since ye can't be certain it'll kill."

"Nay!" Vice Ambassador Kirthos slammed his hand onto the table, revealing part of an elaborately tattooed snake on his wrist. "Krile dust is purest anathema to those who dream the Serpent's Way, Ambassador. We would rather eat glass!"

Azhani knew this to be true, for the followers of the Serpent's Way eschewed poisons and mind-altering intoxicants of all kinds save that which came from the venomous fangs of the snakes they venerated. Even now, though everyone else had drained their glasses, Vice Ambassador Kirthos' sat untouched. "I believe him," Azhani said quietly.

"Then I defer to your judgment, old friend." Turning to the queen, Kuwell asked, "What next? And how can we of Y'Dror help? Perhaps we should search every room?"

Kyrian paled. "Would that not cause widespread trouble?"

"Much as I appreciate your offer, Ambassador Kuwell, I wish to leave this matter with my captain—and Azhani, of course. In fact, consider this your primary duty from now on, Azhani. I will not allow Oakheart to be seen as a haven for poisoners. Root them out and bring them to face my court forthwith!"

Standing, Azhani bowed. "Yes, my queen."

Lyssera stood as well. "For now, I wish the rest of you to return to your normal duties. Stardancer, you will, I hope, see to Ambassador Windstorm's care?"

"Yes, of course."

"Vice Ambassador Kirthos, I trust you have no objection to her presence in your quarters?"

"Of course not. I relish the opportunity to aid the stardancer in healing Walker Windstorm," he said, getting to his feet.

"Good. Prince Allyndev." Lyssera looked to her nephew. "From this moment forward, you are to serve Azhani and Kyrian as you would me. Whatever they need, see that they have it immediately, do you understand? This means no more gardening, at all."

Frowning sullenly, he mumbled, "Yes, my queen."

At the queen's pronouncement, Azhani kept her expression neutral. *I hope Lyss knows what she's doing. Forbidding him his idle pleasure is one way to make sure he focuses himself on what others might presume to be the "proper" tasks of a prince, but it also might fill him with resentment.*

"Ambassador, Vice Ambassador, I hope whatever led to the trouble to begin with will be sorted peacefully?" she said, looking from one man to the other.

"Of course. I believe it was a matter of some possibly false gems?" Vice Ambassador Kirthos said calmly.

"They be not false," Ambassador Kuwell muttered. "I pulled the bloody things from the earth meself!"

"Kuwell," Azhani said quietly. "Why not take them to an appraiser? Is possible we are looking for a thief as well as a poisoner."

"Ah, Twain's Grace, I'd not thought of such a thing." He shook his head ruefully. "That be a damned fine idea. 'Twill be done forthwith."

Azhani breathed a sigh of relief. *At least we won't have them going at each other's throats now.* "Thank you. Let me know what you discover."

"Aye, and if there's anything else ye need, send word." He closed his hands into massive fists. "I believe I've still some head-cracking left in my arms."

She chuckled. "I'll remember that, old friend."

"I'm glad to see we're all in accord. Now, please, find the culprits!" Turning to Kyrian, Lyssera asked, "Stardancer, if you would remain a moment? I would speak with you alone."

"Of course, my queen."

As she exited the Kelani quarters, Azhani mulled over who might be a suspect in the crime against the Y'Skani ambassador. Though she might personally believe him innocent, the possibility of Kuwell's guilt had to be considered. As he'd said, however, krile was an inexact poison. Ambassador Windstorm didn't die, only nearly caused a multi-kingdom incident that would have taken a great deal of diplomacy on Lyssera's part to repair. It also didn't seem likely that Kuwell would use poison—not when he had his axe to hand.

Now Kirthos might have done it out of some desire for power, but as a follower of the Serpent's Way, even a chance to take Ambassador Windstorm's title wouldn't push him to use poison. A laughable possibility was Lyssera herself, but again, why would she do such a thing, especially in the face of an oncoming beast season?

And since it's not Kyrian or me, that just leaves…the rest of Y'Syria and beyond. This could take a while. Her stomach growled. *Damn. Oh well, I'll think better on a full stomach. In fact, I can eat and think at the same time.* "Allyn," she said, getting the prince's attention. "Let's find some dinner. I'm starving and I need to make plans."

"Of course, Master Azhani," he said dully.

Part of her wanted to stop right there and give him a lecture about accepting his duties, but there wasn't time. Right now, she had a poisoner to catch.

"I'll not keep you long, Stardancer," Lyssera said as she resumed her seat. Wearily, she rubbed her face. "You must pardon me, for I am heavy with the burden of this near-death in my court. I fear even the specter of The Great Fields puts me in mind of my beloved twin."

"I understand, Majesty," Kyrian murmured.

"It bothers me too to know of the love she shared with Azhani, for I see its hard echo in our mutual friend and wonder if grief for the loss of that love might set her on a course of utter destruction."

"It is true that she loved Ylera deeply."

"Aye, I expect she could have done nothing less, for Ylera's..." She paused a moment to chuckle softly. "My sister was well-known for her charm. If she wanted someone, then not even altering the course of the wind would keep her from sailing into their bed. But then, I suspect you already know this, don't you, Kyrian of Y'Len?"

She knows... Goddess, has she told Azhani? Blanching, Kyrian said, "Y-yes, I...I know. I have said nothing to Azhani, but yes, Ylera was a friend."

"Classmates at Y'Len, if I recall," Lyssera replied. "I have many a letter from my sister speaking of those she knew and counted among her friends. You were one of the foremost." Narrowing her eyes, she leaned forward and said, "I am greatly disturbed to hear you've kept this information from Azhani, for it would, I think, color her perception of you quite differently."

"That's what I'm afraid of." With a soft sigh, Kyrian nervously tugged at the sleeve of her robe and said, "You have not said anything to her?"

Lyssera shook her head. "It was not my place."

"Thank you," Kyrian whispered, relieved.

"You're welcome, but why not speak of it?" Lyssera asked. "If she knew you shared a loss with her, it might help her to deal with her grief."

At this moment, Kyrian could barely remember her reasons. Ruefully, she shook her head. "In the beginning, I was angry at her. For all that I knew, she had slain Ylera. But she was not the person I envisioned, not the madwoman Arris claimed had done those horrible deeds. The more of her story she shared, the less I believed the rumors and bard's tales." She continued to fidget, looking everywhere but at Lyssera. "We created a trust between us, and mentioning my relationship with Ylera seemed counterproductive. If I said something, I was afraid she might fear my presence was a deception—that I only stayed by her for the chance to stab her in the back. Then I met Elisira and learned the truth. Since then, I haven't found the right moment to admit it. And if I say something now, she might hate me for not speaking sooner and I don't..." She sighed. "I can't have that."

"Reasonable excuses, all, but..." Lyssera leaned forward and held Kyrian's gaze. "You will tell her, won't you?" It was not truly a question, not when the queen spoke with that tone of command.

Kyrian, however, was not so easily cowed. Folding her hands, she rested them on the table. "In my own time, Majesty."

Wryly, Lyssera chuckled. "You're quite formidable, Stardancer Kyrian. I expected, for your age, that you would be more malleable."

"A malleable stardancer is a dangerous one, my queen. We are called upon to make life-or-death decisions at a moment's notice. We cannot dither and thus, we cannot allow ourselves to be swayed by the commands of another—unless those commands are not counter to our own ends." She offered Lyssera a wistful smile. "I may also have the advantage of knowing Ylera. Much like you, she was bred to command and inadvertently taught me how to steel myself against it."

"Ah, and does this mean that you were once one of my sister's many conquests?" Lyssera asked carefully.

Kyrian snorted. "Absolutely not! I was but a lass of thirteen when she and I were friends." Growing pensive, she said, "Perhaps, if Ylera had stayed at the monastery longer, as I grew older, I might have developed an infatuation. As it stood, what I felt for her was respect and loyalty. Of my peers, she was the one who defended me against those who did not feel a half-elven child should have the same access to education as those of pure elven blood."

Lyssera sighed. "That is the great shame of my people and I do apologize. I wish I could say I was free of those prejudices, but I know they plague me from time to time, though I make an effort to stop them when possible."

"Ylera said much the same thing, but Y'Len is fully a third half-elven, my queen, and of those, many are quite ah, beautiful to behold. I believe her desire for company outlasted her bias. It wasn't long before she shed the aura of the court and became yet another belching, farting, snoring student who was rowdy when she was drunk, studious when the teachers were looking, and in all honesty, my best friend." Kyrian smiled at the wonderful memories cluttering her thoughts.

"Yes, she seemed quite fond of you. In letters, she often spoke of you in the tone of a friend," Lyssera said quietly. "And it certainly sounds as though you knew her well."

"Well enough. We shared a room for a couple of seasons. She worked hard to make you proud, my queen. I think she was aware of her destiny as your envoy and wanted to serve in the best way possible. To this end, I suspect that's why she spent so much time with others—she had to learn diplomacy and how best to…" Kyrian frowned. "I like not the word 'manipulate,' but…" She shrugged. "I think it might be the best term."

"Perhaps 'convince' would be a better word for it," Lyssera said wryly. "Yes, Ylera was very good at convincing others to cooperate."

"Yes! I agree completely!" Kyrian said eagerly. "And yes, she 'convinced' me to do many things I probably shouldn't have."

Lyssera blinked back tears. "Will you tell me more of my sister?"

"Of course, Majesty. What would you hear?"

"Anything. Everything."

They spent more than a candlemark talking about Ylera's adventures in Y'Len. Some were worthy of laughter, while others brought groans or gasps of shock, but Kyrian felt that this was necessary, that Lyssera needed to feel close to her sister through the memories Kyrian could share.

"Yes, yes, she wrote of that one. And the time she and her friend 'Kyr' snuck off into the woods and ended up falling into a bog."

Rolling her eyes, Kyrian said, "Oh yes, I remember that too." She sighed. "Somehow, Ylera was always able to talk me into finding trouble."

"Hm, I wonder if she ever dragged Azhani out in the middle of a rainstorm to search for mushrooms and yellow mint?" Lyssera asked teasingly.

Kyrian shifted uncomfortably. The conversation was slipping toward an area she didn't wish to discuss. "She's…never mentioned anything to me of the sort." While not specifically true, it wasn't a lie, either. It just didn't seem right to be telling Lyssera things Azhani had mentioned in confidence.

Knowingly, she said, "No, she wouldn't. Azhani keeps her thoughts close most times. Even with me, she is quite reticent about her life with Ylera. She shares bits and pieces, but never whole cloth. I have tried, and she does tell me small things that help. We…we have been good for each other, I think."

At this, Kyrian tried not to feel jealous, but she couldn't help the flash of sickness that filled the pit of her stomach.

Lyssera gazed off into the distance, blinking slowly as if lost in thought. "When she first appeared in my study, I was full of uncertainty about her. Though I knew the truth, I was still of two minds about it." She shook her head. "I did not want to believe a son of Thodan could be so cruel. It was easier to think my sister had been wrong, that somehow Azhani had fooled her, but what I saw and what I heard that night—that story did not come from a woman who was a killer." Narrowing her eyes, she turned to Kyrian and held her gaze for a long moment. "No, she was just as broken as I, and that is why I fear for her sanity. She has helped me, though she knows it not. Just as you are helping me now. I want to help her—I tried to help her, because…" Touching her face, she sighed. "It has to be hard to look at me and not see Ylera. Yet I am not her. I am not the woman who loved her. I am merely her friend."

The relief that raced through Kyrian at that admission was frightfully strong. "W-what can I do, Majesty?" she rasped.

Taking Kyrian's hand, Lyssera stared into her eyes. "I don't know, but you're doing something anyway, whether you know it or not. From the moment I saw her with you at Tellyn's, it was clear that a spark of life had returned to her. She smiled and it was beautiful. Somehow you have unlocked her heart, and that makes me very happy that you're here."

"And I'm glad to be here," Kyrian whispered. "I missed her, when she was gone." Softly, she admitted, "I worried about her."

"Aye, and I worry now," Lyssera replied as she refilled their goblets. "Azhani talks openly of destroying the rimerbeasts, but of her plans for Arris she speaks little. We both crave revenge and I know she wishes to present me with his head on a platter, but such a gift would not ease the loss of my sister!" she said sharply.

Kyrian winced. "No, it wouldn't. But he should not rule Y'Dan. If he will not step aside for another, what else can Azhani do?"

"He should be arrested by the high king's forces! Let Ysradan deal with him." Lyssera replied. Standing, she began to pace. "If not, there will be war with Y'Dan, which feels ill-omened, especially so soon after we made peace.

Yet this is the road we will go if Azhani seeks violence, for I swore to back her against Arris." In obvious discomfort, she closed her eyes. "Ylera was my best counselor, and now she is gone. I fear my own heart screams for me to join Azhani in a bloody massacre of those who would stand with Arris Thodan, but Ylera?" Shaking her head, Lyssera looked out over the garden. "Ylera would not want our countries to war over her death."

"No, she'd rather Azhani and Arris dueled, for it would appeal to her romantic nature," Kyrian said softly.

Lyssera's sharp bark of laughter made her jump. "Oh aye, you did know my twin well."

"So what will you do?"

Half shrugging, she replied, "Against Arris? Nothing, for now. He is not our greatest threat, the rimerbeasts are." She was silent for the count of several heartbeats, then, softly, asked, "Can I trust her, Kyrian? Can I hope that her hunger for vengeance won't lead her to run off with my armies and leave Y'Syr a perfect target for hordes of hungry monsters?"

"Yes," Kyrian replied quickly. "Azhani's honor is all she has. She has sworn herself to you, and thus she will serve your needs above her own. This much I know about her without any hesitation. Beyond that, her dedication to Astariu is absolute, and we both know Astariu teaches that one must choose the path of the greatest good."

Relaxing, Lyssera said, "Yes, I agree that her honor is paramount, for when I suggested sending a Cabal assassin after Arris, she turned quite pale. And whenever she has spoken of Arris' downfall, it is always in terms of him dying on the end of her sword."

Kyrian was glad the Cabal had not been summoned, though she herself did want to find one of their number and have some rather stern words with them. "That should speak to her loyalties, my queen—and her desires. Though I think it obvious why she wants to be the one to put Arris to a brutal end. He murdered her fiancée."

"Yes, I knew they wanted to marry," Lyssera said as she took her seat again. "Though I suspect had they done so, it would have caused quite the commotion. Many of my people would not have tolerated such a union, for the ink on Thodan's treaty was still too wet."

"And Ylera would have thumbed her nose at them and thrown a lavish wedding party," Kyrian replied quietly.

"Then she would have been thumbing her nose at me, for I, sadly and shamefully, would have found it hard to swallow. I think... I think I might have laughed at them, had Ylera come to tell me what they planned," Lyssera said regretfully.

Goddess, this conversation... I will never tell Azhani what has been said. Never. She respects Lyssera so much. If she knew the queen had, even for a moment, held her feelings for Ylera in such contempt, she would... I don't know, but it wouldn't be good.

Something of her thoughts must have shown on her face, for Lyssera said, "Ah, you think me unkind. Perhaps I am. But I am a queen, Kyrian, and thus must consider every shadow and shape of a situation. Every act, every word, every single, damnable thing I do is subject my people's study and venom. One mistake and the repercussions are infinite." For a long while, she sat there, looking up toward the darkening sky. "Loss has taught me that Y'Syr cannot continue to mire itself in the bigoted, hidebound ways of the past. I would give all I have for Ylera to live again, to love Azhani as she did, and I would celebrate their marriage like no other—if only to have her back. But she is gone. I cannot change that." Lyssera wiped tears from her eyes. "All I can do is help change the future for others and in time, celebrate for them. But now, I must beg you to guide me, to calm my fears and tell me I am not a fool to believe that Azhani is our one true hope against the rimerbeasts."

Feeling like the weight of a thousand moons had just come crashing onto her shoulders, Kyrian said, "I wish words could ease your concerns, my queen. All I can offer are my memories. Will hearing of how Azhani and I came to be friends help?"

"Perhaps it will."

Another candlemark was consumed in the telling, but when it was over, Lyssera looked less troubled.

"And thus, I believe she is right to serve in this manner, Majesty," Kyrian said quietly.

"You are right, Stardancer, and I thank you. Honor is what compels Azhani to walk the difficult paths she takes. This will allow me to be content when her conversations about Arris' fate are filled with dark words, for they are, at their heart, laced with grief and not madness," Lyssera said with a relieved sigh. "Her heart still rests securely in the Twain's light."

"I'm glad you found some comfort in my story. But I have stayed overlong. Ambassador Iften will need me soon."

"Yes. My apologies," Lyssera said with a weak laugh. "Go, and take with you my blessing. I expect we will speak again ere long."

Lyssera was polite enough to wait until Kyrian had seen to Ambassador Windstorm's care before demanding her presence once more. Even a queen could not order a stardancer's actions, but wisdom warned Kyrian that she should do her best to maintain good relations with Azhani's current benefactor. Truly, she didn't mind the company. Although duty pricked her with the need to stay at Ambassador Windstorm's side, his staff had made it clear they were more than capable of following her instructions, freeing her to serve the queen's needs.

A meal was waiting for her when she joined Lyssera in her study. They ate, Kyrian feeling particularly nostalgic when she nibbled on a small fruit pie, remembering how Ylera had attempted to coax Y'Len's baker into making them. Afterward, she and Lyssera sat quietly, sipping wine from crystal goblets and watching the fire dance on the hearth.

Azhani was conspicuously absent. Eventually, Kyrian asked, "Will it take her long to find the culprit?"

With the faintest of shrugs, Lyssera replied, "Perhaps. Thodan once said that she and Rhu'len could vanish for days at a time when they were on the trail of someone he'd tasked them to capture."

"I wish..." Kyrian grimaced. "I would have been happier if she'd taken me with her." The fear that she might be abandoned again tickled at the back of her mind, even though she'd sworn Azhani would not run away from her obligations to Lyssera. *I have to trust her. If I don't, I might as well pack my bags and return to Y'Len tonight.*

They grew quiet once more, the fire's crackle the only sound to interrupt the stillness of the chamber. Lyssera studied her wine glass, circling her fingertip over the rim absently. "You love her." They were innocent, gentle words that might be only simple conversation, but for the knowing cant to the queen's head. There was no mistaking what was being spoken of here. This was not about friendship, but something more, something sharper, deeper. Because of that, the statement seemed to echo madly in Kyrian's ears, whipping her heart into a beating frenzy that made breathing near impossible.

Swallowing heavily, she fought back the urge to deny the truth. "How could I not?" Bravely, she met Lyssera's gaze. "I have laughed with her, cried with her, lived with her, traveled with her, saved and been saved by her." On an uneven breath, she whispered, "I have touched the colors of her aura in all ways, swum the energies of her deepest essence, and opened my eyes to know her as only a stardancer can. She is, without a doubt, a grand and beautiful woman, flawed as only the truly good can be."

Somberly, Lyssera nodded. "Is that what Ylera felt, I wonder?" As she often did when speaking of her twin, she gazed into the distance, her expression touched by sadness and loss. "She was so eager to love, to be loved, to be happy…she looked so hard for it, drawn, like a moth to a flame, to any who could promise her the hope of it."

"All I've learned about Azhani tells me that Ylera had that and more besides," Kyrian replied. "I'm sure she felt cherished above all others, for Azhani is the most focused person I know. She would have devoted everything she had to spare to Ylera." She smiled sadly. "She certainly has tried to do as much for me, as my friend, even if I might wish for more."

It felt strange to admit it, but she couldn't lie, not to Ylera's sister. It would be tantamount to saying the same falsehood to her dead friend, and though Kyrian didn't live and die by her honor like Azhani, it was still deeply important to her.

"Were I not queen," Lyssera said quietly. "I might find myself jealous of Azhani, for you, Kyrian, are…interesting to me."

Kyrian blushed. "Thank you, my queen. Perhaps, in another time, I might have returned that interest."

"Alas, it is not another time and I am who I am. We could not dance openly and I will not love in shame," Lyssera said regretfully. "Perhaps it is why I do not love at all."

"Don't close yourself to it, for even a single moment's taste is better than never sipping of its sweetness," Kyrian found herself telling the other woman. "You are kind, wise, and beautiful—all traits any would find worthy of cherishing."

With a soft snort, Lyssera said, "I am also very aware of the politics of royal romance, Stardancer. Sadly, I am not free to engage in petty affairs of the heart, else my bed might be warm more nights than not. You, on the other hand, should not be so lonely."

Wryly, Kyrian smiled. "I will be fine, my queen. Now is not the best time for me to seek companionship. Not when I have sworn to aid Azhani in her quest to stop the rimerbeasts and deal with Arris Thodan."

Lyssera's answering grin was knowing. "Peace could be upon us, I suspect, and you would still find a way to deter my urge to play matchmaker. Very well, perhaps I will turn my meddling ways elsewhere." She poured herself more wine and then turned to watch the fire again. Soon, she was asleep.

Carefully, Kyrian took the mostly empty glass from her, lifted her from the chair, and carried her to her bed, where she gently tucked her in. "I think, my queen, that Ylera would be most amused by the idea of her 'properly elven' queen of a sister playing matchmaker for a stardancer. Sadly, I fear any efforts on your part would only end in disaster, as Azhani has no more interest in bedding me than she does in dancing with a squirrel!"

Muzzily, Lyssera murmured, "But squirrels are good dancers, just ask the trees," and then let out a snore that nearly rattled the rafters.

Laughing delightedly, Kyrian exited the room.

Oily, dense smoke from dozens of torches and small lanterns filled the dockside casino. Azhani took her time working through the room, playing a few rounds of cards or dice, losing some, winning others, assuming the role of a bored gambler better than she might like to admit. There was a certain thrill to it, not in the winning and losing of coin, but of going undiscovered, of presenting herself not as Azhani Rhu'len, former warleader of Y'Dan, but simply as Zan, a fur trapper down from the mountains for the first time all winter.

"Zan" was a useful tool, one she and her father had developed over the years that they had worked for Thodan. Most here knew her, and if she had one or two new scars ruining her plain, hawkish face, well, none of them cared much to look at her long. They all knew Zan was far too intent on making the coin to fill her packs with enough mead to keep her warm over the next winter.

Someone nudged her ribs and said, "Eh, there, Zan, do ye hev a brick t'keep yer bed warm fer ye?" He chuckled. "Or kin ye barely but afford that, now?"

Casually, she punched him in the gut, took his drink, downed it, and then dropped the empty glass on his cards. "Shut up and play, Torg, or go 'way. Y'breath be like the scorned leavin's o' a skunk's den."

A few of the other gamblers chuckled. Torg spat a wad of kendac into his spittoon and the game resumed. She lost to him three hands later, then completely cleaned him out right after that. Cursing her loudly, he stormed off while she merely tucked a coin into the bodice of the wench who'd been keeping her glass filled, her back warm, and her ear full of gossip for most of the night. From Hedva she'd learned the names and faces of every whore and moneylender in the place. For a price, Hedva would be happy to introduce her to either.

Every wicked desire could be fulfilled inside The Blue Dove if one had coin enough. *Not that I have many wanton needs.* She tried to keep the twist of distaste from her lips, for that would only serve to drive Hedva from her, and she still needed the woman's company—as a shield from those whose motives were even less greed driven, if nothing else. Hedva was a simple woman. She knew Zan's wants and never once had Zan ever asked for a whore. Gossip and news was what Zan needed, and Azhani was quite happy that Hedva was always eager to provide it.

In the past, staying away from whores had been a necessity based in secrecy, but now—now, she looked around the room and found every face wanting. Bared chests and nearly exposed breasts could do nothing to arouse her lust, not when she had the memory of Ylera's hands upon her body to spark heat enough to warm the coldest of nights. *Even Kyrian's smile can get my heart beating faster than this tawdry display!*

Unbidden, an image of her friend filled her mind. Caught in a blaze of sunlight, the amber of her hair burnished to glowing gold, she stood dressed in the thinnest of tunics, flushed from exertion, her eyes sparkling with joy as she looked up at her. Azhani was overcome with the urge to rush back to Oakheart and…and… *And what? Kiss her? Goddess!*

Shaken, she could barely grasp the truth of her lustful thoughts. Guilt poured bile into her belly, making her sick with the need to get away before she went completely insane. *No! How can I be thinking that anyone could be desirable after losing my Ylera?*

"Zan? Be ye all right, darlin'?" Hedva muttered, giving her shoulder a quick squeeze. "Ye look like that last drink were rotten."

Quickly, Azhani swallowed back her emotions and grunted. "Just time fer a break. G'wan, git yerself somethin' pretty." She thrust a few more coins at her before stomping off toward the tavern at the back of the casino.

Kyrian is just a friend. Nothing more. That she is a beautiful, desirable woman is no more or less important than acknowledging that the sun is bright and the snow is cold.

Pushing any further thought in that direction aside, she peered through the smoke and crowds until she found exactly what she was looking for—the pit. Situated in the very center of the tavern, the pit was where those with grudges went to grapple at games of strength instead those of chance. Here, it was not unusual to see two men beat each other to unconsciousness simply for the sake of a few coins. Here also were those who preferred to perform feats of strength—arm wrestling, lifting of heavy objects, and twisting of iron bars to prove their virility.

Azhani found the practice to be equal parts interesting and confounding, for she could see much of it that would be of use to a warrior like herself, but those who devoted themselves to this cult of muscles would never survive a real battle, for their bodies were terribly unbalanced. A warrior needed strength, yes, but speed was their greatest ally. She herself was strong, but it was the fleetness of her feet that had kept her alive this long and would, she hoped, continue to do so for the foreseeable future.

It was not the contests that had brought her here, however, but one of the contestants. Skirting the pit, she made her way to the back corner and straddled a chair across the table from a man who could have made a great deal of coin masquerading as a talking bear.

Naked from the waist up, muscles bulging and gleaming with sweat and scented oil, and decorated with the attractive addiction of an amorous lady friend, Eskyn Dowser was one of the best arm wrestlers in The Blue Dove. Over the years, he had made its owner, Yannev Krolg, plenty of coin serving as the house champion. He was also the best source of information on all things illegal in the city. They had some shared history together, and Azhani had spent years cultivating him as a source. By now he was, if such a thing could be said, a good friend of "Zan's".

"Be right with ya, my friend," Eskyn said, barely pausing the long, lusty kiss he'd been engaged in when Azhani had sat down. Instead, he deepened it, covering the woman's throat and barely-clad breasts with wet, loud kisses until she laughed and shoved at him playfully.

"Don't fall in," Azhani said dryly. "I'd hate for you to lose your tongue before I've had a chance to wet it with a shot of Yannev's best."

Turning away from the woman, Eskyn laughed as he boisterously pounded the table. "Astarus' balls! Zan!" he exclaimed loudly, a large, welcoming smile spreading across his dark-skinned face. Once, many years back, Eskyn had joked they might be cousins, and ever since, he treated her like long lost family.

Giving the wench on his lap a final kiss, he said, "Grab us a couple of beers, love! And tell Yannev I'm off—my best cousin Zan's in town!"

The fact that Zan and Eskyn were as likely to be cousins as Kyrian was to strip down to her garters and sing, "The Lusty Librarian" in Lyssera's court never seemed to bother Eskyn, and Azhani allowed the fiction. Especially since Eskyn knew her actual identity. For whatever reason, he seemed to prefer her as the fur trader.

"You want something to eat, Es?" the woman asked curiously.

Scratching his bald head, Eskyn snorted. "Why sure! Me and the cousin ain't broke no bread in a beast's age. G'wan with ye now, love. And be sure ye tell Yannev to put me off the list."

She giggled and ran off.

Turning to Azhani, he fixed her with knowing grin. "I been wondrin' when ye'd drag yer butt down from Her Royalness' tree to come see me, old friend. I feel like I owe ye a drink for all that shyvot you suffered in Y'Dan."

Azhani made a face. "I'd soon as not think on it. I lost much there."

"Aye," he said, nodding slowly. "But found sommat here, I gather." He glanced in the direction of Oakheart.

She shrugged. "I've no claim to poverty, if that's what worries you."

"Our queen rewards quality, or so I'm told." He pulled out a pipe and lit it with a bit of tinder he took from a box next to a candle. Puffing out smoke, he watched her, seeming content to wait until she told him what she wanted.

Azhani, however, liked making him wait. It was their game, one they'd played many times before and right now, it was a familiar path to tread in a life that was becoming increasingly strange.

As the silence between them grew, Eskyn's wench brought a tray of food over. He thanked her, then sent her away with a handful of coins. Once she was gone, he reached for a loaf of bread, tore it in half and offered some to Azhani, saying, "What can I do for you, cousin?"

Accepting it, she dipped a piece into a plate of spiced oil. "Krile, Eskyn. Who'd be stupid enough to sell it to anyone from Oakheart?"

Eskyn scowled. "Let's say I might know the answer to this, and let's say tellin' ye involves some rather frightening risk—what's it worth ye knowing?"

With a casual flick of her fingers, she sent a heavy gold coin spinning across the table. "This, and more with it, if your information proves sound."

He caught the coin and quickly pocketed it. Hallmarked from the high king's own treasury, it was the purest gold he could ask for without it being in nugget form. For someone like Eskyn, just one of those coins could keep him well fed for several days. That he was being offered more than just one meant Azhani's need was serious. Licking his lips, he said, "It'll cost ye nineteen more for the names ye need—and I'll be wanting someone ye've picked to watch me wife until ye've done with yer house cleaning." He nodded to the pretty woman sitting close to the bard, clapping along to the music he was playing. Cracking his knuckles, he added, "I can take care of meself."

"You'll have twenty-five. And two guards," she said quietly. "Now tell me."

"All right," he said, leaning closer. "Ye'll be wantin' to cast yer gaze this-a-way, then," and took his time telling her a story of greed, corruption, and scandal that had, until that morning, gone largely unnoticed by the upper courts of Oakheart.

When he was finished, Azhani had more than enough information to find the poisoner and give him over to Lyssera's mercy, if any existed for a man who would betray his kingdom for coin.

CHAPTER EIGHT

The chair was hard, but Azhani cared little about comfort right now. Across from her crouched a man. Old, worn, and bitterly marked by life, Jordrakk had clearly spent too much time hunched in crowded spaces, for he glanced around his environs like a rat trapped in a cage. Chains kept him penned to the corner of the cell and he looked exactly as Azhani expected a man who was bound for the gallows to appear—broken.

"I hear you've information for me," she said quietly. "Speak, then."

Slowly, Jordrakk shuffled forward, his chains just long enough for him to touch the bars. "Freedom," he rasped, shaking so much she worried his bones might come apart from the force of it. "I am owed it, for what I know."

"Give me the name I seek and you may yet have it," she replied.

"Var. 'Twas Draygil Var who had the last of my krile, and may he choke on it! His 'good name' won me nothing in this viper's pit! Nothing!" He was so enraged that white flecks of spittle dripped from his mouth. "Let me free and I'll shout it from the rooftops."

"You are certain of this?" Azhani asked. Draygil Var was a baron, and though a minor nobleman, still well-connected enough to cause trouble if these accusations were to be found false. He was also the man Eskyn had named as being someone from Oakheart who'd had a recent interest in krile. It was because of Eskyn that she'd come to see this particular prisoner.

"Oh aye, I'm sure," Jordrakk spat bitterly. "For you'll be knowing it by this." He thrust his hand toward her. Upon his palm was a burn mark in the shape of Var's signet. "'Twas his warning not to be speaking of his business, but I don't care! Bastard's a thief!"

Azhani recognized the mark. She'd seen the crossed arrow heraldry on the arms of several guards stationed in one of the wings at Oakheart. "Thank you, Jordrakk. I will return," she said, turning and marching up to the office of the jail's warden.

Securing the release of the prisoner, however, took time—even when she had Lyssera's full authority to back up her request. It was that delay that ruined her plans, for when she returned to collect Jordrakk, she found a guard kneeling beside his twisted, lifeless body.

"What happened?" she snapped as the man hastily stood and saluted her.

"Sorry, milady, but he just...started shaking and gibbering and finally fell over. I couldn't even get the key to his cell out afore he were dead," he said, shaking his head regretfully. "I dunno what 'e done, but 'e be dead now."

Kneeling, Azhani turned Jordrakk's head to the side and cursed, for his face bore the clear signs of a krile overdose. "Shyvot! No, this isn't your fault, Constable. It's mine. I should have realized he was an addict." Momentarily, she considered cutting off the man's hand as evidence. *No, it's a clue, but Var could claim I forged his signet. Better that I just use what Jordrakk told me to guide me in seeking unassailable proof of Var's guilt.* "See to it that this body is burned."

"At once, Master Azhani," he said, saluting her smartly.

She was now stuck at the beginning, or near to, for at least she had a name. *And since I have a name, it's time to search a little closer to home...*

Court was in full session. Circumspectly, Lyssera rubbed at her tired eyes and tried not to think about how many more candlemarks she would have to remain seated upon her damnably uncomfortable throne. Azhani's predawn visit to her chambers had no doubt sent the court gossips into a tizzy over what their queen was doing with her brand new retainer, but at the moment, Lyssera cared little for gossip and instead, focused on truth—there was a snake lurking in her bower, and she aimed to see its head cut off.

Whispered words flitted from corner to corner of the hall, but Lyssera ignored them, knowing she had to wait until Azhani's investigations bore ripe fruit. At the moment, the warrior slept, or so it appeared to Prince Allyndev, whom Lyssera had sent to check on her nearly half a candlemark ago. With Kyrian in the ambassadorial wing treating Iften, it meant there was little more to be done other than endure the tribulations of court.

Lady Sidar's presence made it more endurable, for she, at least, had possessed kindness enough to summon a page to bring Lyssera fresh tea whenever her cup became empty. One appeared at her elbow now and said, "Lady Sidar asks if you require aught, my queen?"

"Just another cup, thank you," she replied, allowing the girl to pour and then adding a single dollop of honey, stirring it into the darkly brewed liquid and then drinking slowly. It was bitter, heavily laden with the earthy taste of herbs that would keep her alert. *This is one of Tellyn's blends. A good choice.* Lifting the cup in Lady Sidar's direction, Lyssera smiled and nodded her gratitude.

Though Sidar did not reply, she did offer a brief nod of her own. Such was the way of court. Perhaps later, when most eyes had turned away from them, they would share a meal. *And more, if I read the offer in the pattern of flowers painted on this cup correctly.* Lyssera briefly toyed with the notion of taking Lady Sidar to her bed. It would be one way of assuring any misguided feelings of Azhani's were crushed, but she could not find it in her to be so cold—to either woman. *Sidar is lovely and I would be cruel to use her thusly.* Pensively, she looked around her court and studied the men and women who nipped and pecked at the heels of greatness. *Who is it? Who among you is so driven by the greed for glory, you would commit treason to gain it?* One of them had attempted murder in her court, bringing pain and vileness a guest in her home. Thinking about it drove icicles of pure rage into her stomach.

Long had Oakheart claimed its title as the safest castle in all Y'Myran. That this sanctity might have been broken for mere gain sickened her. Suddenly, every face that looked back at her was a devil's mask of potential malice, even that of Lady Sidar, whose appearance Lyssera had, upon occasion, found to be quite pleasing. Now, however, it was merely one more facade in a sea of suspicion. Draining her cup, Lyssera prayed that Azhani would corral the traitor soon. *I cannot breathe while choked with a noose of fear. Oakheart needs to bask in the clean air of peace once again.*

Unbeknownst to Lyssera and the court, Azhani was not sleeping, though she had left the bed curtains drawn to make it appear as though she were. Instead, after obtaining the master key to every door in Oakheart from Lyssera, she snuck off to seek evidence of Baron Var's guilt.

Jordrakk's untimely death had sent her on to another of the names Eskyn Dowser had provided. This time, what she had learned gave her no further evidence, but a fuller picture of who Var was. On the wharves of Y'Syria, he was known as an inveterate gambler with terrible luck and a growing inability to pay his debts. Until recently, he had been mere days away from waking up wearing ship's anchors as slippers. Then his fortunes had changed and he paid every single one of his debts in full, a sum that equaled several thousand goldmarks.

Though she now had both suspect and motive, Azhani still wanted to have proof of both the means and the opportunity for his treachery. Thus, she had acquired the master key. Now, she was hunkered down in the boughs above Var's suite, watching his guards. All she needed to do was wait for court to begin. Once Var left, she would have plenty of time to search his quarters.

She did not have long to wait. The heralds sounded their horns, the summons carrying through Oakheart's halls. Shortly, Var's door opened. He stepped out, looked at one of his guards, and then marched off toward the grand hall. Azhani gave him half a candlemark to be well and truly gone, then dropped from her perch, landing in front of the guard who had remained.

With a silky smile, she said, "Hello," and punched him hard enough to knock him out before he could do more than open his mouth in shock. Wincing, she shook her hand then used the master key to open the door. Swiftly, she dragged the guard inside, tied him up, and stashed him on one of the more comfortable looking chaises. Afterward, she locked the door and went to work, turning the suite inside out in her search for proof Var's guilt.

Fortunately for her, Baron Draygil Var was as poor a criminal as he was a gambler, for in just under a quarter candlemark's time, she had everything she needed to see him hang.

Hidden under the mattress of his bed, she had found a half-empty vial of krile, a sack of coins, and a scroll tube. It was the tube that was of most interest for her, for it bore several sigils inscribed at both ends that she sensed reeked of magick. Luck again was with her, for one end was not fully sealed, falling off when she drew the tube out from under the mattress. A single piece of parchment slid out when she shook it. She read the message scrawled upon it and ground her teeth in frustration.

> *Make every effort to cause a major disruption in the court, Var. Point the eyes of the elves away from their western borders for as long as you can. Serve me well, and your rewards will be endless.*

Though unsigned, there was little doubt in Azhani's mind that the order had come from Arris Thodan, for who else would wish to cause such trouble for the Y'Syran court? Flushed with rage, she growled, "What is that bastard trying to hide?" and tucked the evidence into her belt pouch. Quickly, she made her way to court. It was time to catch a would-be murderer.

Rumor, fleet-footed, poison-tongued, and edged with the harshness of recent distrust, made the grand hall a place of acid words that flowed around Kyrian as she stepped onto the thick, gilt-edged carpet that led to Lyssera's throne. From far at the other end of the chamber, Lyssera quickly came to greet her.

"My aching posterior is grateful for your timely arrival, Stardancer Kyrian," she murmured as they formally embraced.

"It's my pleasure to serve your comfort, Highness," Kyrian said with a soft chuckle.

Lyssera smiled and, in a completely normal tone, asked, "How is our friend, the good Ambassador Windstorm?"

"He is well, Your Majesty. Vice-ambassador Kirthos assures me his crankiness and demands for 'slightly charred cow' are quite normal," she said as they made their way back to the throne. "Though for now, he must be content with just the drippings."

Lyssera took her seat and waited for the page to provide Kyrian with a padded stool. "I have, quite to my surprise, had a letter from Clan Chief Padreg."

"Oh?" Kyrian glanced up at her with interest.

She nodded. "He and his lady send their love to you and Azhani," she said quietly. "Though I fail to understand why he wished me to be certain to remind Azhani of their wager."

Thoroughly flabbergasted, Kyrian could only shake her head. "Wager? Truly, the Twain only know what is meant by that, for I surely do not."

"I am as unsure as you—though perhaps we can ask her ourselves," Lyssera said, gesturing to the other end of the hall.

Striding toward them, her face dark with anger, was Azhani. Whispered phrases heavy with curiosity and accusation followed her all the way to the edge of the dais.

This does not bode well.

Azhani knelt before the throne. "As you commanded, Highness, I have discovered the identity of the one who sought to harm Ambassador

Windstorm." Her clear, plainly spoken words effectively muffled all other conversation. Stillness filled the room until it seemed that all Kyrian could hear was her own heart beating like the thundering rhythm of dwarven war drums.

Rising from her throne, Lyssera looked out at the court and said, "And tell us who this person is, that they might be brought before me to face this accusation honorably."

"Baron Draygil Var," Azhani replied. "And for proof, I offer these, discovered just this day within the baron's own chambers." Calmly, she held up a vial, scroll tube, and pouch branded with the baron's personal arms.

"That is a name known in this court," Lyssera said, no trace of surprise in her tone, though Kyrian detected a slight widening of her eyes as she spoke. "Are you sure you wish to offer it to me thusly, Azhani? For if you are right, then he is guilty of the direst form of treason and must face death. Will you risk your honor to besmirch his name so?"

Kyrian held her breath. She didn't know the baron at all, but if Azhani risked the honor she was fighting so hard to restore, and failed, it would destroy her.

The court's silence was parchment thin.

"Foul!" A man's voice rang out. "I cry foul, Majesty. This oathbreaker lies to gain favor! I beg of you, do not be gulled by her deceitful ways!" Pushing his way to the throne, a richly dressed man gave Azhani a hate-filled glare. "I demand you arrest her for sullying my good name!"

Icily, Azhani replied, "If it is lies that I speak, my lord baron, then pray explain why your personal arms are upon the tube that bears a note upon which your name is written—a note, I might add, instructing you to *Make every effort to cause a major disruption in court.*' Personally, I feel that poisoning the Y'Skani ambassador does take that instruction a bit far, but then you were also told to *'Point the eyes of the elves away from their western borders for as long as you can,'* weren't you?" As Var's face turned a disturbing shade of red, Azhani faced the queen and said, "I believe you'll find that the vial of krile is half empty and that the pouch of coin is quite heavy, my queen."

Lyssera opened the scroll tube, read the note, and then turned to Kyrian. "Stardancer Kyrian, in your opinion, is this vial of sufficient size to harm a man such as Ambassador Windstorm?"

Quickly, Kyrian examined the vial, trying to hide her nervousness as she held it up so that the light shone through the glass and illuminated the greenish contents. "This is quite a large vial. A dose of this drug should be small and yet, more than half is gone. Since Baron Var himself seems not to be exhibiting signs of addiction or poisoning, nor have any others been so affected, save Ambassador Windstorm, I would have to say that yes, this is a more than sufficient amount to have caused his death, had he not received proper care."

"Thank you, Stardancer," Lyssera said, taking the vial back from her. "Well, my lord, what say you to these charges?"

White-faced, he sputtered, "She planted it, of course! She must have!" Sneering in disgust, he said, "This Y'Dani scum is the real poisoner, my queen. I am shamed you allowed such a one into your household. I trust you will have her properly thrashed for her insults."

Outraged, Kyrian just barely kept herself from pulling her baton and walloping the man over the head with it. His lies—and they were pure falsehoods, for his gaze never quite met Lyssera's when he spoke—were just the tinder needed to set the court ablaze.

"Aye, he speaks truth, Highness!" someone shouted.

"String her up!" another one yelled. "Or send her to the damned Y'Danis so they can try again!"

A muscle on Azhani's face twitched, causing the scar to jump. Kyrian wanted to touch it, to calm her friend's nerves and reassure her that she was safe, that Lyssera would not do such a thing. *I wouldn't let her, though it might mean my own banishment.*

The shouts grew louder and louder until, with one upraised hand, Lyssera silenced them all. Stepping down off the dais, she began to circle Azhani and Baron Var. It didn't escape Kyrian's notice that Azhani was still on her knees, head bent humbly, while Var stood with his chest puffed out and his face a mask of haughty self-importance.

"Who serves me is at my discretion," Lyssera said calmly. "Though it should be known that Starseeker Vashyra herself has found Azhani Rhu'len to be a woman whose honor is above reproach. I wonder, Baron Var, if she would say the same of yours?"

He did not reply.

Exhaling sharply, Lyssera glanced down at Azhani. "I will, however, grant that this evidence, while damning, is tenuous. Have you any further proof that might weight the scales in your favor?"

No one but Kyrian saw the panicked look that flashed across Azhani's face before she said, "I—"

"My queen, if I may?" Kyrian interjected. "You have the key to the proof you seek—simply ask a starseeker to subject them both to a truth summoning." Azhani's scant, but approving nod was all the reward Kyrian needed—especially now that she was the focus of so much scrutiny from the court.

Lyssera smiled. "An excellent and timely suggestion, Stardancer Kyrian," she said, sending a page to fetch Starseeker Vashyra. "We will wait for her convenience. Until then, Var, Azhani, I hope you are comfortable."

"Of course, Highness," Azhani replied.

Baron Var, however, gave a longing look to the padded seats of the court's gallery.

Shortly, word came that Starseeker Vashyra would attend them within the candlemark. Lyssera gestured for Azhani to rise and sit beside Kyrian. A similar chair was brought for Baron Var, who placed it across the dais from Azhani's, then spent his time glaring at her as if he wished she would simply drop dead.

Azhani could feel the tension in the hall rising to a fever pitch as they waited. Var stared daggers at her. She pretended to ignore him, but it was difficult. All she wanted to do was strike his head from his lying, dishonorable body, but until Lyssera gave the order, she had to remain calm.

Nervous whispers filled the room as the nobles resumed their usual chatter. *No doubt taking bets as to the outcome,* she thought dryly.

As casually as she could, she turned to Kyrian, nudged her with her elbow, and murmured, "Want to join me for a bite to eat after the manure hits the crowd?"

Surprisingly, Kyrian smiled. "Aye, and while we eat, you can tell me all about the bet you made with Padreg."

The bet? Azhani swallowed nervously. *How did she hear about that? Beast's bones! Blessed Twain, what am I supposed to tell her? That I wagered my services against us falling in love? Something tells me she'd take that about as well as a square wheel turns.*

Another part of her mind urged her to admit the trouble wasn't the bet, but the fact that Padreg might have a shot at winning. This was a whole new jar of mental molasses to open and ponder. Even considering the idea left her floundering. She yearned to remain true to the love she had for Ylera while at the same time, she was beginning to acknowledge that her desire to live had grown. She no longer dreaded waking up in the morning. *And if I can live without her, then... Goddess... I can love without her, as well.*

Shoving aside the urge to bash her head into the nearest wall, Azhani kept her voice steady as she said, "To be honest, I'm not—"

She was saved from having to speak further when, at the other end of the hall, the double doors opened to admit Starseeker Vashyra. Willow thin, with knee length, silver-touched ebony hair that flowed around her body like a curtain, Starseeker Vashyra glided down the middle of the hall as if she were made of air. Heavily embroidered azure robes marked her as one of the most powerful starseekers in the Astariun temple. A star-shaped tattoo was emblazoned on her forehead, boldly announcing to all and sundry that here was a hand of Astariu! Woe betide any who doubted her skill. No one would dare call her testimony into question.

Reaching the dais, Vashyra bowed. "I understand you have need of my skills, Majesty?"

"Yes, and I thank you for your hasty arrival, Starseeker," Lyssera replied as she stood and embraced her.

Humbly, she said, "I am honored to serve the will of my queen."

Stepping back up onto the dais, Lyssera gestured to the court. "There is a matter of law before us, Starseeker. Evidence has been presented that could place the life of this man in jeopardy." She nodded to Baron Var, who glowered at everyone. "If it is falsely offered, it will call into question the honor of this woman," she said, indicating Azhani. "Will you aid me in determining the truth, that the Twain's will may prevail and our kingdom be assured of true justice?"

Starseeker Vashyra bowed. "My skills are yours to command, Majesty." Smiling serenely, she nodded first to Azhani, who smiled back, and then to Baron Var, who managed to summon a grimace. Turning to face the court, she said, "Be assured that I will do everything in my power to separate the lies from the truth."

It was almost comical how everyone in the room seemed to shift about, jockeying for the best position possible to watch the unfolding drama. *Lyssera should sell tickets. She'd fill the kingdom's coffers inside a month!* Azhani nearly laughed as some of the younger, more enterprising courtiers at the very back of the room started climbing up on the gallery benches to get a better view.

Beside her, Kyrian tensed as the queen's guards moved their hands onto their weapons.

Quickly, Azhani leaned over and whispered, "Look at Var—I think he's about to piss on his fancy velvet shoes."

Shooting Azhani an outraged look, Kyrian covered her mouth and hissed, "Azhi! That's awful!"

Azhani just winked at her and turned to watch as Lyssera recounted what they had learned about Baron Var's involvement in Ambassador Windstorm's poisoning, producing the items that were allegedly his at the end of the telling. "The matter that sits before us is this—are these items truly Var's, or is it Master Azhani who is the liar?"

"And so you have summoned me to perform the truth summoning," Vashyra replied gravely. "Very well." Kneeling, she pulled a square of purple silk from her belt pouch and unfurled it over the dais.

From witnessing previous truth summonings, Azhani knew the fabric was embroidered with tiny sigils that had been painstakingly enchanted over many long months. All starseekers possessed one though Vashyra's was the most ornate that she had ever seen.

As she was about to place the pouch of coin on the cloth, Baron Var suddenly shot to his feet and snapped, "No! I refuse to allow this charade to continue." Rushing toward Lyssera, he was barred the guard's pikes. Beseechingly, he held his hands out to her. "My queen, please, you must listen to me! You have been placed under a cruel spell by this vile creature! You must cast her from your home before she betrays you!"

"Goddess, what if he's right? What if she betrays us all?" someone asked, their voice carrying above the mutters and whispers.

"She's already branded an oathbreaker! If she were truly innocent, the queen would have given her a new mark!" someone else said, causing several in the gallery to nod.

Azhani felt ice form in her stomach. Not for the first time she wondered if Lyssera had been wise to make her such a public figure in her household.

"Yes, yes!" Baron Var said eagerly. "Tell her, my friends. Remind our queen of the plumes of smoke we all saw—the week long bonfire that it took to consume the bodies of the slain! Did we all not see Arris' banner fly, telling all who cared to look that the king mourned the unjustly dead?" He began to pace, feverishly waving his hands as he shouted, "Did she not slay our beloved

Princess Ylera?" Turning back to Lyssera, he snarled, "Have you forgotten this, my queen?"

"Silence!" Lyssera's shout was so loud, it rattled the rafters.

Instantly, the whispers ceased.

"Baron Var, you are not above the Twain's law," she hissed, stalking around him. "Starseeker Vashyra has agreed to the truth summoning. Your fate—and Azhani's—are in her hands. I cannot stop this even if I wished it, which I do not." Coming to stand in front of him, she looked him right in the eye. "You will accept her judgment or by ancient law and custom, you will be summarily exiled!"

Mouth agape, he stared at the queen, then began quickly backing away, as if seeking to run, but it was too late. Starseeker Vashyra had already begun to chant. Var's jaw worked, a silent, "No," forming on his lips. Despite his protests, the coin pouch shot from the cloth and fixed itself to his chest. No matter how many times he attempted to shove it away, it refused to come off. Shaking his head, he pulled and yanked, but the vial, too, stuck. Finally, came the scroll, all three objects irrefutably marked as his.

Vindicated! Azhani rose from her seat, reaching for the hilt of her sword as Baron Var's expression went from anger and shock to pure, venomous hatred. Spinning on one foot, he drew his dagger and drove it deep into Azhani's stomach. Twisting it, he hissed, "Tell your whore that Arris sends his greetings," then jerked it free, sending a ribbon of crimson splashing over the dais, staining all upon it with her blood.

In shock, she stumbled back, grabbing for her belly as pain tore her composure to shreds. "No!" she screamed in shock as Var yanked a mirror from his pouch.

Smearing the blade of the dagger over it, he snarled something in a guttural tongue. "Master, attend me!" he cried, flinging the mirror to the ground, where it burst into pieces, sending a plume of noxious smoke into the air around him.

"Azhani!" Kyrian leaped to Azhani's side, driven to help her friend even though duty screamed at her to subdue Baron Var first. As a stardancer, she was trained to protect the innocent as well as heal. Azhani's wound, while dire, wasn't as worrisome as having a maniac on the loose. Thankfully, the queen's guards were already trying to find Var among the clouds of smoke he had unleashed in the hall.

Suddenly, Var appeared, dagger held before him. He dove for the queen, only to be rebuffed by a spell shield Starseeker Vashyra hastily summoned.

Belatedly, Kyrian drew her baton while at her feet, Azhani struggled to sit, blood liberally pooling around her. Raising her hand, Vashyra pointed at Baron Var and spoke a single word, binding him in glowing bands of magickal force.

Above the crowd, the smoke began to thin to a faint haze.

Stepping off the dais, Queen Lyssera stalked toward Baron Var, Starseeker Vashyra at her side. "Baron Draygil Var, hear now my final judgment," she said, her voice ringing clearly in the hall. "On this day, you have proven yourself guilty of the crime of poisoning by krile. For this act, you will serve no less than one hundred mortal years in the mines. Your lands and title are hereby forfeit and you will be struck from the rolls of the nobility. For the crime of attempting to spread fear and chaos in my court, I exile you from Y'Syr for the remainder of your natural life."

Baron Var's face was a twisted wreck of hatred and contempt.

"Finally, you are also found guilty of attempted murder, both of myself and my chosen retainer. And for that, Baron Var, your sentence is death."

Var threw his head back and laughed. "You think I care for your judgments, Queen Listless? Your laws are nothing! Your faith in the Twain is pathetic!" Struggling against his bonds, he screamed, "You must come to feel the glory of Ecarthus! All will taste of his love! All will know his favor!" Somehow, he managed to rip one arm free of the spell and raised his dagger high into the air. "Master Darkchilde, I have done it! I have struck down the one you seek!" As he drove the blade deep into his own throat, he began chanting words that were ugly and dark with evil intent.

Kyrian started to shake as fear wove a net over her heart. *No, what is he doing? Oh Goddess, what has he done!* She screamed as the smoke above the crowd coalesced into a silvery disk that settled over Baron Var and began to spin and whirl with fractured, broken energies.

A bolt of lightning shot from Vashyra's hands and was absorbed by the disk, causing it to grow larger and more stable. Guards grabbed the queen and dragged her back to the dais, putting themselves between her and whatever Var had summoned. Somehow, Azhani had managed to stand, though how, Kyrian could not fathom. This however, was something that could distract her from the terrifying events unfolding around her. She dropped her baton and quickly wrapped her arms around Azhani's body. Softly, she began to hum, pouring Fire straight into the wound and praying it would be enough to keep her friend alive until they could get to safety.

The pain gradually receded behind the wall of Kyrian's chant. Quickly, Azhani looked around, trying to take in her surroundings while at the same time keeping Var in sight. Screams of shock and horror echoed around the court. Nobles and courtiers alike raced to the exits or grabbed for weapons, though most just stood, transfixed by the events transpiring before the throne.

Vashyra continued to blast the disk-like manifestation with lightning, but all it did was get larger and larger, extending beyond the length of Var's outstretched hands. Shimmering bands of energy washed over it, and slowly, a cowled face began to appear. The glassy surface grew to the height of a man and then taller. The face became a figure that casually stepped through the portal and into the throne room.

"Draygil, you fool!" the man snarled. With a casual flick of his fingers, he spat a few guttural words and sent Starseeker Vashyra flying into the crowd, ending her spell.

Azhani's anger twisted into an inferno of hatred. Jerking her sword from its scabbard, she leaped toward him. "You!" she shouted. It had been many years, but she would never forget the sound of Kasyrin Darkchilde's voice.

Her actions were foolish, though, for they took her from Kyrian's healing influence. Fresh blood erupted from the wound in her abdomen and she stumbled, falling to her knees at the sorcerer's feet.

Hollow, mirthless laughter filled the hall. "By Ecarthus' bloody eyes, Draygil, you might actually have done me a favor!" Squatting, he leaned forward and sneered, "How sweet of you to remember me, daughter of Rhu'len."

She spat on his boots.

Grabbing her by the throat, he growled, "Tell me, how does it feel to grovel at my feet?"

She couldn't breathe. Agony raged along every nerve in her body. Thinking was absolutely out of the question, but Azhani still had one thing left, one important, utterly unbreakable thing—pride. "Darkchilde," she rasped. "Your feet stink."

"Demons take you then, spawn of DaCoure!" he retorted, throwing her onto the dais. Thrusting his arms into the air, he hissed, "Vengeance, I summon thee."

Immediately, the temperature within the hall plummeted.

"Yes!" With a mad cackle, he began lashing about him, striking down bystanders with furious blows. "Die! All shall die!" Wind rose, causing the chill to increase. Ice began to form on the banners. "Come, my vengeance. Come and feed," he crooned.

An eerie, terrible moan echoed around them. Growls filled with hate and hunger seemed to come from every shadow. Hideous, malformed shapes began to coalesce. Open maws dripped with poisonous venom and claws coated in toxic slime gleamed wetly. All those remaining in the Great Hall tried to flee, but the doors were now sealed shut, barred by glowing bands of magick.

In the midst of it all stood Kasyrin Darkchilde, his head now bared, a rictus of pure glee warping his face. "Behold your doom, daughter of DaCoure," he yelled, gesturing to the ghostly rimerbeasts that filled the hall. "I'm going to enjoy this almost as much as I did when they tore your father to pieces!"

Staggering to her feet, Azhani found herself once again being aided by Kyrian. "You bastard," she said, gripping her sword as best as she could.

He just laughed and stepped back toward the portal from which he'd emerged. "The kingdoms will remember this day, Azhani. Oh yes, they will forever know how the tainted blood of DaCoure destroyed the Kelani line, and your name will be as a taboo spoken only in the darkest corners for fear of bringing the curse upon their own heads," he said with an evil grin. "And I shall reinforce their every terror."

"No!" Azhani screamed, leaping for him, not caring that the ghostly rimerbeasts were attacking the others, wanting only to destroy Kasyrin Darkchilde before he escaped. She passed right through him, landing atop the dying Baron Var with a grunt of pain.

"Comedy, Azhani?" Darkchilde said, snorting derisively. "How droll. Very well, I shall entertain myself a moment longer." He raised his hand and a sphere of fire appeared in his palm.

"Sorcerer!" Starseeker Vashyra shouted, distracting him. The tattoo upon her forehead glowed as she flung bolts of blue-white light from her hands, striking Darkchilde full in the chest. Chanting loudly, she spread her arms out and the bolts split, hitting every ghostly rimerbeast in the room, stopping them in their tracks, leaving some of the nobles on the very brink of death's door.

"I will not be denied," Darkchilde ground as he tried to move his arm. But the light spread, enveloping him and snuffing the fireball in his hand.

Kyrian appeared at Vashyra's right, adding her own voice lifted in song and spell. At her left stood Queen Lyssera, bearing a golden staff. Stepping off the dais, the queen strode up to Darkchilde and commanded, "Go, foul cretin, and come ye here no more." Violently, she struck him with the staff, sending him flying toward the portal.

Landing in a sprawled heap, Darkchilde staggered upright, shouting, "I will have my vengeance!" as he flung a fireball at Azhani.

This is it, she thought as she tried and failed to scramble away, but then Kyrian was there, shouting Azhani's name as she hurled her baton right into the heart of the fire. Both it and the sorcerer's spell vanished in a blinding flash.

"No!" Darkchilde screamed. "I will not be denied!" Raising both hands, he started to chant only to find himself facing Lyssera and her golden staff.

"Get out of my house!" she yelled, shoving him through the portal. "Now, Vashyra!" Quickly, she leaped away as lightning enveloped the silvery disk and shattered it into nothingness.

Azhani groaned and tried to get up. "I-is he gone? Darkchilde, where is he?" she demanded fiercely, managing to stand. "I-I must kill him."

"I'm sorry, Azhani," Vashyra said as she and Kyrian hurried to support her. "There is no telling where he could be." Her expression was one of deep regret. "We did not truly engage the man himself, but instead his shade, a lesser image of his true form."

Gaping at her, Kyrian said, "So, he could be anywhere? Even—not in Y'Myran at all?"

Wearily, Vashyra nodded.

"Shyvot! Why him? Why now? What, by the grace of the Twain, does Kasyrin Darkchilde have to do with all this? And how has he allied himself with the rimerbeasts?" Azhani rasped. She tried to remain standing, but even with help, the pain was growing too strong and she was too weak to take much more.

"Vashyra, can you not track the sorcerer's location by the foulness of his spells?" Lyssera asked as she joined them.

Vashyra frowned. "I—" Suddenly, she froze. Stepping away from Azhani, she closed her eyes and exhaled slowly.

Stillness settled over the great hall and all within it. No one spoke, no one moved. Everyone was utterly focused on the woman who now stood in the very center of the chamber, lit by a single shaft of golden light. A voice then emerged from Vashyra's body that had none of the sweet timbre of the starseeker's usual speech. No, this voice was older, infinitely more powerful, and for those of elven descent, it was instinctual to listen, to let the words resonate within them like the brassy clang of an ancient gong.

"The breaking is at hand. The Blade, the Heart, and the Pawn shall meet, and on that day the sun will stand still and the stars will no longer spin with time. The Beast will rise to seek his place among mortals. Stand well against the storm, and sages shall sing of thy glory into the mists of Eternity. Fall, and all shall blacken and fade."

As suddenly as it came, the light was gone and Vashyra crumpled. She was caught by a nearby guard and gently lowered to the ground.

"I'm next," Azhani managed to mutter just before her legs gave out.

"I've got you," Kyrian said, slowing her descent. "Just rest now, Azhi. It's over." Tenderly, she pulled Azhani into her arms and began stroking her hair. "I'll take care of you."

With a weak smile, Azhani surrendered to the pain and closed her eyes.

CHAPTER NINE

KASYRIN DARKCHILDE STOOD AMIDST A maelstrom of destruction. Once he had been summarily returned to his body by the elven starseeker's magicks, the energies she had twisted around him had taken an extreme force of will to break, causing everything in the vicinity to shatter. Fragments of her power still lingered, the electric crackle curling along the charred threads of a curtain and causing the fireplace tools to melt into a misshapen puddle of iron.

Face contorting with rage, Kasyrin banished the last of the starseeker's spell. "Damn you!" he screamed, turning and putting his fist through a priceless urn that had somehow survived the original destruction. As pottery crumbled, he snarled, "You will bleed for this, Azhani Rhu'len." Blood smoked on his knuckles as he summoned his army of invisible servants to clean up the ruin of the manor house library. It was all he had power left to do. Drained, he slumped against the charred plaster wall and waited for the task to be done.

A goblet of restorative wine floated toward him and he drank it dry. Feeble warmth pushed him upright and into his bedroom where he discarded his ruined robes in favor of fresh garments. Afterward, he made his way to the Ecarthan temple, taking solace and power from those who cringed away from his dark-robed form.

Yes, feed me your fear, little peasants. Give it all to me for my lord's bright glory! Deliberately, he slowed his pace, forcing himself to look at them, to wait until they, compelled by the innate politeness of the Y'Dani people, looked back. That's when he struck, grinning malevolently, taking a single step in their direction as if about to grab them for some imagined slight. To a one, they scurried away, wordlessly bowing and scraping, never speaking, but their terror was a balm to the wounds the starseeker's spells had scored against his inner shields.

The temple was home to him in a way no other place had been. Here, the sweet smell of burning flesh, the delicious sounds of sacrificial screams, and the tolling of the gong wrapped about him like a warm blanket, welcoming him as nothing else could. It was to his office he hurried, though, for there, he could tap into the raw power those sacrifices generated. Almost immediately, the pain-laced energy chased away his lethargy and allowed him to think clearly once again.

Pouring another goblet of restorative wine, he took a seat at his desk and went over his correspondence. It gave him great joy to read that High King Ysradan's fleet had lost yet another ship to the sea serpents plaguing the shores of Y'Mar. It was an unforeseen but entirely welcome bonus that an entire fishing village had been swamped by the waves churned up in the beast's death throes. Similar, but perfectly planned woes plagued the other kingdoms.

"Yes," he whispered. "Die for me, you worthless cattle!" The messages fed the fire at his back.

Other letters came from the priests who had ventured out into Y'Dan to build shrines and temples to Ecarthus. This news was even more heartening, for they were slowly gaining a loyal following. One even said, *I truly cannot believe your wisdom in this, master. They flock to our halls at the mere hint of His luxuries.* Kasyrin chuckled.

"Of course they come to you, you dolt. They're stupid and poor. Promise them the sweet taste of carnal indulgence with those who would never so much as glance at them otherwise and they will do murder to serve," he purred, crumpling the letter and tossing it into the fire as well. "And they serve my master well, for their lust creates more souls to feed his hunger."

The last of the letters made him forget all about his defeat at the starseeker's hands, for here, he felt, was the fullest proof of his true power—within days, there would be three fully operational temples within Y'Dan, each ready to serve Ecarthus. Every day, zealots presented themselves, their yearning to serve shining from their faces. All were ordained.

From Porthyros he received but one thing, a handbill fresh from the printer's trays. Holding it up, Kasyrin laughed aloud as he read, "'No Nonhumans Need Apply!' Ah, yes, splendid. How very, very splendid." This, of course, was a gorgeously delicious perk to his carefully crafted Nonhuman Restriction Act—a law Arris passed without so much as a blink.

Kasyrin nearly salivated at the thought of all the newly made lawbreakers that would soon find themselves facing steep fines or, better yet—a screaming end as he plunged his dagger into their chests and flung their still-beating hearts into Ecarthus' fires. Since it was law, no one would dare speak out against it, else they too join them. Instead, he expected the people to do exactly as they had the moment Arris became king—accept their lot and carry on doing the same thing as always, grubbing in the dirt.

This only made Kasyrin laugh. "That's right, little sheep. Bury your heads until my lord Ecarthus comes to shroud you in his glorious darkness!" However, the edge of anger returned when he remembered that the Y'Syrans had obviously given Azhani asylum, spitting in the face of the oathbreaker tradition. Frowning, he muttered, "Perhaps Arris ought to send them a reminder that they are now, in fact, breaking the high king's law."

Glancing down at Porthyros' message, he had to smirk, for the next lines were about his pet king. *He has grown quite fond of his visits to the temple, Master, and commented often about how much he enjoys the services. In my hearing, he has told no fewer than twenty other members of the court that he is greatly looking forward to the next time he is called to worship. It has, I believe, made some of those who were most resistant to the idea begin to think twice. I have even seen Lord Vostrel speaking to a priest!*

This was a coup indeed, for Vostrel was one of the few who had refused to attend even the pleasure services. Reading this made the bad taste in Kasyrin's mouth fade entirely.

With the king's support, and the conversion of his court, the rest of Y'Dan would soon follow. This spurred an idea, and quickly he dashed off a message to Porthyros. Why should he wait for conversion to bring them to his doors? Arris just needed to make it law that all citizens over the age of say, fourteen, had to attend services at least once a month. He could even sweeten the pot by ordering his temples to distribute a packet of food to those who did show up—and, just to make it even better, to promise to feed anyone who attended at least one service a day a meal that would always include meat.

Whether that meat was sweet venison or simply pigeon pie would depend on how successful the priests were at capturing the game. It mattered little, for even the possibility would bring the poor to his doors in droves, thus accelerating the schedule of sacrifices, giving Ecarthus—*and myself*—more power to use against their enemies.

::Thy mind grows keener, my servant.:: Suddenly, Ecarthus was upon him, filling him with the burning lust for pain that always accompanied the demon god's possession. **::And yet, when faced with our enemy, that mind failed you. I am most displeased.::** Agony twisted through his body, making him feel as though his bones were splintering. There was a great sigh that burst through his ears like the whistling of a storm's winds. ::**I am, however, a forgiving god.**:: In a heartbeat, the pain ceased, leaving Kasyrin feeling as though something ineffably precious had been stolen from his grasp.

"Master," he rasped, his throat afire from screaming. "I beg of you, forgive me."

::**Do not fail again.**::

Within Kasyrin, it felt as though the demon were pacing, sharp claws tearing at his thoughts as Ecarthus strutted about, his rage near blinding.

::**Azhani must not interfere.**::

Real fear accompanied Ecarthus' thoughts. They were cold, and filled with a dread so unearthly Kasyrin wet himself as it washed over him.

::**The boy is your key. He is but a tool meant for thy use—break him, if thou must.**:: Ecarthus laughed, his mirth hollow, sharp, and ugly. ::**Remember, her desire for vengeance is nearly as great as thine.**::

Images filled his mind then, pictures of Azhani's face when she learned of the death of the Y'Syran whore she was fucking. All her rage, all her hatred was as clear as day. If he were to dangle Arris as bait, she would come racing to catch him, and then Kasyrin could deal with her however he saw fit.

Still, why ruin a perfectly good tool if he didn't have to? "There is no need for that yet, Master. The DaCoure family is, quite simply, afflicted with the worst case of prideful honor I've ever seen. We've no need to worry where she will be, because your children will be her first and only target. They will keep her occupied while our work here will go on exactly as planned—and you know how very useful Arris is in that regard."

::**Very well. I will withdraw. Know that I long for the day when our desires are made real and we are both free of the curse of failure!**:: With that, he was gone, leaving behind fresh power to replace what it had cost to keep him tethered to Kasyrin's body.

As he poured another measure of wine into his goblet, Kasyrin smiled. Yes, the rimerbeasts would most definitely keep Azhani and any allies she might acquire from interfering in his plans. He would do all he could to see that their attention remained focused northward, away from Y'Dan and the spread of the Ecarthan temples. His power would grow until it was too late for her to stop him.

Raising the glass, he said, "To success!" and drained it.

I have to get up. Azhani did not want to move. Her abdomen ached, her ribs creaked and twinged painfully, and the rest of her body felt as though it had been used as the charging dummy at a lancer's tourney. Unfortunately, her bladder was screaming a warning that if she didn't find the chamber pot soon, she'd regret it. Opening her eyes, she groaned and tried to sit up, but discovered she was as weak as a newborn. *What happened?* Hazy memory, laced through with anger, pain, and deep hatred, whipped away the last threads of weariness. *Baron Var…summoned Kasyrin Darkchilde after stabbing me, and then Darkchilde was nice enough to use me as his personal punching bag.* She groaned. *I'm getting too old for this shyvot.*

Once again, she tried to sit, gasping at the stitch of pain that traveled over her belly. "Damn."

Kyrian, who was dozing in a chair next to the bed, woke. Sleepily, she rubbed her face and reached for Azhani. "My apologies. I must've nodded off."

"It's fine." With a quick smile, Azhani motioned for Kyrian to help her. "Just need to use the privy…then you can go sleep in your own bed."

Standing, Kyrian helped Azhani up. "As lovely as that sounds, I'm afraid I cannot," she said with a dry chuckle. "Queen Lyssera ordered me to stay with you."

Azhani frowned. "I can take care of myself." It irritated her to hear that the queen was treating her like a sickly child. "I don't need a nurse." Taking a step toward the curtained alcove containing her chamber pot, she grimaced. "Damn it! I hate this!" Gritting her teeth, she forced her legs to carry her across the room.

"I'm starting to believe this is going to be a routine aspect of our friendship," Kyrian said, sighing in resignation. With seemingly endless patience, she walked Azhani to the alcove, held open the curtain, and waited until she was settled before lowering it to offer her a semblance of privacy. "You get injured and then I have to fight like a dog to get you to let me help you heal."

As relief from one discomfort washed over her, Azhani snorted. "Quite likely." Yawning, she poked her tongue out and grumbled, "Twain's grace, my mouth feels like a shepherd lost his flock inside it."

Laughing softly, Kyrian replied, "There's plenty of water, my friend. You can have some once you come back to bed."

"That might almost be worth how much it's going to hurt to get off this damned pot," she muttered.

"Need help?" came Kyrian's solicitous query.

Embarrassment played dice with thirst and thirst won. "Yes."

To Kyrian's credit, she didn't laugh, just carefully helped Azhani return to the bed, poured her a glass of water, and then supported her as she drank greedily.

"Thank you." She collapsed onto the mattress. "Now, if memory serves, the next thing you'll offer me is bland soup and a cup of foul-tasting, bitter brew that'll make me sleep half the day candle down."

Kyrian smiled warmly and brushed her fingers through Azhani's hair. "Well, I could add some honey to that tea, but don't blame me if it doesn't work as well," she said, going to the hearth. Here, several mugs were lined up and Azhani assumed she must have prepared them earlier. Taking one down, Kyrian poured hot water into it, then, with a teasing wink, drizzled in a generous dollop of honey, stirring it afterward. "Here, drink. You can have soup next."

The strong, fresh smell of the herbs was so powerful, Azhani had to fight a yawn just to take the first sip. Whatever effect the honey might have had on the brew's effectiveness must've been minimal, for it was still bitter. Grimacing, she muttered, "Still tastes like the bottom of a cesspit." She drank it, though, because she knew it would alleviate the pain gnawing at her torso like a pack of hungry wolves.

"Here, suck on this while I get you some soup." Kyrian held out the spoon from the honey dish.

Feeling very much like a child with a treat, Azhani savored the residue of honey, grateful for the way it banished the bad taste of the medicine. "Thank you," she said. "It helped."

Kyrian nodded and then offered her a mug of broth. "It's not much, I'm afraid, but again, it'll help you be more comfortable so you can sleep."

"I know," she said, taking it. After a sip, she smiled. "I don't know how you do it, Kyr, but somehow you manage to make simple broth taste rich and delicious. Join me?" She patted the spot beside her. "Since you won't leave, you can at least share this massive bed with me."

Regarding the bed intently, Kyrian crossed her arms over her chest. "Promise you'll wake me if you need anything?"

With a sleepy nod, Azhani smiled. "Promise."

"Finish your broth first." She resumed her place in the chair by the bed. "Then I'll get you settled."

"All right." For a time, she simply sipped her broth and tried not to think too much about how she hurt or what had happened. But eventually, her innate thirst for knowledge rose to the fore, prompting her to ask, "So…what's happening out there?" Casually, she tipped her mug toward the suite door to indicate the castle environs.

"Chaos, likely. I've heard from Prince Allyndev that the nobles are deeply disturbed by Baron Var's treachery. There's a great deal of finger pointing and accusations being thrown around by those who wish to distance themselves from him."

Azhani scowled. "Of course. I trust Lyssera is handling this?"

"Aye. According to Starseeker Vashyra, the sorcerer's involvement makes it quite unlikely that Var had any other allies in the court. There are a few who are calling for war with Y'Dan, though."

"Even with the rimerbeast threat? They're insane!" Azhani retorted. "I've got to stop them." She tried to get up, but Kyrian put her hand on her chest.

"Easy," Kyrian soothed. "Queen Lyssera has made it clear that we cannot blame Arris for this just yet. While there was proof enough that Var had been in the employ of someone who didn't have Y'Syr's best interests in mind, we can't prove it was the king of Y'Dan."

Putting aside the empty mug, Azhani grumbled, "It was the sorcerer. Kasyrin Darkchilde. Next time you see Lyss or Vashyra, tell them his name. They'll know it." Hatred coiled in her belly, the viper's venom of rage boiling through her blood. "He killed my father," she added grimly.

"Oh, Azhi," Kyrian murmured, then tenderly caressed her face. "I'm so sorry."

She looked away. "He's always hated us. He and my father had a mutual enmity that lasted for years. Then…" She shook her head. "He killed him. The bastard killed him!" she hissed, hands curling into fists. "I'll tear him apart!"

Gently, Kyrian squeezed her shoulder. "You might have that chance some day, Azhani, but if you want it, you must rest."

Numb now, her energy spent on rage and her heart filled with ages-old pain, she pulled away from Kyrian. "I know. Good night." She closed her eyes. A few minutes later, the lanterns were dimmed and the bed shifted as Kyrian settled beside her. "Kyr?" she said softly.

"Hm?"

"I'm sorry."

"It's all right." Kyrian reached for Azhani's hand and pulled it around her in the casual embrace they had enjoyed for most of the winter. "Sweet dreams, Azhi," she added softly. Within moments, she was asleep.

Lying there, the light scent of Kyrian's hair drifting into her nostrils, Azhani stared into dimness, listening to the slow, even breathing of her friend and tried to tell herself to rest. Her eyes, however, would not shut. Tense, she waited to be sure Kyrian was asleep before tugging her hand away and rolling onto her back. She had a moment's peace before Kyrian followed, snuggling up against her and sliding her hand up over Azhani's chest, stopping when she reached her breast.

There was not enough air in the room. Everything narrowed down to that one point of contact. Heat exploded in her belly and radiated deep into her body, triggering desire she had sworn had died with her beloved Ylera. *Goddess! What's happening to me? Kyrian is my friend! How can she make me feel so much? Sharing a bed isn't new for us. I've certainly never wanted her before.*

Sighing in her sleep, Kyrian shifted closer and brought her leg up over Azhani's, pinning her to the bed, her knee dangerously close to very sensitive areas.

Air! Azhani had to breathe or risk passing out, though right then, unconsciousness was something she was more than willing to seek. Panting softly, she moved Kyrian's hand, then her leg. *I'm too weak to get up, so this will have to do.*

"Twain's grace," she whispered as sweat gathered along her spine. The need to curl her hand to Kyrian's face and kiss her awake was so strong that she actually felt the strands of Kyrian's hair against her fingertips before she jerked away and grabbed the blankets instead. Closing her eyes, she willed herself to think of Ylera and only of Ylera, building a blood-soaked picture of her lover's broken, lifeless body until it was crystal clear in her mind—but it faded almost immediately. Instead, she found herself remembering the laughter they shared. The joy, the happiness—all good memories, tinged with a heavy burden of sadness and regret, but lacking the knife-like sharpness that had once carved ribbons of agony in her heart.

Fear, naked, tumultuous, and icicle-cold, lanced through her then. Every muscle in her body was taut with the effort to stay still, to keep herself there, in bed, instead of leaping up and…falling right down again. Part of her was screaming at her to get up, to get the hell away from Kyrian.

And then Kyrian shifted in her sleep and smiled then mumbled something about dancing pigs and handsome frogs, nearly causing Azhani to laugh out loud. Heart full, she closed her eyes and mumbled, "Your dreams must be quite amazing, my friend." Then, feeling daring, she brushed a kiss against the crown of Kyrian's head and settled in to sleep.

For Kyrian, waking up with Azhani's arms wrapped around her was tantamount to being offered the finest Y'Tolian wine and then told she could only admire its glorious color, not taste its sweetly heady bouquet. To be so close to the glimmering richness of her desire, yet forced to thrust her hands behind her back lest she break the unwritten laws of friendship, was nightmarish and yet thrilling. It was pure bliss to feel the tender heat of Azhani's breath lift the hairs at the nape of her neck! Equally delicious was the easy, overly familiar way Azhani's hand rested upon her hip, her fingers lazily scratching her thigh.

Fire crept through Kyrian's guts, roiling and twisting, filling her mind with visions of just how powerful Azhani was and how…incredible it would be for that strength to be focused solely on bringing Kyrian pleasure.

Dizzily, Kyrian inhaled, feeling sick at the direction her thoughts were racing.

Ah, my queen, how sharp you words are. Of course I love her. I'm so lost to the want of her that I'll gladly cling to whatever scraps of emotion she tosses my way. Had Kyrian said as much when Lyssera pinioned her with her all-too-truthful statement of fact, she suspected the queen would have laughed. *Or worse, heaped pity on me for my fruitless desire.*

Still clearly lost to sleep, Azhani moaned softly and slid her hand up to cup Kyrian's breast and for just the space of three heartbeats, she tried to savor the feeling, to believe with all she was that Azhani wanted her. But it was a lie. Carefully, she slipped from the bed, missing the fiery embrace the moment she stood and was greeted by the morning's chill. Frowning, she turned and pressed her lips to Azhani's temple.

As loving as the touch was, it served more purpose than just affection, for through her lips, she could get the best sense of how warm Azhani was and this morning, fever burned within her.

"Damn," Kyrian murmured. "I was afraid that would happen." Going to the hearth, she added another herb to the cups waiting on the mantle. This was an old stardancer's trick, because it cut down on time spent preparing a patient's medicine when they actually needed it. As she gave each mug a gentle shake to sift the herbs together, all thoughts of desire vanished. Now she had to concentrate on getting Azhani well; she could pine later. "Breakfast first." Grabbing her robe, she headed for the kitchens. She'd need her strength to fight the sickness raging within Azhani's wounds.

At the doorway, something made her turn and look back at her sleeping friend. What she saw made her regret getting up all over again, for there, nuzzling Kyrian's pillow, was Azhani, a smile of such earnest joy on her face that Kyrian felt her heart clench. Giving herself a mental shove, she scowled at her own reluctance to move and made herself close the door. *It's Ylera she loves. I'm just her friend.*

On the other side of Oakheart Manor, Queen Lyssera strode through the halls, Starseeker Vashyra at her side, and armed, liveried guards surrounding them. It galled Lyssera to have to put on such a show of force, but after the sorcerer's attack and Baron Var's treachery, the captain of her guard was taking no chances with his queen's life.

"Have you found anything?" Lyssera asked quietly.

Vashyra shook her head. "Only bits and pieces, my queen. This prophecy, as I said, is ancient and obscure. Some of the scrolls I looked at suggest it predates the arrival of the Firstlanders—and could even be from the time of the Alyrr! However, I must wait to hear from the sages of Astarus before I can even offer so much as a guess as to its meaning."

"Keep looking," she replied sharply, then grimaced. "Twain's grace, the last thing I need right now is a damned prophecy added to the plate of bad luck fate has chosen to serve us!" Weariness made her words angrier than she intended. It felt like she hadn't slept since Ylera's death. They paused near a window that looked into a small garden. "I should thank you, old friend, for stepping in earlier. I sincerely believe I was ready to do violence on Lord Volkirk."

Chuckling softly, Vashyra said, "It was my pleasure, Lyss. If anything, what I told them should stop the endless demands from the courtiers that you tear the kingdom apart looking for Darkchilde." She shook her head. "I should have known it would be him. His enmity toward Azhani's family isn't a secret."

"True. But then, between them, Rhu'len and Azhani did manage to amass quite the rogue's gallery of thieves, crooks, liars, and bandits who'd like to see them suffer," Lyssera replied. "We could not have known this one would suddenly decide to aid Arris Thodan."

"Do you believe this to be the case, Highness?"

She nodded. "I can't prove it, but…I've a hunch I'm right. Sadly, there's little we can do about it for now." She turned away from the window and sneaked a sip from a flask of brandy she kept secreted in a pouch on her belt. The potent liquor burned going down, but helped steady her nerves.

A mischievous grin pricked the corners of Vashyra's mouth. "Ah, so that's why you finally lost your temper in the council session."

Lyssera scowled and looked at the flask. "I hope not. I'd hate to think my words controlled by a sip or two of drink."

Gently, Vashyra touched her arm. "I'd not worry on it, my queen. You spoke as you had to—their questions regarding the prophecy had become tedious and repetitive." She smiled then. "It was a stroke of brilliance to command them to look to their own archives for answers. They couldn't have run off faster."

Lyssera laughed. "No, of course not. The idea that one of them might suddenly play a heroic part in these wild times appeals to their pride." She sighed. "At least now we can concentrate on the north, and the rimerbeasts."

"You've summoned the armies," she said. "But who will lead them? You?"

"If I must." Though she had hopes of a better answer, Lyssera was wise enough to know those hopes were pinned on so many nebulous maybes that she dared not speak them aloud.

Vashyra gave her a considering look. "You should rest. I'll come to you if we discover anything."

It was tempting to ignore duty and do as her old friend instructed, but Lyssera was a queen, but right now, the kingdom needed her to guide them. "I'll rest when we're safe. Until then, I've much to do." First and foremost was to see that Stardancer Kyrian had whatever she needed to make sure Azhani Rhu'len recovered from her grievous wounds, for without her, most of Lyssera's current plans would crumble like unfired clay.

Seven long days passed as Azhani recovered. For one week, Lyssera had to juggle all her plans for creating the safest future for her kingdom. Every eventuality needed to be covered and it was during these candlemarks when she missed her sisters most. Alynna, her warleader, would have spent all her waking moments developing solutions to the problems posed by Y'Dan and the rimerbeasts with the least amount of Y'Syran blood shed. Meanwhile, Ylera would have used every one of her diplomatic tactics to coax allies from the shadows.

Word from Kyrian was that both Azhani and Ambassador Windstorm were healing, though the former was certainly far more irascible than the latter. Starseeker Vashyra continued to seek answers regarding the prophecy while Lyssera herself took to the lesser-used halls of Oakheart, strolling through them with her pair of guards, thinking and brooding.

"Ah, Majesty, there you are." Lady Sidar hurried up to them, causing Lyssera's guards to draw their blades. "Oh!" she blurted, stopping immediately. "Peace, gentlemen. I am unarmed." She held out her open hands and waited while one looked her over.

"She speaks true, my queen," he grumbled, and Lyssera tried not to laugh.

"Of course she does," she said, offering the other woman a welcoming smile. "And how might I serve you, Sidar?"

Clasping her hands behind her back, Sidar bowed. "Actually, I came to learn if there was aught I could do for you, my queen. Rumors, like gnats, fly thick and heavy in court, and I am tired of the biting and stinging."

Lyssera grimaced. "And what do my lords and ladies say, then?"

"That you are seeking some long-lost relic hidden within Oakheart's walls," she said as they began to walk together. "A weapon of great power that will smite those who have done such harm against our beloved kingdom."

"Ah, how I wish that there was truth to that." Mirthlessly, Lyssera laughed. "Sadly, my thoughts and actions have little to do with such whimsies."

Sidar inclined her head. "Then perhaps you give hope to those who wish to see the chair at your right shared by one who can give the people of Y'Syr the heirs they wish to dote upon?"

Irritation made her cheeks warm. "I suspect they will have to look to another for the heir—though I'm half tempted to name Allyndev as such, just to spite them." One of the guardsmen choked and nearly stumbled. "Oh, do relax, Gregori—I'll not put a bastard on the throne. I know full well it would mean civil war."

Gregori blushed. "Sorry, Highness. I know you value the boy, but most see him as little more than a nuisance and some wish it had been he and not his beloved mother who had died."

"And those are words you'll not be repeating," she said angrily. "Not in my hearing nor in Prince Allyndev's!"

With a hasty bow, he murmured, "Yes, my queen."

Trying to grasp her temper before it blossomed into a full royal rage, she turned to focus on Sidar, who merely stood there waiting, a calm, unreadable expression on her face. Again, she noted how beautiful the other woman was, and again, she considered allowing herself to become distracted by that beauty. Instead, she said, "Actually, Sidar, there is something I could use your assistance with—I am in need of someone who can liaise with the army as the squads and platoons arrive. Forthwith, I charge you with that task. Gather what you need and see that no one is unduly burdened by my soldiers' presence upon their lands."

"Yes, my queen. Who will I answer to?"

"For the time being, me. In time, perhaps another—we shall see. Go now. I expect a report on your progress by sundown."

Lady Sidar bowed once and then strode off, the heavy heels of her boots thudding loudly on the carpet.

"My queen, if you don't mind me saying," Gregori said quietly, "that is a task for a warleader, not a lady of quality."

Darkly, Lyssera smiled. "I know, but as I have no warleader, I should think a lady of substance will be a more than adequate replacement. Now, I think I'd like to visit with Ambassador Windstorm."

The mood around Oakheart was tense. Though she was mostly confined to her room, Azhani could still sense it. From her window, she could see the colorful fields of tents blooming along the edges of Banner Lake and knew that the drums of war were echoing the heartbeats of Y'Syr's people.

Vigilance was the order of the day. Even the lowest of chambermaids seemed to walk about as if expecting a battle at any moment. Darkchilde's attack had shredded the castle folk's sense of security, and it galled Azhani that she could do little to restore it.

She wasn't surprised when Lyssera began visiting, sitting with her during the late meal, questioning her again and again about everything from defending the city to smashing rimerbeast eggs.

"You'll need more bandages than you can imagine," Azhani told the queen as Kyrian changed her dressing. Absently, Azhani reached to scratch the healing flesh and got her fingertips smacked for it. "It itches!" she grumbled as Kyrian shook her head.

"Yes, I know it itches. It's healing. It's supposed to itch," she said while smearing unguent over the area. "That's why I made this—to help with the itching so you wouldn't scratch yourself raw. Just be patient."

Azhani sighed. "But that stuff makes me smell like rotten milk."

"Hm, could it be the goat's milk I use for the base of the salve?" she replied archly.

Lyssera laughed. "I use a similar concoction to soothe my eyes when they become sore. It does smell horrid—but is very efficacious."

With a grimace, Azhani said, "I truly do not understand why medicine must be so awful. Would it be so difficult to make it pleasant?"

Kyrian carefully placed clean bandages over the wound. "It is my experience that foul things are strong, Azhani. Tempered strength may indeed be what is necessary in many situations, but when it comes to fighting off sickness, you will want every ally possible, even the bad tasting, bad smelling ones."

There was no arguing with that and Azhani knew when to surrender. "I bow to your greater wisdom in this area."

Smiling affectionately, Kyrian chuckled. "Your days of bitter tea and soured unguents are drawing to a close, my friend—for this injury anyway. Soon, you'll be able to drown yourself in honey, if that is what you choose."

Unbidden, an image of Kyrian licking honey off a spoon rose within her mind, and suddenly Azhani wanted nothing more than to be that spoon. Clearing her throat, she tried not to blush. "Thank you, again. I'm grateful for all you've done. Especially in the throne room. Without your help, I'd still be kissing Darkchilde's boots."

Ruefully, Kyrian shook her head and stared out the window, her thoughts obviously somewhere else. "I just wish it had been more—what if you'd had to fight him?"

With a laconic shrug, she replied, "I'd have shoved him at you and made a run for it." It was hard not to smile, and slowly, she felt the corners of her lips rise as the mischief within her escaped as a soft chuckle.

Rolling her eyes as Lyssera hid a laugh, Kyrian said, "You'd have looked like a demented rabbit, hopping away while I tried to dance my away around that sorcerer."

Azhani grinned and poked her fingers up above her head. "That's me: warrior rabbit. Got any carrots?" Kyrian's deep, rich laugh poured over her like cool water. *Ah, Goddess, she makes me feel good to be alive!*

"Sorry, I'm afraid you'll have to make do with a bowl of chicken soup tonight, little bunny," Kyrian replied affably. Turning to Lyssera, she said, "And since she was able to get herself around on her own earlier, I trust you'll rest easier knowing she'll be returning to her duties soon?"

"Yes. That is very welcome news," Lyssera said quietly.

The urge to scowl forced Azhani to grab for her mug of tea and drink down the cold, bitter fluid, just so she could let the muscles of her face collapse as they desired. She'd grown accustomed to Kyrian's presence at night—their closeness was something she savored, even if she couldn't bring herself to speak of the new, raw, incredible emotions roiling just under the surface of her thoughts where Kyrian was concerned. Something between them was changing, though, and someday very soon, they would have to talk. *Or I'll go insane.*

"Did you finish it finally?" Kyrian asked once Azhani set aside the cup.

"Yes," she replied, sticking her tongue out at her.

"Good. Here's your reward." Kyrian smiled fondly as she offered her a spoon covered in honey. "Now, if you will both excuse me, I need to see to Ambassador Windstorm."

Lyssera nodded. "Of course. Give him my regards." Once Kyrian was gone, she turned and watched as Azhani greedily sucked the honey from the spoon. "You have created something special with that one, Azhani."

"I know." Regret, fear, and hope strangled her words. "She is more than I could have hoped for, but…I still love Ylera."

"Of course you do," Lyssera said gently. "But even I can see that your pain has lessened, that you do not grieve as sharply, and we both know this would please my sister more than anything else." She smiled sadly. "There is no shame in wanting to love again."

Putting aside the spoon, Azhani sighed. "Yes, I have…decided much the same, my queen, but—" She looked toward the window, trying to put her thoughts to words.

Lyssera touched Azhani's arm and offered her a gentle smile. "Talk to me."

"Sometimes I feel like she's stealing the hatred that gave me the strength to go on. From the moment I knew Ylera was gone, revenge was my goad. Everything I did—claiming the Rite, then killing everyone who got in my way until Banner Lake ran red with blood—all of it was simply so I could find a way to spit Arris Thodan on the end of a sword. It was for her. For my Ylera." Bowing her head, she murmured, "I'd have died, otherwise. I should have died." So many feelings spun through her thoughts. Anger, regret, the hollow pang of unfathomable loss—and yet, beneath it all, hope grew stronger with every breath. She looked up at Lyssera. "How can love that blazed so hot fade so quickly? How can I even think of wanting another when Ylera lies unavenged?" Weakly, she rasped, "Did I even love her?"

Gathering Azhani into her arms, Lyssera softly said, "Yes, you did. But have you considered the fact that maybe Kyrian isn't stealing anything, but instead, showing you that hatred won't bring Ylera back? That…" She swallowed heavily. "That you can go on without her?"

Everything about the embrace was foreign. Comforting, yes, but lacking anything of the fire that accompanied even one of Kyrian's gentlest touches. As beautiful a woman as Lyssera was, she might as well have been a statue as far as Azhani was concerned. And her words? By the Twain, how they pricked and needled at her!

Still, she was contrary, retorting, "Then how can I even think of loving again? I should be dreaming of ways to make Arris pay, instead I worry over how we are going to destroy the rimerbeasts. Why is that? I'm certainly not afraid of Arris!" she said frustratedly.

Pulling back, Lyssera chuckled wryly. "I do like easy questions, my friend, and this one is quite simple—you're a warrior! Tell me, which is the more dangerous of the two? A beast season, or Arris Thodan?"

There was no hesitation in her reply. "A beast season. Arris is dangerous, but he is still a man possessed of reason and capable of understanding when he is outmatched. Rimerbeasts will never stop. They don't care if all the armies of Y'Myran stand between them and their next meal, they will just keep coming until they are destroyed to the last."

"And thus you have discovered it. Even when your heart is confused, you will make the right choice," Lyssera said calmly.

Pensively, Azhani considered her words. She thought of Kyrian, of how incredible it felt to lie beside her, how much joy she took from laughing with her, how amazing it was to face her on the practice mat, and closed her eyes. *I will always love Ylera. Always. But Kyrian is beautiful. She is my best friend and she is so very, incredibly beautiful.*

Gently, Lyssera touched her shoulder. Azhani opened her eyes, revealing the tears that were gathering there. The queen said, "Allow yourself to heal. You'll be a better warrior for it—and more than able to deliver a proper vengeance to that murderous boy sitting on Y'Dan's throne."

With a sigh, Azhani ran her hand through her hair. "I know. I've lain here, night after night, telling myself that it's what Ylera would say, that seeing beauty in another, feeling the heat of desire and wanting it, was a gift from the Twain themselves." She shook her head. "I thought everything inside me was as barren as the icy wastes, but it's like a miracle." Frowning, she said, "Then I remember that my Ylera, my glorious, beautiful, wise, gentle Ylera is dead and I feel guilty for wanting anything when she can't even feel the simple warmth of the sun."

"There's nothing wrong with what you desire, Azhi. Life must continue, as must the heart." Solemnly, she asked, "If your places had been reversed, would you have wanted her to weep forever?"

"Goddess, no! I'd want her to be loved and honored every day," she replied resolutely.

Grabbing her hand, Lyssera caught her gaze and held it. "Then why don't you deserve the same?"

"I…I don't know!" It was so frustrating to feel like she was going in circles. She wanted so much to break through the cycle of grief, to grab hold of the joy she sensed Kyrian could offer, but at the same time, she was afraid of sullying Ylera's memory and of losing what she might have with Kyrian in the process.

"You could do far worse than to love a stardancer," Lyssera said quietly. "Ylera would be honored to share your heart with her."

Something about the way she seemed so calm, so utterly assured of her words, made Azhani sit and stare. She turned the thought over and over in her head, trying to find anything in it that was wrong or strange and which would give her the permission she needed to wrap a cloak of ice about her heart so she would never have to argue with herself about it again. But there was nothing there. It was honesty, plain and simple, and there was little Azhani could do to defend against it.

"I don't know what to say, Lyss. What I felt for Ylera was unlike anything I'd ever experienced. When she died, it was as though all the love had been leeched from my heart. I had no emotions; they were mixed with her blood and staining the stones of Ydannoch castle." Sorrow and wistfulness colored Azhani's tone as she murmured, "But I really like Kyrian. She is… I can't even find words. Is it love? I don't know. I just don't know."

"I may not be much of a warrior, but I am a queen, and as a queen one has to remember simple things, some of them being possibilities. In this case, I counsel you to allow for the possibility of love." She grinned. "I've heard the bards say that the heart and the mind don't speak the same language, but you know what Ylera used to say to that?"

"With love, translations aren't necessary," Azhani replied. "Goddess. I...I'll have to think on it some more, Lyss." Rubbing her face, she blinked away her tears and added, "How's Allyndev faring?"

Leaning back in her seat, Lyssera smiled. "Needful of having his teacher back, I think. He won a few bouts with some of the younger guardsmen and it's made him an arrogant toad, according to my chambermaid's gossip."

Azhani snorted. "I'll ask Kyrian to spar him. She'll knock the attitude from him quickly enough."

"She is that good, then, that you would trust a student to her training?" Lyssera replied archly.

"Aye. She routinely humiliates me." She grinned wryly. "One of the best I've seen at Goddess Dance." *Though whenever I bring up using weapons, she shies off or freezes. We need to work on that. There's got to be a reason she's so terrible at it when she's otherwise well-studied.*

Both of Lyssera's eyebrows rose. "A stardancer who can humiliate the great Azhani Rhu'len at Goddess Dance? Well then, it should be quite the show. Please, ask her to spar with my nephew. The last thing I need right now is for him to suddenly decide he's Astariu's gift to the Y'Syran army."

Azhani laughed. "Trust me, when Kyrian's done with him, he wouldn't dare make such a ridiculous claim."

"I must thank you, Stardancer, for being so good to me," Ambassador Iften said as Kyrian took the time to plump his pillows and straighten his covers. "I fear I may not have been the most cooperative of patients."

Quirking one eyebrow, she said, "Yes, you've been a bit of a curmudgeon, Ambassador, but I suspect I too would be more than a little off put by similar experiences."

Snorting, he offered her a weary smile. "I'm an old man, lass. That alone gives one the right to a certain amount of grumpiness."

"Ah, so it wasn't the krile that sharpened your tongue?" she asked playfully. Caring for Iften Windstorm had exposed Kyrian to a whole new set of emotions with regard to a patient. Never before had she felt such affection for someone who was, on the surface, uncooperative, troublesome, and often rude. Yet there never seemed to be anything cruel behind his complaints and irritation. Indeed, most of his frustration seemed directed inward and it wasn't long before she felt a great deal of compassion for this noble old man who'd had what was left of his health ruined by a poisoner's heartless act.

"Nay, lass, you may put that claim to the scouring sands of my homeland," he replied solemnly. "The Y'Skani wastelands may be forbidding to most, but for me, they were cradle, hearth, and home. I long for them fiercely, even if I may never return." He coughed and she rushed to help him sit up then offered him some water to clear his throat.

"You'll see them again, Ambassador," she said quietly. "The krile has nearly burned itself from your system."

"That may be, my young friend," he said with something approaching fondness in his tone. "But never again will I walk the sands. Not while I still bear the mantle of ambassador. My duty keeps me here, though my heart yearns to be there. That is ever the cry of the desert walker. When we are amidst the fury of a sandstorm, we wish nothing more than to be in a cool tavern with a wench on each arm and ale in our cups, but the moment we set foot in said tavern, we long for the warm valleys and golden dunes of Y'Skan."

"So you have told me," she replied with a chuckle. Iften had not been shy in regaling her with stories of his adventurous youth. In return, she had told him what it was like growing up among the starseekers and stardancers of Y'Len. She admired him, and saw in him someone with a capacity for great caring which matched her own. They were alike in many ways, though outwardly distinct.

"And will again, I expect. We both know I am overfond of the sound of my own voice," he said with a teasing smile. "Speaking of listening to me—where is my dinner?" His brow furrowed into a frown. "Or have you decided to torture me further by making me wait for my gruel and bread?"

Schooling her face into a mock glare, Kyrian pointed at a covered tray and said, "I wish I'd known you were craving gruel and bread. I'll have to take this back to the kitchen now." With a flourish, she removed the lid.

Iften's mouth gaped at the sight of the steak waiting on the plate. It was small, and with it were a large portion of vegetables and a bowl of broth, but it was still the meat he had been asking for since the moment he woke after the poisoning.

"You'll do no such thing, lass," he replied gruffly, reaching for a fork. "I shall be quite pleased to tuck into this."

Blandly, Kyrian said, "Are you certain? I do recall that there was a rather nice pottage waiting on the hearth. I'm sure the cook would be happy to bring you a burnt portion."

With a plaintive sigh, he murmured, "Do you need to hear an old man beg, lass?" Quickly, he stabbed his fork into the steak and plucked it from the plate, biting into it before she could react. "Ah, by the Great Serpent, how delicious!"

Laughing, she said, "You, Ambassador, are quite the sneaky one."

He grinned. "One does not reach my age without learning a few tricks, Stardancer. Now, did I ever tell you about the time I found the bones of a beast so massive, it must have been as big as Oakheart itself?"

"No." She pulled a chair over so she could sit with him and watch to make sure he did not choke.

Greedily, he tucked into the food, spinning a long, barely believable tale of great lizards that ripped lightning from the skies and shook the ground with their steps. At the meal's—and coincidentally, the story's—conclusion, he wiped his mouth and said, "I trust then, that there will be no more talk of gruel and pottage for my meals? It appears that I will not be food for the worms just yet."

She chuckled, though her joy in his recovery was bittersweet. "No, not yet, though I fear you are not entirely well either, Ambassador. The krile may be fading, but the sandlung is not."

"Aye," he replied, taken by a sudden spasm of coughing. "But I made my peace with that long ago. 'Tis a hazard we of the desert face all our lives, as you well know." Gently, he patted her hand. "Please, you mustn't allow today's joys to be spoiled by the storm clouds of tomorrow." Their fingers wove together, his wrinkled and gnarled, hers calloused but still bearing the flexibility of youth. "You have done so much for me, Stardancer. More than just simply healing my body. You've given an old man a bit of sunshine—allowed me to enjoy the role of a cantankerous granther when I've no littles of my own to dazzle with my stories."

The simple gesture touched her deeply. "It's been my pleasure, Ambassador," she murmured. "Especially as I have no grumpy old relatives to tell me such unbelievable tales!"

"Och, enough of that stuffy nonsense, lass. Let me have the pleasure of my name—or, if you'd rather, you may call me Granther."

It was her turn to stare at him in shock. "You would allow such familiarity, Ambassador?"

Somewhat dryly, he replied, "Lass, you've seen me at my lowest and listened to my wildest tales and not gone running. I've a fondness for you that I can't quite explain, except to say that it is not of a man for his lover or a patient for his healer. So yes, I would quite like it if you were to put aside formalities and titles and allow me to repay all your kindnesses with something besides complaints and surly words."

"Thank you, Amba—er—Granther," she said quietly.

He smiled. "Ah, yes, I do think that is a rather nice ring to it. Now tell me, what puts such a shadow on your face when you speak of the sandlung?" he asked gently.

She sighed. "It irritates the healer in me to know that no matter how hard I fight, I'm going to lose." Shaking her head, she murmured, "I'm not used to battles like that."

"Surely you've lost patients," he said.

"Oh, aye, Granther, more than I like, but never to something so…horrific." She pulled away from him, gesticulating as she spoke. "I can see what it's doing to you, can feel the way it creeps through you, choking you, stealing your strength and…and—" Helplessly, she clutched her hands into fists, unable to strike out at the thing that was killing him by inches.

Covering her hands with his, he smiled sadly. "Do not think on it. The sandlung has been part of my life for more years than you've walked these lands. I've many years yet left to hold off its smothering grip." When she shivered, he said, "Talk to me instead of your friend. How is she?"

"Recovering wonderfully," she said, unable to keep the joy from her voice. "It won't be long before she's prowling the halls again."

"Thank the Great Serpent! I could not have born her death on my conscience. It was so galling to learn that the young man who'd presented himself to me as a friend was little more than a scorpion waiting to sting me into a frenzy!" he said angrily. "And then to hear he'd called upon that sorcerer! No, I just could not have accepted that such a woman could be brought low by my own foolishness!"

Kyrian couldn't fool herself any longer, not when he thought such terrible, untrue things about himself. "No, Granther, it wasn't your fault," she said, her eyes filling with tears. "It was mine."

Startled, he blurted, "What?"

"It…it's my fault," she stammered nervously. "S-she wouldn't have been hurt so badly if I-I'd moved faster, if I hadn't frozen when it all—" She shuddered, even now driven back to that moment and the terror that turned her muscles to stone. "I let my fear win," she whispered. "Again. I'm a coward."

"Ah, lass," he murmured gently, reaching for her. "Come here."

Feeling as though she were drifting through a river of molasses, she fell from her chair into his arms and sank into the warm embrace he so freely offered.

"It's not cowardice to feel fear in the face of danger." He rubbed her back. "For if it was, I'd be a coward a thousand times over."

"T-that's not it," she said, shivering. "I…I-I f-freeze. I-in battle. E-every time," she mumbled, fighting to get the words out coherently. Never before had she said them aloud. It hurt, cut her so deeply that she wondered why she wasn't bleeding all over him.

Soothingly, he replied, "There's no shame in that, lass. I've never been eager to stare certain death in the eye, either."

Sniffling, she looked up. "But you've fought giant scorpions, and raiders, and been caught in sand storms, and—"

He laughed roughly. "Yes, lass, I have done that—and been scared spitless each time, I promise you!" Tenderly, he brushed her tears away. "What you must remember is not that you were afraid, but that you overcame that fear—and I know you did, Kyrian, else Azhani would not be with us today. You told me yourself of how you sang her wounds closed during the conflict."

Oh, how Kyrian wanted to cling to his words, to take them inside and make them truth! They were absolution and comfort, blessing and acceptance. But to allow herself to be forgiven so easily—well, she just couldn't let herself escape punishment that quickly.

"Yes, but—"

"Peace, lass. Life is too precious to dwell on should-have-dones," he said. "Focus instead on the things that give you joy."

Looking away, she murmured, "At night, when she's sleeping, I sometimes wake just to look at her, to remind myself that she's still alive. Lying there, watching her breathe, thinking about what would have happened if she'd died—I'm just so ashamed, Granther! What if I'd failed? I'm a stardancer! We're trained to do our duty to the goddess no matter what! If we have to fight, we fight. If we have to k-k-kill, then we d-do so," she stammered angrily.

Iften shook his head. "You're a good lass, Kyrian, with a gentle, pure soul," he said calmly. "And your heart is too shrouded by the golden silk of love to realize that Y'Syr would have gone on without her. Azhani Rhu'len is a great warrior, but she is far from the only person in the kingdoms who can serve Queen Lyssera as she does."

"It's not the kingdom I care about, Granther!" she blurted weakly.

He nodded. "I know, lass. Your feelings for her are writ large upon your face."

"Please, say nothing of them to her, I beg of you. She doesn't know, can't know—I... I shouldn't feel this way," she babbled nervously. "She's my friend. She loved Ylera...who was also my friend, Twain curse me for it."

Halting her tumbling words with a gesture, Iften replied, "Fret not, Kyrian. Your secrets are yours alone to tell, but mine to carry. My shoulders are strong and I am more than willing to lend them to you."

With a heavy sigh, she murmured, "Thank you," and let him hold her as she told him of Ylera, Azhani, and her inability to admit the friendship she'd shared with her friend's lover. He listened, speaking little and never once offering words of scorn or judgment for her actions. Eventually, she rose and shuffled over to the hearth to add wood to the fire and take a drink of her cooling tea. It had been cathartic to talk to someone, to finally voice the thoughts that had plagued her since meeting Azhani. And there was no doubt that Iften was possessed of greater wisdom than she—perhaps he would have advice on how to proceed, how to live with the feelings crowding so tightly in her heart.

Softly, she said, "I'm not ready to surrender you to the sandlung yet, Granther." It was little more than an excuse to continue to see him, to have time to talk to him, and she suspected he knew that.

"Of course you aren't, lass." He chuckled dryly. "You're a stubborn one—I'd expect nothing less of you."

I nearly got her killed again. If Lyssera hadn't shoved the baton in my hands, I'd have been unable to do anything to help and Azhani would be ashes scattered across the throne room! Bile rose in her throat.

"Lass, if you continue to fall into the quicksand of your own mind, even a dust storm will seem like a blessing." Iften slipped his hand under his pillow and retrieved a flask of carved crystal. Offering it to her, he commanded, "Drink." Wryly he smiled, and added, "'Twill not cure that which ails you, but it will let you forget about them for a time."

Though Kyrian was not normally one to use alcohol as a way to escape her thoughts, the hopeful expression on Iften's face told her that this was more than just an old man offering to share his illicit drink. No, there was something almost formal in it, a gesture that was, she suspected, a way for him to offer her yet another form of comfort. *He's attempting to sooth my shattered nerves.* Without a word, she returned to his side, took the flask, and drank. She began to choke, wheezing at the potent, fiery liquor that burned a path straight to her gut and then exploded through her, making her feel dizzy. "What, in the name of the blessed Twain, is this?" she gasped.

With a charming grin, Iften replied, "Snake piss."

Kyrian shuddered, but took a second drink. It was no worse than the first, and perhaps a bit better—sweeter, though maybe that was because her tongue was numb from the first sip. "Thank you." She sunk into the chair. "I think I needed it." Weakly, she returned the flask. The alcohol had one immediate effect—she wasn't thinking about anything but keeping herself from falling down!

Chuckling softly, he said, "Any time, lass," and took a swig for himself. "A desert walker's life's blood, this is," he told her with a slow, solemn wink. "You'll not find courage in this flask, Kyrian, but perhaps it's not courage you need." He held it up and stroked its smooth sides. "No, what it offers is merely a bulwark against twisting thoughts. A way to gather the wit to understand them better."

"I love her, Granther," she said softly. "I don't need wit to understand it, I need the strength to ignore my feelings because I've tried and tried and—and it's tearing me apart!"

"Why is it you wish to throw away the gifts the gods have given you?"

Kyrian scoffed. "Gifts? How can this…this damned desire be a gift? She'll never return my feelings. How could she? I knew Ylera! She was… Goddess, she was like the sun! I'm but a waning moon when held against her light!"

"Oh lass, you cut yourself too small and forget the truth of love," he said sadly. "In one thing alone are you correct, and that is simply that you will never be what Ylera was to her, no one could be. However, it does not mean she cannot love you, for you can offer her an entire world of joy and experiences she would never have had with Ylera. That is the promise of love."

Hope rose sharp and thick within her, but she shoved it aside, shaking her head. "No. No, it can't be. We're just friends," she said insistently. "Ylera was special. She was important and beautiful and wise and funny and I… I'm not. She found her way into Azhani's heart because she was supposed to. I'm just in the way."

"You can't let the past control the future, Kyrian. You're not in the way—Ylera is gone, and the woman I recall would hardly have wanted one she loved to spend the rest of her days in lonely suffering. You knew her—what do you think she would want for Azhani?" he asked softly.

"Happiness," she replied immediately. "Ylera was so kind, so generous—she'd have hated to see her in pain."

Reaching for her hand, he gave it a squeeze. "And what would she want for you?"

"I…" She was accosted by a memory of Ylera, alive, laughing brightly, pointing at one of the prettier acolytes who was just a bit older than Kyrian, and telling her, "Stop mooning over her, you idiot! Go talk to her! You'll never find any kind of happiness just sitting on your hands and waiting for the Twain to spoon feed it to you!"

Blinking away the past, Kyrian murmured, "She'd have wanted me to grab life with both hands and enjoy every moment like it was my last."

"Exactly. The heart is resilient. It fights for the love it desires. Even Azhani will love again, and you are worthy of that affection," Iften said with a broad smile. "Ah, listen to me! Giving such advice to you! You honor me so, lass! I thought I'd never say such things to someone like you."

Meekly, she said, "I only hope your words aren't wasted, Granther."

He shook his head. "They'll never be a waste, Kyrian. Even if they help you not, I will say them and hope that somehow, some way, they'll offer you comfort." She looked away. "And if my words fail, then perhaps my arms will not," he murmured, reaching for her again. With a soft cry, she sank into his embrace, finding it impossible to resist the urge to hold onto the frail old man. Gently, he rubbed her back. "I don't know what else to tell you, lass, but I do know that love can grow from many foundations, and friendship is often the best of them. Be truthful. Share your honor. Let your heart be your guide and what is meant to be will follow."

CHAPTER TEN

"Ecarthus frees us," the priest droned as Arris looked on dazedly. "Our blood is his blood. To him we gladly go." Below the priest, gray-shrouded acolytes dragged a naked, bound, and gagged man up the steps to a basalt altar. The stone was inscribed with a set of strange lines and runes that made Arris' stomach churn just to look at them. They glistened wetly, and he suspected he was about to learn why. Behind the altar stood a cauldron filled with a tower of flames that gave off a sweet, slightly noxious smoke.

Watching from his balcony seat, Arris hardly knew what to think of this "special ceremony" to which he had been invited. It had begun as all other invocations to Ecarthus had in the past—nubile men and women were waiting, all more than willing to disport for their king's pleasure. There was wine and food a-plenty, and when that palled, Porthyros was nearby to ply him with copious amounts of his favorite tea. He had even been there to hand the king a cup just as his latest conquest crawled away, likely to brag about what an incredible lover he was.

Then it all had changed, and he wasn't sure if it was for the better. A priest had led them down a long corridor, up a narrow flight of stairs, and into a private balcony box overlooking the altar. Here Arris was able to see and experience everything. Standing beside him, his face a mask of pure religious fervor, Porthyros seemed utterly lost to the ritual taking place below them.

What's happening? The sleepy question wafted through Arris' mind just as the priest split open the man's chest with a wicked looking dagger, ripped out his heart, and tossed it into the fire. Blood sprayed everywhere, anointing the grooves and sigils cut into the altar's surface. Arris was momentarily sickened, then a sudden wave of incredible energy surged through him.

Power! This is what his kingship had wrought. The true expression of pure power and control—for he and he alone had been able to grant the Ecarthans the right to worship, he and he alone had enabled their great god to finally take his rightful place in Y'Myran. *I have the power over life and death now. I am...a god maker!*

"Your tea, my king?" Porthyros whispered, and Arris drank deeply of the brew, ignoring its faintly bitter taste. He could scold 'Thyro later for neglecting the honey. This was exactly what he needed.

Grinning, he crushed the cup in his bare hand, not caring that his blood ran down his wrist. Just weeks ago, he'd hardly have been able to crush a beetle, much less a heavy clay mug, but his lessons in swordplay were changing him. New muscle wrapped his once-scrawny body, and now he was no longer merely a boy in a man's mantle. Soon, even his father's armor would be too small for him.

"Exhilarating, isn't it, my king?" Porthyros asked as the acolytes struck the gong to signal the service's end. "Just think—that man will wake in paradise, showered in Ecarthus' eternal gratitude!" he added enthusiastically.

"The ultimate reward," Arris murmured, breathing the smoke deeply. "Shall we go? I long to feel a woman beneath me."

"Of course, my king." He moved the tea cart away and gestured to the stairs. "Your carriage awaits."

As they exited the temple, for a moment Arris felt as though he were separate from his own body. Fog wrapped the city and made it seem as though he and Porthyros were little more than islands of life in a sea of frozen mist. He felt the prickle of danger long before it struck.

A flash of light on a silver blade dazzled him, but he was not frightened—no, he was preternaturally calm as he thrust Porthyros away from him, drew his sword, and ran the attacker through. He watched as his blade emerged from the man's back and blood bubbled from his mouth.

After pushing him away, he viciously kicked the body and said, "Have him hung for the crows." While Porthyros gaped in shock at the still twitching figure of the would-be assassin, Arris boarded the carriage

As calm as he might have seemed on the outside, inside, Arris fumed and fretted about the assassin. Questions tumbled about his mind, making sleep a futile endeavor. Was it a plot? Had he been sent by Azhani? Were there more? Did it matter? He'd kill them all!

Three whores and four cups of tea later, he finally slept, yet nightmares plagued his rest.

In the dream, wind ruffled his shaggy, snow-coated beard. Around him, the mountains of Amyra's Crest rose, their sharp, jagged spires cutting into the sky like broken teeth. Fetid gore covered his armor, and at his feet, half buried in snow and ice, were the bodies of armored soldiers wearing the green and black tabards that proclaimed them as his guards. Blood drenched the ice all around him. Rimerbeasts howled, their wispy gray forms just beyond the edge of his vision. Waning sunlight kept them at bay, but soon, they would press the attack.

Fearfully, he searched for Porthyros, but he was nowhere to be seen. The wind kicked up more snow, making it even harder to see. Practically on hands and knees, Arris went from from soldier to soldier, searching for signs of life, but he was entirely alone. Every one of them was cold and dead, their faces frozen in a rictus of horror and agony.

Wrapped in the cyclone of swirling snow and wind, he didn't notice the sky had darkened into twilight until a victorious howl sent chills of terror racing down his spine.

Grimly, Arris gripped his battered, blood stained sword and prepared to die. The snow cleared as the rimerbeasts circled him, moving closer and closer until they were close enough that he could smell their stink in the wind. Then there came a sound he hoped never to hear again.

The long, piercing wail that cracked the twilight had terrified an entire army of bandits and brigands. Arris was just one man, and yet there was nowhere to run. The thundering of horses' hooves drumming on the ground heralded the arrival of his greatest fear. Out of the swirling snow she came, mounted on a beast the color of darkest smoke. In her hands was a blade of flaming ice, and with it she carved a swath of death through the rimerbeasts encircling him. Terror spawned wings on his feet and he ran, sprinting away from the mounted maven of death, leaping rocks and bodies and anything else that stood in his way until he came to a stumbling halt, staring out over the vast expanse of a gaping chasm. To leap it would be to seek certain death.

Shaking now, he stood, holding his blade before him, waiting to feel the cold sting as Azhani gutted him. But she charged right through him, vanishing into the mists gathering on the mountainside.

In relief, he sank to his knees, throwing aside his sword and sobbing pathetically. "Not real," he whispered. "It wasn't rea—" His words were snapped off as a blade plunged into his back and exploded from his chest.

Toppling sideways, he looked up and gaped in shock. "No...you..." He reached out for her, but could not connect, could not to touch her. His last sight was of a pair of golden eyes that blazed with victory.

"No!"

Arris' scream sent Porthyros diving through the king's bedroom door. He barely stopped himself from being cut to ribbons as Arris danced about the room with his sword, slashing blindly at the air.

"My king!" Porthyros cried, hoping his voice would wake the young man from his stupor. "Are you unwell?" Quickly, he turned up the closest lamp to chase back the shadows in the room.

Naked, Arris stood panting, sweat pouring off his body in streams as he stared at Porthyros unseeingly. Slowly, a small amount of sanity seemed to restore itself in his eyes, for he lowered the sword and blinked. "'Thyro? Ecarthus' balls, man! Where's my tea?" he demanded, flinging the blade from him as he sank into a chair.

"Right here, Highness," Porthyros replied, hurrying to the hearth to fetch the pot that was steeping beside it. *Too much krile. Damn. Almost killed him. Need to be more careful. It's not time yet.* Nightmares were one of the first signs of krile toxicity. It had seemed wise at the time to triple Arris' doses while he was at the temple, experiencing his first inner sanctum ritual, but now Porthyros wasn't so sure he'd made the right decision. *Better lower the dose for a while. Just to be sure. I'll have to see that the guard at the door knows to say nothing of the king's nightmares—perhaps a candlemark or two with one of the chambermaids might buy his silence.*

What Porthyros truly feared, however, was Kasyrin Darkchilde's reaction to what he'd almost done. As he stirred honey into the cup, he mumbled, "Master will not be pleased with me."

There was no sense in lying or omitting his error from the report. The sorcerer would know. He always did. And to lie would only bring worse punishment. Telling the truth might be painful, but he would live through it. Still, he could temper the pain by informing Darkchilde about how well Arris had taken to the ceremony.

And we'll just solve the problem of potential bastards by giving his whores to the priests. No one will miss the filthy little maggots anyway.

CHAPTER ELEVEN

The empty parchment stared at Azhani accusingly. It wasn't the first time she'd attempted to write to Padreg, but condensing her recent experiences into a message meant to be carried by the hands of another had so far eluded her. It had reached the point where she was just going to send a bland, "All proceeds as hoped" and save the rest for another time. A knock on her door spared her that, though, and after quickly sanding the inked date and greeting, she pushed the parchment aside for later.

"Yes?" she called, half rising. Her side still ached, but it was little more than a twinge. Kyrian's healing touch had once again worked a miracle for her body.

A page entered, bowed, and said, "Master Azhani, Brannock Maeven to see you?"

She smiled. *He's early. Damn.* "Thank you. Please show him in."

"Of course," the page replied, stepping out to allow a man dressed in the colorful robes of an Y'Noran trader to enter.

Doffing a ridiculously oversized hat, he bowed floridly. "Ah, Lady Azhani, thy face is the purest expression of this humble man's visions of unearthly beauty."

Hard pressed not to laugh, Azhani stood there, arms crossed over her chest, one eyebrow creeping upward as Maeven continued to heap armloads of praise upon her every feature. This was, she knew, by design, for the page and anyone passing by would only remember an unctuous minor merchant and not whatever business he might have had with her.

After a suitable amount of time had passed, Azhani shut the door. "How in the Twain's name do you dream up all this poppycock?"

He laughed. "As I boy, I spent several years apprenticed to a man who did business in King Naral's court. Let's just say the Y'Tolian peerage have made complimenting each other a game and leave it at that."

"I take it you're good at this game?" she said, then shook her head. "Never mind." Returning to her seat, she added, "I'm afraid I haven't a message to send yet."

Plopping his hat back on his head, Maeven smiled. "I'll be in Y'Syria for a few days, my lady. However, I do have tidings for you." Drawing a scroll from his pouch, he bowed formally and unrolled it. "From the hand of Padreg of Y'Nor, I bring you tidings. Hear now his words."

Somewhat bemused, Azhani glanced up at him. "So formal? I hope it's not a marriage proposal."

In the process of opening his mouth to speak, Maeven began choking. "I think not, my lady. Though if it is a husband you seek, I am—"

"Just read the note, Maeven. I'd like to get back to my work sometime today," she said sharply.

"Yes, of course."

Clearing his throat, he shook out the scroll and began reading.

"My friend,

Word of your battle with the foul sorcerer has reached our tents and left us all to hope that you and Stardancer Kyrian are both well. It should not surprise you to learn that Elisira is most concerned for your safety, and begs that you take great caution with your life. I, too, would add my own voice to this prayer.

My lady has also enjoined me to make clear to you that she is most overjoyed with her new life here in the plains. Twain's grace, my friend, but she has taken to the husbandry of our herds like one born to us!

It will no doubt please you to know that young Devon has found a place with Master Gwytian Delvras, my court mage. He has told me that the young man is deeply gifted in the arts of magick. By the next time you see him, Devon will be well on his way to earning his journeyman status. Aden, Syrah, and Thomas all send their greetings.

No doubt you have heard that we are beset on all sides by the harbingers of catastrophe. Monsters, my friend—truest of the names for creatures of terror and destruction—roam our lands and waters. Myths have become fearsome reality, and thus my attempts to garner aid against the coming beast season have all been for naught.

Of Ysradan, there is little to tell beyond the fearsome news that Regent Madros cannot break through the crush of serpents that patrol the shores of Y'Mar, and thus he will not act without his king's approval. I've some doubt as to the man's honesty in this, but no proof to sway me one way or the other.

It also concerns me that he sent Princess Syrelle to foster with my clan at such a dangerous time, but now that she is here we have done all we could to show her the ways of the plains. I fear, however, that this is not what she expected, for oftentimes she complains of the lack of servants to attend her. My lady, who once eschewed their necessity, has come to share this opinion, and as a result the two have become fast friends while helping each other with their laces and buttons."

Azhani's bark of laughter interrupted Maeven's recitation. "I fear the princess will learn much that will scandalize the high court when she returns home. I am glad Eli's found a friend, though."

"Aye. The two lovely doves do giggle like younglings at their first summer fair," he said fondly.

Pulling the abandoned parchment toward her, Azhani quickly scrawled a few lines upon it, wishing Elisira much joy in her new friend. She also warned Padreg not to forget that the ladies were accustomed to certain luxuries that had been long absent in Elisira's life and were likely becoming a quickly fading memory for Syrelle. Having trained many a nobleman's sons and daughters, Azhani knew this might leave Syrelle sharp tempered and less inclined to cooperate with any instruction she might receive. Once the flow of words ebbed, she nodded to Maeven and said, "My apologies."

"None is needed," he said, taking up Padreg's note once more.

"You must know by now that the monsters which roam our kingdoms are many and terrible, yet what strikes me to the very quick with fear is not their horrid visages, but the dark news that Y'Dan has become a haven for demon worship! Aye, though you must surely be as shocked as I to hear it, let me tell you the worst news yet—our beloved and glorious Twain

are suffered there no more! Arris, the grimy, sniveling bastard, has cast them out and installed this demon known as Ecarthus as the master of his faith.

My spies tell me that this beast, also called the Eater of Souls, now claims many lives in a daily sacrifice. The land you once served is now caught in the grip of terror so paralyzing that few move beyond their towns and villages to avoid becoming a target for Ecarthus' foul priests.

Never lightly is regicide spoken of, for a king who seeks the death of another becomes himself a target for the assassin's knife, and yet what else can I demand? My cousin is not well. His laws are unjust and his rule has caused a weeping in the land that even we of Y'Nor can hear. Had any doubts over Thodan's choice of you as queen arisen within me, they have crumbled under the weight of Arris' actions."

If Brannock Maeven seemed surprised by the contents of his king's message, he did not show it. Padreg would never have chosen someone who was unable to keep even the gravest of secrets.

"I wish I felt as sure," she said aloud, penning a few lines on her message in response to Padreg's words. "The crown was never a burden I desired."

"Surely you would take it to spare Y'Dan's people this nightmare Arris has wrought them," Maeven said quietly.

"Yes, I would. But only if it comes legally to my hand. I would not claim it as battle spoils."

"You humble me, my lady. I do not know if I could be so divorced from the desire for power," he replied.

She offered him a sad smile. "Power is a terrible siren, Brannock. It sings a sweet song when it is beyond your reach, but within its embrace, you serve its machinations like a puppet whose strings are made of strongest steel. I prefer a life free of the manacles of history's expectations."

"I don't understand, my lady. Surely Arris doesn't feel this way."

"Of course he doesn't," she snapped, wincing as her side sent off a fiery twinge of pain. "He's a fool and a tyrant. He sees only his own greed, not the truth of a crown. The bearer is not master of all he surveys, but a servant of all who stand below, gazing up in hope and need. A king is the bulwark against the machinations of Fate for his kingdom. He does not thrust his people before him and hide, hoping the shadows will pass him over."

Maeven bowed deeply. "Padreg does not lie when he says you are the most honorable person he knows."

"Then he needs better friends," she said dismissively. "Was that all there was in the letter?"

He shook his head. "No. There's a bit more." Shifting, he rolled the scroll up to the very bottom and began to read once more.

> *"My prayers are filled with the hope that we shall take swift victory against the rimerbeasts so that we might then focus all our efforts on ridding the kingdoms of the scourge that is Arris Thodan and his unholy god, Ecarthus. To that end, I sought counsel with the sages and seers of my clan, and they, with unified voice, begged me to send you this gift."*

With a broad and somewhat mischievous grin plucking at the corners of his mouth, Maeven withdrew a long, leather-wrapped bundle from under his cloak and presented it to her, then backed away as she unwrapped it. An old, ornately decorated but battle-scarred hilt slowly emerged as he spoke further.

> *"Behold! Gormerath—slayer of demons! Forged by the hand of Lyriandelle Starseeker herself, this blade has been a part of the Keelan family for centuries. Now I give her to you, my greatest friend. May she love your hand as faithfully as she loved those of the mothers of my foremothers.*
>
> *It is my fondest hope that we will soon meet again. Until then, be well and strong."*

Shaking away the remaining wrappings, Azhani stared at the legendary blade and felt struck to the core with gratitude, shock, and a little fear that she wasn't actually worthy of such a prized relic. "He honors me."

"Aye," Maeven said. "There's not a one of us who hasn't heard the stories of Gormerath and Lyriandelle Starseeker."

"Firstborn daughter of Ymaric Firstlander, one of the seven founders of Y'Myran," Azhani whispered, stroking the blade. "Do you know how many books I read about Lyriandelle Starseeker? About how she made this sword from a piece of her father's great ship and used it to lay waste to the monsters plaguing the wilderness of Y'Myran?"

He chuckled. "Probably as many as I did—dozens. Maybe hundreds. All about her and every bearer of the blade after, right until it came to the hand of Padreg's mother Ketri, who packed it away when her son was born."

"And now it's mine." Azhani lifted the sheathed blade and tried to see its history, its fame, its glory, and power. Instead, what she saw was mud, dirt, dried blood, the shells of a few dead beetles, and a lot of dust.

Wryly, Maeven said, "She needs a bit of love and tenderness. Twenty-plus years at the bottom of a tack trunk can't have done her much good."

Azhani scowled. "This is the blade Padreg sent, isn't it? You didn't stop to play a few hands at the Dove before coming here, did you?" She was only half joking.

Lifting both his hands in warding, Maeven quickly replied, "By my beloved mother's honor, I swear I came straight from Padreg's tent to this very door without stopping to sample a single drop of even the rudest of Y'Syr's meads."

As she could see no signs of dishonesty in his behavior, Azhani smiled. "It's fine, Maeven. Here, let me finish this letter and you can take yourself off to the city for that mead you seem to be craving."

Even though her head was spinning with the import of Padreg's gift, she took her time in thanking him, making it clear that she would treat the blade as the treasure it surely was. When she was done, she handed the sealed scroll to Maeven. "Tell Paddy that he has my deepest thanks."

"I certainly shall," he said, packing it away and then exiting the room.

Once he was gone, she fetched her sword cleaning kit and began to remove the grime from Gormerath's hilt. A quarter candlemark passed before shining metal was revealed. Carefully, she knocked the mud and dirt away from the sheath until the blade slipped free.

"Oh!" she gasped, blinking in shock. While the hilt had been crusted in muck, the blade had remained untouched. The beauty of Gormerath was now fully exposed.

"Twain's grace, you are a masterwork!" she whispered, daring to run her finger down the fuller of the most unusual blade she had ever seen. Wedge-shaped and pulled to a needle-fine point, the crystalline metal shimmered with the bands of thousands upon thousands of folds. Yet Gormerath's most arresting feature was its incredible color. Upon first glance, it appeared dark and dull, but when lifted into the light, the blade revealed all the shades of the deep ocean and the night sky.

Lost in a world of scintillating hues, Azhani sat rocking the sword back and forth, mesmerized by the blade. Even the brass hilt now seemed to reflect every hue of butter and gold. In the center of the pommel, a dark blue sapphire was inset on both sides, and each stone seemed to pulse with a hint of life. The handle, a hardwood Azhani didn't know, felt as though it had been made for her hand, though time and use had darkened it to nearly black. *This will need leather wrapping. I wouldn't want it to slip from my grasp when my hands become coated in muck and blood.* It pained her to think such a thing, but practicality won out over aesthetics.

Gormerath was longer than the blade she currently wore. So long, in fact, that she would need to wear it upon her back. Strangely, it felt no heavier than her shorter sword. Standing, she took a few experimental swings, both single and double handed, and found it to be the most perfectly balanced blade she'd ever wielded.

Without thinking, she raced through her forms, finishing them with a laugh of unfettered joy. Wielding it was like racing the leading edge of a thunderstorm in the hopes of making it home before the rain. The blade seemed to sing as she moved, and it truly was almost weightless.

"By the Twain, with this in my hands, I'll slay whole armies of rimerbeasts!"

Suddenly, she was seized by an incredible force. Startled, and a little fearful, she looked down and watched as pale blue strands of power untwisted from the blade and raced up her arms to bind themselves around her body. Images and sounds, smells and tastes—thousands upon thousands of them—crashed through her. She was all at once Azhani Rhu'len, Lyriandelle Starseeker, and every woman whose hand had ever grasped Gormerath's hilt. Her fear evaporated as she came to know them as intimately as she knew her own heart. Every battle, every death, every grief-sworn vow raged in her mind.

And then it was gone and she stood there, utterly dazed.

Spoken by a voice she would never forget, words came to her.

"I am Gormerath, warrior of the people. We will serve them well, Master."

At the same time both chilled and exhilarated, Azhani muttered, "Paddy, next time I see you, I don't know whether I'm going to kiss you or kick you."

Shaking her head, she gently laid the sword on its wrappings. Though she was loath to part with it now, it needed a new sheath and there was no way she'd trust a page to find exactly what she required. Carefully, she covered it up, and carrying it like it was the most fragile of infants, she exited her room and headed for the armory.

"He…sent you…what, exactly?" Lyssera asked as she stared at hilt of the sword that peeked up over Azhani's shoulder.

Kyrian chuckled. "That was almost the exact same thing I said, my queen."

Rising, Lyssera circled around Azhani, who stood stock still while she ran her fingers along the scabbard. "It seems…quite the plain home for a blade so storied."

Taking three steps away from both of the other women, Azhani drew the sword and spun it about experimentally, her skill evident even though this was simply play.

"I like her," she said, swapping the sword from hand to hand, then quickly sheathing it. "She's light, fast, and sharp as shattered glass." With a shrug, she added, "And she feels fantastic in my hand. To be completely honest, I think she might just give us a true advantage against the rimerbeasts, if the tales about her are true." Drawing it again, she slowly twirled it about, creating shimmering, hypnotic patterns of light and shadow that held them all rapt.

Having heard those tales all her life, Lyssera nodded slowly and murmured, "I can't even begin to imagine what could be a gift of equal value, but I shall think of something, surely."

Kyrian sighed. "Azhi, put your toy away—you're lulling the queen to sleep."

Sheepishly, Azhani lowered the blade. "My apologies."

"Don't," Lyssera replied hastily. "I'm enjoying it. I don't get to see you practice nearly enough—and you truly are a master."

As Azhani's cheeks warmed with the praise, Kyrian smiled fondly. "Speaking of mastery—I do believe it's time for Allyndev's next lesson."

Adrenaline raced through her, but it felt wrong, all wrong. Kyrian shook her head and said, "No, no—strike, block, feint then disarm, my prince. Be aggressive, but cautiously so—you want to disable, not kill, your opponent."

Across from her, Allyndev looked incredibly irritated. It was clear he was chafing under her tutelage, but she'd been asked to fill in for Azhani, and by the Twain, that's what she was going to do. "Let's do this again." She stepped back and readied her staff.

The wood felt clumsy and strange in her hands. Staves were not her best or even second best weapon, but since her baton had been destroyed by the sorcerer's spell, she had no other choice. To replace the baton, she would need to travel to Y'Len and have the smiths there craft one for her hand alone. There just wasn't enough time, not when they would soon need to head north to begin clearing the caves of rimerbeast eggs. Though Azhani had not said she wanted to join one of the first expeditions to head north, Kyrian knew Azhani well enough by now to understand where her honor would take her. She also knew that she would go with her, choosing to walk toward the battle she so feared rather than hiding here in safety of Oakheart.

There was another reason why she was using the staff. Allyndev's lessons had garnered an audience, and rather than subject him to the taunts of his peers, she armed herself to spare him any blows to his ego that being defeated by an unarmed opponent might induce.

"Ready?" she asked as he sighed heavily and lifted his sword.

"When is Master Azhani returning?" he muttered. "I was *learning* from her." Taking an experimental swipe at her, he sneered and added, "I beat every guard that came against me! Then you came and made me look a fool!"

It stung to be the subject of Allyndev's disapproval. Mostly because she knew she shouldn't be doing this, shouldn't be teaching a prince of the blood how to be a warrior when she herself could barely keep her wits about her in a fight. But this was what was asked of her, and she wasn't going to let Azhani down—not in this and not ever.

"She'll come when she is healed." She forced herself to remember that his frustration could hinder his learning if she made it worse. Still, if he would just try to take something from her lessons, he might discover that there was as much merit to a sound defense as there was to Azhani's stronger offense.

Allyn circled her, and she found herself comparing the way he moved to Azhani's more lithe and battle-hardened reflexes. Though he was no doubt trying to use every trick his master had taught him, it was clear he had a long way to go before he'd be a testament to her tutelage. Kyrian waited until he'd established a pattern and then broke it simply by twisting when he least expected it and rapping him hard in the side, scoring a strike that would leave a painful, but temporary reminder not to leave his flank open.

"Ouch, damn it!" he hissed angrily, stepping back and lowering his shield.

"Don't leave yourself exposed, my prince," she said calmly. "Now come on, disarm me."

"I'm trying!" he snapped, stepping forward and circling her once more.

She gave him nothing. If he was going to disarm her, he would do so by skill, not because she was some idiot soldier who had known him all her life and thought it amusing that he'd finally picked up a sword. Everyone who sparred with him said he had a natural instinct, and maybe that was true, but right now her job was to teach him and this was what she knew—make her opponent do all the work. Tire them out. Make them try, again and again, until they succeeded—in which case, she would counter it—or failed, allowing her to remain protected.

Finally, he struck, she countered, and he pulled his hand back, shaking fingers that were likely numb from the rapping she'd just given them.

"Are we sparring or dancing, my prince?" She lifted one eyebrow in amusement as he crept back toward the edge of the practice ring, his movements constituting an ever-widening circle that made it look very much like he was trying to run away.

"Sparring, damn it," he growled and lunged suddenly, getting his blade up under her staff and yanking, trying to jerk it from her hands.

She'd have applauded him for the bold move if it had worked. Another time, she would teach him the proper way to catch the stick, but now she shoved the staff against his shield and caused him to stumble back, freeing her. Twirling the staff, she swept it toward his knees, but he blocked, then tried a move that would definitely disarm her, catching her staff. Unfortunately, he tried to shift the grip on his sword and she ripped her weapon free and spun the staff around, rapping him on the elbow sharply enough to cause him to drop the blade.

Holding up his hands in surrender, he said. "I yield, Stardancer." As she stepped back, he sneered at her. "By the First Tree, you should have more respect for me. I'm a prince, damn it! Master Azhani doesn't treat me this sorely."

Just as Kyrian was about to reply, someone yelled, "Run back to your nursemaids, little princeling. War is for men, not halfbreed pretenders!"

"Yeah, get out of here, you useless bastard! You're not worth Master Azhani's time!" another called.

"Go back to your trees, farmer boy! There's no place for quitters in the queen's army."

Wincing, Allyndev picked up his blade and headed over to the bench where towels and waterskins waited.

Kyrian sighed. The jibes were nothing new, and she suspected he'd heard worse—she had, whenever she'd dared to step beyond the gates of Y'Len. Not even the priests could shield her from the casual cruelties of the hidebound and she suspected the same was true for Allyndev. Especially as he was a prince.

"See, I told you he wasn't that good. Just lucky. Waste o' time t'give the little shyvot airs. He ain't ne'er going to have a crown on that useless head of his. Ain't none who'd stand it." After saying his piece, one guard stomped out of the salle.

Lowering her weapon, Kyrian resigned herself to the end of today's session. It was just as well, for Allyndev's temper might have gotten the better of him, and if he'd attacked her with true aggression, she'd likely have frozen, too afraid of her own strength to properly defend herself. One or both of them might have been hurt in the process. *I think, however, that I shall request that our sessions be closed to observers from now on. It won't earn me any friends to take their favorite whipping boy away from them, but the guards need to learn some respect for their prince.*

"So I see insulting your prince is still a team sport," Azhani said as she stepped out of the shadows and into the midst of the jeering guards. "I'm sure Queen Lyssera will be so pleased to know her people respect the Kelani name so highly."

One of them sneered at her and spat, "What do you care, Oathbreaker?"

"Ajep, stand down," another man murmured. "She's been pardoned, remember? Queen's Law."

"So?" Ajep said, curling his hand around the hilt of his sword. "Let her defend herself, then." He thrust his jaw at her.

"Are you insane, man? She'll take you apart and use your bones for beads!" the other man hissed. "That's the Banshee!"

Azhani wasn't sure she should feel so proud of the soldier's obvious respect, but there was no doubt that it felt damned good to hear that tone in his voice.

"So? She's just another shyvot-sucking Oathbreaker as far as I'm concerned," Ajep retorted.

Throwing his hands up, the guard said, "It's your funeral, Ajep. I'm getting out of here."

Calmly, Azhani said, "Apologize to His Highness on your way out, Torvik, and I'll forget I heard you being disrespectful to him." Facing Ajep, she nodded at the salle floor and then folded her arms over her chest disdainfully. "If you're so intent on testing yourself against me, then why didn't you come to practice after that first day?"

One of the others sniggered. "Eh, that's an easy one, Master Azhani. After ye set 'im on 'is arse a few times too many, 'e be scared o' ye."

"Shut it, Deegan!" Ajep snapped. Putting his hand on the hilt of his sword, he stepped closer to Azhani and said, "I'm not afraid of you."

"That's a mistake," she growled, staring down at him, using her height to every bit of its advantage. He twitched, partially drawing his blade. Immediately, she was on him, grabbing his wrist with one hand and driving her other forearm into his throat, pinning him to the wall. Gagging, he fought to breathe. "I want you to remember this, Ajep," she hissed. "I will teach Allyndev everything I know. Every way to hurt, maim, dismember, and destroy another person's body." Slowly, she closed her fingers down around his wrist, crushing it in her powerful grip. The bones and tendons grated and he began to whimper. "And when I'm done, when I'm absolutely certain he's at least my equal, I'm going to stand there and watch as he takes you apart in front of the entire castle. When he's done with you, Ajep, your name won't be worth a single line in all of Oakheart's history books. Now get out of here and go do something worthwhile, like bathing. You stink of the alehouse."

Giving him a shove, she sent him stumbling out of the salle, making a mental note to mention to Captain Evern that Ajep had been drunk on duty. The others quickly dispersed and she descended to the practice floor, her plan for the afternoon already forming.

She'd seen everything, and now she intended to take two birds with one arrow. "Battle conditions!" she snapped, startling both Kyrian and Allyndev. "Face off and don't stop until the kill strike is made."

Though Kyrian's face registered shock, Allyn quickly spun and flung his towel at her, using the distraction to grab his sword and a half-empty waterskin. She dodged the fabric but not the waterskin, staggering back enough that Allyn was able to press his advantage. He jumped past her, snatched his shield from the wall, and then charged her. Recovering, Kyrian twisted out of the way and caught his sword on the end of her staff, using its greater leverage to shove him back.

"Don't let her bully you, Allyndev!" Azhani snapped as Kyrian began twirling the staff around him, cracking the tip against his shield every so often to throw him off balance. "She's just swinging a stick! You've got a sword, use it!"

Fierceness blossomed on Allyndev's face and suddenly he came alive, rushing forward and using his shield just as she'd taught him. Thrusting it like a secondary weapon, he hemmed in Kyrian's ability to use the staff to keep him back.

"Good, good!" Azhani shouted, running around them and watching for Kyrian to fight back, to transcend the moment and show her the depth of her ability.

Slowly, she withstood the battering, earning every inch of space between her and Allyndev with sweat and bruises. Allyn was grinning now and Azhani recognized the glint of incipient victory in his eyes, but she could also see that Kyrian wasn't yet ready to surrender, and she had far more training than he did. This was never clearer than in the way she ran him ragged now, forcing him to waste his strength on powerful blows that never landed, then taunting him with sharp jabs of her staff to his thighs or flank. In Azhani's estimation, it was a forgone conclusion that Kyrian would win—it was only a matter of time.

The moment came when Allyndev missed a critical block and took a hard, painful blow to the elbow that completely disarmed him, sending his blade flying. Instead of delivering the killing strike, however, Kyrian immediately stepped back, holding her staff before her as if expecting him to press the attack. She was visibly shaking.

It's now or never. In frustration, Azhani barked, "I said battle conditions! Finish the fight, Kyrian. Take him down! Make the kill strike!"

Kyrian flinched, but shook her head. "No."

Damn it! What's stopping her? She's more than good enough to do this! The unexpected gift of Gormerath had been exactly what Azhani needed to focus her determination on the upcoming beast season. Since Kyrian had made it more than clear that she intended to follow her lead, Azhani had to know that her friend could defend herself against the rimerbeasts. *I can't be worried she's going to freeze every time we face one of those monsters. It'll get us both killed, and I won't have the blood of another person I care about on my hands!*

"Allyn, hand me your blade—and hit the baths. You're done," she snapped, taking the blade from him once he'd retrieved it. Hastily, he backed out of the practice ring. With a flick of her wrist, she struck the end of Kyrian's staff. "Fight me."

"No."

"Yes. Defeat me, Kyrian. I know you can."

Determinedly, Azhani rained blows down on her, coming at her hard, fast, and from every direction. Kyrian blocked them all, barely seeming to break a sweat, but she would not engage. She would not return the strikes. In Kyrian's hands, the staff was a crippled weapon; an ineffectual shield that was slowly losing its usefulness the longer the bout continued. Again and again, Azhani struck, making each blow or thrust harder and faster than the last until she connected with Kyrian's arm, her leg, and her side.

These were not light, practice hits. No, Azhani went full force, knowing she could hurt Kyrian gravely if she misjudged where her hits landed. But Kyrian was wearing practice armor, she wasn't. All it would take is one blow from the staff and she would be at Kyrian's mercy.

"Fight me!" Azhani screamed almost pleadingly.

"I can't!" Kyrian wailed, trying to escape the ceaseless attacks and failing miserably.

Desperate but determined to get some answers, Azhani drove her into the wall and pinned her there with vicious, powerful blows. Cornered, terror etching her face, something in Kyrian's eyes changed. With a wild, broken scream of agony, she thrust the staff outward, blocking Azhani's strike with all her strength. With a tremendously loud crack, the staff snapped in half.

Now armed with two weapons, weapons that were much more like the baton she loved so much, Kyrian erupted into the fury of the Dance, blocking and returning every one of Azhani's blows.

"Yes, fight me, Kyrian. Make me into whatever is causing you to fear battle and destroy it. Come on," she crooned, hating the sight of the tears that stained Kyrian's face. "You can't hurt me, my friend."

Round and round they went, Kyrian sobbing with every blow, but fighting on until she missed and staggered to her knees.

"I quit," she gasped.

"You can't quit. I won't allow it," Azhani replied sharply. "Get up. Fight me!"

In shock, Kyrian looked up at her, panting and crying, sweat tangling her hair in ugly mats, and screamed, "Won't allow it? What are you doing to me?"

Azhani opened her mouth to reply, but swallowed her words when Kyrian suddenly leaped for her. Killing rage was in her eyes as she flailed her weapons at her—not wildly, though. No, these blows were meant only to kill. If a single one landed, Azhani knew she would not survive it.

Strangely, the threat of imminent death was calming. Blocking the blows now was almost easy.

"Talk to me, Kyr. Why do you hate this?" She couldn't understand it. Couldn't see why someone who was such a master would hate the skills she'd obviously worked so hard to gain.

"I…" Kyrian started to flag, her blows losing power as she automatically blocked Azhani's strikes. "I…"

"Please, Kyr! Talk to me! Please! You've let whatever this is fester for far too long. Surely you, of all people, know how bad that is!" Azhani dropped her blade and caught Kyrian's sticks before they could hit her. Holding them in place, she looked Kyrian in the eyes. "You healed me. You reached inside me and broke open the infection and let it drain and now I can run! Let me do the same for you!" She stepped closer, lowering her voice as she added, "Whatever it is, I swear to you, I'll still be here."

Shaking uncontrollably, Kyrian stammered, "I…I…I…I'm afraid."

"Of what?" Azhani whispered.

Kyrian blinked rapidly. "O…of k-killing someone." She took a deep, ragged breath and whispered, "Again." As if the words were a stone through glass, Kyrian shattered, falling to her knees and sobbing, "Ah, Gods, I killed a man."

Kneeling, Azhani took her into her arms and held her. Slowly, she rubbed her back as Kyrian cried herself out, clutching Azhani's tunic as grief raged through her. "Tell me about it?" Azhani finally said when the sobs quieted.

Kyrian sighed wearily. "I…it seems like forever ago. It feels like yesterday. Sometimes I cry so much about it that I have no more tears."

It was not an unfamiliar admission or feeling. Nodding slowly, Azhani replied, "The first time I killed, I nearly threw my sword into the river. I couldn't bear to touch it."

Softly, Kyrian said, "It took me a month to put my baton back on my belt. Three before I c-could draw it." She shifted in Azhani's arms until she was snuggled up against her. "H-his name was B-barrig. He was a bandit. I-it happened in Myr. I'd taken my students swimming. It was a h-hot day. On our way back to the village, h-he appeared a-and tried to capture the ch-children and I, I stopped him." The story haltingly unfolded, and Azhani found herself being introduced to a part of Kyrian's life she'd never expected to discover.

A teacher. Goddess. And children...she would love them, wouldn't she? She could scarcely match the image of the innocent young stardancer against the haunted, weary woman in her arms. *No wonder she didn't want to go to Myr with Syrah.*

"When it was over, and I stood there, staring at his body, trying to find the strength to sing the pathsong for him, it-it just hit me that I was—that I had taken his life. What right did I have to bless him on his way?" She shook her head violently. "It was then that I knew my greatest sin. Nothing—not one thing I could ever do—would balance the evil of choosing to take another's life." With a long, heavy sigh, she said, "That's why I freeze. In my mind, all I can see is his face. Because of one man, I fear combat more than I fear death."

"Why?" Azhani asked gently.

"Why? What gives me, a healer, the right to kill? What if, one day, I just stop caring? What if, one day, I love it?" she asked, a fevered expression on her face. "The blood, the death, the killing—grinding my baton in the bones of my enemies! Watching the bastards scream in agony!" She shuddered in disgust. "The moment that happened, I'd cease to be a stardancer and become a true murderer."

"No." Azhani gathered Kyrian against her and caressed her tenderly. "No. You could never find pleasure in death. Astariu's Fire burns too hotly within you," she said, believing this with every iota of her being. "This dark path you fear—it will never be yours." Brushing her cheek against the top of her head, she murmured, "You can't allow these fears to rule you, Kyrian. If you do, you'll always be running from them." For a moment, she was quiet, finding the words that she wanted to say amid the maelstrom of her thoughts. "The decision to take a life is...a difficult one, and is a terrible burden to bear. It should be, but you are strong, and wise, and good."

"I...I wish I could believe you," Kyrian whispered, looking away, her posture screaming her guilt and shame.

"You don't need to believe me, just what you were taught as a healer. What do you do with flesh so poisoned with rot that it's killing a limb?"

"You cut it off," she replied immediately, then looked up at Azhani and frowned. "Damn you. You're telling me Barrig was the rotted limb."

"I am," Azhani said calmly. "And so are any who would attack a stardancer or seek to kidnap children for the pleasure of others."

Kyrian sighed as she snuggled closer. "You don't counsel fairly, Azhi."

With a wry chuckle, Azhani replied, "Who said I had to be fair? Where you're concerned, I'll fight dirty to help you get better."

Slowly, Kyrian smiled. "All right, I understand what you're trying to say, but my fears won't be conquered in a day."

"I don't care. I'll still be here." *I don't want to be anywhere else.*

"Then…I have hope." Kyrian tipped her head up and kissed the soft curve of Azhani's cheek. "Thank you."

The faint, almost insignificant touch felt like scalding water was being poured through her veins and it was all Azhani could do not to gasp aloud at the roar of desire that came alive within her. "You're welcome," she whispered, reaching down to brush stray bits of hair away from Kyrian's face.

Closing her eyes, Kyrian bit her lip, then covered Azhani's hand and they sat like that, silent but for the throb of their heartbeats. The future would bring what it would bring. For now, she was content to know that they would both work to keep Kyrian's fears from getting her killed.

CHAPTER TWELVE

Azhani reached over and touched Gormerath's hilt, assuring herself that the sword still sat by her side in the boat. After days of council sessions, Lyssera had ordered them out of the city to enjoy some quiet time away from the chaos running rampant in Oakheart's halls.

"How long have you had it now?" Kyrian asked bemusedly.

Caught, she replied, "A week. It still doesn't seem like a day's passed, and yet I feel like she's been mine all my life."

"You know they say she came to you wrapped in silk of purest ivory, cased in gold, and that when you first drew her, the skies themselves heralded the binding of her to your service."

"Bards," Azhani said dryly. "They do love to embellish the truth. Besides, who would believe that she was so dirty I almost thought she was a fake?"

Kyrian looked at her incredulously. "Really? You didn't tell me that part. When did you know she was real?"

"The moment she was freed from her rotting scabbard." She touched the hilt once more before getting back to the job of guiding their little boat along the shore of Banner Lake.

Dipping her paddle into the water, Kyrian softly asked, "Has anything been decided yet?"

Azhani sighed. Being granted such a gift could have been troublesome, but instead of drawing the ire of Lyssera's council, it had somehow earned her quite a bit of support. "No." She sank her oar into the water roughly. "Except half the council wants me to wear the warleader's mantle and half of them would rather slap it on some unproven second son of a distant cousin twice removed who's only ever held a plowshare before his wife dragged him to Y'Syr when the armies were called up."

Scowling, Kyrian shook her head. "They're insane. You're the best person for the job!"

"I don't want it, but it's a task I'll take if it's offered," she replied gravely. "But let's not think about that. Let's just enjoy ourselves."

"What of Arris and this Ecarthan faith he's spreading?" Kyrian asked then.

Azhani shrugged. "He—and this god of his—can wait. Whatever harm they do pales against the devastation of just a handful of fully grown and starving rimerbeasts. Lyssera has ordered extra guards at the border and sent word to the other kingdoms. If the Ecarthan priests attempt to spread their poison there, I've no doubt they'll be met with a very pointed rejection."

"I hate them," she said quietly. "I've been talking with some of the stardancers and starseekers that left before the new laws took effect, and the stories they tell…" Kyrian shivered. "It's worse when you hear similar but worse tales from the few elves and half-elves that are managing to get out of there now."

"I know," Azhani said grimly. "And we will deal with them, I promise you that." She reached over and squeezed Kyrian's hand. Then she chuckled dryly. "You know, there is an unintended benefit to this."

"A benefit? Are you mad?"

"Not at all. Simply bemused. I heard Lord Gleewyn offer shelter to a family of half-elves who'd lost their father to those damnable priests."

"Paldir Gleewyn? The one who swore by the Twain that we half-elves were an abomination before our beloved gods?" Kyrian's eyes went round with shock.

"One and the same," she replied cheerfully. "Apparently, he's had something of a revision of faith thanks to this Ecarthus."

"Incredible." Kyrian shook her head slowly. "All right, but honestly, one man having a change of heart doesn't make what Arris is doing right."

"No, it doesn't," she said. "But there is little else to be done now. You must agree that the rimerbeasts are the greater threat." Azhani looked at her, wondering if she was about to be surprised by her friend yet again, but no, Kyrian was nodding. No surprises here.

"I agree, I really do."

"Thank you," Azhani said warmly. "Now let's not speak of worldly matters anymore, not when we have all the beauty of nature's comfort to buffer our souls before we travel north to slaughter rimerbeasts."

Kyrian smiled. "You'll hear no arguments from me."

Half a candlemark's rowing brought them to a shaded beach. Grabbing a basket of food, they climbed up the shore and made their way into the forest.

There they found the perfect picnic spot, spread out a blanket, made a small fire, and sat down to enjoy their repast.

"It's so beautiful," Kyrian murmured.

Azhani nodded. "It is. Peaceful. It reminds me of the woods near the cottage." Pensively, she looked at the lush foliage around them, then said, "We're not quite as remote, but there's still something quiet and welcoming about it." She sighed. "When this is over…I might like to go back there. For a little while, at least."

"After Arris?"

"Aye."

They were silent for a time, enjoying their picnic. Eventually, Kyrian stretched out on the blanket, put her arms behind her head, and appeared to drift off into a nap. It wasn't long before she spoke, though. "Azhi? I know you said you didn't want to talk about worldly matters, but…I really am curious—what will you do about Arris?"

This was not a new question. Time and time again, they had talked it over, trying to find yet another way they might deal with the evil man now sitting on Y'Dan's throne.

This time, however, there was something else in Kyrian's question. Azhani couldn't quite put her finger on what made this particular moment special, but whatever it was, her answer was very important to her friend. Toying with the ties on her dagger, she frowned. "I…don't know, Kyr." She shook her head woefully. "You know very well that I was driven by pure vengeance. If you'd asked me that a month ago, I'd have told you I wanted him spitted on a pike and his entrails strewn for the crows, but now…" A leather tie snapped. "Now I just want justice."

Quietly, Kyrian said, "What changed?"

"I did," Azhani replied. Looking up at her, she smiled sadly. "Lyss and I have spent so much time talking. And you know, she made me understand something I couldn't see before."

"And that is?"

"That Ylera would have never wanted me to be a monster," she whispered, blinking back tears. "And I was well on the road to becoming one. And then you—you taught me something, too."

Startled, she said, "Me?"

Azhani nodded. "Yes, you." She grinned as she reached over to tickle her lightly. "You showed me that life is bigger than I thought. That there is joy beyond heartbreak."

With a heavy sigh, Kyrian covered her face and murmured, "She would be so happy, so grateful to know you feel that way."

Azhani frowned. "What do you mean by that?"

Sitting up, Kyrian wrapped her arms around her knees, and, after taking a deep breath, replied, "I knew her. Ylera. She was…my friend."

Azhani's heart was beating so fast it felt like it was going to hammer a hole in her chest. The enormity of what Kyrian had just admitted charged through her like a herd of Y'Noran horses. She almost couldn't grasp it. All of her life slid down to a focal point of one, breathless thought. *She and Ylera were friends?*

It seemed absurd, unreal. How could the woman who had fought so hard to save her life have been friends with the woman Azhani had been accused of slaying? *No one is that pure-hearted. No one looks upon a sworn oathbreaker and sees only a patient to be treated. And most certainly no one, stardancer or not, befriends that person, the woman who was accused of the heinous murder of a friend.*

Incredulous, Azhani stared at Kyrian, whose face was etched in a stark ruin of fear. Terror made her seem almost child-like, and suddenly Azhani understood. *She said nothing because I would never have trusted her, and she needed me to trust her to save my leg. She put aside her grief because she saw something in me worth saving.*

Softly, she asked, "How did you know her?"

Kyrian swallowed quickly and rasped, "We were classmates a-at Y'Len." She blinked quickly and in that moment, Azhani knew she could not be angry with her, not when all she wanted to do was gather Kyrian into her arms and soothe away the tears that were escaping the corners of her eyes.

For the space of several heartbeats, Azhani let herself sink into thoughts of Ylera, wondering what it had been like for her at the temple. How had she met Kyrian? Were they close? How close?

A strange twist of fear and jealousy rose within her then. Fear that they had been intimate and jealousy of *Ylera* for having had the chance to love the woman she now looked at with growing desire. *Oh, don't be ridiculous! Kyrian's a great deal younger. She would have been barely a child when Ylera was schooling with her!*

Kyrian hid her face against her knees and Azhani shook herself from her thoughts, saying, "She would be glad to know we are friends, then." Gently, she brushed her fingers against Kyrian's arm. "You know, she often spoke of introducing me to those who were…important to her. Perhaps, in some strange way, that's why I happened to be there on that snowy road when your kidnapper rode past."

"Oh Goddess, Azhi," Kyrian whispered. "Thank you."

"For what?"

With a forlorn smile, she replied, "For not hating me—for not being angry even though I've kept secrets."

"I could never hate you, Kyrian. No matter what, that is the one thing I can promise." She slid closer and took her hands. "You had so much faith in me! You risked exile to heal me and I will never, ever forget that!" she said intently. *You're so important to me! How can I tell you how much you've come to mean?* "Before anyone knew the truth, you believed in my innocence. That was such a gift, Kyrian. Such an incredible, amazing gift."

"It's my sworn duty to heal those in need," Kyrian replied, but she smiled warmly. "And it was my honor, Azhani. You saved my life when your own was nearly over. No one who had been guilty of the crimes you were accused of would have done such a thing. I knew then that there was more to the story than was being told, and I had to know the truth. For Ylera's sake."

Azhani smiled. "Then for Ylera's sake—and my own—I am grateful that we have become friends."

"So am I." Shyly, Kyrian reached for her and they embraced, hugging for a long time.

Eventually, Azhani released her. "It's getting late. We should return before darkness falls and makes crossing the lake hazardous."

She forgave me. She isn't even angry with me! By the Twain, have I been worrying at this for nothing? Standing quickly, Kyrian began cleaning up their picnic site, all the while mulling over the fears that had kept her mum about Ylera for so long.

Was I stupid to keep it from her? Should I have said something earlier? Goddess, this is just so…so unexpected. I thought… How many candlemarks had she fretted and brooded over this choice, this seemingly terrible lie of omission, only to have Azhani act as though it were, well, all right? Faster and faster she worked, hurrying for the sake of burying herself in the effort. Returning to Oakheart seemed like a very good idea—if only because there, she could throw herself into her room or talk to Iften, who might be able to offer some grandfatherly insight that would calm the butterflies buzzing in her stomach.

"Hey, hold up a moment," Azhani called as she finished packing and was about to head for the lake.

"Hm?" Kyrian turned to face her.

"You've, ah, crumbs." She reached for Kyrian's face and delicately brushed something from her lips.

It was an incredibly intimate touch, and Kyrian felt herself lean into it, opening her mouth slightly as Azhani bent forward. She could barely breathe. Her heart felt like a ball of jagged thorns, banging and beating against her ribs and lungs, stealing even the ability to move. Closer and closer Azhani came, still caressing her lips as Kyrian stared up at her, fascinated by the way Azhani seemed truly mesmerized.

Is she...is she going to kiss me? Every inch of Kyrian's body screamed for this to be it, to be the one time it finally got what it so deeply craved.

Their lips brushed. Kyrian tasted a hint of apples and honey from the cider they'd drank.

"Hello?" Prince Allyndev's voice sent them reeling apart. "Master Azhani? Stardancer Kyrian?" Crashing sounds followed the queries. "Are you out here?" Suddenly, he appeared, twigs and bits of underbrush stuck to his doublet. "Oh, there you are," he said brightly, hurrying over. Jerking a scroll from his belt, he shoved it at them and said, "Aunt Lyss needs you back at court."

Azhani took the message, opened it, scanned the contents, and then cursed. Crumpling it, she tossed it onto the fire, watched as it burned, and then kicked dirt over the entire thing until there was nothing left but some smoke.

Though her lips throbbed and her head was spinning with what she'd just experienced, Kyrian found sense enough to ask, "What is it?"

Azhani cursed again. "A few of the lord councilors have gone mad. They want Lyss to lead the army."

"Twain's grace!" Kyrian gasped. Though there was no doubt in her mind that Queen Lyssera was a competent warrior, it was idiocy to suggest that she abandon her throne when there was barely a thin strip of water separating Y'Syria from a kingdom currently ruled by a madman. "They can't truly think she'd go, can they?"

"I've no idea, but I think it's time to remind them of the realities of a beast season," she said darkly.

Snickering wickedly, Allyndev said, "I can't wait to see what you do, Master."

"I won't *do* anything, Highness," Azhani said. "People who are that stupid need to be *shown* their ideas are wrong. In fact, you're going to help me teach them a very valuable object lesson, Prince Allyndev."

"I am?" he asked eagerly.

"Indeed. You and Kyrian need to locate Lord Jantis Morgan."

Allyn's eyes went wide and Kyrian tried to place the name. "Wasn't he…" She frowned. "Wasn't he King Maddrell's warleader?" she asked quietly.

Slowly, Allyndev nodded. "Aye. He retired after the beast season that took Granther Kelani's life." He turned to Azhani, respect heavy in his gaze. "He'll rip those councilors to pieces, you know."

A thin smile curved Azhani's lips. "I know. Come on, let's go. I'd rather get back before the mosquitoes decide we're their supper."

"You are all idiots," Jantis bellowed as he limped around the room, his heavy cane making a distinctive thunk on the floor with each step. The same beast season that had taken King Maddrell had also ruined Lord Morgan's legs, causing him to lose one at the knee and face a lifetime of agony from the scars crisscrossing the other. Stopping in front of the map, he slammed the tip of his cane into the center of Y'Dan, he said, "That is an enemy, not a nuisance! And this—" He dragged the cane tip to the Crest of Amyra. "This is Hell. We are facing a fight on two fronts. You do not send your *queen* off to face Hell and leave the throne open for an *enemy* to take!"

One of the councilors cleared his throat and stood. "Lord Morgan, we don't argue this point. My concern is, who do we trust? Surely we can't expect this *boy* here to do it?" He pointed to Allyndev.

The entirety of his aunt's council stared at him. Worryingly, he felt his cheeks start to warm. This was not the time to show any weakness. Wanting to squirm, he forced himself to remain still. If they were to take him seriously, he had to act like he belonged. That was something Master Azhani had taught him—behave as though you're supposed to be somewhere, and most of the time, no one would question your right. Well, right now he was acting as though he wasn't scared to death that someone was going to decide *he* should be warleader of Y'Syr.

"Of course not, you wine-addled sot!" Jantis growled. "And no, I won't do it either. I'm almost four hundred years old and I'm no more a warrior than you, Lord Barrendar, are a philosopher."

Allyndev nearly choked on his own tongue at that. Lord Barrendar's dislike of books was almost legendary at Oakheart. Drinking, carousing, and hunting—that was how the southern lord chose to spend his days when he wasn't making trouble for Lyssera in council.

Barrendar scowled, but it was Lord Paldir who then stood and said, "I say we end this nonsense about our queen risking her life. The Kelani line has dwindled too much as it is—why should we risk the future of Y'Syr when there's a perfectly reasonable answer staring us in the face?"

"Surely you don't mean that damnable woman!" Lord Bethelsel grumbled as a page filled his wine cup.

And why not Master Azhani? Allyn wanted to scream. *She can turn you all into pig slop inside six breaths! She's perfect!*

Azhani, he noted, hadn't spoken a single word either for or against herself. Neither had the queen, though both sat at the head of the table, their gazes fixed on whoever was currently speaking.

"Why not?" Lady Sidar asked sharply. "She's a proven leader. My own father fought at her side for years—and were he here today, he'd gladly stand and do it again!"

"I am with Sidar," Lady Zishara said as she pinned Sidar with an icy stare. "Which is strange, I know, but the Y'Dani warrior is a butcher when it comes to rimerbeasts, and frankly, I'd rather have her out there slaughtering the monsters than here, making us a target for that horrid sorcerer."

It might have been Allyndev's imagination, but he thought he saw a slight hint of amusement flicker across Azhani's face at Lady Zishara's argument.

Lord Bethelsel scowled, but nodded. "You have a point, Zishara."

"Moreover, if you're so against Azhani," Lady Sidar said as she quickly stood. "Then one of you should volunteer to go. Surely one of you is brave enough, skilled enough—nay, even Twain-blessed enough—to take up your blade and the mantle of warleader against the rimerbeasts!"

With a snort, Jantis said, "Don't waste your breath, my lady. They're all a bunch of summer heroes, and fighting rimerbeasts requires someone with winter in their bones." He turned and bowed to Azhani. "It would be my honor to pass what was once mine to this able and Twain-touched warrior, but you will all decide how best to destroy the kingdom yourselves, I wager. Do it without me. I'm tired." With that, he hobbled to a nearby chair and pulled off the carved prosthetic that was a visceral reminder of his sacrifice.

Fascinated, Allyndev watched as Jantis winced and massaged the nub of his leg. Kyrian moved to kneel beside him, pulling a salve from her pouch and carefully applying it as the entire council looked on, almost all of them glancing away when the thickly scarred stump was fully bared.

Azhani stood and gestured to Jantis. "Look then, my lords and ladies. Look upon what a beast season wrought and ask yourselves if this is the fate you would risk for your queen."

Allyndev held his breath, for her words were a blatant challenge.

"The point has been conceded," Lord Barrendar said after several drips of wax from the day candle had spilled down its sides. "Queen Lyssera should not lead the armies of Y'Syr."

Side by side, Azhani and Lyssera exited the council chambers. Behind them, echoes of the day's arguments still rang. They had continued right up until Lyssera stood and demanded that they end deliberations for the evening, but Azhani could only feel the dizzying sensation that fate had once again grabbed her in its claws and was dragging her right into a life she wasn't sure she wanted, but had to live.

Quietly, she said, "At least that nonsense about you leading the armies has been put to rest."

Lyssera snorted. "Aye, but what will they think up next to avoid the obvious?"

"Barrengar looked ready to drag poor Jantis up and slap the mantle on him right then."

"Right up until Jantis threatened to cut off his most prized possession," Lyssera said with a sour laugh. "It has to be you, my friend."

"I know. It's going to change everything, though. And you'll need to make it painfully clear how much power I have."

They shared a glance. No warleader should ever have to say that. All tradition stated that the warleader was the ultimate head of a kingdom's army, but there was no way the nobles of Y'Syr would consent to allowing Azhani full control.

"I'll find a way to word it so they can choke it down," Lyssera said sadly. They paused outside the door to her quarters. "If it were my decision alone…" She shook her head. "You'd have been wearing the mantle from the moment you pledged yourself to me."

"Your confidence means everything, Lyss."

She smiled. "Ylera loved you, Azhani. That bought you my trust no matter what else you may have done. Are you ready to face it?"

"I have to. Y'Myran is beset on all sides, and if Y'Syr fails to stop the rimerbeasts, then who else would try? No, whatever is behind this curse of monstrous plagues is counting on my not being there. I can feel it." Her expression hardened. "I'm going to make sure they get a nasty surprise."

Gently, Lyssera kissed Azhani's cheek. "Good. Now, I must eat! Tomorrow, I will tell the council my decision. After that you will have five days before the ceremony."

Azhani nodded. "I understand. Good night, my queen," she said, bowing respectfully before turning and walking away, her mind roiling with thoughts of her future.

The shadows of Y'Syria were a familiar home to Azhani as she prowled from street to street, drinking in the fog-dusted vista of the lake. Blinking back visions of the past, she studied the structures she had first seen twenty years ago, when she and Thodan had come through Banner Gate to sue the elves for peace.

Then the sights, sounds, and smells of the city had been foreign; now they were a comfort. At one time in her life, she had planned to share them all with her beloved Ylera, but Ylera was gone—a heartbreak she thought she would never survive, and yet here she was.

Falling. Twain's grace, she could feel herself stumbling right down the same path that had ended in Ylera's arms, but the face she saw this time wasn't shaped like Y'Syr's queen. No, what filled her with a longing she could no longer deny were golden curls shrouded by stardancer crimson and half-hiding Kyrian's impishly wonderful smile. All Azhani had to do was close her eyes and Kyrian was there in her mind's eye, looking over her shoulder as they rode toward Y'Syria, the joy and awe she felt at entering the city of trees so bright it nearly stopped Azhani's heart to see it.

The kind, gentle, warm, and most of all feisty young woman had taken Azhani from a broken, dying shadow to a strong warrior who was once again ready to don the mantle of warleader. *Astariu moves in many ways, and most are more mysterious and cunning than I can ever fathom.*

Worn brick became weathered wood under her feet as she made her way to the docks, stopping to buy a mug of hot cider from a cart parked near a warehouse. A fisherman's bench was her goal, and there she sat, staring into the fog, and quietly admitted a truth to herself that had been growing for weeks.

"I am in love." Speaking the words aloud, even if only to a sleepy gull perched upon a nearby pylon, felt like pure relief. It was also terrifying.

For months, all she had been able to feel was hate and grief. Slowly, shred by shred, life returned to her heart. First had come the kindness of an old woman, then Kyrian's fierceness in healing her, then finding Elisira and her crazy but beloved Y'Noran king in the wilderness—what a boon that was! Without that meeting, she might never have been given the sword that rested against her shoulder. Gormerath was a king's gift, from the hand of a king who called her friend.

Padreg had known, had somehow seen what was happening between her and Kyrian. *That ridiculous bet. I was so sure of winning.* She shook her head, wondering what he'd say if he knew where her thoughts were today.

She closed her eyes and conjured an image of Ylera lying dead in her arms. Pain clenched tightly in her chest—pain that would never truly leave, she suspected. But it was tempered, even shielded, by an immediate memory of Kyrian looking up at her and grinning as she tickled her nose with an owldragon's feather.

Kyrian's lips had tasted like honey and tart jam. Azhani touched her mouth and shivered, wanting to race to the castle and taste them again just to remind herself that it had been real.

The fact that Kyrian and Ylera had been friends had been stunning at first, but somehow, it felt right. Perfect, even, that her first love should have known her new one. She wondered if Ylera would approve. Thought maybe she might, given how well Lyssera and Kyrian got along.

Azhani wanted Kyrian, craved to learn if there was something behind that first, tentative kiss besides rapidly beating hearts and the wild heat of lust. What she needed was the courage to pursue the answer.

Draining her mug, she turned to look back at the massive complex of trees that made up Oakheart, and wondered whether if she gazed upon it long enough, the answers would write themselves in its leaves.

Kyrian stirred. The knocking was so subtle, it could have been nothing more than the brush of wind against Oakheart's branches. It was insistent and carved into her dreams, pulling her from her bed in a drowsy tumble. Mumbling sleepily, she tugged a robe off the back of a nearby chair and slipped it on, shivering as the faint chill in the air penetrated its thin layers.

Most denizens of Oakheart kept themselves fully covered in the event of a nocturnal summons, but Kyrian could not bring herself to be restricted by the thick layers of cloth most of the wealthy ladies wrapped around their bodies before bed. Thus she had only the single garment, but it was enough to satisfy the bounds of propriety. Rubbing her eyes, she made her way to the door, expecting to see one of the pages waiting on the other side with news of an illness that required her skills. What she found instead was Azhani standing there, her expression carved into a mask of desperate need.

"Azhani?" she said, startled and more than a little worried.

"I watched all night," she murmured, hanging her head. "But learned nothing. So I came to you, hoping you would let me in."

Stepping aside, Kyrian smiled warmly. "I am always here for you."

Azhani stumbled inside, wobbling about unsteadily until she reached the bed, where she dropped onto its edge as if her legs could no longer bear her weight.

Concern roared to life as Kyrian quickly closed the door and hurried to join her. "Are you…drunk?" She mentally rummaged through the cures she could concoct for the inevitable hangover.

Azhani laughed. It was such a rich, beautiful sound that Kyrian's breath caught in her throat. "Goddess, no. If I was, I might be better able to understand what's going on inside me." Turning, she offered Kyrian a winsome smile and then just *stared* at her.

To be caught in that gaze—it was like having Azhani's hands slide all over her body, material be damned! Kyrian's cheeks heated and she swallowed heavily, her mouth suddenly dry. The pit of her stomach contracted and she wanted, so much, to lean in and kiss her again, to discover if she still tasted of apples.

"W-what do you need?" she whispered, biting her lip and feeling very shy of a sudden.

"You," Azhani replied, lifting her fingers to trace the curve of Kyrian's cheeks. "I need you."

Air vanished. The distance between them evaporated as she sank against her. Kyrian's whole body was made of hunger and fire and all she could do was fall endlessly into Azhani's indigo eyes. Shadows danced, wrapping them both, and Kyrian felt like the pale moon against Azhani's lush darkness. She wanted to melt into her, but uncertainty kept a wall between them.

"I—" she rasped.

Azhani stilled her with a touch. "You kissed me."

Oh Goddess. "Yes." She blinked, working up the nerve to speak again. "You kissed me."

"I know," Azhani said softly. "Do you love me, Kyrian?"

Stunned, Kyrian could only sit there, gaping. How could she ask that? How could she want the answer to that question? Every fiber of her screamed at her to say yes even as her thoughts cowered in fear. *What if she doesn't want me?* They had kissed. Was it wrong? It had felt so right, so perfect, but was perfection enough?

"Azhani…I…" There was no forcing the words out. Not now, not when she was damn near stripped bare.

Standing so quickly that Kyrian nearly fell, Azhani strode away. "I'm sorry to have awakened you. I will see you at breakfast."

In horror, Kyrian watched her go, every line of her body twisted into shapes of dejection and forced pride. "Azhani!" Air rushed beneath her feet as she threw herself upright and reached for her. "No, please," Kyrian whispered, arresting Azhani's steps just as she got to the door. Slowly, she turned, the room's lamps casting golden shadows over her dusky skin. Kyrian moved closer, stretched her hand out, and, throwing fear to the wind, said, "Goddess, yes, I love you." Then she froze as she realized what she'd said. *The secrets between us are vanishing.* "Do you… I hope you—" She gasped as Azhani grabbed her and spun her around, pinning her to the door.

Without speaking, Azhani touched her, stroking her throat, her ears, her cheeks, and then slowly shaping her lips, tracing them over and over until Kyrian felt like she was going to be incinerated by desire.

With a sudden, impish smile, she reached up, slipped her fingers into Azhani's braids, and tugged, tipping her head up to brush her mouth against Azhani's. It was everything she had craved, but now, now she had to have more. Moaning softly, she thrust her tongue into Azhani's mouth, exhaling sharply when she felt the fabric of her robe slip aside and Azhani's hand slide down her body, blunt nails scraping at her abdomen and ribs in ticklish, tantalizing patterns that left her dizzy and aching.

"Goddess," she groaned, diving into the kiss with an intensity that should have frightened her, but only made her want more. Their teeth clashed. Her lip tore and the pain was momentary, yet also incredible, because it was lust unbound—the same lust that sent her hands questing to map the curves of Azhani's ass.

"Kyrian, oh my Kyrian," Azhani whispered, kissing her again and again, cupping her breast and sliding her thumb in ever-tightening circles around Kyrian's nipple.

"Azhi, oh Azhi." She couldn't stop touching her, tugging at the fabric of Azhani's clothes and the buckles to the baldric that, even now, hung over her shoulder. "Got to—get this off!" she said, shoving her away.

A bit sheepishly, Azhani mumbled, "Sorry," and slid the sword off. After setting it in the corner of the room, she returned to Kyrian, capturing her face in her hands and kissing her hungrily.

"Yes," Kyrian hissed, wrapping her leg around Azhani's and grinding against her wantonly. Surrendering to the liquid pulse of need that flowed around them, Kyrian threw her head back and moaned loudly when Azhani covered her throat in wet, languid kisses. Azhani's doublet finally opened and, with a grateful cry, Kyrian pushed her hands inside, caressing her breasts eagerly.

"Oh Goddess," Azhani whispered, sudden tears streaking her cheeks. "I never thought I would feel so much again."

"But you do." Tenderly, Kyrian touched her, shaping tiny whorls and spirals over Azhani's skin.

"Yes," she growled, crushing their mouths together, fusing them in an embrace that was as desperate as it was passionate.

She whimpered in sudden pain and Azhani nearly leaped away from her. "Did I hurt you?"

Ruefully, Kyrian smiled, then touched her lip. There was blood. "It's split," she said. "But it's all right."

Azhani cursed. "I'm so very sorry."

With a soft laugh, Kyrian shook her head. "Don't be. I'm not." Licking the soreness away, she smiled invitingly and purred, "Kiss me again."

Hesitantly, Azhani shook her head. "I…no. I don't ever want to hurt you," she said, delicately touching the tiny wound before drifting feather-light kisses over Kyrian's cheeks, nose, and chin.

"You won't," Kyrian said, but Azhani shook her head again.

"I'm scared," she murmured.

"I know." Things were changing. The passion that had possessed them was tempered now, though not destroyed. Kyrian kissed her, curling her fingers around the nape of her neck and scratching slowly. "It's too much, isn't it?" Inside, Kyrian was going insane, wanting, needing this to continue, to hold onto every moment as if it was the last. Yet she couldn't force it, couldn't make Azhani take that last step that would forever silence the ghosts of the past.

"It's too raw. Want…so much," Azhani rasped, brushing her knuckles against Kyrian's breast. "And so afraid." With a sigh, she pulled her hand away. "I should go, before we…" Ruefully, she grimaced.

"Stay," Kyrian said firmly. Stepping back, she caught Azhani's hand and tugged her to the bed. "Hold me. Put your body against mine. I need you here in the morning so I know this isn't a dream." When she still seemed reluctant, Kyrian half turned, winked playfully and said, "I'll even put honey in your tea."

"Kyr…" Azhani whispered, taking a few steps with her. "If…I stay. It's… this isn't temporary."

"Goddess, I hope not," Kyrian replied with a heartfelt grin. "Because I plan to wake up next to you every day for the rest of my life. Now get over here and get into my bed. I'm cold!"

Azhani remained where she stood and Kyrian went to her, wrapped her arms around her waist and rested her head against her shoulder. "I won't make you stay if you truly must go, but I'm scared too," she murmured. "I don't want to wake up tomorrow and find you gone, again—nothing more than a wraith who excited all my most secret of longings."

Azhani drew in a shuddering breath. "I'll stay."

"Thank you." Tenderly, she kissed Azhani's chin, then stepped away and let the robe slide off her shoulders. "Your turn," she said, pushing off the doublet and inhaling sharply.

They had seen each other naked dozens of times before, but tonight it was different. Tonight they were not friends but lovers, and that made every curve, every muscle and endless stretch of skin brand new.

"It is cold," Azhani murmured while chewing her lip shyly.

Kyrian stared. How could she not, now that she could? Years as Thodan's warleader had carved scars into Azhani's dark brown skin and behind every one of them, Kyrian knew there was a story, a moment in time that had almost taken this very candlemark away from her.

Self consciously, Azhani crossed her arms over her body. "I know, there are a lot of scars."

"They're beautiful," she said. "You're beautiful. I've always thought so."

Azhani snorted. "You, beloved, are a shameless flatterer who should look into a mirror, because you are definitely the beautiful one of the two of us," she said, moving close enough to catch Kyrian in a quick but heated kiss.

"Azhi, if you want to sleep, you need to stop that," Kyrian murmured when they broke apart.

"I'm not the one looking at me like she wants to do naughty things," Azhani replied with a chuckle.

Kyrian laughed. "Point, but I'm not the only one whose thoughts aren't entirely focused on being good." She reached for Azhani's belt and released it, then tugged at the laces of her breeches and shoved them off. "You did knock at *my* door."

"I did," she replied, shoving the covers over so they could lie together on the bed. "And I will never regret it," she added as Kyrian curled around her.

"Neither will I." Pushing herself up, Kyrian looked at Azhani and smiled. "I want this, Azhani. I want you. I love you."

"And I love you," Azhani replied softly, pulling her down for a kiss that seemed to go on and on until only the urgent need to catch their breath drove them apart.

"Sleep. We are going to sleep," Kyrian rumbled fiercely.

"Yes, sleep, my love." Azhani sighed in contentment.

This felt right. Waiting, no matter what their bodies demanded, meant that they could see each other by morning's light, and if this was wrong, they'd know it. In the moment, both were so sure, but how could they be absolutely certain? Kyrian knew what she wanted, but what if Azhani didn't? Wasn't it better to allow her skittish heart time to grow accustomed to the idea that the love blossoming within it was true and real and not a mirage of shadows? *Yes, waiting is right. I don't want a moment's need to destroy a lifetime of joy.* They settled into each other's arms and slowly relaxed, trading occasional sleepy caresses. With the sound of Azhani's heart beating under her ear, Kyrian fell asleep.

Thank the Twain Lyssera gave me those five days. Azhani studied a thin strip of light peeking through the bed's curtain. Like a knife made of fire, it lanced over them, turning the dimness of their cozy confines into a truth she hardly dared believe. There, tucked against her, lay Kyrian, her face seemingly relaxed into the peace of sleep. However, when Azhani lightly ran her fingertips over her nipple, Kyrian gasped softly, shifting so that more of her was available to be touched.

Fascinated, she continued caressing her, letting her fingers drift over Kyrian's milk-pale skin, gooseflesh rising in the wake of her touch. Reverently, she traced the muscles of her arm, shaping every curve all the way down to her fingers, then lifted her hand and nestled a kiss against the palm as Kyrian smiled and turned to brush her lips over Azhani's collarbone, nipping the brief prominence of bone gently.

Her stomach contracted as desire raged like a whirlwind through her body. Trying to focus, to keep from turning this first morning into something cheap and tawdry, Azhani shifted and touched kisses to Kyrian's temples, brow, and finally, briefly, to her lips. "Good morning," she murmured, voice still rough and grumbly. Waking with Kyrian in her arms had knocked the edges off her worries and made her more sure than ever that this, this love, this life, this woman, was what she wanted more than anything.

Kyrian reached up and tugged on some of Azhani's braids. "I think I owe you some tea, love."

"Mm. Only if you can make it from right here." She smoothed her thumb over Kyrian's hip. "Goddess, I can't believe how amazing this feels."

Languidly, Kyrian stretched. "I agree."

"I could wake like this every day for the rest of my life and it wouldn't be enough," she said, feeling the truth of that settle into her like an oath.

"You, Azhani, are a romantic." Kyrian kissed the tip of her nose, then sat up and grabbed a waterskin from the nightstand. "And fortunately for you, I cannot bear to wake with a dry mouth. It's not warm, but it's definitely wet and sweet." She offered her the skin after taking a swig.

A tart reply sat atop her tongue, but Azhani forbade herself from saying it. There would be another time for such bawdy terms, but not today. Today was special, important. Today, she would reclaim the whole of her heart and heal the last of the wounds Arris had inflicted upon her soul.

The tea was mint, strong and sweet enough to please even her palate. "This is good. I might have to inveigle you to make this every night once we're in the mountains. It can get quite stuffy in a tent as the sun rises."

Between them, they drank the tea, playfully fighting over the last drops until Azhani pinned Kyrian to the bed and settled over her, the empty skin hitting the ground with a weak plonking sound.

"Goddess Azhi, just kiss me," Kyrian whispered as Azhani stared down at her intently.

She did, blurring their mouths together gently, then carving wet lines over Kyrian's throat and collarbone. Every inch of Kyrian's body was hers to explore, though she held herself thrall to her throat and mouth, unable to let go of the tether that held her to this near-chasity.

With a groan of pure frustration, Kyrian hooked her leg around Azhani's and flexed, twisting them around until she was the one who sat astride, looking down at her with a wicked grin dancing on her kiss-bruised lips.

"Kyr?" she murmured, scratching Kyrian's thighs lightly.

"I'm not going anywhere, Azhani. I want this. Do you?"

Azhani's heart froze. Right now, right here, the future waited. This is what she had looked for in the trees and found in the sweetness of Kyrian's kiss. "Yes," she said, reaching for her. "I want you, Kyrian."

Her mouth was seized and held in a kiss that left her utterly unable to do anything but hold on, wrapping her legs around Kyrian's hips and grinding against her fiercely. This was living. This was healing.

Her face was explored, Kyrian's faint, teasing touches making her giggle. She was kissed and she returned those kisses eagerly, looking into Kyrian's eyes so much that the color became hypnotic. Green, so much vibrant green pulling her deeper and deeper into this lyrical flame of a woman who danced above her to a song that made her bones throb with the need to be with her.

Kyrian found every scar and touched it, the sear of her focus making Azhani squirm. "Ticklish?" Kyrian asked bemusedly.

"Perhaps a little. And…the way you're touching me…" she said, losing her ability to speak when Kyrian kissed her again.

"How am I touching you?"

"Like I'm—"

"Beautiful?"

"Special."

"You are," she said, smiling then. "I love you."

It was unreal, hearing those words again. Feeling them, knowing them, reveling in the answering surge of love that caused her heart to pound giddily. "I love you."

Uncertainty made them both hesitant at times. "Your breasts," Kyrian said, brushing them lightly.

"Please," Azhani said, then moaned deeply when Kyrian covered her nipple and sucked slowly.

Later, when it was Azhani who had Kyrian beneath her, gasping for air, as she trailed her tongue over the soft curve of Kyrian's belly and down between her pale thighs, Azhani looked up and whispered, "Kyr?"

"Twain's grace, if you stop now, I swear I'll have Vashyra turn you into a toad!" Azhani bit back a laugh and moved lower, much to Kyrian's ardently vocal delight.

"You're intoxicating," Kyrian whispered as she splayed her hands over Azhani's belly.

Azhani smirked. "Better be careful, then. Wouldn't want you to get a hangover."

"Oh no, I want to be drunk in you." Kyrian stroked her deftly, tracing shapes that made Azhani shiver and tremble with each tantalizingly teasing touch.

"Goddess, Kyr," Azhani whispered, arching into her. She felt caught between an inferno and a whirlwind and was ready to fling herself into both, just so she could burn in the heat reflected in Kyrian's eyes. Had loving Ylera been like this? Had she ever felt so completely wanton? Nothing mattered. Not the rimerbeasts, not Arris, not anything but the way Kyrian curled her fingers in a slow, torturous rhythm that made every nerve in her body scream with delight.

She was ignited by ravenous kisses. They flowed into each other, becoming a shadow play of hands, bodies, and mouths. Skin was marked and bruised by teeth too eager for pleasure, muscles were left quivering and shaking as ecstasy poured like warm honey over them. Azhani was unmade, undone, and unmasked, stripped bare to the truth of her heart. Love, this was love. It did not matter that what they shared wasn't made in the dewy, gilded petals of bard-sung romance, for what she shared with Kyrian was equally precious and true. To it, Azhani vowed to cling, for it was the Twain's gift, and to deny this truth would be to repudiate their blessing in her life.

"We should probably make an appearance," Kyrian said much, much later. The day candle was half way burned and her stomach was providing reminders that it did not like missing meals.

"You're right, of course," Azhani replied, though she didn't move. Instead, she rolled to one side and began tracing delicate patterns along the inside of Kyrian's thigh.

Bemused, Kyrian shifted. Her stomach, it seemed, was going to wait. "I am?" She chuckled, then gasped when Azhani's fingers grazed a sensitive spot.

"Mmhm," Azhani murmured. "But I don't want to stop," she added, making her intentions unavoidably clear.

Kyrian moaned. "I don't think I want you to."

"Good." She shifted again and Kyrian found herself held in the most exquisitely, intensely pleasurable embrace she'd ever experienced.

"Oh Goddess, Azhi!" she cried as ecstasy uncoiled within her. "I love you!"

Lowering her to the bed, Azhani smiled and kissed her tenderly. "And I love you, my Kyrian. I so very much love you."

CHAPTER THIRTEEN

If Kyrian or Azhani had thought to keep the shift in their relationship a secret, they should not have pursued each other in Oakheart Manor, for by midmorning the next day, everyone in the lower halls was abuzz with the news. Lyssera herself heard her maids gossiping about it and found herself in turns equally pleased and dismayed. Though she had actively pushed the two women together, she now feared that blooming affection might find itself tragically cut short by the upcoming campaign against the rimerbeasts. Still, she was determined to give the two lovers every candlemark's peace that she could. In her prayers, she asked the Twain to see that between them, they learned that no subject was too sacred or profane to address. *Above all, let them be honest with each other, for only in truth will they find the most unbreakable of affections.*

Unfortunately, three days were all that could be spared to them. On the afternoon of the third, she went to Kyrian's room and found them putting away baskets full of freshly delivered laundry. That this was a job for a servant seemed not to bother them. They laughed and played together, and for a moment, Lyssera stood in the doorway and watched as joy suffused Azhani's face while Kyrian mimicked one of the most cantankerous stardancers attached to Lyssera's court.

Huddling inside her crimson robes, Kyrian screwed up her face into a sour grimace and croaked, "I tell ye, Vashyra, this kingdom is doomed! When ye have to settle for a paltry Y'Maran white instead of a true Y'Tolian red, why then, what's the use in living?"

Lyssera laughed. "You've Stardancer Deshka's inflection perfectly, my friend."

Kyrian blushed. "I've spent a great deal of time in his company. He's in charge of the stillroom at the temple."

"Ah," she said knowingly. "And a right old miser he is with the keys, or so I'm told."

"Aye! You'd think caring for Ambassador Windstorm would have earned me the respect of my own keys, but no—every time I required an herb, I had to roust the old man from his bed so that he could measure and grind them himself. It got to the point that I ended up fetching my herbs from Tellyn Jarelle, even though I had to pay for them," Kyrian said ruefully.

Stepping into the room, Lyssera chuckled softly. "And now you understand why many in the court frequent her establishment rather than taking themselves to the temple."

Azhani nodded. "What brings you to see us, Lyss?"

She smiled warmly, but felt uneasy at interrupting their privacy. *Twain grant they are not separated now that they have found one another.* Her smile slowly faded as the import of her news weighted her tone. "Arris has sent a messenger."

"Ah, and what does Lord Loose Breeches desire of you, my queen?" Azhani asked flippantly.

Taking a nearby seat, she shook her head in bemused disgust as she replied, "First, he proclaimed Ecarthus as True God, Master, and Lord of all and decreed that our beloved Twain, Astarus and Astariu, were little more than lies fed to us by the cursed priests of the Firstlanders. Then he went on to inform me that, as he was the most powerful king in all of Y'Myran, he was taking it upon himself to lead a chosen group of heroes north to hunt for rimerbeasts this winter. As merely a woman, an elf, and a paltry queen of an insignificant realm, I should hand over the bulk of my armies that he might use them as a 'hammer of death' to glorify his god by claiming a full and complete victory over the rimerbeasts."

Both Azhani and Kyrian gaped at her.

Rubbing the bridge of her nose to keep her headache at bay for just a few moments longer, she continued, "And, finally, he demanded, on pain of violent retribution, that I extradite you, Azhani, and anyone found in your presence, to his custody immediately. He means to have you drawn and quartered."

"Twain cast him into a river of shyvot that he might drown in it!" Kyrian cursed angrily.

Azhani gazed out the window, looking across the bay and in the direction of Y'Dannyv. "Shall I pack my bags?"

"Don't be foolish!" Lyssera snapped. "I told him I would sooner give my armies to the care of a blind drunk than to him. Then I made sure he understood that an icicle had more chance of surviving a midsummer's day in Y'Skan than he did of getting me to cooperate with him in any fashion. Furthermore, if he attempted to wrest you from my protection by force, he was making a full and open statement of war on Y'Syr, and in that event my armies would march on Y'Dannyv and burn it and his beloved Ecarthan temple to the ground."

Azhani blinked in shock. "That will earn you no friends in the Y'Dani marketplace, my queen."

"I've no interest in goods tainted by hate." With a sigh, she offered them a wry grin. "In any event, I did not come just to share this ill news with you, but to tell you that it has prompted me to adjust our plans. I can give you but one further day of peace before you must take up the mantle again, Azhani. The kingdom needs you."

"And I am here to serve her, my queen." Azhani bowed deeply. "As you will it."

"Good. Right now, my will is that you and Kyrian spend all the time you can in this cradle of joy," she said as she stood. "Let it be your bulwark against the storms of tomorrow."

A day of peace. Azhani stood upon a hastily erected dais in the center of Y'Syria, surrounded by the queen, her court, and as many members of the general public as cared to gather to witness an unlikely yet momentous event. Lyssera's heralds had done their job well, for as far as Azhani could see the square was packed with people. Only a single, narrow aisle remained open.

The crowd was noisy, the hum of their chatter so loud Azhani could barely hear, but when Lyssera stepped up to the edge of the stage and held out her hands, they quieted.

"My beloved people!" she called, her voice projecting by some means Azhani could not understand. It was not mystical, but rather intentional. Kyrian had tried explaining it to her the night before, but she had only been listening with half an ear. Besides, what did it matter how it worked, so long as it did? Lyssera's clear, strong voice pulled her back to the moment. "You have watched as the armies of our fair kingdom gathered around our beautiful city, and today I stand before you to announce that they come not for tourney or tribute, but for battle. Rumor, I am sure, hath carried upon its wings whispers of rimerbeasts, and I am afraid that this rumor is truth."

The crowd gasped in shock and fear.

"But, who will lead our brave men and women?" someone shouted. "Warleader Alyssa be gone to the Great Fields."

Lyssera smiled at the speaker. "A fine question. Who indeed should take up the mantle of my beloved sister? Should it be I, your queen? Will you send me off to slog through the wilderness, leaving the throne empty for a pretender's arse to fill?"

"No!" the crowd roared.

She nodded as she paced across the dais. "Aye, I am in full agreement. It shall not be me."

"But how can we be facing rimerbeasts, my queen?" a woman shouted. "'Tis not a beast season."

"And what of our cousins in Y'Nor? Do they not stand against ogres? And I have heard tell of dragons, kraken, and even giant scorpions!" another man called out. "What will we do to fight these fiends?"

Now the crowd grew ugly and Azhani tensed, readying herself to act if the need should arise. More questions swarmed about the square like angry wasps.

"Nay, it is not a beast season, but the truth of it has been proven to me— the caves of Amyra's Crest are choked with the eggs of those most vile beasts." Lyssera glanced around at those assembled around the stage. "Nor are we unaware of the troubles that plague the other kingdoms. This is why we must have a warleader, someone who can best serve Y'Syr by understanding the threats we face and dealing with them accordingly."

A weak cheer wafted through the square.

"This is why my choice, though perhaps confusing to some, is what it is." Lyssera half turned and gave Vashyra a quick nod. She and Azhani strode over to her and Azhani knelt before the queen.

"All know of the heroism of Azhani Rhu'len. Say what you will about the events of Banner Lake, but remember this—this woman is the same warrior upon whose shoulders the great and beloved King Thodan the Peacemaker rested his trust. We know Thodan and his honor—we know the deeds Azhani has done. We know we have found her innocent of any wrongdoing in the death of our sister Ylera, and thus we choose to claim her as our warleader!"

Lyssera shouted, dropping her hand down on Azhani's shoulder and squeezing it roughly.

Muttered phrases tumbled through the crowd. "Are you sure? Can she trusted? Will she betray us? She's a hero. Worked for peace. Saved hundreds."

Variations on those subjects abounded and Azhani found that she almost appreciated the controversy. It would be too easy, too unreal if they all loved her just because the queen ordered them to. *Better that they question my fitness openly than seethe and stew about it privately. That way sows the seeds of assassination.*

To Starseeker Vashyra's right stood Kyrian, a massive crystal bowl clutched in her arms. In it was water drawn from a blessed well in the temple courtyard. Vashyra dipped her fingers into it and then dusted them over Azhani's brow.

"Before the Twain, I cleanse thee, Azhani, child of Rhu'len," she intoned sonorously.

Solemnly, Azhani replied, "In their eyes I am clean."

Sunlight washed down over the square, bathing it in golden glory. Vashyra smiled and winked at her. Then she and Kyrian stepped back as Lyssera lifted a sheathed blade from the arms of the page who'd born the burden for the last candlemark. Holding it out to Azhani hilt first, she said, "Our land is benighted by minions of the dark and we, by Fate's choice, are without one who can lead our people to victory. Thus, I stand before you, and ask if by the sword Gormerath, friend-gift of Chief Padreg of Y'Nor, do you, Azhani, daughter of Rhu'len, scion of the House DaCoure, swear to defend Y'Syr and its people? Will you accept the mantle of command and pledge your life to uphold our honor?"

Feeling caught in the moment, Azhani lifted her head, looked Lyssera in the eyes, and gravely replied, "I will."

Lyssera curled her hand around the hilt of the blade and pulled it from the sheath. How easy it all seemed, this taking of oaths. Once before she had stood before a ruler and sworn such a promise of service. Azhani closed her eyes briefly, remembering, letting the past wash through her one last time before the future came to claim it's due.

The taste and smell of copper had clung to her tongue as she'd stood, drenched in blood, surrounded by fallen friends and foes. King Thodan, astride his great charger, looked down at her with pride in his huge smile. He'd dismounted, grabbed her arms and shaken her fiercely, loudly declaring, "By

Astarus' thumbs, Azhani, you are a fine testament to your father! You deserve nothing less than his mantle! Will ye take it?"

She should have been shocked, but all she could feel was numbness. *I did it, Father. I drove them back for you.* After Rhu'len's death, she'd done her best to step into his shoes and join Thodan in ending the beast season that had taken his life, but it had not been without its price. The bodies of the slain were mute testament to how deeply the rimerbeasts had cut into the armies of Y'Dan and Y'Syr, and yet somehow she'd brought them together, human, half-elf, and elf, and saved Thodan from being killed by an ambush.

Azhani remembered asking if she'd had a choice—after all, warleader was a hereditary title. *Thodan probably thought I'd lost my mind.*

Indeed, his response had been to laugh and tell her to stop asking such foolish questions. Then they'd gone and gotten drunk. *Somehow, I doubt Lyss is going to want to finish three kegs of dwarven brandywine tonight. Goddess, is this really happening? Have I earned my honor again so easily?* She looked to the crowd and saw plenty of hope on the faces below her, but there were also more than a few expressions that were dark with hatred, anger, and dissatisfaction. *No. Not yet. It won't be easy. The elves won't tolerate me any longer than they have to.*

"By the grace of our beloved Twain, I bid you rise, Azhani Rhu'len, warleader of Y'Syr!" Lyssera intoned as she tapped the flat of the blade against Azhani's elbows, then presented it to her hilt first.

Accepting it, Azhani turned to face the crowd. Raising the sword high above her head, she shouted, "By Astariu's name, I will guard you with my breath, blood, and bone until they have become naught but ashes!" The blade shimmered, then blazed to life, limning her in chromatic fire.

The stunned crowd slowly started to cheer.

As Azhani lowered the blade, Starseeker Vashyra began to chant, pacing around her in circles. After nine circuits, she clasped her by the shoulders, and pressed a gentle kiss to Azhani's forehead. "From this moment on, all you past deeds, for good or ill, are cast into the forgotten realms of history. By the light of our beloved Twain, I call you reborn, Azhani Rhu'len, and bid thee to live with honor, serve with grace, and love with faith."

The brassy call of a horn pierced through the cheers filling the square. "Let all now stand and bear witness, for the warleader is chosen! Long live Azhani Rhu'len, long live the queen! Hip-hip huzzah!" cried the herald.

"Huzzah!"

Azhani shivered at the power of the voices that now cheered her name. The scar on her cheek burned.

"I knew you'd find a good use for that old relic!" a familiar voice boomed out over the crowd.

Striding down the aisle that stretched before the stage came Padreg and Elisira. Both were clad in finery befitting royalty of Y'Nor, though only Padreg wore a crown. Elisira's hair had been braided to reflect the style of her adopted homeland and hung in a single plait down the middle of her back. Both looked tanned, healthy, and ecstatically happy.

At the edge of the aisle, they stopped and bowed to Queen Lyssera, then to Azhani. Amid their entourage behind them, stood a tall, fine-boned young man and a young woman dressed in the colors of high king Ysradan's family.

Is that Devon? Azhani was hardly able to recognize the assured, handsome man who had replaced the gawky boy she had said goodbye to just a few months ago. *And that must be Princess Syrelle.*

Descending from the platform, Lyssera greeted Padreg and smiled at his introduction of his future wife. "We are always pleased to greet our cousin from the south," she said cordially. "And I bid you welcome, Lady Elisira. Your deeds are not unknown to me."

Elisira blushed as Padreg replied, "And I am always pleased to stand within your fair city, cousin, though need and chivalry doth press me to beg a refreshing draught for the ladies."

Lyssera chuckled softly. "I believe drinks are definitely in order, old friend. Come, let us repair to the castle."

"I'm glad you were able to come," Azhani said quietly as they strolled along the streets of Y'Syria. Surrounded on all sides by guardsmen in the livery of two kingdoms, she felt almost safe enough to relax, yet still she kept herself alert. The moment she let her guard down would be the one time her enemies would strike.

"Peh, a few paltry ogres could not keep me from standing at your side, my friend," Padreg replied jovially.

Elisira snorted. "More like he wasn't about to let you cover yourself with glory without painting himself with a bit of it by proxy."

"No matter what his motives, I am still glad to have him," Azhani said as Padreg scowled.

"You will note that I have not come to the party empty handed, perhaps?" He gestured to a small city of Y'Noran tents that were populating the fields south of Y'Syria.

"Your generosity has been noted," Azhani said as Kyrian slipped between a pair of guardsmen and handed her half of an apple. Absently, she murmured, "Thanks," and kissed her.

"Oho! What's this?" Padreg said, only to wince as Elisira elbowed him in the ribs.

Azhani chuckled. "An apple," she said dryly, lifting one eyebrow as if daring him to say more. "Care for a bite?"

"I—no, thank you," he said, though by the mischievous twinkle in his eyes, Azhani sensed this would not be the last time she would have to discuss her love life with Padreg Keelan.

Damn me and that Twain cursed bet!

The young woman currently attached to Devon's side was indeed Princess Syrelle, daughter of high king Ysradan. From Elisira, Azhani learned that she was older than Devon, though perhaps a year younger than Allyndev. For one so young, Syrelle carried herself with grace befitting a princess of the Ymarych house and spoke in calm, measured tones whenever a question was put to her.

Looking upon her, Azhani felt that Syrelle favored her mother in appearance, for she was slight, with a shock of gloriously bright red hair that fell past her waist in carefully plaited braids. It was her eyes that marked her as Ysradan's daughter, for they were of a shade of teal so vibrant they seemed like gems plucked from the heart of a dwarven mine. Many a passerby stopped to stare at her and Devon, Azhani noted, was utterly and completely smitten with her. *And if the look on Allyndev's face is any indication, he finds the princess just as beautiful.*

When the party stopped to admire a troupe of minstrels and jugglers, Padreg touched her shoulder and murmured, "I believe, my friend, that I have won. However, since your service has been given to another, I shall take two of Kushyra's foals instead."

She inclined her head, but did not speak. Kyrian glanced up at him, her eyebrows arched in curiosity. "What are you talking about?"

By the Twain, now what do I do? Heat prickled in Azhani's cheeks as she looked from Kyrian to Padreg, feeling quite uncertain. In her experience, women generally didn't like being the subject of chance games.

Chuckling softly, Padreg crossed his arms. "Seems you may have forgotten to mention something."

Meanwhile, Elisira rolled her eyes. "You must forgive my lord his smugness. He is over proud of his ability to sense the workings of *korethka*." Casually, she draped her arm over Kyrian's shoulder and told her, "In a moment of what we might consider sheer lunacy, he made a wager with Azhani that she would discover her heart was not completely sundered by Ylera's loss and that, in you, she would find purpose and joy that would stand equal to what had been taken."

"And I thought he was crazy," Azhani said regretfully. "But I've never been happier to be proven wrong."

Glancing between them, Kyrian replied, "I'm not sure if I should be offended—after all, I'm surely worth more than two untested foals!"

Padreg laughed. "Aye, lass. Ye be worth the whole herd!"

Quietly, Azhani said, "Personally, I believe you to be priceless."

It was Kyrian's turn to blush as Elisira chuckled. "I see that serving in Lyssera's court has given you a chance to hone the silver side of your tongue, Azhi," she said warmly.

With a completely straight face, Azhani offered her a florid bow. "One must do what is necessary to serve."

"Well I am glad of it," Kyrian said as she kissed her. "Don't be a sore loser, my love—and worry not, for I see no harm was meant."

"Thank you for understanding." Azhani was supremely grateful that her partner was so gentle-hearted. Another might not have been so forgiving. She turned to Padreg. "I'll not be breeding Kushyra this season, but when I do, her first two are yours."

"And I will come make sure your healers are as skilled as they can be," Kyrian said calmly.

Smiling brightly, Padreg thrust his hand out to them. "That is more than a fair bargain, my friends."

They shook on it.

Prince Allyndev is sure taken with the princess, Kyrian thought as they made their way through the city. *If the gossips get hold of this, it'll set the tongues of the court to wagging. A merger between the Kelani and Ymarych families would be very favorable, even if Syrelle is human.*

"She is like Astariu," Allyndev whispered, causing Kyrian to suppress a snort of laughter.

Moving closer to him, she put her hand on his arm. "My prince, your eyes give away your interests. Perhaps you should invite the princess to a meal?" She nodded over at Syrelle, who had stopped with Devon to peruse the wares at a clothier's stall.

A pained expression washed over Allyndev's face. "I dare not. Aunt Lyss has always told me to be careful who I favor with my attentions, for others might read alliances where none exist." He sighed wistfully. "Perhaps she will be among the camp followers when we go north."

Pinning him with a stare, Kyrian said, "Were you not paying attention when Padreg said that she and Eli were responsible for skewering at least three of the ogres that attacked their caravan on the road north? I daresay she'll demand a place on the front lines!"

"Truly?" he replied, obviously stunned by the information.

"Aye. 'Twas the three of them, in truth—Elisira, Syrelle, and Devon. Go—ask them about it. If Devon is like any young man his age, he'll be eager to tell the tale to a curious listener." She gave him a push toward the others. "And Allyn," she said quietly. "To the beasts with what anyone thinks. You are no prince of glass, too fragile to let others touch. If there is aught about them that draws you, then befriend them. There is no greater reward in life than sharing joy with others."

He stared at her a moment, then hurried over to the clothier's stall. Kyrian watched as he and Devon clasped arms and he offered Syrelle the most courtly of bows. There was, she could see, some hesitancy on both sides, but they were all of a similar age, and shortly, the three were laughing as each of them picked up various items and held them up for the opinions of the others.

"Clever, my love." Azhani slipped her arms around Kyrian's waist and rested her chin on her shoulder. "I had wondered how I might inveigle them to work together. Devon has been trained by me, Syrelle no doubt by her father or one his masters-at-arms, and Allyn, of course, is also a student of mine, which leads me to think that education will continue even as we travel.

All three will do much better if they have each other to see as comrades and competition."

Kyrian chuckled. Half turning, she kissed Azhani's jaw. "Oh love, you are always thinking tactically. I merely wanted Allyn to make some friends—especially since he seems quite taken by the princess."

"Ah, yes. But then, so is Devon. I hope that will not cause problems." Azhani scowled in concern. "I do not wish to be a mender of broken hearts."

"Then perhaps you will be blessed by Astariu and they will choose to take a different road together," Kyrian said as the three new friends wandered over to a wine seller's cart.

In time, they arrived at Oakheart. They were met by Queen Lyssera's chatelaine, who took charge of Padreg and his entourage, leading them to their rooms while Azhani went off to meet with the captains of Lyssera's guard in order to discuss battle plans.

Kyrian wrapped her courage around her like a shield and went to visit Starseeker Vashyra about a rather delicate matter that needed to be resolved before they went north.

Having lost her baton in the struggle with Kasyrin Darkchilde's shade, Kyrian discovered she felt almost naked without the comforting weight of the weapon at her side. Though she chose not to seek battle, if one found her, she intended to be able to stand as strong as any of Azhani's soldiers.

"Ah, friend Kyrian," Vashyra said, holding her arms out in welcome as she entered the temple sanctuary. "It is good of you to visit."

"Thank you, Priestess," she replied, bowing deeply. When she straightened, she smoothed her hands over the front of her robes, trying to soothe away her nerves, and said, "I-I am here to request a new baton."

A stardancer's baton was a special object. In fact, most average Y'Myrani had no clue as to the exacting specifications the followers of the Twain used to craft the deceptively simple weapons. Sages studied them, blacksmiths spent years perfecting them, and yet only a few were ever made each year, for they were fitted to the wielder. This meant that no two batons were ever alike, though they all bore a similar form. Each had to be crafted to the wielder's needs, for each must serve their bearer without causing them to stumble in the Dance while still being strong enough to crush a man's skull if need be.

Vashyra nodded. "I've been expecting you. Come." Leaving the sanctuary, they made their way to the temple armory. Here they found racks of swords, maces, and other armaments meant for the brotherhood of itinerant scholars who pledged themselves to Astarus, but none of the old trunks or chests yielded a rune-scribed baton blank.

Kyrian sighed. "I should have been more careful with the one I had."

"Don't be so hard on yourself," Vashyra said gently. "You acted as you should have, and your reward should be pride, not shame. I will simply have a new baton made for you and that will be that."

Kyrian scowled. "But…won't it take weeks to forge one? I'll not be here to see to the proper rituals," she said in protest.

"Aye, it will, but as I am going north, I see no reason why I cannot forge you one as we travel. It is not so hard to make a smithy when one is camped amidst an army—I shall simply begin the process here and finish it on the road. When you are needed for a ritual, I will send an acolyte to fetch you." Vashyra pushed up her sleeves and entered a storeroom. Here, she retrieved several steel bars. Weighing each, she chose three and stepped back into the hall, saying, "Come. We will begin by seeing which of these has the spirit to match your own."

Kyrian flushed slightly. "I hate to be so much trouble, Priestess."

"Oh, don't be foolish! It will give me great joy to craft such a simple and beautiful thing. Now, touch these, and tell me if any sings to you." She held the bars out to her.

Warily, Kyrian reached for the first one. Though the bars, in theory, all looked the same, there was one that was just a little bluer to her. Blue calmed her. Maybe it was because of Azhani's eyes, or because she had such joy for the blue skies of summer; it mattered little. "This one," she said, touching it lightly. It was cool, but not cold. The others seemed lifeless and yet this one…hummed.

Nodding as if she expected this, Vashyra smiled. "A good choice. Now, go and fetch yourself a staff. I'll not have you going without arms when we ride toward the uncertainty of a beast season."

Kyrian shivered. The last time she'd held a staff, she'd nearly beaten Allyndev bloody with it. "No, I'd prefer to rely on my skills at the Dance, Priestess. Staves are far too encumbering."

"As you chose." She inclined her head briefly. "Here," she added after returning the unwanted steel to the supply closet. "Wear this. The dweomer it bears is a small one, but it will help should you find yourself a target of attack." In her hand, she held a simple talisman in the form of the Astariun rune.

Crafted of silver and gold, it was not much different than the one Kyrian already bore except for the faint trace of magick that made her fingers tingle when she put it on. "Thank you," she said quietly. It felt odd to wear two talismans, so she removed the one she'd had since she was a child and tucked it into her pouch. Later, she would stitch it to her backpack, adding it to the beads and charms she'd collected during her travels.

Vashyra chuckled. "Don't thank me, my friend. Consider it my insurance against having to face Azhani with the news that you've been hurt."

Kyrian swallowed. They were going off to battle. Either one of them could be hurt or killed. *Oh Goddess, please keep her safe!* "Then on behalf of my beloved, I thank you," Kyrian replied.

"Now, shall we go find ourselves a nice cup of tea?" Vashyra gestured toward the door that would lead back to the sanctuary. "I admit to being possessed of a thirst, and I would like some time to rest after this afternoon's ceremony."

Nodding, Kyrian said, "Yes, I think tea would be wonderful. After you." *And I'll just have to pretend it's something much, much stronger.*

There was a grand celebration, of course. Visiting monarchs were not so ordinary that Lyssera could get away with a simple public greeting. No, her entire court had to turn itself out and show the so-called "barbarians" of the south how elves treated their honored guests. Following a grand feast, the major players in the upcoming northern campaign met to hear the strategy that would be presented to them by their newly mantled warleader.

Seated around the table were Padreg of Y'Nor; his consort-to-be, Elisira Glinholt; Ambassador Iften Windstorm of Y'Skan; his vice-ambassador, Kirthos; Ambassador Kuwell Longhorn of Y'Dror; Lord Jantis Morgan, the former warleader of Y'Syr; and the members of Lyssera's council, including Lady Sidar and Lord Bethelsel. To represent the temple of the Twain, Starseeker Vashyra and Stardancer Kyrian were also in attendance.

For Kyrian, being included in the proceedings was quite strange, but she was here at Azhani's request. It was nice to be able to greet a friend she had not seen for several days.

"It's good to see you up and about, Granther," she said quietly, giving Iften a gentle kiss on his weathered cheek.

"You did not think I would absent myself from the entertainment, did you?" he asked with a merry smile. "After all, as ambassador I have at my disposal a considerable retinue of, shall we say, young men and women with a fondness for weapons that might find themselves happy to display their prowess under the command of a famous warleader like Azhani Rhu'len."

"A clever way to circumvent any political maneuverings on the part of your queen, old man," Lord Bethelsel grunted. "I like it. Azhani," he bellowed then. "This fool just tossed a couple handfuls of desert grit into your machine. Way I see it, that just might keep most of those soft easterners on their toes."

Lady Sidar bristled. "Surely you are not implying that those of the east are incapable of fighting, my lord."

"It is not a matter of *if* they can fight, my lady," he replied blandly, "but whether that battlefield be draped in silk or dirt."

Lady Sidar scowled. "I assure you, my lord, that they are more than passingly familiar with the notion of a true warfare. Unlike our friends of the west, we train for something besides stealing cows."

As Lord Bethelsel began to glower, Azhani neatly stepped in. "My lord, do you have the reports I asked for?"

Startled, he looked away from Lady Sidar and then nodded. "Aye, Warleader." He shoved a collection of scrolls toward her. "Though what you'd want with our snow tallies for the last two winters I've no clue."

"I like to be prepared," she said calmly, then turned to Iften. "Your people will be very welcome, Ambassador, but please do remind them that snow is cold and rain is wet."

The ambassador roared with laughter. "Aye, Warleader, I shall make sure they understand that they should mimic their northern brethren, no matter how strange it may seem to wrap themselves in layers of smelly fur."

Azhani snorted. "And you, Kuwell—are your people are ready as well?"

"Aye," he said with a broad smile. "Our blades are sharp enough to take a hefty bite out of the beasts when you command, Warleader."

"Excellent."

Once everyone had settled around the table, introductions were made. Devon and Allyndev, serving as the group's pages, went around the room pouring wine for those in attendance. In a swirl of silks and velvets, Queen Lyssera swept into the room, accompanied by Evern Roshani, the captain of her guard, and Jerrad Beshar, the elven scoutmaster. Lyssera took her seat at the head of the table while Azhani stood and began to pace about, waiting until near silence descended.

"We are here to speak on what is to come," she said calmly, nodding to the scoutmaster. "Jerrad, if you would."

Rising, the deeply tanned young man crossed the room and stood before the map of Y'Myran that dominated the length of one wall. "My men and I have spent the last few weeks in the Crest and have discovered that here, here, and here…" He tapped areas that were distressingly close to the northern borders of Y'Syr. "…are several caves filled with rimerbeast eggs." Moving his finger west, he struck the area above Y'Dan. "Trappers and hunters have told us it is the same here, as well. Nests fill the caves."

"What of Y'Dror?" Kuwell asked quietly. "Very little word has come to me of late, but with the dragon, I cannot be certain if it is caution or catastrophe that keeps my kin silent."

"I have heard nothing of the dwarven lands, my lord," Jerrad replied solemnly. "My scouts are just now moving east. However, I would not rule out the possibility, as the beasts breed like flies."

"'Tis what worried me," Kuwell said with a grimace.

Iften frowned. "Forgive me, but I have not faced a rimerbeast before. Are they so terrible?"

"Worse than a rain of scorpions in the middle of a sandstorm, Ambassador," Azhani replied.

The old man gave a start. "By the Serpent! I had heard the tales, but…" He shook his head in disbelief. "How is it that these creatures have not destroyed us all?"

For a long moment, Azhani looked down at her hands, seemingly lost in thought. "The honor of Y'Dan's, Y'Syr's, and Y'Dror's thrones, the courage of their soldiers, and the meticulous plans of all the warleaders before me who took every lesson they learned in the heat of battle and made sure they were passed on to those who came after them." Saluting the scoutmaster, she said, "Thank you, Jerrad. Captain Evern, we'll hear from you next."

The elven warrior rose and bowed stiffly, his expression hardened with distaste. Kyrian recalled that he'd been one of those who had protested Azhani's appointment as warleader, though she didn't know if that was due to desire for the position himself or his distaste over a half-elf wearing the mantle. His loyalty to Queen Lyssera must have been more powerful than his disagreement with her choice in warleaders.

Gruffly, Evern said, "Those of our army who we will spare for this campaign have been assembled. Fully ten thousand archers, five thousand rangers, fifteen thousand cavalry, and thirty thousand regular infantry fill the fields and forests outside Y'Syria, awaiting the warleader's orders." He looked at Azhani pointedly. "We are ready to march," he added, just a touch of contempt slicing through his tone.

Sixty thousand soldiers. By the Twain—I can scarce conceive of such a number! Kyrian tried to envision it, but could not equate the amount with the flesh-and-blood men and women who would fight and die for safety of the kingdom. *And this does not account for those who come from Y'Nor, Y'Skan, Y'Dror—the temples, or even the Y'Dani men and women who've been practically throwing their swords at Lyssera's feet on the mere the chance that she might help them win back the homes Arris took from them with his Twain-cursed laws.*

"Thank you, Evern." Lyssera gestured to his seat.

He sat, his armor clanking noisily.

Standing, she began to pace about the room, looking at the faces of all present. She offered Kyrian a gentle smile before stopping beside Starseeker Vashyra. "Are the mages ready?"

"Yes, my queen," she replied softly.

"Good. Then our supply lines are guaranteed," Lyssera said grimly. "Whatever Arris may or may not do, my people will not freeze or starve in those damnable mountains."

Curiosity ate at Kyrian. How would they manage this feat? She wanted to ask, but was too timid. Lady Sidar, however, had no such reservations.

"Pardon me, but why should that be? I have studied war, my queen, and it seems to me that supply trains can easily be cut off or stolen by a determined enemy."

"May I answer this, my queen?" Vashyra asked and Lyssera nodded.

"By all means, Starseeker," she said, returning to her throne.

"It is true, my lady, that in the past, vast supply lines would have been necessary. I understand this to be so in other kingdoms, but we of Y'Syr are perhaps a bit more devoted to the mystical nature of Astariu's teachings, and thus we have developed spells that will allow—at certain intervals—the transport of goods and people across vast distances. This will be costly in terms of our magickal efforts, but I—and the mages of Y'Syr—feel that this beast season warrants such effort," Vashyra said calmly. "However, it will mean that many services others have come to rely on from the mages of the temple will become quite scarce. Please recall this before you send your complaints."

"Of course, Starseeker," Lady Sidar said. "Is there aught those of us who are not mage-gifted can do to aid you in this effort?"

"Pray. No prayer is ever wasted, for the Twain treasure our words of love and view them as they would a field of newly blossomed flowers," Vashyra replied. "And practice patience with others, for if we are to weather this, we must do so as a united force, not divided by petty arguments and agendas of profit." This last, Kyrian suspected, was directed at Lord Bethelsel. The old man grunted, but said nothing.

"Stardancer Kyrian, how fare you as liaison to the healers?" Lyssera asked then. "I have had word that more stardancers will come from Y'Len, but four days remain ere they arrive."

"All goes well, my queen." Kyrian felt uncomfortable as the scrutiny of the entire room landed on her shoulders. "W-we are engaged in the production of kits for each soldier that will contain battlefield-ready pain draughts, bandages, and antidotes for rimerbeast venom."

Nodding, Lyssera smiled. "Excellent. Do not fear to seek aid or assistance, for this may well save lives."

"Stardancer, if I may?" Lady Sidar said. "There are members of my house who I can spare to aid in the construction of those kits. I myself would be willing to offer a candlemark or two for the purpose."

Surprised, Kyrian said, "Oh, well, thank you, my lady."

This spurred others in the room to offer similar arrangements. Within moments, Kyrian had far more volunteers for her project than she knew what to do with, but she was grateful to have them, nonetheless.

Lyssera chuckled, then turned to Azhani. "I believe you have a plan to show us, Warleader?"

"Yes." Standing at the map, she demonstrated how the forces under the Y'Syran banner would quite literally cover every inch of the Crest of Amyra that they could reach, systematically destroying caves full of eggs until they began to hatch. After that, the army would separate into specialized units that would spread as thinly as she dared let them in order to keep the rimerbeasts from breaking through their lines and invading the vulnerable villages and cities south of the mountains.

The discussion went late into the night. Kyrian found herself dozing off many times, though she tried to listen and drank so much tea that she felt sure she could have floated to Y'Mar. Poor Devon and Allyndev ran themselves ragged fetching food, drink, and scrolls from the archives as everyone present offered advice on every subject that could be debated.

"There is news of the prophecy." Starseeker Vashyra's words jarred Kyrian to wakefulness. "I was uncertain whether it was worth sharing, but felt that holding it back might be equally damaging."

"Go on," Lyssera said.

"We had been going through what were thought to be documents pertaining to the Alyrr when, in a scroll nearly as old as Y'Syria itself, I found a line that echoes that which was heard the day of the sorcerer's attack. 'Forgotten by all, the banished will seek to break the chains and stride among mortals.' There was more, but it had faded to incomprehensibility."

Azhani scowled.

Lyssera offered the starseeker a respectful nod. "You have our thanks, Vashyra. Please, keep searching. Perhaps you will discover more that will shed light upon what we face."

"Could it be talking about the rimerbeasts themselves?" Kuwell asked as he put tinder to his pipe and filled the room with sweet-smelling smoke. "Are they not banished each season? And are they not our ancient foes? Would they not, if they break the line of battle, fill our cities, thus 'striding among mortals' and subsequently making a buffet of our flesh?"

Darkly, Azhani said, "If that's the case, then I'll be here to see that they choke on every bite. Vashyra, if you could see that a copy of that scroll is sent to my quarters? I would like to study it myself."

"Of course," she said. "Now, Kuwell, your dwarves will fan out here." Azhani tapped the map showing the easternmost parts of Y'Syr. "If any mountain clans remain, you'll gain their trust faster than my people ever would. The same goes for the tribes of the north."

Snorting, he replied, "You can't seriously believe those savages are still up there, can you? It's been over a decade since anyone has seen one."

"One thing I've learned, old friend, is never to count an old enemy—or a potential ally—as truly gone until you've seen their corpses burned and sung the pathsong," she said grimly. "Kyrian, in those kits, will you be including those honey lozenges you were telling me about the other day?"

"The ones for coughs and sore throats? I can, why?"

"Because I guarantee every single person will have need of the damned things before we've been a month in the mountains. And let's make sure we have plenty of lungwort, as well," she said dryly.

Kyrian chuckled. "Oh trust me, my love, that was the first thing I packed."

Though only Padreg and Elisira laughed with them, Kyrian was grateful for something that lightened her mood. It made stepping out of the room as dawn burned into her bleary eyes a little less exhausting. They had, at least, a plan. One Azhani took pains to assure everyone was as flexible and inclusive of all the advice given as she could make it. *Now all we have to do is execute it and make sure to get all of them before Arris decides an unprotected Y'Syr is a more interesting target than hordes of terrifying monsters.*

CHAPTER FOURTEEN

Like all things, war—or in this case, a cohesive military action against an invading horde of monstrous entities that lacked even the most rudimentary of leaders—took time. Though the beast season might be early, the life cycle of the creatures seemed to be following the traditional patterns observed over hundreds of years of dealing with the creatures. Because the rimerbeasts appeared to be spawning normally, this predictability allowed Azhani to utilize all her years' of experience to train the soldiers to fight them. This ensured that the Y'Norans, Y'Drorans, and Y'Skani could all work together. Tactically, it meant that when those units were deep in the hills and mountains, cut off from their traditional commanders, they would cooperate with each other out of habit, rather than by circumstance.

Over the weeks that passed, many people became familiar to those serving under the Y'Syran banner. Princess Syrelle was such a person, as she had demanded to take on the task of acting as one of Azhani's messengers. She had even procured a suit of the simple livery worn by the pages who served the army, eschewing the richer robes and gowns her royal status would normally allow.

"By the beast's bones, Devon, just take me to meet her, you silly oaf! I want to help," Syrelle snapped irritably.

Azhani looked up from the report she was studying to see Devon and Syrelle facing each other, Devon looking quite pale while Syrelle was flushed and scowling.

"But Princess," Devon replied quietly. "Wouldn't your father object—"

"The day my father objects to my desire to help a fellow citizen of Y'Myran is the day my mother kicks him from the marital bed for a week!" she retorted. "Now take me to see Stardancer Kyrian or get out of my way."

Tucking her report into her belt pouch, Azhani decided to intervene before things got too heated. "Trouble?"

Syrelle sighed. "It's only that this lunkhead believes me too tender of stomach to deal with the sight of the chirurgeon's tent, Warleader." She tossed one of her thick braids behind her shoulder and rolled her eyes.

Quickly, Devon said, "I just didn't want you to be deprived of your fastest messenger, Warleader."

Azhani snorted. "Dev, there'll be more than a few times when she'll be sitting on her arse with little more to do than pick her nails. If she wants to use those candlemarks helping Kyrian, I'm not going to stop her—and neither will you."

Sullenly, he lowered his head. "Yes, Warleader."

Prince Allyndev quietly stepped forward. "I'll take her, Master Azhani. I was going there to take this load of bandages to Stardancer Mistri anyway." He held up a basket marked with the weaver's guild emblem. In it were dozens of balls of newly woven gauze.

"Thank you, Prince Allyndev." Syrelle offered him her arm. Turning to Devon, she said, "Coming?"

"Well, I—"

Allyn smiled. "Come on. If we pitch in long enough, Stardancer Kyrian sometimes makes these amazing little bannocks."

Sudden longing filled Devon's face. "Oh! I remember those. They're delicious. I'm coming!"

Laughing, Allyndev said, "Great—can you get that, please?" He pointed to a second basket of gauze that was waiting on the ground next to him.

Clever, my prince, Azhani thought as the three walked away, chatting amiably. *You're still a little rough around the edges, but there are the makings of a fine man lurking within you.*

Of course, both young men had eyes only for Princess Syrelle. Much to Azhani's amusement, the young princess seemed utterly oblivious to their attentions. *And well she should be,* Azhani told herself the next afternoon when she spotted Elisira training Syrelle how to use a short blade. *King Ysradan would have my hide if his daughter was killed while mooning over a couple of lads.*

It did bother her a little that Syrelle seemed so determined to master even the most martial sides of war, but by Azhani's standing order, no one associated with the army would go unarmed at camp. Even the lowest pot boy, messenger, or laundress was to carry a long knife, a short bow, and a quiver of arrows. Rimerbeasts were only the most obvious of the dangers lurking in the Crest of Amyra.

Discipline, the bane of any commander of armed men and women, was tackled head on when Azhani instituted daily competitions allowing everyone the opportunity to exercise their aggressions in nonlethal bouts that awarded small prizes to the winners. Favorites developed among the spectators, and Y'Syria's gamblers blessed this new occupation at which they could throw their coin.

It did offer a new set of headaches when bookies vanished before paying their debts. This was one of the troubles listed on the reports that constantly filled Azhani's pouch. She would solve it—but until she did, it would niggle in her thoughts, burrowing and biting at them until, by night's fall she was crawling into bed with Kyrian, her head pounding and aching, too tired to do more than fall into an exhausted sleep while her lover gently rubbed her back.

She always apologized by morning's light, spending much of the first candlemark past dawn showing Kyrian that she was treasured beyond all things.

"You," Azhani said as she drew faint designs in the pale skin of Kyrian's abdomen with her lips. "Are my sanity."

Framing her face with her fingers, Kyrian smiled. "No, my love. I am merely patient."

Azhani laughed. "Are you? Who is it then that keeps trying to push me lower, hm?"

"The owldragon in the corner," she replied, winking at her. "And she's growing very impatient."

"Is she?" Azhani drifted lower still, bypassing Kyrian's hips in favor of the tender skin at her knees. The kisses she left here were wet, open-mouthed, and meant to steal the fierceness from Kyrian's glare.

"Beast!" Kyrian swore behind a fast, heavy gasp. "Oh!" she exclaimed in the next, her breath catching when Azhani drew her tongue along the soft curve of her thigh. "Oh, please, Azhi," she whispered, feathering her fingers over Azhani's brow. "Please..."

Her next words were inarticulate, which only made Azhani smile as she focused on all the bright and beautiful reasons she loved the woman beneath her and gave her every key to bliss she had to spare.

The week ended with the first of several small groups of soldiers going north to establish base camps and begin the arduous process of denuding the mountains of rimerbeast eggs.

Three days after that, another delegation from Y'Dan arrived. The Ecarthan priest in charge marched into Lyssera's throne room and demanded that she immediately hand Azhani Rhu'len over to him.

"And why would I wish to do that?" she asked with a vaguely amused smile. Azhani stood beside the throne, her arms crossed over the gleaming armor she now wore everywhere she ventured.

"She is a murderer and an oathbreaker! Arris demands his justice!" the priest snapped as he glared at her.

Lyssera flicked her fingers at the priest as if he were a particularly loathsome bug. "You speak falsehoods and lies, priest of worms. Azhani has been found innocent by the highest law in this land and all others, so take yourself and your liar's tongue back to your worthless master and bury yourself in the vileness of his shyvot. You'll get no satisfaction here."

The priest stiffened arrogantly. "I'll not leave without her!"

"Yes, you will." Lyssera nodded to her guards, who surrounded the priest and his retinue.

"You'll regret this! We will come, whore-bitch of the Twain! We will come and we will purify this tormented land for the greatness of Ecarthus!" the priest shouted as he was dragged from the hall.

"I think it's time for our naval lords to have some fun, don't you agree, Warleader?" Lyssera said as she turned and gave her a calculated look.

Saluting smartly, Azhani grinned. "Aye. I'll instruct Lord Imberlain to set sail at once."

"Good. Inform him that no ships bearing the colors of Y'Dan are to cross into Y'Syran waters." That said, Lyssera smiled a warm greeting at the next courtier awaiting her attention.

The moment Imberlain's ships set sail, Padreg sought Azhani out. "Is it time?"

"Aye. It has begun. Shall I have Maeven summoned?"

Chuckling, he said, "No, I think I'll give the old scoundrel a fright and find him myself."

"Have fun." She smiled briefly. "Just make sure he knows how important this is, Paddy. If Arris attacks us from behind, we'll be forced to fight a war on two fronts, and that's a recipe for sure disaster."

"I know. Maeven's never let me down—after all, he got that old piece of junk to you in one piece," he said amiably.

She reached up to touch Gormerath's hilt lightly. "I'd hardly call her junk." Closing her eyes, she added, "She sings, you know. Softly. A little hum that never quite silences, even when I am sleeping. It was disconcerting at first, but now…I'd not be without it. Or her."

"Mother said she would sing for you if she liked you. I'm glad." Moving closer, he reached for the hilt, then drew back, scowling. "I believe I've just been warned," he said, rubbing his hand lightly.

"Oh?"

"Aye. She bit me. Or rather," he said, holding his burned fingertips out for her to examine. "Stung me."

"That's…unexpected," Azhani said, wondering if it was something she should be worried about. "Kyrian's never been hurt—nor Lyssera. Both have lugged her about with no trouble at all. I wonder what she has against you?" She tried to ignore the fact that she was talking about the sword as if it was alive and had feelings. *Some things are not meant to be questioned, only accepted. Gormerath is a blessing sent by Astariu herself. I'll not be angering the goddess simply because it's behaving oddly.*

Padreg seemed unconcerned. "Our lore tells us that Gormerath is very… particular about who touches her. As a boy, I carried her just as you described, but now I am a man, and I bear a man's blade." He placed his hand on the hilt of his heavy broadsword. "Perhaps she was just reminding me that I am no longer a boy."

"Perhaps," she replied thoughtfully.

"If it troubles you so, speak to Starseeker Vashyra. She could certainly unravel the mystery."

The next day, Azhani set out to do just that, but found that Vashyra was too busy to see her. An acolyte politely asked her to return the next day, and by then, Azhani had forgotten the matter altogether as more pressing business took precedence.

With little to occupy his time now that his lessons with the mage, Gwytian Delvras, were postponed, Devon found himself incredibly bored. Gwytian had remained in Y'Nym to help Padreg's forces there against the ogres. Normally, Devon would be with Syrelle, but since she'd thrown herself into the war effort, he was at loose ends. In the mornings, he had lessons with Azhani and

Kyrian, but it was well after luncheon and no one had thought to saddle him with a task. So he wandered Oakheart Manor, constantly marveling at the incredible magicks that had gone into its construction.

Every path held a new wonder. There were archways that opened onto impossible-seeming terraces and gardens cradled within the branches and foliage of the grand trees that housed the castle. No matter where he went, clusters of chattering courtiers, none of whom ever seemed to notice him, were gathered, performing any number of "important" tasks—though to Devon's eye, those tasks seemed to include a great deal of chatter. Minstrels plucked the strings of their instruments for ladies bent over tapestries or sewing, storytellers held groups of noble children enthralled, and everywhere—absolutely everywhere—servants in Lyssera's livery hurried by, carrying out their daily duties at a pace that was dizzying to the former page.

In Oakheart's halls, gossip abounded. Round one corner and he could hear that Lord Stethen was cuckolding Lord Vertras, go around another and he would learn that Vertras himself was seducing someone else. Money was a frequent topic of conversation, for there was much gold to be made because of the upcoming conflict. Men and women whose holdings included vast herds of cattle, ore for weapons, grain—all were gleefully counting the coin they felt sure would be pouring into their coffers because of the off-cycle beast season.

None of it was of the slightest interest to Devon, who found the machinations of those in power as boring as plating grass for baskets and not nearly as useful. He supposed that he could be studying. After all, there was a grand temple of the Twain here—surely the starseekers within would allow him to sit in on classes with their acolytes. If not, Master Gwytian had sent him north with an entire trunk full of books—some magickal, others simple histories that were meant to fill his head with the practicalities of what he was learning—but he'd already finished reading two and written full reports on them. He didn't want to run out and have nothing to anticipate. Besides, he desired company, not the dusty realms of academia!

Pausing at the entrance to one of the many gardens, Devon was startled by what he saw. Kneeling before a cluster of flowering bushes was Prince Allyndev, diligently plucking weeds from the flower bed. It was altogether the strangest sight Devon could imagine discovering in this place of amazing things, for the idea that a nobleman of any stripe, much less a prince of the blood, would be sullying his hands with laborer's work was enough to make him doubt what his eyes were seeing.

Confused, but willing to seize the opportunity to speak to his new friend, he smiled and stepped into the courtyard. "Ho there, my prince! What ails the plants that you must forsake the bounds of propriety and see to their tending?"

Allyndev leaped to his feet, acting as though he'd been caught doing something wrong. Hunching his shoulders, he mumbled, "'Tis no concern of yours."

This was so unlike the Allyndev that he'd come to know that Devon scowled. "That may be, but here you are—dirtying your good linen trews. Are Oakheart's gardeners so lax in their duties that you must make up for their lack?"

Fury washed over Allyndev's face. "Oakheart boasts the finest gardeners in all Y'Syr, and were I not a man of calm heart, I would thrash you for suggesting otherwise!"

Quickly, Devon held up his hands in a warding motion. "Hold, my prince. I meant no offense."

Sullenly, Allyndev glared at him.

"Peace?" he said, extending one of his hands hopefully. Maybe they could go get a drink and laugh it off. He was starting to like Allyndev—he seemed to be more like old King Thodan in the way that he treated the people around him.

Allyndev, however, barely glanced at Devon's hand and instead coldly asked, "Was there something you required?"

Lowering his hand, he sighed. "No, I suppose not. My apologies for disturbing you, my prince." Bowing hastily, he turned and hurried away, feeling the burn of shame rising to his face. *Guess it's time to read another book. Maybe I'll try that treatise on flame spells. I can always learn better control over those.*

Sitting at her desk, Azhani stared at several maps, using different colored inks to mark where each unit of her soldiers would be deployed. When she was done, Devon would diligently copy them and send them to Lyssera. The originals would be in Azhani's pouch at all times. Only she and the queen needed to know all of the army's troop movements, though smaller versions would be given out to the captains and sergeants leading the soldiers.

The door to her study opened. Glancing up, she smiled in some confusion as Lyssera entered. The queen calmly pushed the door shut, locked it, and then made her way over to the wine cabinet. She then filled two large tumblers with a very potent brandy.

Bringing them to the desk, she sat and downed half the contents of one glass.

What's going on? Azhani frowned as she waited for Lyssera to speak.

It didn't take long. Pushing the other glass across the desk, Lyssera solemnly said, "What I am going to tell you now cannot ever pass out of this room, old friend, but I feel it is of such vital importance that the secret can no longer rest easy in my heart."

Intrigued, Azhani took the other glass, but did not drink. Instead, she merely offered Lyssera a curious smile and inclined her head. "What is it, my queen?"

Pensively, Lyssera stroked the rim of her glass. "There are some secrets one keeps because they are shameful. Some because they are scandalous. Others, you hold onto because if they were known, things would change in ways no one is prepared to handle. This is one of those secrets."

Feeling something akin to fear, but closer to anticipation, Azhani took a large drink of her brandy and began to listen. Over the next candlemark, Lyssera spoke. Her tone never rose much above a whisper, forcing Azhani to strain to hear every word, but after the first few phrases, she absolutely understood Lyssera's precautions.

When Lyssera was through, Azhani set her now-empty glass aside and laughed softly. "That scoundrel!" Incredulously, she shook her head. "I can see it, though. It makes so much of what he was doing, what he said, how he pushed…" She blinked back tears. "He was always so happy for me. I thought he was just being a good man." Rubbing her temples, she sighed and said, "This changes so much."

"Nothing," Lyssera said firmly. "It changes nothing."

Scowling, Azhani shook her head. "No, my queen, it will change everything."

"No, damn it. It wasn't supposed to be known, ever! I told you because I trust you and I want…" She pinched the bridge of her nose.

"You want the same thing I do. Peace. Prosperity. For everyone." Leaning forward, Azhani said, "And you know this is one way to ensure it. Just as I do."

"I know no such thing!" Lyssera retorted, but there was no force in her tone, just weary resignation.

"I swear, I will keep it to myself unless it's absolutely necessary. I know you want what's best, Lyss, but this…I can't let something like this sit in my arsenal unused."

Wanly, she smiled. "Ever the tactician, old friend?"

Spreading her hands, Azhani shrugged. "It is my nature."

Lyssera's face became a mask. "Then do not waste what you know, for it will be ruinous if revealed at the wrong moment."

Gazing through the windows at the mountains that could just be seen in the distance, Azhani nodded. "I shall make every effort to see that it is put to the best possible use, my queen."

At that, Lyssera stood. "Forgive me, but my hope is that you will find other, less distressing choices."

"I will do what is right for as many as I can—though I know you would choose otherwise," she said solemnly.

"Thodan said you were the most stubborn woman alive," Lyssera muttered. "I often thought he was mistaken, but perhaps I was too hasty in my judgment."

Azhani laughed. "A trait I'm told I inherited from my mother, Twain bless her soul."

"Speaking of your mother, do you have any desire to recognize your elven kin?"

"None whatsoever." Her tone was dry and empty of even a shred of emotion.

Lyssera nodded. "Then I'll consider the matter closed." Lightly, she touched the top of the desk and leaned forward, biting her lip. "As to the other—do as you must, but please, remember that some secrets are better left alone."

"I understand," Azhani replied softly.

And then Lyssera was gone, leaving Azhani to mull over everything she'd just learned. She did not like it, but this was something she would have to put aside for another time. There was too much else to do. *I will keep your secrets, my queen, but you should know as well as I that they have a way of escaping, even when you bury them deep.*

The day came when, with Azhani in the vanguard, the remainder of the army rode north. With her went all those who were closest to her. At her right, Kyrian was astride Arun and wearing a brand new set of robes made of patches of thick, deep-red leather that had been augmented with metal rings. The armor had been a gift from the couple riding at Azhani's left, Padreg and Elisira, each of whom wore the armor common to the Y'Noran plainsmen.

Woven leather that had been formed and treated to be nearly as hard as steel caged their bodies and boasted of the skill of their armorer.

Azhani's own armor was a gift from Lyssera. Made of interlocking metal scales shaped to resemble the clustered leaves of Oakheart's branches, it fit like it had been painted over her skin, and weighed so little she could scarce believe she was wearing it. Even Kushyra had armor, though the warhorse's barding was leather and thick rings, not metal scales. Of all of them, only the horse seemed at all excited to be facing the prospect of battle, as she practically pranced through Y'Syria's gates, tossing her head proudly when the crowd of gathered citizens cheered.

Part of Azhani was just as excited, but mostly, she was sick with fear. People would die. Never had she fought a beast season when dozens, if not hundreds, did not perish. Some would be those she knew and treasured, perhaps even loved. Her stomach rebelled at the idea that she might lose someone like Kyrian, and more than once she had almost ordered her to stay in Y'Syria with Lyssera just to be safe.

But Kyrian had made her choice plain to her the night before, when they were checking through their saddlebags one last time before sending them down to the stables.

"Azhi, please, stop looking at me like that," Kyrian said as she leaned over, unhooked a waterskin from Azhani's saddle, and handed it to her. "Drink. And try not to glare when they cheer again."

"Look at you like what?" she muttered.

"Like you wish I was back there, waving at you from the dais beside Lyssera. I belong right here, at your side," she said sternly. "And nothing will keep me from this place."

Azhani sighed. "I know. I'm just—"

"Worried. About supplies going bad, about who will live or die, about what we'll face—I know, my love." Kyrian touched her thigh gently. "Believe it or not, the rest of us are thinking about almost the same things. But we're here. We believe in our warleader. You should too," she said with a fond smile. "Because she's pretty good at her job."

Azhani snorted. "Pretty good, huh?"

"Mm, so I've been told." Kyrian took a drink from her own waterskin. "I mean, she's obviously scared Lord Loose Breeches enough that he's sent, what, three delegations to try and convince the queen to send an innocent woman to his dungeons? I'd bet on her victory any day of the week."

"You would, hm?"

"Every last coin."

Shaking her head, Azhani laughed. "Thank you. I needed that." She took Kyrian's hand and kissed her knuckles quickly. "Do you have any idea how grateful I am that you're at least half as stubborn as I'm rumored to be?"

Kyrian's cheeks glowed with her pleasure. "No, but I'm hoping you'll tell me."

Indulging her, Azhani replied, "You make all of this…" She gestured to the world at large. "Bearable. No, joyful. Because of you, I wake with happiness in my heart."

"Goddess, I do love it when you talk to me that way, because you're so much better at saying what I'm feeling," Kyrian said with a broad smile.

"Ah, beloved, I daresay we'll not need half the honey you packed for our tea—not with these two to sweeten the pot," Padreg said loudly.

Elisira merely laughed and swatted his arm.

The closer they got to the mountains, the louder Gormerath's song became, until Azhani was sure everyone could hear the blade, but no one else ever mentioned it. None of the mages she spoke to knew what it meant, so she ignored it. The hum wasn't unpleasant, just ever-present, like the constant grind of the waterwheel at a mill.

Days passed quickly. Nights and mornings before camp was struck were given over to instruction, with Kyrian sharing her healing knowledge with any who chose to come listen while Allyndev continued his lessons under Azhani's tutelage. Allyn was not her only student. Many wanted to learn from the warleader, and their numbers eventually swelled the camp so much that she recruited others to teach just so she could get some sleep at night.

Though the forest and foothills teemed with life, Azhani made sure her hunters knew not to denude the areas through which they traveled, else the people that actually lived there would suffer for their passage. Amazingly, many warriors—some from Y'Dan, others near-granthers in armor made of piecemeal and patchwork—met them on the road to beg for a chance to protect their kingdom. Most were sent to garrison the tiny villages that dotted the northern frontier, but some were given tabards and added to the ranks waiting for their chance to destroy the rimerbeasts.

They entered the mountains on a warm, cloudless day. From the very moment that the earth beneath their feet became more stone than dirt, Gormerath's song changed, becoming a near-painful howl that set Azhani's teeth on edge.

Wincing, she grabbed the hilt and tried to pull the pommel away from her ear. She was startled when something jerked the sword toward an opening in the rocks some dozen or so feet above her head. Instinct, always a warrior's friend, pushed her to halt the army, gather a small group of men, and climb up to the cave. She barely had time to find her footing on the ledge just outside the entrance when the stench of partially-hardened rimerbeast eggs slammed into her face.

The fear and disgust it inspired was primal. She lit a torch and held it high, revealing row after row of leathery, slimy boulder-shaped objects. "Follow me," she said as the others joined her. "Move quickly, but break every shell. Do not get the contents on your skin. If you do, leave immediately and seek a healer's care."

"Aye, Warleader."

Jamming the torch into a notch someone had carved into the cave wall long ago, she nodded grimly and drew Gormerath. "Let's get to work." As the blade cleared its sheath, the cave was lit by a brilliant, bluish-purple glow. Azhani was so surprised, she nearly dropped the sword. "By the Twain!" she gasped as her men started cheering.

Somehow, she maintained her composure and swung, shattering the first egg. The moment the blade came into contact with the shell, the jangling, painful shriek became an exultant cry of joy. It got louder and louder with every egg she destroyed. Soon the cave was filled with the sound of breaking shells.

A candlemark later, they staggered outside, the noxious, disgusting job finished. Taking a wad of rags from her pouch, Azhani cleaned the blade. Kyrian and Vashyra strode past her, hands joined, both already chanting the phrases that would cleanse and bless the cave, sealing it against a secondary infestation. The beast season had truly begun.

CHAPTER FIFTEEN

The air was fetid with the odor of burning rimerbeast eggs. Exhausted, scalded in a dozen places by the acidic slime, and aching from head to toe, Azhani trudged down the path toward camp, her squad behind her. Destroying rimerbeast hives was nasty, messy work. From sunup until sundown every day, she and her soldiers carved their way through the leathery sacks, denuding every cave they could find. By nightfall, they were all so tired, they could barely make it back to camp and surrender to the care of their brethren.

Half the army was always left behind to wait, to warm salves and prepare food and beds for the men and women whose day's work would hopefully save lives come winter, when the caves they couldn't reach erupted with full grown beasts.

This time, this moment when she walked into camp, shoulders bent and bowed, was Azhani's favorite. This was when Kyrian would greet her with a beautiful smile and a cup of hot, sweet tea. It made the drudgery worthwhile to have this comfort, this love to sustain her. Never before had she experienced it, and it made all the difference. Now she understood why so many of her soldiers had partnered, finding comfort and love even in the ugliest of seasons.

For weeks, they combed the hills and mountains, destroying eggs, killing bandits, and even stumbling into a den of hoblins—nasty, feral humanoids that were more common to the eastern part of Y'Myran. Discovering them here in the west had been something of a shock for some, but not Azhani. Such was the nature of a beast season. Anything that found succor in the misery of others would crowd into the Crest of Amyra, hoping to scavenge the leavings of the rimerbeasts. Azhani set patrols to hunt the hoblin packs down so that they wouldn't harry the army's flanks as it moved westward.

Almost all those assigned the duty seemed glad of it, eagerly racing off to slaughter the creatures. She never had to ask for volunteers, for there were always plenty.

"It really is too bad you have to kill them," Kyrian said after she related the latest totals from the "hunting packs," as they called themselves. "Hoblins are intelligent—they use tools and make weapons, unlike rimerbeasts. I feel like you should be able to talk some sense into them."

They were at a stream, scrubbing beast slime off Azhani's armor. Glancing over at her, Azhani said, "I would parley, but they don't speak a language we know. It's been tried. It may be that they just hate us, who knows?"

"I find it odd that an entire race would hate another just for existing," Kyrian replied skeptically. "Even the differences between Y'Dan and Y'Syr have a historical beginning."

Azhani snorted. "What, you think we stole one of their cows in some distant past?"

Kyrian made a face. "I don't know. It just seems—" She stopped speaking the moment Azhani held her hand up in warning.

Footsteps, faint ones, but with the tread of the armed and armored, made the ground beneath Azhani's feet vibrate. Suddenly, four hoblins leaped out from the underbrush, bows drawn, and fired.

Screaming, "Kyrian, get down!" Azhani drew Gormerath and knocked all but one arrow aside. It found its mark in Kyrian's left bicep. "You bastards!" Azhani yelled, racing toward them, swinging her blade indiscriminately. She decapitated one, then spun and skewered a second before they had a chance to nock more arrows. The third turned and ran, but was felled by an arrow fired by Princess Syrelle, who came charging through the trees, Elisira and Padreg at her back.

Trapped, the fourth hoblin drew a short, curved blade and slashed at Azhani's stomach. Swiftly, she used the body of the dead creature still impaled on her sword to block him. Jerking Gormerath free, she took hold of the blade, half-sword style, and parried several more vicious blows while Syrelle and Elisira each took aim with their bows. It was Padreg's arrow that hit, though, plunging deep into the hoblin's throat.

Without stopping to thank them, Azhani turned and rushed back to Kyrian's side. She found her sitting by the water, casually bandaging the wound. Both the arrow and shaft lay on the ground, having been cleanly removed. Dropping to her knees, Azhani asked, "Are you all right?"

She nodded, though she was quite pale. "I…I'm fine, I think. It was…the wound isn't deep." Picking up the arrow, she held it out to Azhani. "And these aren't complex arrows. It was simple to remove."

With an inarticulate cry, Azhani plucked the thing from Kyrian's hand, hurled it into the stream, and then wrapped her arms around her. "I was so damned scared," she murmured into her hair. "I'm so glad you're all right."

"Y-yes, I'm fine," Kyrian stammered, holding onto her tightly. "Just a little sore. I…I even remembered to pack the wound with antiseptic herbs first."

Elisira and the others arrived. "Here," Elisira said, thrusting a wineskin at Kyrian. "Drink. It's dwarven and should put some color back into your cheeks."

Kyrian shook her head quickly. "No, no, I have something, if I need it. Right now, I think I just want to finish cleaning Azhani's armor so we can get back to camp."

"I'll take you back," Elisira said with a smile. "Paddy and Syrelle can stay and help her."

"No, that's all right," she said quietly.

Scowling, Azhani murmured, "Go, beloved. I'd rather you were safe right now. I'll be back shortly."

Kyrian looked at her, then sighed. "Of course, yes. I'll go. Thank you, Eli."

Helping her to stand, Elisira started walking Kyrian back to the camp that was just a few hundred yards away.

Once they were gone, Azhani growled, "Padreg, I'm putting you in charge of hunting them all down. Take your best—I want every last hoblin from here to the border eradicated."

"My pleasure, Warleader," he said as he started scrubbing her gorget, then hissed and shook his hand as a scale pinched his thumb. "Ah, beast's bones, that stings! Those scales are gorgeous, but I think I prefer my leather."

"Stick your hand in the water," Azhani muttered. "It helps. I've done it so many times now it's become habit."

He winced as he plunged his hand into the freezing water. "I'm shocked they got so close."

"Prince Allyndev says they move like whispers." Syrelle made a face. "He also says he hopes the rimerbeasts are easier to track."

"They are. Rimerbeasts don't care who knows they're around. Hoblins do. Just another example of their intelligence, I suppose," Azhani said as she cleaned hoblin blood off Gormerath.

Padreg snorted. "They're not very bright, attacking you and Kyrian. Suicidal is more like it."

"Perhaps so." She ran a dry cloth over the blade before sheathing it. "I still want them dead."

"And so they shall be," he replied with a nasty grin. "And I shall be glad to be seeing to it. It's high time my sword arm got more work than making rimerbeast omelets."

Summer storms wrapped the mountains. Rain dappled the night, making Devon's current task that much more miserable. His boots were coated in rimerbeast slime. It was so hot he barely had the energy to do more than make a few half-hearted swipes at the ichor before giving them up as lost and pitching them into the burn barrel. Not even the rain could do more than offer a brief hint of cool relief before the ever-present heat pulled more sweat from his body.

Closing his eyes, he sat drinking stream-cooled water until someone cleared their throat. With a sigh, he wiped his face and then gave Prince Allyndev an inquisitive look. Allyn was a strange animal. One minute he seemed almost friendly. Certainly he was nice enough to Princess Syrelle—Devon would have to be blind not to notice that both he and the young nobleman shared a similar affection for her. But with Devon, Allyndev seemed to run hot and cold. At breakfast, he would be all smiles and friendship, but by supper he was snappish, rude, and sometimes, cruel. It left Devon confused as to how he should treat the other young man.

Syrelle herself seemed not to notice Allyndev's behavior, for the few times Devon had tentatively brought it up with her, she'd laughed it off as ridiculous—something that only served to make him feel, well, horribly jealous. *Not that Sy would ever bother with me when she has someone as handsome as Allyn to moon over. No, I was born a servant and no matter how far I go, she'll never see me as anything more than Padreg's scruffy apprentice mage. Allyndev, though—he's a prince. I bet her father would be more than happy to have something besides the rule of law binding his house to the kingdom of Y'Syr.*

Devon stared at Allyndev, waiting for him to speak. The last time he'd bothered to say anything to prince, he'd been treated with such disdain that at this point, he'd prefer the company of a smashed rimerbeast egg. It might smell, but at least the stench was obviously offensive.

Shifting nervously, Allyndev returned the stare, saying nothing.

Nearly rolling his eyes, Devon just sat there, letting him stew. *Why does he have to be so damned handsome? I could tolerate it if he didn't look like some hero from a bard's tale. He's tall and golden and I'm…less tall and scruffy, to boot. And he's got better lips, too. Syrelle's always talking about how soft they look and she's right. Meanwhile, my face looks like someone glued sand to it. No matter how many times a day I shave, it just grows right back. It really isn't fair.*

The staring contest continued until Devon could stand it no more. "Did you want something, my prince?"

"Ah, er…I…" Like a fish flopping about on a line, Allyndev seemed unable to settle himself.

Devon sighed. *This is not going well at all, is it?*

Making friends had never been easy for Allyndev, especially with others his age. Most either treated him as a ticket to power or an object of ridicule. That Devon had not seemed interested in either confused him. Added to what he had to put up with from the soldiers in his unit, and it made a recipe for disaster by day's end. Oh, he started the mornings just fine, but after a full day of being belittled, berated, sneered at, teased, and told that he was an unwanted bit of flotsam most of his people wished the queen had quietly locked in a dungeon somewhere, well, he just longed to go home and tend his trees.

Princess Syrelle was one of his bright sparks. Just being near her was a buffer to the harsh words. It killed him every time she'd go off to spend time with Devon, because he was so warm and friendly and could make her laugh with just a few well-timed quips while Allyn always felt so tongue-tied and lost. *He's adorable. She says it all the time and she's right. He reminds me of a tiger cub, only his claws are so much sharper, because I've seen him burn a cave in less than a quarter candlemark. Yet I still have this crazy urge to pet him just to see if he purrs.*

It suddenly occurred to him that Devon had been speaking while he was woolgathering and now he had no idea why he was standing there except Devon had the warmest, most friendly eyes and he really wanted to stop putting his foot where his mouth was.

"Ah, er…I…"

There was a flash of disappointment on Devon's face. "Are you lost, my prince?" he asked dryly. "If you turn that way and walk five steps, you'll find your tent."

Allyn winced at the sharpness of the words. "No, I...I'm not lost," he replied softly. "I...I just..." Helplessly, he stared at the other young man.

Blinking slowly, Devon reached for his waterskin and offered it to him. "Here, drink. I think it's hot and we both need to sit and cool off a while."

Warily, Allyn accepted the skin and drank. "Thank you," he said with true gratitude. "It is indeed far too hot. I've often thought of sleeping in the stream when it's like this."

Devon laughed. "I did—or very near—three nights ago, before the storm broke. I filled one of the tubs and soaked myself in it half the night. Kyrian told me I looked like a waterlogged corpse when she found me the next morning."

Tentatively, Allyn chuckled. "Some of the men in my unit snuck away the other day and climbed to that peak that still had snow on it. Sergeant Matthias nearly ran their soles bloody when they got back. He was livid."

"Probably just jealous." Devon drained the skin and then got another out of his pack. Studying it briefly, he flicked his fingers over the leather, causing it to glow faintly. After taking a drink, he grinned and said, "Ah, here we go. Perfect." Innocently, he passed it to Allyn, who took a long drink and nearly choked when instead of lukewarm liquid, out came ice cold ale.

"By the Twain!" he rasped, coughing in surprise. "You're amazing!"

Devon shrugged. "It's a simple spell. Master Gwytian would say it was a waste of effort, but I doubt he's suffered this heat. So..." He ventured a shy smile. "Why did you come looking for me, my prince?"

All his nervousness came stumbling back as he mumbled, "Ah, well, er... you and Syrelle are close, right?" *Of course they are, you ninny. She talks about him all the time!*

Surprisingly, Devon shrugged. "I serve the man who is fostering her. We've even shared a few lessons, so I guess, yes, we are friends. Why do you ask, my prince?"

"Allyndev—or Allyn, please. I-I don't need to be treated like I matter," he said quietly.

"You matter," Devon replied immediately. "Trust me, my prince—Allyndev—you matter. Everyone matters."

"Tell that to them," he muttered, indicating the area where his unit was camped. "Or most of Y'Syr. I'm half Y'Dani." He touched his faintly rounded ears, then indicated his face, which bore the unmistakable stamp of those of the western kingdom. "It's tainted blood."

"Beasts take them," Devon replied sharply. "That kind of shyvot is what King Thodan and Queen Lyssera were trying to change."

"The sentiments of centuries don't go away overnight," Allyn said, shaking his head sadly. "It's of no matter now. Forget I mentioned it."

Devon eyed him, then shrugged. "All right. So, you were asking about Syrelle?"

"Yes, ah…is this hers?" he asked, pulling a distinctive purple scarf from his pouch and showing it to him. "I found it caught on a branch by the stream. I seem to recall seeing her wearing it, but if it's not hers, I'd rather not embarrass her by making her think I'm offering some kind of courting gift." *I only wish I was free to offer such gifts to a woman like her.*

Taking the scarf, Devon studied it, then nodded. "Yes, it's hers. Elisira gave it to her shortly after she arrived at Padreg's spring camp. If you'd like, I can return it to her for you."

Jealousy surged through him, but Allyn grabbed onto the beast before it could spring from his mouth in a spew of hateful words. "Why don't we both take it to her?"

Devon chuckled. "Ah, my prince, you prove to be the better man." He returned the scarf. "Very well. We shall both go."

Surprised at the other young man's acceptance of his solution, Allyndev replied, "Lead the way, then." *Well, that went better than I expected.*

Over the weeks that the army had been crawling the mountains, the original scouting parties slowly returned, bringing news of what they'd discovered. Several men and women had to be sent back to Y'Syr to recover from terrible injuries, but only four were lost. Still, Azhani felt those deaths like a wound. Even as the others celebrated, she sat in her command tent, staring at blank pieces of parchment for a long time before dipping her quill into the ink pot and composing letters that would return to their families along with the scouts' recovered belongings.

This was just another in a long line of duties that crept in and stole her free time. No more did she teach evening weapons classes—there just wasn't enough candlemarks in the day. Many times, Padreg counseled her to delegate more, but she was determined to prove to the stubborn elves that an Y'Dani woman was worthy of the title of warleader.

Every part of the army's organization was her doing—from changing the scattered, uncoordinated camps clustering in the hills to a well-guarded pattern of concentric circles, housing the most vulnerable in the very center and the strongest in the outer perimeter. She also insisted that there be communal stew pots available for anyone to sup from and that their water supply be constantly refreshed. All of this was to ensure that every man and woman had plenty to eat and drink. She even inspected each tent just to make sure that the soldiers had comfortable beds. There would be no losses due to someone sleeping on a rock and being cranky before they started climbing up to the caves.

Eventually, she finished with her tasks and set out for her camp. It was constructed in a rough square and situated in the outer perimeter of the ring fortifications, for she would be no warleader if she was not willing to be first to defend those who would die for their kingdom. She and Kyrian shared a tent on one side of the encampment, Padreg and Elisira had another, Devon and Syrelle a third, and Prince Allyndev had one that sat on the border between Azhani's camp and that of Sergeant Matthias' unit, which was Allyn's current assignment.

Poor Allyn, she thought, looking at the tent that was the hereditary wartime sleeping quarters for a Kelani of his rank. *I'm glad he refused to put up the banners. It already screams, "Look at me, I'm an important person. Eat me first!"* The tent itself was the most hideous shade of bright green satin Azhani could imagine, though after it had been rained on a few times, the color had mercifully faded to a dingy, bilious hue. It took twice as long to erect as the regular round tents she and most of the rest of the army used and was stiflingly hot at night. It also leaked.

Unfortunately, there was nothing she could do about it until the next shipment of supplies—making sure they had enough food was far more important than a brand new tent for Allyn. It had a roof, the windows could be opened to allow for a breeze, and pots could be set out to collect the rain. At least he, unlike the many of the footmen, had an actual bed instead of a thick pad on the ground.

"Azhi, help me with this, would you?" Kyrian called, distracting her from her contemplations.

"Of course, love." She turned away from the travesty that was Allyndev's tent and went over to help Kyrian put up the oiled tarp that kept most of the rain out of their own tent.

"Thanks," Kyrian said once it was secured. "I noticed you rubbing your knee earlier, so I thought I'd try to get this up on my own. I didn't want to wake up with a face full of rain water."

Azhani winced. "Aye. It's been aching all day. How's your arm?"

"I'm ready to pull the stitches. Want to help with that, too?" she asked, smiling winsomely. "I'll be so glad to get rid of them. I still can't believe how lucky I was with that hoblin arrow."

"Aye, though had you been wearing your armored robes—"

Kyrian rolled her eyes and waved her hands. "Yes, yes, I know. And have I left camp without them since, beloved?"

"No, and you know I'm very happy about that." Wrapping her arms around her, Azhani kissed Kyrian with undisguised passion. "Now, why don't we see to fixing up that arm of yours, hm? Then maybe you can put some lineament on my knee so I won't wake up stiff tomorrow." She gave her a hopeful look.

Kyrian wrinkled her nose. "You know I hate the way it smells."

"It's not my fault you mixed up such a potent batch—or that it's the only thing that will put an end to the aches and pains in my legs," Azhani protested softly.

"No, no, I know. I really need to write Tellyn about it, though. She might know something I could add that would neutralize the odor without destroying its efficacy," she said as they entered their tent.

"If you get the letter to me before evening tomorrow, I'll make sure it goes out in the dispatch."

"I will, thank you." She removed her armored robe and sat on a stool while Azhani lit a nearby lantern. "Now, let's get these things out of me before I scratch another hole in my arm."

Devon and Syrelle's tent was of plains manufacture and, like the other Y'Noran tents, eminently suited for providing shelter from any weather. Waterproof, it was easily cooled by the simple expedient of rolling up the sides and was built on a sturdy frame that would take a great deal of force to flatten. Come winter, it would be an even greater boon, for there were felted panels that could be attached to insulate it further.

Large enough to house six and their gear, for Devon and Syrelle, it was akin to a palace. They'd hung a pair of extra blankets to divide it, giving each other some privacy while allowing them the freedom to open the space up when they had company. Tonight, however, there was little entertaining in mind when Syrelle rushed inside, rain dripping from her hair and clothes. Beside her, looking miserable, was Allyndev.

Wracked by an uncontrollable cough, Allyn managed to gasp, "My tent collapsed."

"I'm not letting him stay in that wretched piece of garbage one more night," Syrelle said sternly.

"I'm not going to argue." Devon stood quickly. "Let me go see if I can find some spare bedding at the quartermaster's tent."

A candlemark later, Allyn was sleeping in a freshly constructed rope bed, having been dosed to the eyeballs with one of Kyrian's foul-tasting herbal potions.

Syrelle studied him thoughtfully, then turned to Devon. "At least he doesn't snore like you do."

"And he's not quite the clothes horse you are." He grinned and nodded to the five trunks of gear that took up much of Syrelle's part of the tent.

"It's not all clothes and you know it!"

"No? You always seem to have a pretty new dress to show him."

She rolled her eyes. "Just because I don't wear the same two robes day in and day out doesn't mean I'm a fluff-headed noblewoman with no care other than my next visit to the royal seamstress."

"It's not the same two," he replied quietly. "You know very well it's—"

"Does it really matter who wears what when?" Allyndev mumbled. "You both look great. I'm the one who looks like a something the hunting cats coughed up."

"Hush," Syrelle said tartly, but she went to him, perched on the edge of his bed and used a damp cloth to wipe his brow. "Stardancer Kyrian said you need to drink as much of this as you can." She offered him a mug.

Allyn wrinkled his nose. "It smells like beast shyvot."

"It probably tastes like it, too," she said as Devon chuckled softly.

"Tell you what, Allyn, you drink the whole thing and I'll give you some of that apple cider I've been hoarding," Devon coaxed.

"Thought you said it was gone." Slowly, he drank the mug's contents. "Twain's grace, that's foul." He made a face.

"I lied," Devon replied blithely. "I was saving it for the right moment."

Coughing into a cloth Syrelle provided, Allyn fought to catch his breath as she gently rubbed his back. "And now, when I feel like I've been beaten by every stick in the forest, is the right time?"

"Yes." Devon produced a small flask and dumped some of it into a small cup. "Small sips. Sy, did you want some?"

"Aye. I think we all need a little helping hand to sleep tonight." Daintily, she sipped from the flask. "Oh, that is very good. Let's not waste it, though. We should share it again when we can all appreciate it."

"I…agree," Allyn mumbled, his eyes slipping closed. "I promise I'll be out of your hair in the morning," he added as sleep took him away again.

The next morning, however, Allyndev discovered that his friends had a surprise in store for him. A night's sleep and Kyrian's medicine had gone a long way to restoring him, but when he slipped out before either of them woke to go put his old tent back up, he found it gone. His equipment had been carefully stored under a heavy oiled tarp.

"What did they do with it?" he muttered, scratching his head in confusion.

"Well, I wanted to burn it, but Syrelle talked me out of it," Devon replied, startling him.

Spinning around, Allyn gaped at him. "You—but where will I sleep?"

Syrelle ambled up, yawning. "Isn't that obvious, Prince Allyndev?" She looked over at the tent he'd just exited. "There's already a third bed in there."

"But—" He didn't know what to say. People didn't just treat him like he was normal, like he was someone who could be, well, just like everyone else. He was either a prince or a pariah, never something else entirely.

Grinning, she said, "Don't make me beg, Allyn. With you between me and the snore monster over there, maybe I'll finally get a night's peace."

"I do not snore!" Devon grumbled.

"Actually, you do," Allyn said. "But it's all right. I don't really mind it," he quickly added.

Devon grinned then and clapped him on the shoulder. "So, will ye be staying with us then, lad?" He mimicked Padreg's voice almost perfectly.

"Yes, please, do stay." Syrelle moved closer and plucked a stray leaf from his hair. "I'll even give you a decent haircut."

"But, I, you, we—are we friends?" he blurted, feeling utterly confused.

"Yes, I think we are," Devon said as Syrelle chuckled.

"Yes, Allyn, we are most definitely friends." She kissed his cheek fondly. "Now, come on, let's get all this gear of yours moved indoors before it starts raining again."

Heart full to bursting with emotion, Allyn turned and picked up the first thing he saw and started carrying it toward the tent.

Behind him, he heard Devon say, "Don't I get a kiss?"

"Maybe, if you carry that box there. I nearly broke my back trying to drag it out last night. What's in there, bricks?" Syrelle asked with a groan.

"Armor, I think," Devon said affably. He grunted and Allyn winced, because if it was the trunk he was thinking of, then Devon was right.

I can't even bring myself to feel jealous. He deserves a kiss for picking that thing up. Beast's bones, I might kiss him!

"Prince Allyndev!" The tone of voice of the man calling his name told Allyn that the speaker had been doing it for quite some time.

Shyvot, that's the sergeant! Snapping to a perfect posture, he turned and saluted the rapidly approaching man.

Sergeant Layvendrel Matthias was a person with no patience for anything, much less Prince Allyndev, a fact he'd made plain to Allyn on a number of occasions. He also loathed Y'Danis, though he'd never said why. It had, however, made Allyndev's time under his command quite uncomfortable.

"Sir." Allyn waited for him to speak.

Angrily, Sergeant Matthias snapped, "When I call you, I expect you to respond double-time!"

"Yes, sir," Allyn replied immediately, wondering what horrible task the sergeant had dreamed up for him today. Last time it had been to dig a new set of latrines for the unit in the rain, alone. "I will do better in the future, sir."

"See that you do." Sergeant Matthias looked over at Devon, who was carrying Allyn's armor trunk into the tent, and said, "You're billeting here, now, my prince?" Somehow, he made the title seem like an insult.

Allyn nodded.

"Fine. Eat and get yourself ready. You're on first patrol now," he snapped. Turning, he took a long, leering look at Princess Syrelle's cleavage before marching back to his camp.

Syrelle grimaced. "I do not like that man. He makes me feel like I'm no more than a cheap whore to him."

"You don't have to like him," Allyndev said woodenly. "He's the sergeant. It's not his job to be liked. His sword arm is one of the best in the kingdom." With that, he ducked back into the tent and started putting on his armor.

"Patrol already?" Devon asked, scowling darkly. "I thought you weren't on until nightfall."

"Not anymore. I've been moved to first," Allyn replied. "I have to eat. Keep your boots clean, Devon. Be safe, Syrelle," he added, then hurried out before either of them could speak.

Allyndev tried to hide his wince as his patrol leader told yet another bawdy joke. One of the others laughed and called, "You seen the landscape over at the warleader's camp, Hawkins?"

"Oh aye," Hawkins replied, then elbowed the soldier next to him. "A man could burst his breeches smelling all the flowers."

"Nah, nah, don't be burstin' them, leave 'em lie on the tent floor and enjoy a good fucking," he replied, laughing hoarsely.

Though disgusted by the crass, brazen conversation, Allyndev felt like he couldn't speak up. The few times he'd tried had led to trouble he wasn't willing to deal with out here, far from the main camp where a soldier's life rested in the hands of the men and women of their patrol.

For the past three days, they'd traveled to over two dozen caves, some so small they'd had to crawl through the openings just to get inside. His patrol, a group of crusty ne'er-do-wells, had drawn third straw and were the last into a cave before the priests and mages burned it. Nearly every stitch of clothing Allyndev had with him had been ruined by rimerbeast slime.

It was punishment, of course. Sergeant Matthias had made that quite clear when he'd assigned him the duty. What made it worse was that the patrol's leader, Orindal Hawkins, was well aware that he had earned Sergeant Matthias' ire.

Which was why, when Hawkins thumped him on the shoulder and said, "Hey, Prince—why don'tcha give us all a little 'tour' of the garden you get to enjoy back at camp, hm?" Allyndev didn't punch him in the mouth like he wanted to.

Instead, he kept silent, hoping the game would pall. But luck was not with him today.

"We're waiting, my prince," Orindal said sternly as the rest of the soldiers leaned in close, their faces alive with eager curiosity. "You've been gettin' freebies from us for the last three days. It's your turn to tell us a bedtime story." When Allyn remained quiet, he murmured, "Unless you would prefer I tell Sergeant Matthias you were uncooperative?"

Torn, Allyndev sat there helplessly. Was this how soldiers were supposed to behave? Everything Azhani had taught about honor and respect seemed like a completely foreign concept to the people crowding around him. What was he supposed to do? He wanted to fit in, to be a part of the patrol, not the outsider who was always digging latrines and last person out of the caves.

Maybe, maybe if he became more like these men and women, if he showed them he wasn't some kind of snobbish nobleman, they might accept him, might even like him.

Taking a deep breath, he said, "Well, um, Princess Syrelle has a really, uh, nice arse. A-and her..." He licked his lips and then, to his private horror, gave them a detailed and very crude description of Syrelle's body. He left nothing out, not even the imagined paleness of her breasts.

By the time he was done, they were blissfully hanging on every word. Afterward, Hawkins clapped him on the shoulder again. This time, he smiled approvingly and offered him a flask of strong mead.

"Aye, that's a vision t'put a man into his bed for the night," he said with a broad grin. "Or into his tentmate's bed, if'n they be of a mind to share." He nudged Allyn's ribs roughly and then stood and wandered into his tent. It wasn't long before Allyn was alone, staring at the fire and wondering if he'd just made a terrible mistake.

But they listened to me. They liked me. Hawkins gave me mead. I'm one of them now. I'm a soldier.

In just under three weeks' time, Allyn found himself moving from Hawkins' patrol right through the ranks to serving under Sergeant Matthias himself. With his promotions, though, came an attitude change that he privately hated. Yet the more he behaved like one of the coarse, ribald soldiers at his side, the more they treated him like he was a welcome member of the group. Even Matthias seemed to act as though Allyn were worthy of some respect, putting him in the coveted position of egg spotter—first to enter the caves they discovered.

"Hard boiled, Sarge," he called after carefully prodding a leathery shell. That meant the eggs were too dense for swords and the others would need to use maces to break them open. Toward the back of the cave, he stopped and yelled, "Wet 'n ready!" about a clutch of eggs that were so soft, he could almost stomp them to bits with his boots. "Just like yer favorite wench, Sarge," he added, causing Matthias to bray with laughter.

As utterly disgusted as he was for saying such things, Allyndev couldn't bring himself to stop. Finally, finally, he had a place where he was more than just Alynna's bastard or the queen's charity case. Here, in this unit, he was Allyn, the soldiers' brother-in-arms.

Standing atop a rocky outcrop, Azhani stared down at the constellation of fires that represented her army and smiled. Pride flooded her. *This is what my knowledge has wrought.* They were a truly cohesive force. Y'Syrans, Y'Norans, Y'Drorans, Y'Dani, and Y'Skani alike had come together into a powerful army that had let nothing stand between them and the total destruction of every beast-infested cave that riddled the mountains.

This is where I belong, not on some damned throne. I want to be out here, in the field, doing something. Beyond the few administrative duties that were part and parcel of her command, she wanted nothing to do with the actual ruling of people. She would much rather raise a sword in their defense than put pen to paper and attempt to write the kind of speeches that tapped into the veins of history.

A light breeze, one touched by a faint hint of cooling air, dried the sweat on her brow. "Winter's first kiss," she murmured, looking to the west. They had still yet to breach the mountains north of Y'Dan.

Torchlight below caught her attention. A returning patrol—Prince Allyndev's, by the standard proudly carried by one of the riders. They'd been gone for over three weeks and she was interested to know how he'd fared under Sergeant Matthias' command. Layvendrel had not been her first pick for someone to give Allyndev the experience he desperately needed, but there'd been no other choice. None of the other elven commanders were willing to take the prince—either because he was a nobleman or, more likely, because he was part Y'Dani. She hoped he'd been able to bond with the men and women of Sergeant Matthias' patrol in a way that taught him some level of self confidence. It was an important trait for a prince to have.

"Astariu's tits, but that was an incredible run!" Allyndev exclaimed as he sauntered into the tent he shared with Devon and Syrelle. "We smashed those shyvot-sucking eggs into puke!" He flopped onto his bed and pulled a flask out of his belt pouch. Taking a massive swig, he belched loudly and continued telling them about his latest patrol, expounding on every disgusting detail to the point that both Devon and Syrelle sat staring at him, their faces masks of pure shock. "And then Katchyva had to scramble to get undressed and let me tell you there wasn't a one of us who wasn't ready to help her! Beast's bones, she made me ache to look at her—"

"Allyn!" Devon snapped, then glanced at Syrelle, who was blushing fiercely.

"What? Oh. So what? It's not like she doesn't have a pair of her own to play with." He tossed aside the empty flask lazily and then practically fell off his bed before he could get upright.

"You're drunk," Devon said distastefully.

"What of it? I've just spent the last three weeks crawling around in rimerbeast shyvot and slime." He tugged off his scorched boots and tossed them through the tent flap, then shed the rest of his clothes, not bothering to stop when he reached his loincloth.

"Oh!" Syrelle gasped when the burn scars that covered Allyndev's legs, lower back, and thighs were revealed. They were faint, but it was clear he'd been through something nightmarish. "Allyn, what happened?"

Looking down at himself, he shrugged. "What, those? Those are nothing. Sergeant Matthias said I wasn't good enough to get the easy jobs, so I got sent in last, to do clean up, the first week. He was right. I wasn't good enough, but it doesn't matter, because I got good enough." He smirked. "And now I go in first."

"Didn't the healer see to your wounds?" Syrelle opened her trunk and removed several jars of salve.

"Why? Only babies go to the healer, Sy. I'm no tit sucker," Allyn replied angrily. "I'm a soldier."

"You're an idiot," Devon said in irritation. "Sit down and let us get this stuff on you before you end up looking like ground meat forever."

Dropping onto the bed, he stretched his legs out and grinned wickedly. "You wanna put your hands on this body? Go right ahead." He leered at them. "Not like I haven't earned it."

Devon turned bright red and stormed out of the tent, snarling, "Do it yourself, then, my prince!"

Allyn curled his lip. "Some friend."

Scowling, Syrelle dropped a set of clean clothes on the foot of his bed and set the salve atop it. "He's right. You can clean yourself up, Prince Allyndev." Icily calm, she walked out of the tent, leaving Allyn to stare at the pile dumbfoundedly.

"Where's my hero's welcome?" he muttered, snatching the salve. The burns did hurt. *Pain is good. Pain means I'm still alive. Sergeant Matthias says I need to be a man. I need to put aside stupid dreams and take what I want because nothing will ever be given to me for free.* Well, the first thing he wanted was a damned bath. Grabbing the clothes and a towel, he shrugged on an old, knee-length tunic and made his way to the nearest stream.

Outside, Devon and Syrelle watched him go. Quietly, Syrelle said, "I used to like him, Dev. Quite a lot, to be honest."

The admission felt like a knife to the heart, but Devon only nodded. "I used to like him, too." With a sigh, he added, "Before he left for that patrol, he was, well, we were getting to be friends. Now I don't even know if he sees me as anything other than a glorified servant."

"You are definitely more than a servant, Devon Imry! You are a mage, and a damned good one!" Syrelle said intently. "You deserve everyone's respect—including Prince Allyndev's! You certainly have mine," she added, and then, to his surprise, kissed him softly. "Maybe he'll be different after he's been back for a while."

Daringly, Devon slid his arm around Syrelle's waist. "Maybe. Or maybe Azhani will notice and say something. You know how she feels about that kind of thing."

Chuckling, Syrelle said, "Or you could turn him into a turnip—they're perfectly bland and inoffensive."

"For you, my lady, I shall indeed make him into a turnip of grand proportions, flavored only with the finest of manures," he replied as they sauntered toward the center of camp.

A bath did little to restore Allyndev's mood. Not only was he feeling particularly grumpy for not being treated like the other soldiers swore their camp followers treated them, he was filled with jealousy at the sight of Devon and Syrelle sitting together on a log bench, trading bites of each other's food and laughing at some joke they clearly weren't sharing.

Suddenly, Devon pointed over at Allyn's boots—the pair he had yet to replace—and said, "You know, my prince, perhaps you should leave your friends up in the caves." He pinched his nose delicately. "They're quite offensive."

The words were harsh, but Allyndev was willing to let them go—mostly because they were true. Then Syrelle giggled and that made it a thousand times worse.

Angrily, he grabbed the hilt of his sword and snapped, "My boots earned their scars honestly. You will respect that, *apprentice*, else I be forced to teach you the error of your thoughts."

There was no mistaking the look of hurt that flashed over Devon's face before he got up and walked away.

"That was rude," Syrelle said harshly. "Devon was just joking with you."

"I don't require his childish humor, Syrelle. He owes me the respect due a soldier proven by the scars he's won in battle," Allyndev retorted, and then belched loudly.

"I hear the words fluttering from your lips, but they are not the statements of a prince and a man who bears the title of friend. You are being mean and spiteful," Syrelle said scathingly. "And I shall not bear your presence any longer!" Standing, she glared at him. "For I do not consort with brutes nor savages. Until such time as you have shed this terrible face and returned to the person Devon and I cherished, then I charge you to seek your companionship—and shelter—elsewhere!" With that, she stalked away, going in the same direction as Devon had earlier.

Great. Now who's going to tell me I'm a hero? Who's going to listen to my stories? Sing bawdy songs with me? Maybe I should go see if the Hawkins and the boys have any good ale. Stuffing a hunk of bread into his mouth, Allyn stared at the fire, weighing his options.

Padreg clapped him on the shoulder. "Looks like ye'd best think of a proper apology, boy."

"Why? She's just a woman. He's just an apprentice." Allyn soaked his bread in his stew. "They don't really matter. They're not soldiers, like us. Hell, they aren't even Y'Syran."

Suddenly his vision was filled with two armor clad legs. Looking up, he was greeted by Azhani Rhu'len's stern, hawkish visage. A cold spear of dread spiked him in the stomach.

"Come with me," she commanded. The word, "Why?" was on the tip of his tongue, but he never got a chance to speak it because she added, "Now, soldier."

Refusing a direct order from the warleader could get him hanged, so he quickly set aside his half-finished meal and followed her to the edge of their encampment. Azhani nodded to the sentries as they passed them, then continued into the forest beyond. Once they were well out of earshot, she spun and gave him a look that made him heartily wish he were anywhere but right there.

"Prince Allyndev, would you care to explain to me exactly why you are behaving like a spoiled child?"

"No, warleader, I would not," he replied respectfully.

Pacing around him, Azhani crossed her arms. "I have, I think, come to know you, Prince Allyndev. Our time together these last few months has given me some insight into you, and I have to say, at no time have I ever seen you act like such a terrific fool! Your behavior today was so unbecoming of a prince of Y'Syr or any of the seven kingdoms that I've half a mind to send you back to Y'Syria, because it's quite clear to me that the stress of serving with the army is too much!" She stopped less than half a foot away from him and snarled, "So you'd best tell me why your head has suddenly become lodged in your backside, or I will return you to the queen and tell her that you are to be sent to the nearest nursery and placed in swaddling clothes!"

Stunned, Allyndev whispered, "No." Shaking with fear and feeling deeply embarrassed, he mumbled, "Please, please don't send me home, Warleader." That would be the final agony. He'd never live it down and Lyssera would be forced to send him to some tiny estate far away from anyone just to make sure the stench of his failure didn't taint her honor.

"Then give me a reason not to," Azhani retorted.

He curled his hands into fists, and stood shaking, all the pent-up emotions suddenly exploding. "I hate this! I hate getting up before the sun just so I can crawl through something not even a pig would eat. I hate that I'm either cold and wet or hot and sweaty." He kicked a nearby rock and watched, with some pleasure, as it shot through a pair of nearby trees. "I hate that everyone treats me like a prince to my face and a pariah to my back!"

Azhani did not reply, simply stood there, listening.

Hugging himself then, he looked down and whispered, "Master Azhani, they make me wish I'd never been born. They make me feel like I am nothing!" He looked up at her defiantly. "But Sergeant Matthias, Hawkins, the others—they all treated me like I was one of them once I started being just like them. So I'm going to be just like them! I'm going to act like a complete arse, because otherwise I just want to crawl into a hole and never come out!"

If Azhani was surprised by his words, she didn't say. Instead, she made her way over to a log, sat on it, and indicated the empty space beside her. She waited until he sat before pulling a small leather flask from her belt. Taking a quick swig, she passed it to him. As he tried a sip of what turned out to be simple cider, she said, "It's nothing like the legends and tales, is it?"

Clutching the flask, he whispered, "No, it isn't."

Gently, she patted his thigh. "I wish the answers for what you're feeling were simple, Allyndev. You are half-elven and the human that sired you was Y'Dani, just like mine was. Sadly, to many Y'Syran elves, this makes you something to despise. They treat you as though you were less than a person, but you are not. You are Prince Allyndev Kelani. Your mother was a princess—your father, well, I expect you realize that his name is a mystery for a reason."

"No one cares who fathered me," he replied. "Because admitting his name would only highlight my mother's shame."

She nodded. "For many of Y'Syr, that is the truth. It is also a sad truth that doing what we do—being a 'hero', if you choose to name it that—is not about glory. It's painful, ugly, dirty, fetid, and disgusting. Most days, the best you can hope for is not to end up spitted on the end of your enemy's sword—or in the belly of a hungry beast. In wartime, you start and end your days wrapped in death and no one—but *no one*—will give you true respect unless you've earned it. And you do not earn it by being a complete arse to your friends!"

"But—but what about Aunt Lyss?" he replied weakly. "Everyone loves her! They'd treat her like she's perfect even if she were a complete arse. Twain's breath, they sing her praises even after what my mother did!"

"That, my young student, is because she has dedicated most of her life to the care of every single citizen of Y'Syr. Why do you think her court sessions are so long? No one is ever turned away when they approach the doors of the great hall—if they come seeking audience, she will grant it to them. If they ask for justice, they will receive it. Boons, more often then not, are given and in exchange, she receives their loyalty and respect. It's why when she decreed that I was innocent of Ylera's murder, most accepted that judgment," she said.

With a heavy, disheartened sigh, Allyndev scuffed his feet in the dirt. "I wish they would just let me be! I didn't ask to be born prince. I'd rather be a gardener!" Tears sprang to his eyes. "But I failed there, too. I don't have the gift. I have nothing to give Y'Syr but my blood in battle." Woefully, he shook his head. "When I was a boy, Aunt Lyss once told me that I should learn to be a good ruler, because one day I might sit on a throne. If she had heard, even once, the things my instructors said to me, she wouldn't have bothered to tell me such fairy tales." Oh, how he had hated his father as a child. Whoever he was, he'd branded him more deeply with the scars of shame than even an oathbreaker would bear.

"Whether or not those words were fairy tales, they were well-spoken, my prince," Azhani said quietly. "For there is truth in them—learn to lead well, learn to be strong without needing the honeyed words of false friends, and demonstrate your skills by guarding those who would spill their own blood to save you pain, and then you will have earned your place."

"I will?" he replied hopefully.

Solemnly, she nodded. "And I will help you with these lessons as best I can, which, I'm afraid, means you'll need a bit of knocking about," she said, and then, to his utter surprise, shoved him off the log.

Stunned and more than a little outraged, he stared up at her. Tiny rocks jabbed into his backside.

Smirking, she crossed her feet. "Well, lad, are you going to sit there like a flower and eat dirt or are you going to get up like a soldier and defend yourself?"

Oh. Oh no. That feeling of dread he had experienced earlier returned tenfold. He was about to get taught a very, very painful lesson. If—and only if—he were lucky, he might be able to crawl back to camp when she was done with him. Whimpering softly, he charged her, knowing that if he waited much longer, she'd attack first and then it would really hurt. Pain, he decided, wasn't his friend at all.

Half a candlemark later, he moaned, "Mercy," and prayed. Every joint in his body felt as though she'd tried to wrench them apart. They'd only wrestled, but it was unlike any kind of sparring they'd done before. Amazingly, she had stopped after each move and showed him what she'd done. The moves, he learned, were all dirty, underhanded tricks that would earn him far more respect from the soldiers in his unit than foul language and a bad attitude.

"It's skill, Allyndev." She sat back on her heels. "Soldiers respect a warrior who can best them, even if the combat is simply wrestler's play. Tomorrow,

I'll teach you some things you can do with your blade and shield—and other tricks that will, I suspect, prevent you from having to behave like a complete boor just to keep them off your back. For now, let's return to camp before they send the cavalry after us."

As she helped him stand, he nodded. "Yes. I believe I have a couple of friends who are waiting for an apology—if they're still my friends."

"I believe they are—and they'll prove it, by accepting your apology—but you'd best be sincere, my prince, for Devon and Syrelle care about you and you have hurt them deeply with your words and actions," Azhani replied as they made their way back to camp.

"I know. I'm an arse," he said regretfully.

She chuckled and tousled his hair affectionately. "An arse you may be, Allyndev, but one who has, I think, learned an important lesson."

"Aye, Master," he said with a sardonic grin. "Don't be an arse."

CHAPTER SIXTEEN

Azhani's army went as far north as they could safely climb, then turned west, leaving a trail of blackened rock and plumes of gray smoke streaking the sky behind them. Ahead, the Western Sea beckoned. Behind, spring became summer and summer slipped by until fall seemed just around the corner. Days stretched out, becoming one endless round of search, destroy, burn, and bless.

Time and random encounters with bandits and monsters were not their only enemies, much to Kyrian's surprise. Because the weather could shift from scorching heat to freezing cold in the course of a day, the healers and chirurgeons had to treat a seemingly endless parade of illnesses. On top of that, they had the usual injuries brought on by carelessness or battle. She received a true battlefield education in trauma and triage, honing her skills until she could diagnose four different kinds of illness just by listening to the way a person sounded when they coughed and could set a broken arm and stitch up a sword cut in practically the same breath.

Ystarfe Pass was just beyond the crest of the next mountain. This was their halfway point, and according to Azhani, the location of more than three hundred small caves and crevasses that were perfect for rimerbeast breeding. Kyrian was not looking forward to having to climb hundreds of feet of rope.

"Stardancer Kyrian, we're ready for you," a soldier called from outside her tent.

Today, it was her task to sing the blessing chants that tradition said would prevent the rimerbeasts from returning to the same cave. With this odd beast season, she was no longer so certain the chants held any sway over them. Still, it was better to sing them and be protected than to forget or ignore that ritual and discover that it was simply some anomaly brought on by the carelessness of the previous beast season's cleansing.

Collecting her haversack, she stepped outside and offered him a bland smile. "Thank you, Sergeant." Together, they headed for the cave currently in need of cleansing. *I almost wouldn't mind half as much if I didn't have to do this with him for company.* She glanced at her so-called "guardian" and tried not to roll her eyes. Sergeant Matthias was utterly repugnant, the epitome of everything King Arris represented for the Y'Danis, despite being Y'Syran. He was a hateful, spiteful, jealous man who encouraged his fellow soldiers to treat Prince Allyndev and others of Y'Dani blood as little more than second class citizens. In some ways, she found Arris' blatantly prejudicial laws more honest than the sergeant's rude bigotry.

There's nothing I can do about that now, and at least Allyn doesn't have to suffer being that man's practice pell anymore. Azhani did the right thing and to Hell with anyone who thinks he hasn't earned the right to fight at the warleader's side.

Upon reaching the caves, Kyrian let out a sharp groan of dismay. She had thought it would be at least another week before she would have to climb so far, but it was evident by the amount of rope hanging off the mountainside that she'd have to ascend nearly half a mile up sheer rock.

Hooking his thumbs into his belt, Sergeant Matthias gave her a leering grin. "Sorry about the inconvenience, Stardancer. Damned 'beasts ain't the most accommodating bunch." Disdainfully, he added, "I suppose I could fetch someone else, if you'd rather not bother."

Somewhere behind her, another soldier chuckled. "How much ye want t'bet Master Azhani's tart ain't gonna wanna get herself all banged up?"

"Shut it, Kag. Ye want t'get us horsewhipped?" another soldier hissed.

Masking her face in serenity, Kyrian smiled at Sergeant Matthias. "No, I can do it. Thank you, Sergeant."

He did not reply, only helped her into the safety harness. Following behind, he kept watch as she clambered over the uneven surface of the cliff side until they reached the caves. Once inside, Kyrian spent candlemarks blessing every corner she could reach. It was a lengthy, arduous task. By the time she was finished climbing through the various chambers of the cave, she had twisted her back into so many knots that she felt as though every muscle had been molded into rocks. Worse, her throat burned from chanting while inhaling the acrid smoke that filled the cave.

Pain made her dizzy. Somehow, she managed to get down the mountain without falling or relying on Sergeant Matthias for help. By the time she reached the level ground below, she was nauseated and ready to collapse. There was no way she would allow herself the luxury of doing it here, where they were all watching her like vultures just waiting for its prey to drop. Instead, she continued back to camp, Sergeant Matthias dutifully ambling along beside her, whistling a cheerfully bawdy tune that made her want to reach over and rip his lips off.

Suddenly, Allyndev appeared. "By the blessed Twain, Sergeant! Where are your damned manners? Have you no respect?" he demanded, hurrying up to Kyrian and putting his arm around her. "Let me help you to bed, Stardancer. You must be exhausted."

"No, it's all right, my prince, but thank you," she replied softly.

Sergeant Matthias snarled, "Do not speak to me as if I were your underling, you prattling, halfbreed mistake! A tainted parasite like you has no idea what true respect is!"

Icily, Allyndev replied, "I knew more about respect in my cradle than you will in your grave, Sergeant. Now move off."

The ring of a sword clearing its scabbard sent a chill of fear racing through Kyrian. "Prove your words upon my body, boy, or are you too cowardly to face a pure man?"

"Wait, no, don—oh!" Kyrian gasped as pain seared through her. The world spun dizzyingly and spots danced in her vision, causing her to forget even the most basic of calming meditations.

Allyndev clutched her and glared at Matthias. "I have better things to do than engage in pointless brutality, soldier. Go back to your unit and brag about the size of your…" He paused and looked right at the sergeant's belt. "Courage, because we both know it's the only thing smaller than your mind."

"Bastard!" Matthias snarled, taking a step forward. "I'll have satisfaction of you, boy, or I'll run you through where you stand!"

"I don't normally approve of duels, Sergeant Matthias."

No other voice could fill Kyrian with such relief and no other arms were as welcome as those of her beloved Azhani as she wrapped them around her gently. "It's all right, Allyn," Azhani said quietly. "I've got her."

"Thank the Twain," Kyrian whispered, going limp and knowing Azhani could hold her weight.

"However, I seem to have much more important matters to attend to, so please—by all means, gentlemen, work this out. Now. And Sergeant? No matter the outcome, if you ever treat another person the way I saw you treating Kyrian and the prince, I will have you horsewhipped and sent back to Y'Syria in disgrace." Then she turned away and helped Kyrian back to camp.

The moment Azhani was gone, Matthias rounded on Allyndev and hissed, "I swear by the Twain, you will not walk away from me, you whoreson Y'Dani bastard! You and all your tainted brethren are the reason why everything is a stinking pile of shyvot! If I had my way, this damned army wouldn't stop until the entire kingdom of Y'Dan was nothing but a smoking ruin!"

Stunned by the man's seething hatred, Allyndev gaped at him. "Do you really believe beating up a half-grown boy is going to make you feel better, Sergeant? I don't know why you hate me or the Y'Danis so, but surely there is a better target for your anger?"

Rage twisted the sergeant's face. "Draw your blade!" he screamed, spittle flying from his lips as he swung his weapon at Allyndev.

Allyn easily evaded the wild blow, but did nothing else to defend himself. Soldiers, drawn by the commotion, had gathered and he intended to show them that he could stand up to the other man without having to resort to mindless violence. All the lessons Azhani and Kyrian had taught him gelled in his thoughts and allowed him to quickly react to Matthias' anger-driven blows. Dropping into a crouch, he flexed his fingers and waited for Matthias' next move.

He struck, flicking his sword toward Allyndev's belly, a triumphant grin curving his lips. "I'll see you bleed!"

This is a fake. Look at his eyes. He's not seeing the blade in my belly, he's going for my face. He wants to scar me, leave his besting of me where everyone can see it. I think not! Allyndev jerked to the side and kicked Matthias in the elbow, hard. Without waiting to see what was going to happen next, he grabbed the man's wrist and twisted it sharply, ignoring the snapping of bone and the man's howl of pain as he stripped the blade from his fingers.

Armed now with Matthias' sword, Allyndev stood and waited, watching as Matthias clutched his wounded arm and cursed loudly. Hate lurked in his eyes and Allyn wasn't quite ready to trust him.

The gathered soldiers began to murmur, "Is he going to kill him?"

"He should. Bastard challenged him to a duel and lost. Serve him right to end up skewered on his own sword!"

"Ye daft? Prince hadda have cheated!"

"Are you blind, man? The prince just proved his master's teachings are true!"

On and on they went, some for Allyn, others for Matthias, but most agreeing that Allyndev had just won the bout.

Quietly, Allyndev said, "I could kill you, Matthias."

"Do it. Go on. Show them what a man you are," he said disdainfully. "Killing an unarmed opponent."

"You didn't seem to have such a crisis of honor before," Allyn retorted. "But then, I am not you." Slowly, he offered Matthias the sword's hilt. "Yield to me, Sergeant. I am not your enemy. I am neither above nor below you. I am a boy who is learning to become a man. What will you teach me? Are you nothing but hatred? What does that say about those who taught you? Come, Layvendrel, son of Mairi and Korsahn, yield and let this enmity of yours die here, now. Our true enemies are out there, waiting for us to come break their damnable shells!"

"I..." He stared at Allyndev, astonishment flooding his face. "But..." Shaking his head, he murmured, "You shame me, Prince."

"No," Allyndev said quietly. "I remind you. I don't know what happened to poison you, but I know you were not always who you've made yourself to be. Queen Lyssera would never have chosen such a man to serve her."

Sighing heavily, Matthias suddenly looked horribly tired. "No, she would not. I..." He lowered his head and went to kneel. "I yield, my prince."

Allyn grabbed him and kept him upright. "No. Do not kneel for me. I have not earned it, not yet." Carefully, he slid Matthias' blade into its sheath. "Let me help you to the chirurgeon's tent. They'll need to set that arm."

"Thank you, my prince," he replied, respect filling his voice.

"You are most welcome, Sergeant." Allyn offered him equal respect. Victory sat uneasily in his belly. The gathered soldiers walked all around them, escorting them through the camp, some peeling off to spread word of what had just happened. From time to time, one of them would look over at him and his or her face would be a mirror of Sergeant Matthias'. Allyn had won their respect, but at what cost?

I should not have broken his arm. Kyrian will not be pleased that I used her sacred dance to harm an ally. There had been no other way. Azhani was right, they had needed to work it out. Sergeant Matthias was a good warrior, but he needed to lead by example—and if he continually disrespected Allyndev and the other half-elves, what would that teach his soldiers about the chain of command? *No, I did what I thought was best, even if it got someone hurt. I just have to live with it now.*

Pain made concentrating on putting one foot in front of the other difficult, but with Azhani to steady her, Kyrian managed. "Goddess, what a stupid, pig-headed idiot I am," she grumbled, wincing as stumbling on a rock sent cramps racing up her back.

"We're almost home," Azhani said soothingly. "And stupid was Layvendrel not warning you about the difficulty of the climb. Why didn't you ask for help?"

Sheepishly, she replied, "Pride, of course."

Azhani frowned as she pushed aside the flap to their tent. "Kyrian." She shook her head, then laughed ruefully. "We're a pair, love."

Kyrian sighed. "Aye, we are. I think I pulled something in my back."

"Then let me take care of you for a change." Azhani brushed a kiss over her brow. Carefully, she helped Kyrian to undress, then had her lie on the bed while she warmed oil over their small brazier.

As it was rubbed it in, Kyrian relaxed, sometimes directing Azhani to a particularly sore muscle, but mostly just letting her work uninterrupted. Soon, relief spread through her. "You would have made a good chirurgeon. You've gentle hands," Kyrian said.

"Mm, that's because I love you," she said, kissing Kyrian's shoulder blade.

Grinning, Kyrian half turned to look at Azhani, arching her eyebrow as their gazes met. "Are you implying that your affection for me influences your dedication to this task?"

"No, I'm saying that you're the only woman whose naked body I want to put my oily hands upon!" Azhani gave Kyrian's bottom a playful, but gentle, swat. "Of course my feelings influence my choices."

"I see. In that case, please continue to let them have sway," Kyrian replied contentedly.

Once the massage was finished, Azhani stripped down and slid into bed. Wrapping her arms around Kyrian, she kissed her tenderly before contemplating her in silence.

"I love the way you look at me," Kyrian said with a contented sigh.

Azhani smiled. "How do I look at you?"

Feeling shy, Kyrian ducked her head down and giggled softly. "You'll think I'm silly, but—when you look at me like that, it's as though everything around me fades to nothing for you. Like I'm the only thing in existence right then."

Gently, Azhani kissed her. "That's because in that moment, you are the only thing that matters."

"Oh." Kyrian blushed darkly. "Well, good, that's very, uh, good."

"I'm glad you feel that way, because I really do like looking at you," Azhani said, her voice resonant with amusement.

Kyrian made a face. "I have no idea why."

"Really? But you're beautiful, Kyr." Delicately, she caressed her cheek. "Breathtaking, even."

"Goddess," Kyrian whispered, shivering each time Azhani touched her. "With you, I feel so special."

"You are." Azhani kissed her, brushing her tongue against her lips until all Kyrian could do was moan as desire raced through her. "You make my soul sing, Kyrian."

"Oh, Azhi," she murmured, all pain forgotten as the need to lose herself in Azhani's body overwhelmed her. "Please. Love me." They drew closer, their kiss deepening, and she moaned when Azhani shifted and began to nibble her way down Kyrian's throat to her breasts. "Oh, my love, she whispered, sinking her hands into Azhani's hair as she sucked and licked Kyrian's nipples until Kyrian felt like she was going to burst into flames. Chuckling wickedly, Azhani glanced up at her, then slid lower, causing Kyrian to open her legs, but the small motion sent a small flare of pain through her back and she hissed softly.

Immediately, Azhani pulled away. "We can stop…"

Kyrian let out a bark of laughter. "No! Love me!" Eagerly, she reached out and grabbed Azhani's shoulders, pulling her down for a hard, passionate kiss.

Each time they made love was a gift. Kyrian sometimes wondered if Azhani felt the same depth of emotions that she did—if she truly burned as hotly as she claimed. The way she felt for Azhani was so intense, so all-consuming that it seemed impossible that Azhani could echo her—not when Azhani had already felt so much for Ylera.

With all that faced them each day, Kyrian decided that she would wait until they had a future that was safe from monsters and madmen before she faced that demon. Until then, she would lose herself in the wonderfully loving arms of her beloved warleader.

"You're hurt. Maybe we should stop," Azhani murmured as they separated briefly.

"No!" Kyrian insisted. "I want you, Azhi. Pain isn't going to change how much I need you right now." She eagerly rose up to kiss her. "Don't waste our time, love. This is a gift, let's not squander it."

Azhani returned the embrace tenderly. "All right, but we'll take it easy. A gift this may be, but it's one I want you to enjoy completely."

"Oh, trust me, love. I'm definitely going to enjoy it." Kyrian pulled Azhani down atop her. "I plan to enjoy it many, many times."

Azhani laughed softly. "Insatiable beast."

"Yes. Love me, Azhani. I'm yours." She looked down as Azhani scattered butterfly kisses over her sternum. "Always."

Azhani rested her head against Kyrian's chest and sighed. "Always. I love you, Kyrian."

"I love you, too."

As the last of the long, hot days of summer drew onward, many tales of heroism on the part of individual soldiers came to light. Hardly a week went by when Azhani wasn't shaking the hand of a man or woman who had performed a deed noteworthy enough to demand her attention. Today, for instance, she held the hand of one Jadrielle Enias, a flame-haired young lass from southern Y'Nor who, according to her patrol, had single-handedly driven off an entire pack of hoblins with the skill of her bow alone.

"So I hear you're a bit of a hero today, Jadrielle," Azhani said with a warm smile.

With a diffident shrug, she replied, "'Tis little more than a body should do, given the circumstances." She glanced over at the rest of her patrol. "I warrant this bit of display is more for them than me. Seein' as how they were caught with their drawers in a bind," she added, winking at Azhani.

The corner of Azhani's mouth curved upward. "Indeed?" She knew the circumstances, but was interested to hear Jadrielle's take on it.

"Aye. We'd found a pond, and since it's been hotter than a smith's forge, there was a bit of a lottery cast to see who'd be stuck out while the rest soaked their heads and arses—I lost."

"Ah, well, I'd say in this case that losing has indeed become a win, my friend," Azhani said warmly. "I'm promoting you to my patrol. I can use a bowman who thinks fast on her feet." She clapped the young woman's shoulder. "Welcome. You can toss your gear anywhere there's space."

Jadrielle gaped at her, then grinned. "Thank ye, warleader!" She ran off, leaving Azhani to chuckle softly.

It was rare that she got to feel so good about moving people from one patrol to another. Usually, personal issues were what found her shuffling one soldier for another, but she liked what she had heard from Padreg about the young woman and thought she'd make a fine addition.

And this has nothing at all with transferring the attention away from you, does it? The unbidden thought pecked at her all the way back to her command tent, for the crux of the answer was simply, "Yes, actually." Ever since that first time Gormerath filled her head with song while burning a distinctive shade of blue in the presence of rimerbeasts, rumor had spread. A legend that was a combination of truth, history, and fancy, was forming around her, and Azhani wasn't at all sure she was comfortable with it. She could hardly demand it stop, however, for the tales inspired morale in a stunning way.

There wasn't a soldier in the army who hadn't heard of how the warleader's patrol, led by Azhani and her mystical blade, found more rimerbeast egg-riddled caves than any other. Thanks to a few unwary comments on Azhani's part, the sword's "song" was even becoming a part of the tale. Kyrian found the whole thing quite amusing, but Azhani was worried that by portraying her as some untouchable hero, it made her less effective a warleader.

Jadrielle's presence in the patrol, with her more visible and tangible glory, might just be what the soldiers needed for their storytelling, and would leave Azhani to simply be the warleader and not some mystical "Bearer of Gormerath". Mysticism was all well and good when it came down to blessing caves and healing the sick, but as a warrior, Azhani much preferred something she could see for herself, such as someone's prowess with a weapon.

She looked east and studied the thick column of smoke behind them. The stench of burning egg slime filled the air. It was a scent she hated, she decided while making a sour face. All trace of sourness lifted, however, at the sight of Kyrian striding toward her with evident purpose.

They embraced warmly. "Hello, love. How is your back?" she asked, feeling a twinge of concern. The last cave had been little more than a vertical descent into a narrow crevasse.

"It's fine," Kyrian replied easily. "Allyn and Devon were kind enough to rig a pulley to lower me into the cave." She laughed. "I'm sure I made quite a sight—floating down like a queen on a rope divan."

"I'm sure it was a lovely and inspiring sight," Azhani said with a fond chuckle. "You do know you're not required to volunteer for cave duty, right?"

"Of course, but it was within the boundaries of camp—I thought it might be nice to give the further-ranging stardancers a break," Kyrian said quietly. Her disinterest in joining a patrol or placing herself in any situation where she might find herself facing combat was a subject barely breached between them, though both knew why she was so reluctant to venture beyond the safe confines of the army's encampment. Never once did Azhani ask her to take duty beyond the candlemarks Kyrian sacrificed to the chirurgeon's tent, though she herself was often gone for days at a time, traveling deep into the mountains to burn out as many caves as could be reached.

"Well, I believe we are all due a break. Midsummer comes and I've plans," Azhani said with a smile. "Come, let me regale you with my ideas and you can improve them." Wrapping her arm around Kyrian's shoulders, she led her off to tell her about the celebration she had devised.

For three nights, the army rested, celebrating the longest day of the year by enjoying games of skill and chance, bardic competitions, and feasting on a seemingly never-ending river of sweet cakes and watered wine. In comparison to the grand festivals held in the cities and towns they were trying to protect, their simple distractions were sure to be found wanting by some, but overall, they offered a calm point each soldier needed to shield them against the rigors to come.

Crossing into the Ystarfe Pass brought two things—tangible signs of autumn's approach, and the grim discovery that, in the highest of the caves littering the mountains, some rimerbeast eggs had hatched. Though no actual attacks had been reported, Azhani immediately ordered all patrol and guard shifts doubled. No one was to travel outside their camp in groups smaller than two.

Summer's flame was truly extinguished one blustery night when the army was pressed into the side of a mountain by a bone-chilling storm. Without pause, the soldiers traded warm weather gear for oiled wool and fur and pressed on, driven to do as much damage as possible to the beasts before more hatchings occurred.

Even in cold weather gear, though, the army was a panoply of color. Mages in saffron, starseekers in blue, stardancers in scarlet, and the chirurgeons in their green and white could be seen darting between soldiers in the arms and armor of their kingdoms. Often of a morning, Azhani would stand on a bluff and look down on the army and see not a machine of death but an ocean of hues all blending into a field of violent flowers. It amused her to think that her roses had such potent thorns.

"Goddess, you are a vision," Kyrian said as she watched Azhani don her armor. Lying in bed, still naked and flushed from lovemaking, she felt decidedly decadent as her lover fastened buckles and tightened straps.

"I am?" Azhani settled the tabard that marked her as warleader over her shoulders, making certain the Y'Syran oak tree with its golden crown was centered and unmarred by wrinkles or damage.

"Mmhm." Kyrian wished Azhani didn't have to go. "If I could, I'd lure you back into this bed so I could explain to you in exacting detail just how beautiful you are," she said, standing and sauntering over to her. "But I'll just have to settle for this." She rose up to her tiptoes to kiss her deeply. "Return safely to me, my love," she whispered, then stepped back so Azhani could begin her day.

Reaching out, Azhani cupped her hand to Kyrian's face and smiled. "With a command like that, how could I do anything but race back here to your arms, beloved?" she said before ducking outside to begin her day.

On the other side of camp, Elisira and Padreg took turns helping each other to don their armor, though by the surly expression on his face, Padreg took no pleasure in tightening the belt around Elisira's waist.

"I fail to see why you chose to bear these arms, my love," he grumbled as she smoothed out her tabard. Emblazoned only with the Y'Dani wheat sheaf, it was a symbol of a bygone day, for Arris had done away with his father's heraldry after the former king's death.

"Because something of Thodan's spirit should rise against the rimerbeasts, my love. Because there are those in this army that still honor the wheat sheaf and I will have them know that we have not forgotten them."

At once proud and ashamed, he lowered his head. "You are a wiser person than I, my love, for I had not considered that."

"Ah, Paddy," she said fondly. "It is not that you lack of wisdom, it's simply that I thought of it first." Shaking out his tabard, she checked to be sure the rearing Y'Noran horse had not suffered any damage before draping the fabric over his head. She picked up his belt and showed it to him, grinning when he spotted its new buckle—a working of the wheat sheaves around a horseshoe. "See? Together, we will show everyone that we honor what Arris has forgotten."

Exuberantly, he kissed her. "Every day, my love, you prove how blessed I am to have you as my *korethkyu*."

She laughed and returned his kisses joyfully.

Pressed between Allyndev and Devon, Syrelle clutched the young men to her and tried not to show them how afraid she was. Soon, they would join Azhani for the first patrol since hatched eggs had been discovered. Every corner of the camp was abuzz with the word that had come down from the warleader's tent that morning—tonight, rimerbeasts would hunt! Above them, the sky rapidly darkened, and with every drip of the day candle's wax that puddled on its pedestal, Syrelle felt her heart sink further and further.

Terrified, she alternately fought back tears and blazing anger—how dare the beasts choose to attack this year, when she'd finally made real friends, people she loved like no other! That both returned her affection in measures she was afraid to judge only made it harder. One day she would have to choose, and in so doing, break someone's heart.

She could not do that. "You must be safe," she murmured, hugging them both tightly.

"It'll be fine, Sy." Devon brushed his lips across her cheek. It was not quite a kiss, more of a caress, and still it made her shiver. He pulled back and winked at Allyndev. "Heya, stick-swinger, I'll wager I kill one before you."

Allyndev snorted. "It's a bet, twinklefingers!"

Syrelle rolled her eyes. "And I wish you both a boring night, that you might return to me in one piece and not reeking of beast stink."

"Like I said, it'll be fine." Devon checked over his weapons once more. Though he was armed with a sling, a staff, and a short blade, Syrelle prayed he wouldn't need anything more than the spells he'd practiced night and day since the campaign had begun.

"I hope so." She wrapped her arms around Allyndev tightly, wallowing, just a little, in the warm strength of his embrace.

He petted her hair as she rested her head on his shoulder. "Master Azhani will keep us safe."

"Just…don't be a damned hero." She grabbed them both one more time and kissed their cheeks before shoving them out of the tent, waiting a moment for the urge to sob like a child to pass. Only then did she hurry after them to join Kyrian and Elisira outside.

"It's hard to watch them go, isn't it?" Elisira said quietly. "Knowing they carry the best parts of your heart with them."

"Goddess, yes," Kyrian said with a sigh. "Are you off to do your turn at close patrol then, Eli?"

"Aye. Seems such a small thing, but if any get through the lines, you stardancers will be glad of the warleader's planning, though it pains my lord to ride without me."

Syrelle couldn't bring herself to add to the conversation. After all, how could she when she couldn't decide which man held the greater portion of her heart? As Elisira strode away, she turned to Kyrian. "What can we do to pass the time?"

"Prepare bandages and wound salve. There will be injuries. Make absolutely certain the acolytes crush the roots into a fine paste this time—it needs to spread as thinly as possible."

"Of course, Stardancer," she said, making herself look away as Azhani's patrol vanished in the gathering gloom.

CHAPTER SEVENTEEN

The constant burr of Gormerath's song might have driven some mad, but for Azhani it was the greatest boon she could have ever received. Over time, she had learned to understand the sword's arias. Any tone at all meant danger, but the pitch and strength told her how much and sometimes how far it was from her. When it was just the eggs, the sword had been content to whine, but now that they faced true beasts, the blade screamed its hatred whenever they drew near.

And right now, it was practically deafening her.

Gripping the hilt in her right hand, she used the other to hold Kushyra's reins as she scanned the area. Just as she caught a flash of gray fur, rimerbeasts erupted from the bushes. Immediately, the creatures began to circle the patrol, keening their eerie croon and taking a few cautious swipes at Azhani and her warriors.

Poisonous slime dripped from their fangs.

She suppressed a shudder of fear. Just one bite or claw could spell disaster. They had to be quick, they had to be sure, and most of all, they had to survive to fight again.

Thankfully, she had her own claws. Pointing Gormerath at the nearest rimerbeast, she shouted, "Fire!" and charged in swinging. Behind her, bowstrings twanged. Arrows hissed through the air and the demonic bodies sprouted feathered shafts. Some dropped, their lives quickly ended. Something flashed in the corner of her eye and three of the beasts burst into flames, rapidly burning to cinders.

She laughed. Most days, she hated magick, but when it could do that, well, she'd learn to love it.

"Take 'em down, lads!" she called, laying about her with the sword, trusting Kushyra to keep her in the saddle.

The moment Gormerath touched rimerbeast flesh, the blade erupted into flames and the sword's song rang in her ears. Compelled to join the aria, she threw back her head and let loose the Banshee's cry.

Her soldiers cheered.

A haze settled over her then. Battle became strike, parry, dodge, kill. Keep moving, keep moving, duck, weave, nudge Kushyra this way or that, and ignore the gore that she was soon swimming in, no matter how disgusting it was. Signal arrows flew. Other patrols had encountered live rimerbeasts. The season was now upon them.

It didn't take long before the thick, sick-sweet, coppery scent of blood filled the air. Wheezing, gurgling screams and whimpers, pleas for help and the plaintive cries of soldiers watching their friends die drove knives of anger deep into Azhani's heart, but she was unable to spare even a moment to mourn them. She had to press on, to destroy every single rimerbeast in her way.

A horse screamed its last and she turned in time to see Prince Allyndev knocked to the ground.

"Shyvot!" Wasting no time, she turned Kushyra and charged the rimerbeast looming over the prince. Hitting it at full speed, she sent it flying into the mountainside, where it struck the rock with a sickly crunch. "Get on!" she yelled, offering Allyn her hand. They couldn't ride double for long, but afoot, he was a dead man.

He grabbed her hand and leaped up. As he settled himself sideways on the pillion pad, she spared a moment to feel sorry for the more tender bits of his anatomy that were about to take an uncomfortable bruising. It was an awkward position for both of them, but it was the only way either had a hope of being able to fight.

"Ready?" she yelled over the clangor of battle.

"Go!" He aimed his bow at another rimerbeast.

She went.

The fighting raged through the night. Azhani and her patrols chased the rimerbeasts through the mountains until false dawn sent the remaining beasts racing into high caves to await nightfall out of their reach. Exhausted, she called for the patrols to retreat back to camp, discovering along the way that all but three horses and one soldier had made it through the night. No one had escaped injury, though. Field dressings covered gaping wounds and bound broken bones. Those riders without horses had to walk whenever possible, riding only when they faced combat.

Eventually, they turned back for the main army encampment and the moment they rode passed the first sentries, they had healers and stardancers swarming over them, caring for the worst of the injuries.

"You've all done well this night," Azhani announced before dismounting. "I'm proud of each and every one of you. You are all heroes. Go now. Find your friends and warm tents. Eat. Sleep. Nightfall comes again soon. Twain bless you all."

"Twain bless you, Warleader," they shouted back wearily. She smiled as they dispersed. These were her people through and through and she would do all she could to see them to the other side of the season alive.

Barely able to stand, Azhani staggered into her tent and sank into the first chair she could find. Though her wounds were minor, they were numerous and painful. Anywhere her armor had slipped, the damnable beasts had struck, leaving her covered with dozens of scratches. The worst by far was a long, shallow gash extending from her left hip to the knee, making each step feel like her skin was being slowly peeled from the muscle.

Biting back curses, she filled a pot with water and set it on the brazier to warm, then pulled off her armor, setting it aside to mend later. *Need more plates around my shoulders, elbows, and hips. Need to reinforce the leather on my breeches and make sure everyone uses a pillion pad. Allyndev would have died if I'd forgotten mine.*

Pen and parchment waited on the table, so she quickly jotted down her ideas. She also made note of the dead soldier's name, knowing that one of her first acts upon waking would be to write the man's family. *Need to ask someone how Jadrielle did. She survived, so that's some indication that my choice was correct.*

She'd just finished her notes when a familiar and welcome voice called, "Azhi? Are you in here?" Kyrian ducked into the tent, a warm, loving smile forming on her face as she added, "I didn't see you arrive…" Her words trailed off as she frowned, looking first at Azhani and the wound on her leg, then the pot heating on the brazier. "By the Twain, what are you doing, love?"

"I'm hurt," she replied. "But not badly."

"You're hurt, and I am a stardancer." Kyrian clucked her tongue disapprovingly. "And that makes me eminently qualified to decide if it's bad or not—and that, my love, is no scratch." Lifting the now-steaming pot from the fire, she quickly mixed cleansing herbs into it and knelt beside Azhani's chair. "So why not let me tend it, hm?"

"It really is just a scratch—and there are others who need your care more." Though she couldn't help but be relieved she wouldn't have to stitch herself. It would scar less now that Kyrian was here to do it properly, and leg scars could impede her ability to move in a fight.

"And those others have gotten what care I can give them for now. For the record, this," she said while cleaning out the wound, "is technically a laceration, not a scratch. Now hush and hold still." She hummed as she examined it. "Did you clean it at all on the field?"

"I think Allyn splashed some whiskey on it when he was treating his own wounds." Azhani squinted as she tried to remember, but the fog of battle was too thick.

"Goddess, if it was that stuff we got from Kuwell, I'm shocked you're not still screaming. I had one man claim he poured it on a cut and almost sliced off his hand because it hurt worse than the beast slime," Kyrian said wryly.

Azhani snorted. "I was too busy trying to stay alive to notice. There were far more of them out there than I liked, love."

"Mm, that's what everyone is saying," she murmured, then looked up, her brow furrowing into deep lines of concern. "Should I be more scared than I am?"

"No," Azhani said hastily. "No, I'm sorry. I didn't mean to frighten you. It's nothing unusual outside the fact that this whole season is unusual." She sighed ruefully. Seeing the purple circles under Kyrian's eyes, she reached down and sifted her fingers through her hair. "Have you rested at all?"

"Some. We've been busy. Some of the other squads weren't as lucky as yours. And one beast got close enough that Eli had to put it down—but only after it gutted poor Villikandra."

"Damn," she muttered. "He's one of Iften's, right?"

Kyrian nodded. "Aye. He's one of the morgedraal clansmen. Quiet. Vashyra said she'd take him back when she returned to Y'Syria. He'll die if we keep him here."

"At least we have that option," Azhani said as Kyrian finished stitching the wound closed.

"Mm." She nodded. "You're all done. Now, you should eat and rest, just like you told everyone else."

"I will, but first." Azhani coaxed Kyrian to come sit on her good leg. "I want a little time with you before I go meet with the other patrol leaders."

"All right." Kyrian cupped her hand to Azhani's face and kissed her lightly. "What did you want to do?"

"Just this," she replied, holding onto her, taking comfort in her presence, in her life, and in love itself. "Just be with you."

The quiet enclosed them, leaving them adrift from time until, finally, Kyrian exhaled slowly. "I'm glad you're all right."

"So am I," Azhani said quietly. "I should go. Do you want to join me?"

"I should rest, but yes, I think I will. I'd rather spend as much time with you as I can now. Besides, if any of the others are hiding wounds, I'll know it and can see to it that they're dealt with properly."

"Again, thank you." Though her desire to have Kyrian at her side had been selfish, her lover had proven once again that they were well-matched by finding a good reason to give in to their mutual need to be close.

The list of casualties struck Azhani a much harder blow than she anticipated. Twelve dead, one hundred thirty-six wounded. Numbly, she stared at the tally sheet and tried to place faces to the names, and couldn't. They swam in her eyes with the tears she told herself not to shed. Nearby, Kyrian slept, exhaustion having carried her off long before the last of Azhani's field commanders had finished their reports. Besides the two of them, few others populated the mess tent, though a kind cook had brought over a plate of easily nibbled snacks for her to muddle through while she contemplated the letters she would need to write.

One for every name. She had thought to put it off earlier, but now—faced with the true totals, she just couldn't. They each deserved the very best honor their warleader could give them. So, after forcing herself to eat, she sat and focused on the names until, one by one, she found their faces in her mind and could set words to paper. She told their loved ones just how important each of them had been to the effort to rid the kingdoms of the rimerbeast invasion.

Halfway through the letters, she had to stop, to distract herself with another task lest she become mired in self-castigation. To that end, she began laying out orders to tighten security around camp. Though they would move west in three days, it would serve them well to learn new habits before things got worse.

Someone cleared their throat and she looked up to find a row of messengers waiting to take her orders to her commanders. Over the next few days, some of her people would be riding to the villages and communities that owed no allegiance to the kingdoms in the hopes of warning them before they were attacked by the rimerbeasts. Much as she might like to lead every warning party, she had to leave it up to others to delegate that responsibility to the few soldiers they could spare for the task.

Through the open tent flap, Azhani could see Starseeker Vashyra standing on the low dais the mages used to move from camp back to Y'Syria in what seemed a blink of an eye. In reality, she knew that the magick cost them dearly, and quietly she ordered one of the few soldiers milling about to stand and wait in case Vashyra needed aid after her spell casting. As she suspected, the moment the spell was ended, Vashyra started to sag. The soldier quickly dashed up onto the platform, catching her and helping her to stagger into the mess tent where one of the cooks hurried up with a cup of restorative tea. Another starseeker and two stardancers who were carrying a man on a stretcher dashed through the magickal rift that had opened and vanished. The rift then closed behind them.

Vashyra looked at Azhani and smiled. "Your doing, Warleader? My thanks."

"You're welcome. Is there anything to report?"

She shook her head. "Sadly, no. I wish I could tell you more about that blasted prophecy, but it is as cryptic to me now as it was weeks ago."

"Pity—but I won't let that stop me from moving on," Azhani said with a sigh. "You should get something to eat—and let that nice young man help you back to your tent when you're done. The ground makes for an uncomfortable bed."

She chuckled. "Oh, trust me, I'll not let my pride keep me from leaning on such a handsome crutch."

Azhani smiled and went back to her paperwork. Some time later, a cup of hot tea was set before her and she looked up to find Padreg standing there. His expression neatly conveyed his curiosity, yet he still cocked his head, crossed his arms, and asked, "What are you doing here? The day candle's almost spent."

"I've got so much yet to do, positions to fill," she replied wearily.

Gently, he placed his hand on her shoulder. "No. Go to bed, my friend. It is time to take your lady and hold her against your heart. Tomorrow, we will rise once again and send the bastards back to the abyss."

"I wish I could, my friend. But there will come a time when this task will have to fall to another. For now, though, it is my burden to bear."

Padreg frowned, but she knew he understood, for instead of speaking further, he merely nodded and left her to work. It was time to finish what she had put up earlier. Once more, she dipped her quill into the ink pot and began writing. *To the family of Ariana Wintersky: It is my sad duty to inform you that…*

When all her work was finally done, she drained the dregs of her tea and shook Kyrian awake. "Kyr, love. Let's go to bed."

Rousing slowly, Kyrian sat up, rubbed her eyes, and fumbled around in her haversack a moment before presenting Azhani with a small jar of lozenges. "Here. I forgot I made these earlier. For your throat."

Accepting the bottle, Azhani opened it and sniffed the small candies, then smiled fondly. Honey, lemon, and herbs—all perfect for soothing her sore throat after battle. "Thank you. Come, let us get some much needed rest."

Wincing, Allyndev groaned softly as Syrelle washed dried blood from the wound in his shoulder. One careless moment had left him open to attack, and now he bore the marks of a rimerbeast's claws.

"Hurts," he grumbled, jerking away from her when her ministrations became too brutal.

"Hush," she said tartly. "Had you not been woolgathering, I'd not have to do this!"

"Sy!" Twisting away, he yanked the bloody cloth from her hands. "You're hurting me more than the damned rimerbeast!"

"Damn it, Allyn!" she hissed, her face going red. "If you had seen the way you looked when you came in—if you had felt what we did…" Anger made her voice harsh as she looked over at Devon, who was carefully grinding herbs into a paste.

He sighed. "She has a point, Allyn. You were woolgathering."

"I wasn't, I swear it," he said weakly. Though he was on the mend, it seemed his friends were still just as scared as they had been that first night. "I thought it was dead."

"Oh, of course you did. You've said nothing else for the last three damned days!" Syrelle retorted bitterly. "But Devon was there, and if he says you were woolgathering, well then, what am I to believe?"

Sullenly, Allyndev looked back and forth between his friends. Though there was some anger on Syrelle's face, both of them did seem to be acting out of concern for him. Schooling himself to patience, he tried to put aside his frustration, but failed miserably. "Can't you just bandage this so I can go do something?" he asked plaintively. After three days lying in bed, he was restless and longed to be back out on the field, patrolling with Master Azhani. Though only four days had passed since they'd first encountered live rimerbeasts, the lust for battle was raging within him.

"Oh, by the Twain! Devon, just give me the damned poultice! Allyn, I swear, you are impossible!" She packed the wound and then bound up the bandages once more. "And you are not going anywhere. Sit, and wait for me. Your hair's a fright." Then she sighed and caressed his face, whispering, "Whatever am I going to do about you?" before hurrying off.

Stunned, Allyndev sat blinking dumbly, and then shook himself. "Goddess," he mumbled. "How does she do that?"

Devon chuckled. "I wish I knew—maybe then I could find some way to counter it."

They shared a look, their gazes remaining locked a hair longer than perhaps was comfortable. Allyn blushed suddenly. "I, ah, if you and she are, er—"

"We aren't," Devon rushed to reply. "But I...she's so beautiful and kind and I've never known anyone like her...or you, really. I've never had friends like you," he said softly.

"Neither have I." Allyndev smiled. "I'm a pretty lucky fellow, Dev. I have you and Sy and Master Azhani and Stardancer Kyrian and...and I'm happy."

Moving closer, Devon sat beside him and offered him a mug of tea. "Here. It's that stuff Stardancer Kyrian made up. Tastes awful, but I dumped enough honey in it to make it drinkable—if you swallow quickly," he said with a wry smile.

"Thanks." Allyn took Devon's advice and drank fast. It was hot, but it was better to get it all down so he could follow it with the mug of mulled wine he could see in Devon's other hand.

"You're welcome. You know, it's not looking quite so puffy anymore," Devon said. "That's good, right?" He gave Allyndev's hair a friendly ruffling. Bits of dried blood and dirt fell away. "Oh, gross. I think we're going to have to figure out some way to get you washed up soon, before you stink us out of the tent."

Allyn made a face. "You do that and I might have to kiss you."

Devon blushed. "Ah, er, well, I don't know that you'd need to go that far…"

Dryly, Allyndev snorted, then shook his head. "My apologies. I just feel so useless, Dev."

"I understand." He gave Allyn's back a brief pat. "It's hard to rest when you want to work, especially when the healers are so busy with other patients."

Allyn nodded. "There are others who need them more than I, and it would be dishonorable of me to use my station to demand aid when others are more gravely injured."

"I see you've taken some lessons to heart, my prince," Azhani said as she stepped into the tent.

"You've taught me practicality, master. The skill of my arm in battle is meaningless against the lives the stardancer's magick can save," he said quietly.

Azhani scowled. "Ah, so it isn't wisdom, but self-pity that burns in your gut. Well, once you're done wallowing, report to Kyrian in the chirurgeon's tent."

Allyn nearly knocked Devon to the floor in his haste to stand. "I'll attend her at once!" Grabbing a clean shirt, he tugged it on and rushed out, narrowing avoiding Syrelle, who was carrying a heavy bucket filled to the brim with steaming hot water. "Sorry, Sy," he said, offering her a cheeky grin as he pushed the tent flap open.

"Allyn, wait!"

"Don't bother, Sy," Devon said as Allyndev bounced from foot to foot impatiently. "He's off to see Kyrian."

"But I was going to wash his hair!" She looked down at the soapy water in her bucket.

Allyn bit his lips uncertainly, then offered her a quick smile. "That's…I really want that, but…" He glanced through the open flap at the chirurgeon's tent across the camp. "Kyrian can heal me, Syrelle!"

With a wry chuckle, Azhani said, "Go on, Allyn. I'm sure the water will be here when you get back, right, Princess?"

Rolling her eyes, Syrelle replied, "I suppose."

Devon wrapped his arm around Syrelle's shoulders. "Come on. We can go make a real bath for him."

"Oh, all right." She put the bucket aside. "Just try not to trip on your own two feet in your haste to get to Stardancer Kyrian!" she called after him as he took off running.

"I won't, I promise!" he gleefully yelled back. Finally, he was going to be able to get back out and patrol! He couldn't wait for nightfall.

Kyrian laughed at him when he stumbled into the tent, stripped off his shirt and knelt to present his wounded shoulder to her. "I'm ready, Stardancer," he said in between gasps of breath.

Shaking her head wryly, she replied, "You could have stopped to put shoes on, you know," and began undoing the bandages.

He flushed. "I didn't want to keep you waiting." Nervous and excited, he shivered when she pushed his hair out of the way and began to sing. Slowly, he sank into a peaceful, blissful haze in which all pain vanished, leaving him floating in the calming sea of her voice and Astariu's Fire.

When he once again woke, he was back in the tent he shared with Devon and Syrelle, his head suspended over a tub of steaming water. Blinking in surprise, he looked up to find Devon beside him, carefully supporting his head while Syrelle washed his hair.

"Easy now," Devon said softly. "Kyrian said you'd be a big groggy from the Fire."

"Feel a bit dizzy," he mumbled, flexing his hand. When not even the slightest twinge of pain bothered him, he grinned. "Didn't hurt."

"Kyrian's really quite gifted with the Fire," Devon replied. "She saved Azhani's leg."

"Uh-huh, I heard the story." Allyndev's stomach rumbled loudly. "Goddess, I'm starving. And thirsty enough to drink the bathwater."

Syrelle snorted. "Drink this instead." She dropped a waterskin on his chest. "Stardancer Kyrian made it."

Gratefully, Allyn sucked cool, sweet tea from the skin. The herbs in it tasted different from the stuff he'd been drinking earlier and he hoped it wouldn't make him sleepy. "Thank you," he said once his thirst was slaked. "And thank you for...well, this," he added, tugging at a lock of wet hair that was stuck to his forehead.

"You are very welcome." Syrelle helped him to stand after rinsing his hair out. "Dev's prepared a bath for you, as well."

"Aw, Dev." He grinned as he toweled his hair vigorously. "I'm going to wear out my thank yous."

Devon laughed. "Better that than wearing out our noses with your stink."

Rolling his eyes, Allyn tossed the towel at him, then caught him up in a bear hug. "Seriously, you both have been so wonderful to me. I don't know what I'd have done without you." He turned to pull Syrelle into the hug as well.

Syrelle smiled fondly, then kissed him. "I very much approve of this version of you, Prince Allyndev."

"I agree," Devon said quietly.

Conscious of the feelings they both had for Syrelle, Allyndev knew his friend must be uncomfortable, but couldn't bring himself to relinquish the embrace just yet. Camaraderie was something that was still so new to him that he ate up this feeling, this amazing sense of belonging that flowed around them so easily.

It was Devon who pulled away. "I'll go fetch some supper for us," he said quickly, hurrying out of the tent.

Allyn sighed as Syrelle turned aside and began cleaning up from washing his hair, starting with the basin that held the dirty water. "I can't believe how hungry I am," he said, trying not to feel self-conscious as he stripped off his breeches and climbed into the tub on the other side of the tent.

"The stardancers tell me it's pretty common after a healing."

"I've never needed the Fire before," he said while scrubbing his arms. "Still a bit of stiffness, but otherwise…it's incredible how different it feels now."

Clean clothes appeared on a bench just on the inside of the curtain that separated their bathing area. "Warleader Azhani said you'll be able to patrol tomorrow," Syrelle said quietly.

Aware that Syrelle was worried, Allyndev replied, "Good—though there will be no more woolgathering, I promise you!"

She sighed.

"Sy?" He shifted so he could see her, standing with her back to him. "Aren't you glad I'm better?"

"Of course I am!" she hissed, half turning and glaring at him. "Why would you think otherwise?"

Climbing out of the tub, he padded over and cupped her face gently. "You're so angry, Sy. I can practically feel it—and you certainly don't seem very happy that I'll be able to get back to defending Y'Myran tomorrow."

A tiny noise of frustration got caught in her throat as she pulled away. "I'm perfectly elated that you are healed, Prince Allyndev." Pushing her hands through her hair, she grimaced. "Do not, however, mistake that joy as pleasure for the fact that you'll soon be in jeopardy once more!" With that said, she grabbed a handful of damp towels and stomped out of the tent, leaving him to stand there, naked, dripping water all over the floor.

"What am I supposed to do?" he whispered, turning to climb back into the tub and finish washing.

When Syrelle went storming past him, Devon nearly called out to her, but he knew she was particularly prickly right now. When Azhani had informed him that he and Allyn would ride tomorrow, all the color had drained from the princess' face and she'd spent most of the rest of the afternoon acting as if she were mad at him for the news.

She just cares, that's all. Goddess, she probably loves Allyn. Twain knows I do. I love her, too. Foolishly, perhaps, he carried a tiny hope within him that she loved him too, and that one day she might kiss him as she did Allyndev.

Pasting a cheerful smile on his face, he pushed into their tent, holding up a loaded tray and calling out, "Dinnertime! Venison stew tonight."

Allyn took one of the bowls, huddled over it on his bed and ate mechanically, muttering his thanks while tearing a hunk of bread off the loaf on the tray.

Devon was torn, wanting to go to his friend, to ask what had drained the cheer from him so quickly. Somehow, he knew the answer would involve Syrelle. Looking at her empty bed, he sighed. Would there be any way for their friendship to survive the entanglements of their hearts without causing one of them more pain than they could bear? *Maybe it would just be best if it's me the rimerbeasts take next time. Save us all some heartache.*

CHAPTER EIGHTEEN

Arris Thodan was not a patient man. He had, over many years, learned to trust his mentor and now closest adviser, Porthyros Omal. When he gave counsel on matters pertaining to the crown, Arris listened. With regard to the rimerbeasts, Porthyros' calmly spoken words of caution had kept Arris in Y'Dannyv, dealing with matters of state until autumn paid call to the kingdom.

Scowling darkly, Arris stared at the man standing before him and snarled, "Now, shall I go north?"

"Yes, I think now is a perfect time for you to journey northward, Majesty," Porthyros replied solemnly. "After all, the men will need to resupply and to renew their hearts to face the long winter ahead—and they will be overjoyed to see that their king stands with them against the tide of battle."

"Yes!" Arris shot out of his chair and marched around the room, his head filling with visions of battles yet to come. "It will be glorious! I shall pack at once!"

And thus, the remainder of Y'Dan's army went north.

Much to his dismay, Arris discovered that the work of egg smashing held little glory. It was, however, quite satisfying to watch the foul things crumble. When the ichor spat and hissed against the leather of his boots, he felt more alive than in any other moment. The aftermath of such a task was even better, for he found much to delight him in the arms of his mistress, Batizha. She had been more successful at distracting him from thoughts of Azhani Rhu'len than any other woman to cross his path.

One afternoon, while Arris was enjoying a meal, a messenger burst into his encampment. Heading pell-mell for the king, he slid to his knees the moment he came into Arris' view. Quickly, he bashed his head against the ground and blurted, "Hail to thee, Arris Demonslayer, overlord of Y'Dan."

The glee that curved Arris' thin lips into a smile felt far too good to hold back. He'd earned that name, and by Ecarthus, he was going to revel in it!

"Say your message and be off with you!" Porthyros commanded.

"Rimerbeasts!" he gasped. "Rimerbeasts attack! Hundreds of the foul beasts have flanked our eastern divisions, Majesty."

Afire with battle lust, Arris surged up out of his throne. "That's wonderful…I mean, terrible, terrible news! We must be off at once to defend our people!" Looking from Batizha to Porthyros and back, he waited until both smiled at him before grabbing the messenger. "More, you must tell me more!"

Trembling, he stammered, "A-a scout, he c-came to c-camp, dying. H-his wounds were horrible, my king. T-there was s-so much blood, b-but he h-had this." He produced an ichor-stained, broken sword.

Grabbing the hilt, Arris held it aloft as though it were a blade of legend. "Rimerbeasts." He dipped his fingers into the ichor staining the steel, cursing when it burned his skin.

"I will send for your squad leaders," Porthyros said quietly.

For a long moment, Batizha stood silent, giving Porthyros an odd look. Then, she merely bowed to Arris. "And I shall pack our tent, my love."

Porthyros sniffed and flicked his fingers at her as if he were shooing away a distracting gnat. "I will attend to that, as well. You should return to the city. The king has no need of you now."

Arris snapped out of his communion with the broken sword. "No, 'Thyro. Let her come. I…enjoy her company, of a morning."

Something odd passed over Porthyros' face, but he nevertheless bowed respectfully as he said, "Of course, Majesty."

"And make me some tea. I'm parched!" Arris tossed the sword aside and took hold of Batizha's goblet, draining the contents quickly.

"As you command, Majesty," Porthyros said stiffly, hurrying off toward the larger camp.

"I could pour you more wine, my king," Batizha said with a solemn smile.

"Ah, my Batizha, you are so very lovely," Arris murmured, caressing caressed her face lightly. "And so good to me, but no. I must keep a clear head. No more wine will pass my lips. 'Thyro's tea alone will sustain my thirst until the last of the foul creatures lies dead at my feet." Turning to the messenger, he smiled broadly. "Mark this moment, boy—I will save you all."

Bowing, he replied, "Yes, of course, Majesty. Will that be all?"

A piercing scream echoed through the camp and was followed by the dull tolling of a gong.

Arris smiled. "Make your obeisances to Ecarthus, and rest. I will need you to carry word of my coming to our benighted soldiers."

"At once, Majesty."

The gong tolled again. Arris turned and bowed northward, murmuring, "Ecarthus frees me. My blood is his blood. To him, I gladly go."

"To him I gladly go," Batizha said quietly, though she was not looking quite perfectly northward, but rather at Arris himself.

"To him, I g-gladly go," the messenger whispered, than ran off.

Ystarfe Pass was a memory lost in a haze of too much rimerbeast ichor. Azhani assigned three patrols to remain behind and mop up any remaining monsters while she moved the bulk of her army westward. The weather changed and with it, her strategy. As it grew colder, it became less and less likely that they would discover egg-laden caves, forcing their patrols to work night and day hunting the beasts themselves, killing so much and so often that not one suit of armor or pair of boots in the entire encampment was free of ichor burns.

They lost two thousand soldiers in the first month of full combat.

Each loss was another splinter of failure digging deep into Azhani's heart. Though the smoke from their funeral pyres choked her lungs, she stood there every single time and sang the pathsong at Kyrian's side, her face carved with tears. No name was lost, no sacrifice forgotten, not even when she eventually had to turn to others for help in the writing of the letters that flowed back to Y'Syr in a river of sorrow-filled parchment.

Kyrian did all she could to offer solace, but often, it was not her tender care Azhani seemed to crave, but her body and that, Kyrian willingly gave her. On the battlefield, death was a powerful motivator, and for days following a funeral, Azhani was a menace so fearsome that rumors began to spread that she'd been infused with the spirit of Lyriandelle Starseeker herself.

"It's otherworldly," one soldier said as Kyrian knelt to change his dressing. "The fury that takes her is like nothing I've ever seen."

Another, an Y'Dani soldier who'd risked everything to escape Y'Dannyv and join up with Azhani's army, just laughed. "That's our Banshee."

"I'll follow her to Hell," the first soldier said. "And when she drags my ass home, I'll follow her wherever else she leads."

Kyrian stared hard at him, startled by the man's devotion. He was elven, and of one of the families that had doubted the queen's choice.

He must have noticed her expression, for he touched his fingers to his chest. "Twain's truth, Stardancer. I'd not have thought it possible before, but I'll not doubt Warleader Azhani ever again."

"She won't ask you to do anything she wouldn't," Kyrian replied solemnly.

"I know. Why, I heard she held back a wave of the bastards after her patrol went down the other day—the whirlwind of death they call her. They say her cry sent the beasts fleeing into the night," he said proudly. "Thirty-eight soldiers came home that night."

She smiled, though fear still clung to the back of her throat at hearing the tale again. "Aye. But you know what will haunt her?"

He shook his head.

"The two that didn't. Aldran and Thorvald were good men." Kyrian closed her eyes against the memory of Azhani staggering back to camp with the bodies of the two dwarves thrown over Kushyra's shoulders, her blood-stained face bleak with grief.

The other soldier coughed softly. "They've made a song of it, you know. They're calling her Astariu's vengeance."

Kyrian tried not to wince. Azhani preferred to let others wear the glory. Given the chance, she would spend candlemarks countering the bard's songs of her heroics with even more detailed stories featuring the actions of the least of her soldiers. It didn't take long for the songsters to fall upon this feast of information and fill the ears of their comrades with tales honoring all those whose exploits meant that the army had one more day of victory to celebrate.

"It's a good song—but I prefer the bawdy tunes," she said with a grin. "I'd much rather sing about good ale, wouldn't you?"

Both soldiers chuckled at that.

"I'd have thought you'd be singing that one 'bout your Fire, Stardancer," he said wryly.

There was even a song for the healers. It had been written by a soldier Kyrian had coaxed from the brink of death with the help of the other stardancers, calling upon Astariu's Fire to cleanse the fever of the rimerbeast's bite from his body.

She shook her head. "It's flattering, but I'm Astariu's servant, not some avatar of her divinity. I'll leave that task to someone who doesn't have anything better to do. Right now, I've got bandages to burn." She rose and took the wadded, fouled cloths with her.

Though she'd avoided combat thus far, Kyrian had seen its results so often that she could judge by looking whether a soldier's wounds required the Fire or just a good scrubbing and stitching by the chirurgeons. Their tireless work made it much easier for the stardancers to see to those most gravely injured. So far, thank the Twain, she'd not had to do more than tend minor wounds on Azhani herself, and part of her suspected that it was thanks to Gormerath's mystical nature. Whatever kept her lover safe, she blessed it and prayed daily that it would continue to do so, for the thought of losing Azhani was enough to make her sick with fear.

It made every moment they had more precious than any jewel. Every word they spoke, every touch they exchanged, every kiss, every joke, every shared laugh felt like it was being forever etched into her heart, and she clutched them all like they were made of spun gold.

Just keep her safe. I want to spend my life with her.

Barton was gone.

In its place, death shrouded the once-thriving community like a funeral pall. Not a single building stood unmolested. The ruins of a half-built wall bore the remains of the defenders, their bodies torn to shreds by the rimerbeasts that had ravaged the town.

Scattered fires still burned in the wreckage of the houses, adding a thick, oily smoke to the noxious atmosphere. Nothing moved, and Kyrian couldn't bring herself to look down at the streets, not when her nose and the twisting of her stomach told her that they were thick with gore.

No one spoke, though many faces were stained by tears or hardened by anger. Shaking uncontrollably, Kyrian followed Azhani to the center of town. Here, an aura of evil so thick it made her skin crawl lingered. The starseekers were waiting for them. Standing shoulder to shoulder, they raised their staves high as everyone began dismounting. With a single word, the crystals set atop each staff came ablaze, shoving back the darkness.

Carefully, Kyrian picked her way through the rubble to stand beside Azhani and her commanders, all of whom were peering down into the remains of a well. Most were praying along with the starseekers. The water had been fouled with the remains of the slain.

Kyrian wrapped her arm around Azhani's waist and closed her eyes, saying her own prayers for the dead.

Azhani sighed. "I...have no words for this." She pulled Kyrian close.

"What are we going to do?"

Azhani blinked back tears. "Assign men to clear and burn. I won't let disease destroy this place of rest."

Someone cried out. As one, they all turned to face the commotion coming from the other end of town. Four scouts burst through the soldiers, carrying a makeshift stretcher. Upon it was a man garbed in the purple of an Astariun brother. All five were liberally splashed with blood. A jagged, horrible wound in the priest's throat wept a steady stream of blood.

Kyrian raced to meet them, her hands outstretched and glowing with power. Holy prayers formed on her lips. Her fingers met his flesh and she began to sing. Behind her, several other stardancers joined in, each reaching out to touch her, lending her further power while the starseekers prayed.

Fire enveloped Kyrian, limning her and her patient in the brilliant sorcery of Astariu's power. Her soul leaped and flew with joy as the world around her vanished and she grew lost in the passion of the spell.

Slowly, heartbeat by heartbeat, Kyrian healed the priest. When she opened her eyes again, the terrible bleeding had ceased and he was smiling up at her.

"A gifted one you are, Stardancer," he croaked softly.

Before she could reply, Padreg pushed his way through to her side. "And a lucky one you are, Jalen."

"Ah, 'tis good to see you again, old friend," Jalen said as they moved him out beyond the village boundaries to where their camp was being erected.

"Aye, though I could wish it were under better circumstances."

Behind them, Azhani was snapping out orders, sending men running ahead to the chirurgeon's tent to get a cot ready for the priest.

Jalen sighed and blinked back tears. "We couldn't stop them, Paddy. They came in the dead of night—by dawn, it was..." He shook his head.

A strangled groan caused Kyrian to turn in time to see Azhani bury her face in her hands. Quickly, she went to her, pulling her into her arms as Azhani wept, whispering the names of her friends. "Paul, oh Goddess...Orra, Mattie...they're gone."

Kyrian's eyes burned as she cried with her lover. Allyndev thrust a wineskin into her hands, saying, "It's not an answer, but it might help."

Between them, she and Azhani drained it.

"Surely they're not all gone," Padreg was saying. "We haven't found that many bodies."

Jalen coughed. "We…sent the children, the elderly, and the sick to Y'Syr three months ago. Paul and Orra took them the moment they heard the mines were infested. A few of us stayed behind, to guard the shrine." Someone gave him water. "Those accursed Ecarthans drove me out of Y'Dan, but Barton was mine, damn it!" His face hardened. "The Twain's memory had to remain alive in Y'Dan. I swore an oath on it."

Padreg touched his shoulder gently. "You did well, old friend. Rest now. You're safe."

Nodding slowly, Jalen replied, "Aye. Sleep. Thank the Twain you're here." He sighed and then closed his eyes as they carried him into the waiting tent.

"Azhi." Kyrian cupped her hand to her face. "They're safe, love. Come on, we've work to do."

Straightening, Azhani dashed away her tears. "Yes, we do—but you need rest. Allyn, please escort Kyrian to our tent. Devon, go with Vashyra. I want this place burned free of all rimerbeast taint by dawn. Padreg, I want a three mile wide clear zone around us."

"What can I do, Warleader?" Syrelle lifted her bow to salute her.

"You're in charge of the hunters. We all need fresh meat—partly for hunger, partly to kill the smell coming out of Barton," Azhani said calmly. "Bring in as much as possible, but keep within that three mile boundary."

"Aye. You, you, and you." Syrelle pointed to three different soldiers. "You're with me. I need to find the hunter's camp now."

"Aye, princess," they replied, snapping her quick salutes.

One of the scouts coughed softly. "What of the shrine? It's intact and has a functioning well."

"Elisira," Azhani called.

"Yes, Warleader?"

"Go see to the shrine—if it's as fit as he says, we can make that the central hub of camp," she said as Kyrian's head began to spin. As always, using the Fire had worn her out.

"Of course." Elisira offered the scout a warm smile. "Care to show me the way?"

He nodded, and together they hurried off.

"Kyr, go sleep now," Azhani murmured, kissing her tenderly.

"Are you sure?" she blinked sleepily.

"Yes. We'll be fine, love. Thank you."

"Be careful," she said, then turned to lean on Allyn's arm. "Go slowly, my prince. My feet are suddenly unsteady."

"I have you, Stardancer," he said with a smile. "I won't let you fall."

She relaxed some, turning to glance back at Azhani, who stood outlined by the glow of the mage's fires, her hawkish face burnished in shadows, her blue eyes diamond bright.

"Warleader's patrol, to me," Azhani yelled. "Let's go see if we can find some survivors out there!"

"Aye, Warleader, we come!"

Please let her find someone, Kyrian thought wearily. *Or she'll never forgive herself for leaving in the first place.*

Tangles of arcane energies rippled and fluxed above the ruins of Barton. All through the night, Azhani could look up wherever she was and see the progress of the mages and starseekers as they cleared away the miasma of evil left in the wake of the rimerbeast attack.

The glow of the army's fires dotted the forest and hills. Once the town was declared safe, those soldiers whose desire for comfort outweighed their distaste of scavenging soon took up residence in the newly cleansed town.

As far from the town as possible, a bonfire burned. Here, the remains of the residents were sent, while Kyrian and the other priests sang the pathsong to ensure that each person found their way to The Great Fields. Azhani spent as many candlemarks as she could spare praying with them, trying to offer her apologies to the ghosts of those she had failed.

Under the rubble of the town, many useful objects were discovered and, though some argued that it was looting, were absorbed into the war machine of Azhani's army. They even found a large cache of food in the cellar of what had been the Barton Inn.

Besides Brother Jalen, the only other living beings they discovered among the wreckage were a gaunt, near-dead hunting cat and her litter of kittens. A few soldiers, wise to the ways of dealing with the massive cats, coaxed them into their camp. Soon, the antics of the kittens became a treasured delight among the weary men and women of the army.

Some felt the animals were a burden, but Azhani couldn't be more happy to have them. Once the mother was healthy, her skills as a hunter would help put meat in their stew pots. Even the kittens were capable of bringing down small birds and squirrels.

"I tell you, they're no ordinary cats, Agrid," Azhani overheard one of her men tell a dwarven blacksmith. "Just the other day, I watched Avisha bring down a buck all by herself! It was an impressive sight, I'll tell you!"

Agrid snorted and spat. "Bet she damn near took yer arm off when ye went t'take the kill from her, Rythak."

Rythak shook his head. "Nay. She's been well-trained. Waited 'til we gave her the innards, then took off after another one quick as lightning."

Approaching them, Azhani said, "So Avisha's the reason I've been eating better of late, then?"

Snapping to attention, the two soldiers quickly saluted her while Rythak replied, "Aye, Warleader."

"I'm glad to hear it. You know, I once heard they were the companions of the Firstlanders."

Rythak nodded. "Aye. Bred special for their wit, strength, and loyalty to their chosen hunting partners. There'll be no shortage of those waiting to see if the kittens will choose them."

Now Azhani chuckled. "As Avisha chose Devon?" she asked, earning a heavy sigh from the hunter.

"Aye, though there's more than a few who claim the mage captured her with one of his spells."

"Devon would do no such thing," she replied so sharply that Rythak winced.

"Peace, Warleader, I meant no offense. Perhaps she is only acting as she is named, as to be chosen is quite miraculous."

"Please just try to remember that Devon's as confused by the 'miracle' of her choice as you are, Rythak." She consciously stressed the Firstlander word that was also the translation of Avisha's name.

"Aye, Warleader. I'll pass the word," he said, saluting her again.

Within a week, all the kittens had chosen their two-legged partners except one, a small gray male who had a habit of moving from fire to fire, never staying more than a night or two with one person. Because of this, he was named "Zhadosh," or "Ghost."

Staring at a sea of reports, Azhani rubbed the bridge of her nose and bit back a groan. Rimerbeasts still roamed the area around the remains of Barton. Between rotating soldiers in and out of patrols so no one was overworked and the seemingly daily list of the injured, it was all she could do to keep enough people in the field to hunt them down. Even now, she had to weigh which duties called to her loudest. Anything she wanted was cast right out the flap of the tent. Sleep was for when she could hardly stand upright any longer. Eating happened when someone remembered to shove food at her. She couldn't remember the last time she'd bathed or worn clean clothes.

An ache deep in her heart poked and prodded at her, urging her to throw it all aside and rush back to her family's cottage. Honor and duty held her fast to her seat, where she spent candlemarks reading and writing reports that would then be sent back to Y'Syria. She did, however, pause long enough to assign Padreg the southern quadrant patrol. He would understand the importance of checking that area thoroughly.

The tent flap rustled and Azhani looked up as Starseeker Vashyra stepped in, a grave expression on her face. "There is trouble in Y'Syria, Azhani."

"What is it?"

"Black-sailed ships captained by Ecarthan priests war with the Y'Noran and Y'Syran navies on Banner Lake." She took a seat across from Azhani. "There are heavy casualties. The queen cannot spare any soldiers to bolster our ranks."

"Damn it. Do we need to send some units back?" She wondered where she was going to find a few hundred men and women to reassign.

Vashyra shook her head. "They've achieved a stalemate, of sorts, and some of Ambassador Iften's relatives are helping to fill the ranks that patrol the shore."

Relaxing only marginally, Azhani sighed and tossed her pen aside. "What's going on, Vashyra? Where did all these damned Ecarthans come from?"

"Best I can tell you, from what I've pieced together, is that they were cultivated by the sorcerer, Kasyrin Darkchilde. How he came to be associated with Ecarthus—and just exactly what Ecarthus is—well, we're still trying to figure that out. The brotherhood of Astarus is in charge of ancient knowledge like that, and when even they are having a hard time finding references, I think you can understand how difficult it is for me to answer your questions."

Azhani reached for a pot of mulled wine and poured them each a mug. "All right. Do you think they're related to the rimerbeasts, ogres, sea monsters and the like?" she asked softly.

Vashyra shrugged. "Who can say for sure? Our auguries are…unusually difficult to read of late. I dislike such coincidence, though."

"As do I. All right, thank you. Here is what I am ready to send to Lyssera today. I should—"

"Sleep. You should sleep, my friend. You can't lead if you can't think."

Azhani wanted to argue, but it was late and it had been at least fourteen candlemarks since she'd seen Kyrian. "You're right. Sleep sounds perfect."

"It's where I'm headed," Vashyra replied with a grin. "Thank you for this, though." She drained her mug. Standing, she shivered visibly. "It's getting colder."

"It'll be colder still before this is done, Starseeker," Azhani said as she cleared her table and covered the brazier for the night. "Rest well, my friend."

"You too."

In the days that followed, they learned that not only were the Ecarthan priests attacking their allies by water, but that they were also invading Y'Nor itself.

Azhani, Padreg, Elisira, and Kyrian sat huddled around a pile of messages from Y'Nym, each one bleaker than the last. Death tolls, herd losses, and of course, the dire news that the other kingdoms were suffering troubles of their own. Worse, Brannock Maeven had written, no one had heard from High King Ysradan for weeks.

Quietly, Azhani said, "If he's dead, it'll be utter chaos."

Padreg nodded while Kyrian and Elisira each moved closer to their loved ones. "Aye. I've ordered the princess to stay in camp at all times. She was quite displeased with me."

"Better unhappy than dead," Azhani said sourly. "And if Ysradan's gone, Ysrallan is going to need her."

Kyrian took a breath. "If…King Ysradan is dead…what will that mean in terms of Y'Dan, and of Arris?"

She shook her head. "I wish I knew. Ysrallan is too young to rule alone. Likely, someone will be named as regent, and whoever that is will make the decision in Ysrallan's stead."

"Which means you'd be dealing with Pirellan Madros," Padreg said distastefully. "And that nodwaffler wouldn't know how to keep a promise if Astariu herself commanded it."

The four of them sat glumly, each wondering what the future was going to bring.

Good news, when it came, was fleeting, but nonetheless cause for celebration. Ambassador Kuwell and his allies sent word that the mines and caves of Y'Dror had been scoured clean of all traces of rimerbeast activity and none of the monsters had made it into the forests south of their section of the Crest of Amyra. Because of that, he and his men were marching west and hoped to join the Y'Syran army soon.

Knowing the dwarves were at her back allowed Azhani to breathe a little easier. They would sweep the mountains to the east for any stragglers or strays that had eluded her patrols.

Hard on the heels of Kuwell's missive, however, came a single, deeply distracting piece of intelligence.

King Arris was coming.

She had known that, since crossing into this section of the mountains, the Y'Dani army was actively working to drive out the rimerbeasts—though their patrols had never met, the signs were easy to read for someone who had trained with a good number of the soldiers now crawling along the western ridge of the Crest of Amyra.

This morning, however, word had reached her that Arris himself commanded Y'Dan's army and he was leading them in her direction. If she did not change course soon, they were going to meet in the mountains north of the village of Ynnych, something that could be devastating for both sides of the conflict. She was duty bound enough to realize the rimerbeasts were the greater threat, but she suspected Arris would throw aside any pretense of defending his kingdom and commit all his forces to attacking hers just so he could hurt her again. That thought was enough to make her stomach roil.

A cup of steaming hot tea was set before her. Looking up, she was treated to Kyrian's warmest, most loving smile. "Keep scowling like that, love, and your face will turn to stone."

Azhani took the cup, sipped the sweet, hot beverage, and sighed. "Thank you."

"You're welcome. You appeared to need it."

Nearby, Brother Jalen lifted his own mug and saluted her. "Have I mentioned today how grateful I am you came this way, Azhani?"

Azhani chuckled. "At least once, Brother Jae, but I'm glad too." Glancing over his shoulder at the shrine, she smiled warmly. "You've done a beautiful job with it."

Turning to look at the small building, he nodded. "It was work worth doing—and how else could I repay Astariu for Her healing?"

"She asks for nothing like that, Jalen," Kyrian said quietly. "You know that."

"Perhaps I do, but still—I felt it had to be done," he replied.

Azhani stepped inside the shrine and walked up to the altar. Kneeling before the statues of the Twain, she used a piece of tinder to take flame from the oil lamp and touch it to a pile of incense, releasing a sweet scent into the air. Behind the altar, a massive crystal bowl overflowed with fresh water. This filled a pool that was designed to feed a variety of plants that grew out of pots concealed in the walls of the temple.

Spreading outward from the central altar were the bedrolls and cots of the priests and mages who had taken shelter within the shrine. Some were occupied, but for now, most were empty. Here and there, someone would shift in their sleep, revealing a hint of saffron, azure, or crimson fabric. With a slight shiver at the concentration of so much potential magick, she touched her hands to the altar, murmured a soft prayer, and quickly exited the building, returning to her seat by the fire.

Not too far away, Allyndev, Syrelle, and Devon sat on a blanket, a single plate of food shared between them and with Avisha, who was curled up at their feet. Acting like a queen receiving her due from her loyal subjects, she took tidbits whenever they were offered. Mostly, though, it was a race to see which of the three could eat the fastest, with Allyn and Devon outpacing Syrelle by a good deal.

Bemusedly, Azhani watched as Devon snatched the last small, meat-filled pie and held it just out of Allyndev's reach.

"Hah, just try to take it now, my prince!" he crowed teasingly.

Smirking, Allyn grabbed his arm, jerked him closer, and bit the pie in half, then licked his lips with a satisfied smile as Devon gaped at him.

Syrelle just smiled fondly and shook her head.

They're going to create a few waves if they ever figure out their feelings, Azhani thought wryly.

Kyrian touched her arm. "Hungry, love?"

"Aye, but I'll fetch something. You sit and rest. It hasn't been that long since you healed our good brother here." She nodded to Jalen, who was proudly showing off his work in the shrine to one of Azhani's lieutenants.

"Thank you." Kyrian dropped onto a nearby log bench with a relieved sigh.

The meal was simple, but filling, and afterward they gathered round the fire to listen to Brother Jalen regale the group with the tales of his adventures. While Azhani and Padreg repaired their armor, Kyrian and Elisira darned several pairs of socks and patched as many pairs of breeches as could be rescued.

More than once, Azhani found herself smiling over some of the priest's exploits, but it was Kyrian who burst into gales of laughter. "I can't believe you snuck into the king of Y'Tol's private cellar!"

With a beatific smile, Jalen replied, "I do not sneak, my dear. My entry into that hallowed chamber was by invitation—after all, he had offered me a reward for discovering the cure to that particularly nasty infestation of beetles. I simply chose to take it in the form of three bottles of one of his finest vintages."

Woeful, Padreg shook his head. "Maybe I should just hand the key to my cellar over to you next time you visit Y'Nym, Jae."

Jalen snorted. "You've not got a cellar, Paddy. Besides, I care little for ale or mead."

"Ah, your palate's too refined for my barbarian brews, hm?" Padreg slyly retorted.

In a sheepish tone, Jalen said, "Nay, 'tis not that at all. 'Tis only that they make me belch."

Everyone laughed and the conversation flowed in different directions until Jalen asked Padreg when he and Elisira were planning to wed.

Somewhat pointedly, Azhani said, "Midwinter, wasn't it?"

With a rueful shrug, Padreg looked to Elisira, who smiled fondly and replied, "Originally, that had been our thought, yes. However, we've decided to wait until we've returned to Y'Nor. Both of us want to be home and focused only on the joy of the event, not…" She glanced at the armor in Azhani's lap. "Other things."

"Understandable," Azhani said quietly.

Padreg smiled. "And what of you and Kyrian, hm? Will you stand before Astariu and pledge your lives together?"

Made a bit uncomfortable by the query, Azhani peeked at Kyrian, who sat with a needle held between her teeth, staring at Azhani with a curious expression on her face. Eventually she took the needle from her mouth. "While I hope Azhani and I will be among your guests, I suspect that we aren't yet ready to speak such oaths."

Putting her armor aside, Azhani took Kyrian's hand. "I am ready, my love. I've been ready since the night I came to you." She smiled then and turned to Padreg and Elisira. "I pray your day of bonding is as full of joy as you could hope."

"Thank you," Elisira replied solemnly.

Padreg nodded. "You have my thanks as well, my friend."

Their softly spoken words barely penetrated Azhani's thoughts as she slid from the tree trunk to her knees. Looking up at Kyrian, she took her hand and brought it to her lips. For a long while, she knelt there, just staring into Kyrian's eyes. The world narrowed to heartbeats and a glimmering, fire-touched sea of green.

Eventually, she took a deep breath and said, "Not a single day passes when I do not thank the Twain for your presence, beloved."

Kyrian blushed and reached out to caress her cheek.

Azhani smiled. "When it seemed that my soul was lost to darkness, you were the light that came and soothed the hurts of my body and heart. I was friendless and then your hand was there, reaching for mine and taking it, pulling me back from the abyss that threatened to destroy me. Through you, I found the will to live again." Gently, she kissed Kyrian's palm. "Now, you are my most blessed love—the most cherished friend of my heart, the most beautiful song in my soul, and the brightest light in my life. Words do not exist to tell you more, my love. I cannot carve more truth with my tongue than the most simple fact that I love you," she said, cupping her hands to Kyrian's face and taking another deep breath. "And that there would be no greater gift, no finer honor than to stand at your side on Winter's Solstice and pledge to the Twain that you, Kyrian, are my wife. Please, please, I hope you will do this. Will you share my life? Will you claim the right to cherish our love as long as the stars spin in the heavens above?"

Distant thunder rumbled overhead and suddenly, the skies opened up, covering them with rain as Kyrian slid into Azhani's arms and fervently kissed her.

As the deluge soaked them, Kyrian laughed. "Oh, my beautiful love." Leaning her forehead against Azhani's, she said, "Everything and the universe—that's what I see whenever I look into your eyes." Softly, she chuckled. "You can even make me forget the rain. It always feels like the sun is shining whenever I'm in your arms." Tenderly, she kissed her, then murmured, "Yes, I will marry you. Now, come on! I'm soaked to the skin and freezing!"

Laughing, they both rose and ran to the shelter of their tent.

Padreg Keelan liked to think of himself as a man raised to speak honestly and humbly, but having just witnessed Azhani give her heart so freely to Kyrian, it was all he could do not to throw himself at Elisira's feet and beg her forgiveness for not offering her the same truth. Instead, he surreptitiously scrubbed at the tears scalding the corners of his eyes and watched as the two women made their way across camp to the warleader's tent.

"'Twas truly a most wondrous and moving proposal," Elisira said with a heavy sigh.

"Aye." He felt thick-tongued and numb-witted in its wake.

"I'll not hear its like again, I expect," she said, her tone lightly teasing as she elbowed him in the ribs. "Though certainly, if someone could approach its sweetness, I might be so inclined to eat my boot."

Padreg snorted. "Have you acquired a taste for old leather then, my lady?"

Softly, she laughed. "Nay, but—"

"Make no wagers in haste." He turned to brush his lips over her cheek. "Else your purse may become quickly flattened."

"By whom?" she retorted archly. "There are few enough with mastery of wit and words to match Azhani's. I sincerely doubt any could outdo such purity and eloquence."

Aware now that she was baiting him and loving her more for it, Padreg simply shrugged. "Of a sureness, my lady. 'Twould be of light labor."

"If the labor be so light, then why has it not yet been done?"

Sliding now to his knees, he took her hand, brushed a kiss over her knuckles. "For as much as I am a fool, and thought to avoid even such timid tasks due to the obviousness of our grand affection…" He bowed his head. "You have my deepest apologies, for you are, without doubt, due every word that shapes the legacy of my heart's truest and deepest feelings for you, Elisira Glinholt."

Joy suffused her face. "Oh, Paddy—"

"From the very moment when I beheld you, I knew you were made of the Twain's blessings. You spoke with educated grace and your words held more than simple merit—they had sense. As a woman raised to cart and carriage, you sat astride a horse meant to race the plains and carried yourself like you were born in the saddle. No bird in Arris' squawking flock could match your beauty, and when you smiled, oh, by blessed Astariu, I was truly and utterly lost!" He shook his head ruefully.

"No more lost than I," she murmured, but he shook his head to forestall any further comments.

"Over the years, many counseled that I seek the hand of a beloved in marriage, but no matter where I traveled, from Y'Mar to Y'Tol and all the cities and places that exist between, there were none who could make my solo road a partnership—until you." Again, he kissed her hand. "For now I know the journey has been worth the ride. I pray, with every breath, you feel some semblance of similar feeling and ask—nay, beg—that you, my beloved Lady Elisira—consent to wed this foolish man."

Elisira's gaze was locked firmly on his. Her eyes glittered brightly in the flickering firelight, and for a long, long moment, they stared at each other as she caressed his face. Finally, she took a deep breath. "Glad I am we did not make a wager, my lord, for I would have lost." She kissed him then, and he fell into it with fervent glee, feeling her answer even before she spoke. "Yes, so many times, yes, my love. I shall wed thee."

Gossip is the currency of all gatherings of people. From neighbors, to courts, to vast armies, nothing spreads faster or carries with it such penchant for salacious joy. Within candlemarks of Azhani's public proposal, the soldiers were crowing over the news—and when they learned of King Padreg's similarly romantic proposal to his lady, it was tantamount to a grand victory, such was the celebratory nature that flowed through them.

This might have given Azhani pause to worry over the focus of her soldiers, but Elisira counseled her to let them have their whispered giggles and bawdy jokes.

"They'll find other fodder for the grist soon enough, my friend," she said affably. "For now, our happiness is theirs, if only for a short time."

"But I don't understand why," Azhani replied with a sardonic shake of her head. "What does it matter to them that I am getting married?"

"Hope." Kyrian stirred honey into her tea. "We've given them a reason to believe that we are winning."

"We have? How?"

"By making plans for the future," Elisira said calmly. "We are saying that we expect to see them through."

She snorted. "Have they not heard that plans don't always work out as created?"

"Of course they have," Kyrian said. "But they need to believe otherwise. I say we let them."

"All right, but the next soldier who makes a lewd reference to the glory of your breasts is going to find himself on latrine duty."

Kyrian blushed so hard, her cheeks were the same color as her robes.

Days passed and talk around the fires narrowed to three subjects—the cursed rain, the bloody rimerbeasts, and the blessed event that would take place at midwinter. Harvest came and went, its passing almost unnoticed in the blur of nightly battles. The only chance they had to celebrate was when supplies from Y'Syr included a bevy of fresh fruits and vegetables that honored the season.

Worryingly, word trickled north of rimerbeast incursions that had devastated the outlying villages of Y'Syr and Y'Dan. Each attack left Azhani angrier and more bitter than ever before, for had she still been Y'Dan's warleader, with all the resources of the combined armies, she might have been able to save them.

When winter finally came, it slammed into the mountains on the wings of a snowstorm, making frostbite the second most terrifying enemy the army faced in the Crest of Amyra.

"We are lucky that we quartered here in Barton," Azhani found herself telling Kyrian late one night. "We have some shelter. Without it, we would be forced into the very caves cleared by the last beast year."

Huddled under their covers, Kyrian shivered and moved even closer, kissing Azhani's shoulder gently. "I'd rather be here. I know those caves should be safe, but—"

"But nothing about this is as it should be," Azhani finished for her. "I know. Vashyra has given up searching for anything in the histories that could tell us why they are attacking. All she can say is that this 'breaking' referred to in the prophecy has something to do with the demon god Ecarthus."

Kyrian nodded. "I know. And…maybe it's better that we know so little. We do what we must, and we are doing every possible thing we know. It is all we can do."

Turning, Azhani slid her hand over Kyrian's hip and kissed her. "Yes. And we will do it until it is over. But for now," she said, before deepening the kiss. "Let us leave the worrying aside."

"Gladly," Kyrian whispered as she tangled her legs with Azhani's and gave in to the flame of desire sparking in her belly.

Late one night, Azhani and her lieutenants were gathered in what was once Barton's town hall. The scouts had just returned from a lengthy patrol and they needed to know whether their plans for the next day were changing.

Tal Gwyeth, the leader of the scouts, stood and saluted the assembled group. "Greetings. We're all tired, so I won't bother with the pleasantries." He strode over to map that had been tacked up on a nearby wall and pointed to a valley at least three days' march west. "This is the furthest point of our last mission. From here to there I can state with certainty that all the caves are empty. Only broken shells remain."

A soft murmur went around the room and Azhani grimaced. She knew that Gwyeth meant that the eggs within had not been destroyed, but rather that the creatures incubating there had hatched.

"Here, here, and here, King Arris and the Y'Dani army have engaged the demons," Gwyeth went on, tapping the map at points near the coast and slightly further inland. "They have managed to make some progress, but their tactics are, frankly, unsound. He spends lives like copper. Without reinforcements, he will be overrun in a month." Several of the assembled cursed softly at this. "Beyond that, we have seen evidence of small groups led by desperate villagers, but encountered only one—a group of hunters from Ynnych brought down half a dozen of the bastards on their own, but lost eight men. We sent them home and told them to mind the walls of their village."

"Thank you, Tal," Azhani said as he resumed his seat. Standing, she began pacing the room. "If we do not stop them, the rimerbeasts will go south. Without Y'Dan's army to stand between them and the populace, I fear the kingdom will quickly fall. From there, they can move into Y'Syr, Y'Mar, and Y'Nor, going until all of Y'Myran is either dead or fighting. We cannot let that happen."

Everyone in the room erupted into a flurry of heated questions that were hurled back and forth as they debated the best way to stop the invasion.

Meanwhile, Azhani merely listened and tried not to get too caught up in the image of King Arris as a warrior. She remembered him as pale, weak, and barely able to lift a short sword, much less command the respect of an army.

Is he trying to defend Y'Dan? She could hardly believe it. The murderous king was risking everything to save his people from the rimerbeasts. *Why does he bother? How can he even care? He's the one who sold his people to Ecarthus. Is he throwing away even more lives just for glory?*

For the longest time, she had thought Arris' request for Lyssera to join forces with him was nothing more than treachery in disguise, but…could she have been wrong? Would he have accepted another as Y'Syr's warleader and worked in tandem to defeat the rimerbeasts? Had her own blind need for vengeance doomed Y'Myran to die under the claws of the monsters?

A darker, softer voice came to the fore of her thoughts, whispering, *"What if his presence is yet another ploy to lure you to him? What if he is here not to fight them, but to get to you? He did so much to hurt you—and he knows you alone carry the truth about Thodan's chosen heir."* If this were the case, then it would be prudent to do nothing. Let the rimerbeasts have him. She could keep her men back, continue to sweep this area, and wait until the Y'Dani army was little more than a bloody smear on the mountains.

The idea made her sick.

A lull appeared in the conversation and, quietly, she said, "Return to your units and choose three of every ten men. In two weeks, we will ride to aid the Y'Dani army." If any were surprised by her orders, none dared speak of it. Instead, they saluted, rose, and exited the building.

"May the Twain have mercy on us all if I am wrong," she whispered before putting out the last of the lights and closing the door.

Kyrian turned to her then. "When you go, I will be at your side."

Brought up short by the announcement, Azhani frowned in confusion. "Kyr, you've yet to see combat. Why expose yourself now?"

"Because you will need me," she replied, her conviction evident in her tone.

"And if you are attacked?"

Kyrian squared her shoulders. "I'll do what I must—but Azhi, I swear, I'll try to stay out of the way. You don't have to worry about any heroics on my part." She smiled ruefully. "But I will be there when you need me."

Softly, Azhani replied, "I always need you."

"Then I'm here." She wrapped her arms around her. "Always. You have my word on it."

Devon and Avisha raced across the camp. He was late. Patrol was leaving soon and this would be the last night Azhani would lead them in the hunt for rimerbeasts. Tomorrow, she was taking a hand-picked platoon and heading west to aid the Y'Dani army.

A flash of red hair distracted him. Coming to a stop, he peered into the shadows between two tents. Avisha sat at his feet and rubbed her jaw on his knee. Absently, he scratched her ears as he watched the two people the torchlight illuminated.

"Be careful," Syrelle said as she buckled Allyndev's sword belt tightly. "I don't want you to get hurt again."

Taking her hands, Allyn smiled and brought them to his lips, brushing gentle kisses over her knuckles. "I'll keep my mind on my surroundings and not get caught woolgathering again, I swear it by the Twain."

Syrelle pulled her hands away. "I don't need your oaths, Allyn. I just want you…" She sighed and looked up at him, and Devon felt his heart shatter at the expression on her face. Never had she gazed at him that way. Gently, she touched Allyndev's cheek and said, "I just want you to come back."

Covering her hand, he closed his eyes and murmured, "Sy—" All of Allyndev's emotions were in that one, precious breath of a word.

Devon wanted to curl up right there and become one with the dirt. Only Avisha's jarring purr kept him steady, made him know that this was reality, not some awful dream.

The dream became nightmare when Syrelle smiled and said, "Kiss me," and tipped her head up to meet Allyndev halfway.

Oh, oh, how it hurt! The moment that should be so beautiful, so perfect for his friends, was for him utter torture. *And I cannot even tell myself that I envy only Allyn, for I would not turn away the press of his lips on mine, either. Or hers. Goddess, what a mess!*

In frustration, he cursed softly and ran to where the horses were picketed, Avisha loping along beside him. He could not begrudge his friends their happiness, only wallow in the sick knowledge that he would not share it.

At last he found a horse marked with the saffron cord that denoted its ability to carry a rider lost in weaving spells and unable to do more than keep his feet in the stirrups. He mounted and began the calming meditations that would make his mind ready for casting.

Someone's out there for me. Just look at Azhani—she loved Ylera so much, and yet even she was able to find someone when she lost her. I just need to be patient. It was so damned hard, though, when everyone around him seemed to have someone to fill out that empty space in their lives.

Avisha leaped up onto the pillion pad and loudly meowed at him.

"Yes, yes, I've got you, you little beggar," he said with a chuckle, turning to hand her a chunk of dried venison. "And you are quite the beautiful little thing, so I suppose I'll have to be content with that for now."

Allyndev's heart was beating so hard, he wasn't sure it would stay inside his ribs. "Goddess," he whispered, caressing Syrelle's face and exchanging several more small kisses with her.

It was wonderful. Perfect, almost. It just felt like something was missing.

"Be safe, please," she said, sighing softly. "I wish I had time to find Devon and tell him the same thing."

"Devon?" he said, feeling a bit dumb.

She swatted his chest. "Yes, you idiot. Devon. Our friend whom we *both* love!"

"Oh. Oh!" he blurted, looking at her in shock. "Devon?"

Suddenly shy, she said, "You don't agree?"

"No, I—"

Someone yelled his name.

"I need to go, Sy. We'll talk about this later!"

"Yes, we will," she said firmly, giving him a push toward the horses. "And stay safe, both of you!" she yelled as he ran off.

Racing toward where he could see Devon waiting, he called, "Hey, don't leave without me!"

Devon made a face. "Whyever would we do that? We'd be lost without your heroic magnificence."

"Oh, very funny, twinklefingers," Allyn retorted, mounting quickly.

"Sy's waving."

Turning, he smiled as she lifted her arm and grinned brightly. "Yes, she... she kissed me. And she wants us to be safe. And we're going to talk later," he babbled as his heart performed a weird little tumble in his chest. *Talk. We, the three of us. We're going to talk. What will we say? What...oh, Goddess...* Heat rose through his face as he started to realize that perhaps "talking" wasn't what Syrelle had meant at all.

"Congratulations," Devon grumbled.

Confused, Allyndev turned to say something, but was cut off by Azhani's sharp whistle.

"All right, my lads and lasses, listen up. The weather watchers have said tonight's to be a bad one, so be on your guard. 'The colder, the deader,' isn't just a joke during beast season. The bastards will be out in force and they will be starving." She looked to each of them in turn, her gaze fiercely pointed. Allyn felt as though she were peeling him open like an orange and making certain he was ripe enough to handle whatever came next. When she shouted, "Are you ready to serve your kingdoms?" he yelled, "Aye!" like everyone else.

Lifting his hand in salute, Tal Gwyeth said, "We serve for the honor of our queen!"

Azhani nodded. "Then let's ride."

The patrol was following a northward trail when the eerie howl of a rimerbeast pack raised the hair on everyone's necks.

"Look sharp now," Azhani called.

Her command spread down the line as they slowed, loosening weapons and readying bows.

Pre-battle jitters made everyone nervous as they scanned the sides of the trail, searching for any hint of hidden monsters. Something made Devon turn just in time to see a pair of eyes. Without thinking, he struck, unleashing the power of the thunderbolt on his target. Out of the corner of his eye, he saw Allyndev wheel his horse around and draw his blade. He was about to shout a warming, but in the space between one breath and the next, a flurry of rimerbeasts erupted from the bushes. Azhani's war cry ricocheted around them, chasing off all thoughts but the battle.

"For Y'Syr!" Allyndev shouted, charging the pack.

Bolts of lightning crackled from Devon's fingertips, striking a pair of beasts and sending them tumbling right into a fireball launched by Jasyn, the squad's other mage. Both monsters burst into flames.

Pulling his blade from the back of a dying rimerbeast, Allyn grinned at the mages and yelled, "Good work!"

Jasyn threw up his arms in a show of victory, and in horror, Devon watched as a rimerbeast leaped up and grabbed him.

"Help!" Jasyn screamed as he tried to get free of the beast dragging him to the ground.

Roaring, the rimerbeast rose up on its knees and drove its claws deep into Jasyn's shoulders.

"No!" Devon screamed, grabbing his sling. Chanting a quick spell, he dropped a charmed bullet into it and let fly. It struck its target right in the head, connecting with a startlingly loud pop. For just a moment, the beast went still, then slowly toppled to the side.

Leaping off his horse, Devon raced to Jasyn's side and frantically tried to pull the dead rimerbeast off him while around them, the battle raged.

"Dev," Jasyn gasped, his face contorted in pain and fear.

Devon looked up and paled as three rimerbeasts converged on them.

"Run," Jasyn whispered. "Save yourself."

"No!" Fury and frustration raced through him as he tried to come up with a solution. "I won't leave you." He stood and screamed, "Help!"

At the sound of Devon's voice, Allyndev spun about and drove his mount toward the frantic cry. He caught sight of his friend just as magickal energies blossomed from Devon's fingertips and crashed into the rimerbeast nearest to him. Two more quickly took its place.

Faster, I need to be faster.

One day he would sit and think about this moment, and then he would find the man who trained his horse and shower him in a rain of gold coins, for not once did the beast flinch, not even when Allyn forced him to jump a rimerbeast caught in its death throes.

"Come on!" he yelled, pushing the horse to go faster as Devon and the two rimerbeasts clashed.

Avisha screamed, the cat's inhuman cry so startling that Allyn actually flinched. Then he grinned as she leaped on one of the rimerbeast's heads and started clawing and biting at its eyes.

There was no time for relief, though, as Devon screamed in agony.

Gape-mouthed, Allyndev watched in horror as a rimerbeast grabbed Devon's leg in his mouth, bit down and then shook him like a dog with a rodent.

"No!" Allyn shouted, grief-struck as Devon's body was flung across the clearing. "Devon!" He threw himself from the saddle and charged the rimerbeast, all thought of skill or finesse gone in the killing rage that swept through him.

Hammering the rimerbeast with dozens of blows, he sobbed, "Die!"

He hamstrung it, sending it to its knees. Swiftly, Allyndev scrambled up its back and, taking hold of his sword's hilt with both hands, he drove it deep into the monster's neck. It choked on a feeble roar, then crashed into the ground. Tumbling free, Allyn tugged his sword from the beast's body and raced to his friend's side, gasping at what he found.

Devon's leg was a ruin of bone and flesh.

Lessons pounded into him by Kyrian sent Allyn fumbling to yank his belt off and wrap it around Devon's thigh, tightening it to the point that the bleeding slowed to a sluggish dribble. "Don't you die on me," he growled, grabbing Devon's bloody hand and pressing it to his face. "I need you, Dev."

There was no response. Choking back a sob of grief, he scooped Devon up and looked for his horse, only then realizing the battle was over. Another soldier was tending to Jasyn, getting him onto a travois. Someone was bringing a second toward him.

Avisha was still hissing and biting the rimerbeast she'd killed, her muzzle and forequarters soaked with blood and ichor.

"Put him on this," Azhani said as she set the travois down.

"But—"

"Allyn," she said gently. "We need to get him to Kyrian as fast as possible. This is the best way."

He looked down at Devon's face, his precious, stupid face. Blood flecked his lips, and his normally tanned skin was sallow and getting paler by the heartbeat. "Don't die," he whispered, laying him on the travois. "Don't you die!" He pressed a quick, nervous kiss to Devon's temple. "You'll break our hearts if you die, Devvy."

Devon coughed himself awake. Blinking weakly, he tried to move and found himself strapped in place. Overhead, stars danced and spun. Beneath him, the ground bounced and juddered. His feet itched terribly. Raindrops hit his face, making him shiver.

He wanted to speak, to call out, but it was too much effort. It was cold, and getting colder. Suddenly, everything stopped moving. Someone's face swam into view, but he couldn't name them. Words floated through the air and tried to get into his head, but it was all garbled gibberish. His legs started to throb and his whole body began to burn.

Several times, he opened his mouth. Water. He was thirsty. Raindrops touched his tongue and he savored their sweetness. Someone cried out and briefly, just briefly, he felt a hand brush his. His name—he definitely knew his name. Someone was crying it loudly.

Chanting came. A hand touched his face and he began to drift toward a warm, peaceful place where pain and confusion ceased to exist. Darkness came, then nothing.

CHAPTER NINETEEN

"Blood and bones! Die, damn you!" Arris screamed as he laid into yet another rimerbeast. Evading a paw bristling with wickedly gleaming claws, he drove his horse forward and lashed out with his sword, carving a chunk of flesh and fur off the attacking monster. He cackled at the blood that spurted from the fresh wound and slashed the beast again and again before it collapsed, emitting an eerie, rattling moan as it died.

Spinning around, Arris yelled, "'Thyro, did you see that?"

There was no reply. Further away, battle sounds momentarily distracted him before he threw up his arms and yelled the scholar's name. Still no answer. It had been two days since anyone had seen Porthyros—and three days since Batizha's battered, lifeless body had been found stuffed in the latrine. Rage burned through Arris once again. Someone had killed his woman. No one in his army would come forth and admit to the crime, so Porthyros had volunteered to investigate the matter himself.

Another rimerbeast died and Arris snarled as the creature slid free of his sword, then looked around to make sure none of his soldiers were too close. He couldn't let anyone get near him. If they had killed his woman...well... Fear rippled through him. *They can kill me, too.*

"Damn you, 'Thyro. Why did you abandon me now? I need you!" he whispered as he stopped to drink from the last of the flasks of tea Porthyros had left for him.

The faint sound of laughter made his skin crawl.

Oh no, not again.

He tried to shut his eyes and cover his ears before the phantasm appeared, but it didn't work.

You're a murderer, son. The weary, disappointment-filled voice was his father's, of course, though Thodan was nowhere to be seen.

Quickly, Arris shook his head, then searched the battlefield, hoping for the distraction of another rimerbeast to kill. This area, though, was quiet. Further ahead, combat raged. Rubbing his eyes, he sighed and wiped the caustic blood off his blade. The once-gleaming metal was pitted and scarred, much like his armor.

Killing, he'd discovered, was tiring work. Nothing he had ever faced prepared him for the utter exhaustion of raising and lowering his blade again and again and again all while keeping in the saddle for nine, ten, even twelve candlemarks a day. He was tired, he was sweaty, and his mouth was so dry, he might as well be chewing mouthfuls of lamb's wool instead of draining the last of his precious tea.

Tossing aside the flask, he opened his mouth to yell for more and realized, again, that Porthyros, his oldest and closest friend—the only one who could make the simple, yet special brew was gone. For a moment, he felt like a child again, listening to his father explain that his mother was gone, gone forever...

No one wants to be around a murderer, Arris. Not even a mother can love a killer like you. This time, the voice belonged to Ambassador Kelani and her tongue was acid sharp, burning with the sting of pure hatred.

"Shut up!" Arris growled as he grabbed his head in an effort to still the voices.

Water. He needed water. He had a skin of it somewhere. It should be tea, but every batch he made was awful, so terrible that it was better to drink the piss-warm crap that hung off his belt rather than subject himself to his own incompetence. The voices, though, they kept at him. Babbling, garbled words boxed his ears again and again, just as they had since Porthyros left.

He drained half the skin, then dug his heels into Tyrre's sides, racing into battle once more. Blood would silence the voices.

Killer. Killed me, killed her, killed them all—you're a murdering bastard, Arris Thodan, and everyone knows it!

"I'm no bastard," he growled. "I have a father."

I should have strangled you in your sleep. Thodan's contempt stung so much that tears blinded Arris, forcing him to scrub them away.

"But you didn't," he snapped, laying into the first rimerbeast to present itself for the slaughter. "And now I'm king!"

A soldier turned, saluted, and said, "Do you require aid, my liege?"

"No, you complete dolt! Kill them!" Arris retorted, chasing the fleeing beast.

"Sir!" Quickly, the soldier saluted and ran.

Giggling, Arris lifted his head. "See, Father! They obey me now!"

They follow a madman, my son. Thodan's voice was heavy with sadness. *How can you not see what evil you have wrought?*

The tone in his father's voice was so real, so familiar, it made Arris pause and shiver. He'd heard it so many times before, and yet this time, in this place, it was a trigger—a key that unlocked a river of memory.

Ydannoch Castle's every corridor and chamber was as familiar to him as the back of his hand. As a child, Arris had lurked about, hidden in corners and ignored. Here he was the master, and every moment, every heartbeat was his to own. Here, in this room, he had condemned a woman to die.

At his feet, the once-vibrant woman who had been such a presence in his father's court was sprawled. In his hand, a knife that dripped with her blood. Across from him, almost lost in shadow, Porthyros stood, a smile of such warm approval on his face that Arris nearly cried for the joy of it.

Power rushed through him. This was his victory, his moment to grab the crown that had almost been torn from his grasp. Dropping to one knee, he touched her face with the blade, tipping her chin up so that she could look him in the eye. "You can make it stop, Ylera. Sign the document. Name Azhani as a traitor and I promise you'll go free."

He should be believed. Porthyros had worked with him for years to make sincerity one of his best lies. Yet it was hard, for with all that was racing through him right now, pity for this interloper was the last thing he wanted to feel.

A fat, wet glob of sputum and blood struck him in the face as she snarled, "Rot in the abyss, you bastard!"

"Bitch!" he growled, punching her hard enough to knock several teeth free.

She hit the ground and stayed there, huddled in a heap, sobbing. "Azhi," she whispered weakly.

"You will not speak the name of my beloved!" he screamed as he drove the dagger into her body.

When she was little more than a motionless hunk of meat, he stood over her cleaning his blade as Porthyros carefully signed the confession.

"Soon, my love. Soon, I will make you beg to be my wife," he whispered while Porthyros went to summon the guard to give them the documents. "Y'Dan is mine."

The vision was bitterly clear, and yet Arris could hardly believe it was real. How could he have done such things? Felt such terrible feelings? The words, the actions—they weren't his, were they? He was a hero, not a murderer!

"No," he whispered, horrified, wishing that this wasn't the first nightmarish vision that had tormented him. Last time, it had been even worse, for in it, he had watched himself deliver a cup of poison to his father night after night until Thodan died of a mysterious wasting disease.

When he'd gone to Porthyros and asked about the visions, his old friend had gently reassured him that the nightmare was nothing more than a spell cast by the starseekers Azhani had corrupted into serving her ends.

This is no spell, Arris. It is the pure truth of your memories that you see, not the weavings of a mage bent on your destruction. His father's voice again, stern, insistent, and frighteningly real.

"Oh Gods, no," Arris whimpered.

Yes. Ylera Kelani's voice invaded once more, dragging him right back to that hideous moment when he'd ended her life.

Shaking violently, he screamed, "No!"

::Yes. It is as thou hast seen, boy king. Now, go and kill for me, for thou art mine!::

Mine...mine...mine... The words echoed in Arris' ears.

"No, no, no," he mumbled, slamming his fists into his helm.

The voice, still tolling like a dark, evil bell struck in his soul, would not end, would not vanish. It could only belong to one being—Ecarthus Soul-Eater. No other could cause such pain with just a simple whisper.

"What have I done?" he sobbed.

It was real. Every nightmare, every horrible memory, every terrifying image of himself as a minion of evil—it was all true. Sickened by the realization, he toppled from his horse and staggered to the bushes, vomiting violently.

Some time, later, he wiped his mouth and returned to Tyrre, taking up his reins. *"Kill for me,"* Ecarthus had commanded.

Very well. Arris mounted, steely determination rising within him. *I'm just a pawn. So be it. If my beautiful Batizha taught me anything, it's that pawns are extremely powerful. You just have to be willing to sacrifice them.*

Giving Tyrre the signal to charge, he raised his blade and rode for a knot of soldiers, yelling, "To me!"

If death was what Ecarthus demanded, then he would give it to him—but hopefully not in the way the demon god was planning.

A fresh wave of rimerbeasts poured into the valley as Arris and the soldiers slammed into them. Every heartbeat spent in combat was a moment where the voices in his head were silent.

He fell into a routine. Slice, dodge, run, slash, kick—over and over, killing and killing, slaughtering any rimerbeast that came before him. This is what being a king meant—standing before the hoards of chaos and stopping it from destroying his land, his people, and all those who looked to him to keep them safe. He was born to do this, to be the bulwark against Ecarthus' evil. Somewhere along the way, he'd had that birthright stolen from him.

No more. He'd failed the people of Y'Dan long enough. "Father, I will make you proud!" he screamed, giving himself over to the frenzy of blood and death.

Driven by the knowledge of his past wrongs, Arris did the one thing he knew was right—he fought. All night, he drove his army through the mountains, killing wave after wave of rimerbeasts until everything was a red blur of blood and pain.

Near dawn, he fell off Tyrre's back and staggered off to vomit again. Kneeling between scrub bushes, he clutched his head and moaned softly. *Ah, by the Twain, 'Thyro, you shouldn't have left me. I can't stand this hole in my head.*

Someone shoved a skin of stale beer into his hands and he drank, grimacing at the bitter taste. Without thinking, he shoved it back at the soldier and grunted his thanks, then stumbled back to his horse. In the distance, a horn sounded, and hope flared within him. Was it Porthyros? Had his old friend returned after all? Did he bring reinforcements?

Rubbing his eyes, he let himself daydream for just one fragile moment. All he'd suffered would be over, for that horn would, he prayed, herald Porthyros' return. There would be tea and forgiveness and all would be well. He would be a hero once more.

The horn blew again, closer now. Arris turned, ready to greet his old friend with a smile. But it was not a friend who rode toward him at the head of an army, her face a bleak mask of death.

Oh Goddess, no.

Arris' guts clenched into tight knots of pure terror, for toward him came Azhani Rhu'len. Illuminated in magelight, surrounded by heavily armed and armored soldiers, and looking far more regal than he had ever managed, she sat atop a gorgeous warhorse and proudly wore the armor that marked her as Y'Syr's warleader. Bile rose in his throat even as his loins clenched and tightened. His heart stuttered and silently, he yelled at himself to run, to hide from the one person he'd wronged most.

He could not move. Crazy thoughts spun and twisted in his head. Maybe, maybe she'd come back to him. Maybe she was ready to be his bride and she'd come to pledge her troth—they would be wed and they'd rule together, wisely, turning Y'Dan into the paradise of peace his father had spent his entire life trying to achieve.

The same paradise I shat upon the second my poison had done its work.

Hope, however, was stronger than his own self-loathing and he started toward her, only to stagger back when she glared at him with such a hate-filled look that it felt like a physical blow. All his dreams died. Azhani had not come to love him. No, today judgment on a horse's back had come to collect its due.

Suddenly, Azhani and her entire army veered away. Momentarily stunned, he watched as they attacked a fresh wave of rimerbeasts. The shock only lasted a few heartbeats. "The wounded," he cried, mounting his horse. "Get them out of here, now!"

"Yes, sire!" Several of his soldiers raced off to escort the injured away as he spurred himself into battle once more.

Arris was close to exhaustion, but he could not let himself fall, not now. Not when he needed to show Azhani that he was trying to be better. He had to do this—it was his destiny.

Snow began to fall, turning the ground into a slippery, treacherous morass. Staying mounted became his second battle, making the endless waves of rimerbeasts that much harder to repel. The screams of the injured and dying echoed all around him, but he fought on, throwing himself at every rimerbeast that rose, seemingly from the stone itself, until it was dead.

Crimson-coated claws appeared out of nowhere, raking through his boots and burying themselves deep in Tyrre's throat. As they dragged the dying horse to the ground, Arris rolled away. Raw anger snapped his mind, and in an enraged frenzy, he charged the monster, hacking it to bits.

Somewhere ahead, the Banshee screamed. He ran toward the sound, death racing alongside him as he blindly carved a path straight to her side. For one moment, they stood back to back, fending off the waves of beasts. She was beautiful, terrible, and magnificent. It was everything he'd ever dreamed, ever desired, ever longed for. This was the Azhani Rhu'len that had fueled his nighttime passions!

Quiet wrapped around them. They turned and faced each other. Arris fell in love all over again. Her eyes, bluer than the bluest sapphire; her skin, the glorious hue of the midnight sky; her narrow, hawk-like features the opposite of his human roundness—all were part and parcel of her total perfection. He wanted her.

She ignored him. Her attention was elsewhere, likely seeking another enemy.

Words puddled in his mouth, drowning his tongue, but his voice had deserted him. What could he say? How could he defend his evil actions? What pathetic excuse would put the pearls of forgiveness into her heart so that she would forget how he'd stolen her life, her love, and her honor?

I love you. Feeble, idiotic, and impossible—she would never believe him, never see him as anything more than her enemy. He laughed brokenly.

Was he crazy? Reality seemed as twisted as the visions Porthyros once claimed were merely nightmares. He couldn't grasp it—every time he tried, it shivered and fled his touch like a wild hawk flees the falconer's jess. Without his tea, he was completely lost.

That cursed tea! He remembered refusing to drink it as a child, but his father had insisted that he follow Master Porthyros' teachings, and he wanted so much to please Thodan, to make him proud of his sickly, weak son. So he drank deeply, growing to love the sweet liquid as a drunk loves his wine. It made him calm, gave him confidence, and soon he could stand before the mighty Thodan and not feel like a total failure.

What was in that damned tea, anyway? Did it even matter? No amount of Porthyros' tea would help him, not when Azhani Rhu'len was staring at him like she was trying to decide if she was going to peel him first or run him through just to get it over with quickly.

Yet his mind just couldn't let it go. Now that it was in his thoughts, he had to chase it down, had to try to understand all of what had been done to put him here, now, in this place where everything was going so terribly wrong. The wind shifted. A rimerbeast's cry distracted him.

Azhani snarled, "I'll deal with you later," and ran for it, but he was at her side. He could not leave her.

The resounding shock of his sword slicing into a rimerbeast's hide was familiar now, so much so that he felt disconnected, almost apart from the battle. His body fought, but his mind searched through memories, trying to match symptoms with something, anything he'd read in all the books Porthyros had shoved into his hands. Round and round his thoughts spun, dragging through half-remembered visions of dozens of books and scrolls until something fleeting slid past his inner eye. An apothecary's text—one that had long been banned in Y'Dan—had been found in the castle library. The maid who'd discovered it was terrified. He had not cared, but Porthyros—he'd been insistent that he turn the book over to him.

What was it he'd said? Something about too much knowledge being dangerous? No, no, that was his father's maxim. *No, Porthyros had said…had said…* It was there, floating at the edge of his thoughts, dancing out of reach every time he had to duck or weave or strike out at an attacker.

Damn it to all the hells!

Slowly, the words came to him. *"All knowledge is useful to the mind willing to use it, my king. Would you deny yourself access to power simply because weak-willed idiots fear it?"*

Caught as he was in the scholar's web of words and control, he'd eagerly granted him custody of the book—but not before he'd read it himself. It was in this book that he'd learned about…

His mind went blank. No, not just blank, but forcibly pushed him to think of something, anything else but this. Excited, nervous, and more than a little dizzy, he tried to get past the block. Was it magickal? He couldn't tell. All he knew was that something was trying to stop him from following this train of thought, and right now, he had to know! Sweat poured from his brow in rivers, stinging his eyes and half blinding him. In agitation, he pulled off a glove and scratched his hand, worrying at an old, half-healed wound on his wrist. It struck him as odd that his nails looked so bruised, even though the cut was high up on his wrist.

Oh Gods. Revelation unlocked memory and the answer filled his mind.

"Krile," he murmured, utterly stunned. It all made sense now. Krile for his father, krile for his tea. Toxic amounts for a king, taming levels for a feckless boy who was too weak to tie his own boots, much less rule a kingdom—or earn the love of a beautiful warleader whose heart was destined for the hands of a gorgeous ambassador.

I'm going to die. Calm settled over him. Krile was deadly, even in small doses—especially in small doses, for without the tiny amounts he'd been given all his life, his body would begin to wither, just as his father's had—and nothing in Y'Myran could save him.

Clarity struck then. This battlefield would be his tomb, for if he was going to die, it would be by his choice, doing the one thing that would maybe buy him a small amount of forgiveness.

Taking a last look at Azhani, he saluted her with his blade and turned away, ready to face the next monster.

Azhani surveyed the battlefield and tried to make her sluggish thoughts come together. Dawn's gray light crawled over the mix of blood, snow, and gore, sending the rimerbeasts scurrying for their caves. Aching from head to toe, she nearly dropped where she stood. A full day of riding, then fighting all night had left her utterly drained.

Across the path from her stood King Arris, looking just as exhausted. Covered in ichor and bleeding from dozens of wounds, he seemed barely able to stay upright. Their gazes locked. She expected to feel herself crawl with hatred, but instead she was just numb. Half his face was sheeted in blood from a scalp laceration that was so deep she could see the white of bone.

Kyrian needs to see to that.

"Oathbreaker," Arris croaked. At one point, the word would have been a taunt, but now all it sounded like was the plea of a broken man.

Curling her lip disdainfully, she snapped, "We're not on Y'Dani soil, Arris. As far as I'm concerned, you can take your lies and plant them in a privy!" Angrily, she lifted her hand and offered him a very rude gesture as she added, "You're lucky I haven't the strength to rip your intestines out and feed them to the crows."

Arris sighed and looked away. "I've no more quarrels with you, Azhani," he said wearily. "I…" Shaking his head, he glanced down at his sword. "Gods, there's so much blood. How can there be so much?" Grief twisted his face into a rictus as he sobbed into his hands.

At the sight of the king's tears, Azhani felt a myriad of things ripple through her. Pity, hatred, disgust, sorrow, anger—it all twisted in her thoughts, rooting her to the spot.

"Azhi?" Kyrian said softly.

Startled, Azhani looked away from Arris, startled by the sight of her lover standing there covered in blood and gore. In her eyes was a kind of shocked weariness that Azhani knew all too well from the faces of soldiers who've seen too much of battle. *I should have made you stay in Barton, love. You should be with Devon, not here, surrounded by all this death.*

"He's hurt," Kyrian said, nodding to Arris. "Should I…do something?"

In that moment, Azhani could not love Kyrian more. She knew how hard it was for her to ignore her own calling to heal and leave Arris' fate in the hands of another. Part of her wanted to be magnanimous, to give Arris the healing comfort she herself had been denied, but all of a sudden the lust for vengeance raged anew. "Leave him. He's not worth your time." With that, she turned away, taking in the mountain vista as it was painted in pale amber hues by the morning sun.

"Azhi, I… don't know if I can," Kyrian whispered unsteadily.

"Then do what you must." Azhani pulled a flask from her belt and drank deeply of the fortified wine within. "I won't stop you."

Through the tears burning his eyes, Arris watched as the crimson-robed stardancer strode toward him. She was red, so red, red like blood. The thick, coppery fluid stained every part of him, choked his eyes and his mouth and gagged his thoughts. There'd been so much blood. Every candlemark since taking the throne had been thick with it—from the altars of Ecarthus' temples to the linens on his bed, his reign had been painted with the essence of other people's torment.

Quavering in fear, he shrank back. She would see. Stardancer, servant of the Twain, beloved of Astariu. This vision of throbbing life would know every single dark deed Arris had took lustful pleasure in and she would…would…

The rising sun glimmering off her Astariun token blinded him. *Oh, Twain… Gods. Good. Astariu, blessed lady of life and healing, hear our sacred plea…* The chants of childhood echoed in his mind, breaking through his terror.

"Ss…" His mouth couldn't form words. Staggering toward her, intent on throwing himself at her feet to beg forgiveness, he almost missed it, almost overlooked the danger, but something inside him screamed the moment the bushes rustled. "No!" he shouted as a massive, gray-furred creature leaped out, snarling and reaching for the stardancer.

Somehow, he summoned the energy to raise his sword as he grabbed her arm and pulled her behind him, shielding her with his own body.

The rimerbeast hit him full speed. It skin popped and bubbled in the sun's light, its howls of pain and terror so terrible that Arris wanted to clap his hands over his ears, but he ignored it, beating back the nightmarish thing as it pawed and clawed him.

Arris' armor was useless. Acidic rimerbeast ichor had eaten massive holes in the chain and plate and down to his skin. Every time the blood touched his tender flesh, he sobbed in agony, but he couldn't stop, couldn't let the beast hurt one of Astariu's Own.

Pain-maddened and dying, the rimerbeast charged him again, bowling him over and tearing a great, gaping wound into his belly. With a roar of victory, the beast leaped over him and batted at the stardancer.

"No!" Arris gasped as light flashed before his eyes. "There will be no more blood on my hands!" With the last of his strength, he thrust upward, burying his blade in the rimerbeast's heart. The beast shuddered once and died.

Shoving the body aside, Arris looked up at the stardancer, smiled wearily, mumbled, "It's...done," and passed out.

Someone was singing. The song was sweet, tender, almost a lullaby. Arris nearly wept for its gentleness. Opening his eyes, he watched the stardancer as she knelt beside him, her hands mere inches above his abdomen, an aura of pure gods-touched magick wrapping them in a shade of yellow so bright, it was painful to look upon without flinching. Then she touched him. Agony shattered his body and he screamed.

"Oh Gods, stop, please!" he begged raggedly.

Confused, the stardancer immediately pulled away and looked up at Azhani. "I don't understand. I can't heal him."

Arris whimpered as his muscles slowly stopped seizing.

"Maybe the wound is too great even for Astariu's Fire?" Azhani said quietly.

Slowly, Arris shook his head. It wasn't that. He knew down to his very core that his injury, while devastating, wasn't so great that a gifted stardancer couldn't heal it. No, this was something worse, much, much worse. Coughing softly, he rasped, "It's not that, Stardancer."

Instantly, she turned to him. "What is it, Your Majesty?" she murmured.

"I-I belong to Ecarthus," he whispered bitterly. Weakly, he tugged at his tunic—his armor had probably fallen off by now—and displayed a scar burned into his sternum. "The Twain cannot touch my soul." Pain coiled through him like a river of fire. "Ah gods, what have I done?" He pounded his fist against his chest. As Kyrian moved to stop him, he looked at Azhani. "You hate me. I don't blame you."

Something dark and terrible crept through him, stealing all his warmth. As shivers began racing down his body, he rasped, "I would beg you to forgive me." Blood dribbled from his mouth. "But it's too late." Colorless spots slid over his vision and he tried to blink them away. "Just...promise me, Warleader. Promise me that you'll save them." Slowly, he pointed south, toward Y'Dan, toward the home he had sacrificed to his pride and jealousy. "Save my kingdom, Azhani Rhu'len." Grabbing Kyrian's arm, he hissed, "I need a witness, Stardancer! Call one of my men, now!"

She did, and a soldier raced to their side.

"Niemeth," he sobbed gratefully. "I'm glad you survived." He tried to smile even as more blood flowed over his lips.

"Don't talk, my king," Niemeth said as he knelt and took his hand. "We've sent for the priest."

"No, no there's no time. You must hear my words, must know my will. Ecarthus is a lie. It was all a lie. Everything was…my fault," Arris sobbed. "All of it. My f-father, A-ambassador K-kelani—"

Azhani gasped and Kyrian grabbed her hand.

"I did it. Azhani is innocent. N-never was a c-conspiracy." He looked Azhani right in the eye and said, "Azhani Rhu'len, I revoke the charge of oathbreaking and restore all your rights and titles. You are, as you have always been, Y'Dan's warleader. Niemeth, follow her as you would me."

"Yes, my king!" Niemeth replied, saluting him.

"And Niemeth." Arris grabbed the captain's arm tightly. "Kill the damned priests. Every last one of them. Let no working of Ecarthus stand whole on Y'Dani soil."

Niemeth wept. "It shall be done, my king."

He was growing colder. Shivering again, he muttered, "Damn Porthyros for running. What I wouldn't give for a hot cup of his tea now."

Wordlessly, Azhani tipped her flask into his mouth and he drank, most of the liquid running into his ears. Choking on it, he pulled away. "Too bitter. It's all too bitter."

"Try mine, my king." Niemeth offered him a waterskin, but Arris shook his head.

"It's all right, Niemeth. I'm not thirsty, just cold. So cold." Snowflakes touched his face, coating his lashes. Blinking them away, he sighed. "I can feel Him, Ecarthus. He's…inside me now." Every breath hurt. Shards of pain lanced through him with each passing moment. He looked to Kyrian then, fixing his gaze on her sweet face and the token of the Twain that sat against her chest. Weakly, he rasped, "He's eating my soul." Smiling beatifically, he mumbled, "I wonder…what it will be like…to die."

Arris Thodan took one, final shuddering breath and spoke no more.

Shaking her head sadly, Kyrian covered him with his cloak. "He might have been a monster, but he saved my life."

"I know," Azhani said quietly, then stood and motioned for Niemeth to join her. "It's been a while, old friend."

"Aye. I'm pleased you are well, Warleader," he replied.

As Azhani and the Y'Dani soldier walked away, Kyrian pushed the king's eyes closed and whispered, "I hope you find peace, Arris of Y'Dan." Gently, she stroked the fine black hair from his face, marveling at how young he truly was. *Younger than Allyndev, I suspect. They should have been friends.*

Death is not kind to the body, though, and Kyrian wanted to have Arris washed and readied for the pyre before too long. Taking his hand, she went to cross it over his chest and stopped when something caught her eye.

Scowling, she studied the blood and muck-coated skin, wondering why something seemed so off. It was only when she used a corner of his cloak to clean his fingers that she realized what it was—his fingernails were a ghastly shade of greenish black, the primary sign of long-term krile poisoning.

She gasped, "Oh Goddess!" It would explain so much! Immediately, she searched for other signs of the toxin, finding stains on the insides of his mouth, his teeth, even his toenails, that confirmed everything. Someone had systematically poisoned Arris with krile—probably for years.

Who would do such a thing? Not Thodan. It would have to be someone close, someone no one would suspect. She shook her head, angry and frustrated that this was a mystery she might never solve—a story she might never know. *Wait, wait...he called for someone. Portyrosh? No, no, Porthyros. That's it. Now, Azhani's mentioned a Porthyros Omal—Arris' teacher. He would certainly have access to the prince and as a learned man, he would know of krile. Could he have... but why?* "You poor boy." She caressed Arris' cheek, then pulled a bottle of blessed water from her haversack and sketched the Astariun sigil over his brow. It might mean nothing—but she could not simply let Ecarthus win unopposed. "You never had a chance, did you?"

With a sigh, she stood and waved to several waiting soldiers. As they began wrapping Arris' body in canvas, she hugged herself and and looked over at Azhani, who was helping with the injured. *She has to be told. It's not absolution for him—nothing will ever change what he did—but maybe, maybe she might be able to forgive herself.*

CHAPTER TWENTY

Arris the king was dead. The rimerbeasts had fled for the day, allowing Azhani to spend several candlemarks with soldiers from both armies, listening as Captain Niemeth spread the news of Arris' confession and her reinstatement. Once the shock had passed, she found great joy in greeting old friends. By midday, they were joined by the remainder of the Y'Syran army. A small garrison had stayed in Barton while Padreg led the rest west.

This was not unplanned. His arrival was meant to be timed to provide support should she have found herself facing a battle with the Y'Dani forces. Instead, she was now commander of two armies, one of which had recently been an enemy.

With nightfall fast approaching, there was no time to blend the armies into a single unit, so she ordered that each side occupy half the valley they were in. The chirurgeons' tents were placed at the very center, where they would be best protected. Patrol that night was, at best, scattered, but they managed to get through it with minimal amounts of injuries.

Still, Azhani found herself deeply confused when wounded Y'Dani soldiers wept at the sight of stardancers, healers, and simple herbalists waiting to take them into a tent for care.

"I don't understand," she said as Captain Niemeth made the sign of the Twain over his heart. "Why are they crying?"

"They're relieved, Warleader. The Ecarthans butchered those they felt weren't worth saving." He looked to the southwest, where firelight illuminated the form of a black-robed priest hanging from a scrubby tree. "Many stopped asking for help after battles for fear they might be put to the knife to feed Ecarthus' unending hunger."

"Make sure they know that anyone who needs healing is free to come ask for it," she said, angered and disgusted all over again. "And tell them we have both stardancers and starseekers among our ranks."

"I will, though I doubt many have missed seeing them—your Kyrian has been ferocious in forcing each of us to bare our chests. Half my men thought she was propositioning them! I had to knock a few heads about, but when they found out she was searching for the mark of Ecarthus, everyone volunteered to disrobe for her on the spot. I myself just came from being blessed by Starseeker Vashyra." He closed his eyes as tears crept over his cheeks. "I feel clean again."

Azhani nodded. "I'm glad. No one deserves what those bastards did to you." They both stood in silence a moment, thinking over those who had been lost to Ecarthus' fires. Eventually, she said, "Have there been many complaints about me?"

"Some," he replied. "I've been allowing the dissenters to take what's theirs and go. A few formally resigned, but most are just fleeing ahead of whatever justice they fear facing."

Padreg approached them. "I could get up a group and track them down, if ye'd like, Warleader."

"No, let them go. They've seen enough of death," she said quietly.

"Aye. So've we all." Shivering, he said, "Be glad when it gets a bit warmer."

"It's winter, Padreg. We're not likely to feel the balmy kisses of spring anytime soon," she replied dryly. "But this day does seem colder than others."

"I find myself in agreement with you, Chief Padreg," Niemeth said sadly. "Though there is strange joy to be found here, as well."

"I can't fault you for feeling that way," Azhani replied. "Get some rest. It'll be no warmer tonight." She looked toward the east, where soon, the sun's rays would skate across the sky, bringing the relief of dawn.

Both Padreg and Niemeth saluted, then left her to make her way to her own tent.

Her sleep was fitful, and after only a few candlemarks she had to escape the cloying confines of her shelter and stand outside, staring out at the army. A nagging sense of dread crawled her spine. It was still strangely cold and dark enough that she wondered if they might be facing a storm. Looking up, she gasped softly. The sun, their guardian against the predations of the rimerbeasts, was slowly disappearing behind a shadow so dark no light emerged from behind it. The sky itself was a flat, ugly gray—the color of twilight, when the rimerbeasts started creeping out of their caves to hunt.

"By the Twain," she blurted sharply.

Startled awake by Azhani's voice, Kyrian pulled on her robe and ducked outside, finding her staring up at the sky. It took her a few moments to realize that it there should be sunlight overhead. "Goddess, what's happening?"

Azhani shook her head. "I don't know. I need to find Vashyra."

"I'll come with you." Kyrian quickly belted her armored robes closed.

"No. Sleep. It's probably nothing," she said, though something in the tone of her voice told Kyrian she didn't believe it.

"Azhi—"

"No, it's all right. I just need to talk to her—find out if this strange darkness will affect the rimerbeasts," Azhani said gently. "Go see Devon, if you can't sleep. I'd like to know how he fared the journey."

Kyrian sighed. "All right, you win. But only because I'm curious as well. If you need me, send someone to find me."

"I will." Azhani kissed her tenderly.

They parted, with Azhani going toward the starseeker's encampment and Kyrian going toward the center of camp. She was concerned about Devon. Even after she'd saved most of his hip and thigh, he still seemed not to care about anything, even food. Though they hadn't said anything, she knew Allyn and Syrelle were equally worried.

Upon entering the tent, she found both of them curled up under the blanket of Allyndev's cloak, their heads resting against the side of Devon's cot, asleep. Devon himself just lay there, staring at the tent roof, his expression so carefully contrived she would have sworn it was a mask.

A bowl of stew sat on a nearby tray. *I see they still haven't gotten him to eat.* Quietly, she woke the sleepers and sent them to lie on one of the empty cots. Devon watched them snuggle up and then turned away, pain making his eyes crease. From her perch at the foot of his cot, Avisha softly grumbled at his movement, jumping down and sniffing at Kyrian's knees before butting her head against her thigh.

Gently, she scratched the cat's ears. "Hello, Avisha."

The cat purred softly, then returned to Devon's cot, settling by his foot.

"She's very protective of you." Kyrian moved the blankets aside and began examining Devon's bandages. "How do you feel today? Any itching? Soreness?"

Sourly, he replied, "I feel like my leg's been chewed off."

She gave him a look and he sighed, covering his face with his hand.

"I'm...alive. Jasyn's alive."

"But?"

He looked over at Allyndev and Syrelle. "Maybe it would have been better if I wasn't."

"You don't mean that." She mixed a batch of herbs for him.

Shaking his head, he said, "I think I do. I'm…broken. A burden." He sighed. "At least they're happy."

Tenderly, she caressed his face. "You are only as broken as you let yourself be, Devon Imry. Have you told them how you feel?"

"Gods no," he hissed, pulling away from her. "Sy…I think she suspects. She always seems to know how I feel, no matter how I try to hide it. But she's kind enough to let me keep my peace. I don't want Allyn to know. He'd just feel even more guilty than he already does."

"You're a good man, Devon, but they care about you. Maybe you should try talking to them."

He shook his head. "No. I know what happens then. I won't allow it. Please, don't say anything," he begged.

"I won't, but if you need to talk, I'll be here."

"Thank you." He gave her hand a tight squeeze. "You're a better friend than I deserve."

"You're—" Her reply was interrupted when he, and every other mage in the tent, suddenly screamed in agony.

A mournful, shrieking sound pierced the air, rising and rising and slapping against her like ice-kissed winds. Shivering in mindless fear, she abandoned what she was doing and raced to find the one place she knew was safe in the entire army.

"Azhani!" She burst outside, then stood transfixed at the sight of the darkened sky. *What is going on?* Her heart squeezed painfully as her terror redoubled and nearly forced her to her knees.

Somewhere, an alarm sounded. *Oh Goddess, rimerbeasts are attacking!*

The beasts quickly swarmed the guards, penetrating the camp and killing anyone in reach. Kyrian's training tore through her fear and forced her to reach for a weapon, but she encountered only empty space where her baton should hang. *Oh no. Oh Twain, no. Not now, not when I need to fight…*

"Kyrian!"

She spun and gaped at Devon, who stood propped against a chair, his face white with the effort it had cost him to move so far. Blood soaked his bandages. Growling and huffing, Avisha paced back and forth, her tail lashing angrily.

Quickly, Kyrian raced to his side. "Devon, you damnable idiot, what are you doing?"

"H-here," he stammered, thrusting a baton at her. "V-Vashyra and I, we m-made this. For you. She finished it in Barton. I-I was going to give it to you later."

Numbly, she accepted the weapon, nearly dropping it when it felt almost hollow. Yet the longer she held it, the more it made her hand tingle.

Surprised again, she said, "Is it—?"

"Magickal? Yes." He smiled. "L-Like I said, V-Vashyra and I made it. S-She said she h-had to, and that I h-had to help. Can't explain everything. Just…go. Find Azhani. She'll need you."

Torn between leaving and staying, Kyrian stared down at the weapon in her hand as all around her, soldiers battled for their lives.

Death stalked them. Chaos destroyed what little peace they had secured. Above the shrieking of blood-maddened rimerbeasts, she could hear her heart pound like a set of war drums.

"I-I don't know, Dev," she whispered, her old fears blackening her vision.

He grabbed her wrist and shook her. "You have to go!" he shouted, making her look at him. "Azhani needs *you*."

"I have to go." She blinked slowly, tightening her hold on the baton's hilt. It was much easier than she could remember. Resolutely, she nodded. "But you—"

"I'll be fine," he said firmly. "Avisha will protect us."

"No, I'm not going until I know you're safe." She pushed past him, storming into the tent. There she found Allyndev and Syrelle already up and helping the other mages.

"Sy," she said, grabbing her. "Get your idiot tent mate back into his bed and change his dressing."

Syrelle didn't speak, just grabbed Devon by his tunic, hoisted him over her shoulders like he was a sack of grain, and carried him back to bed.

"Allyn!" Kyrian snapped.

"Yes, Stardancer?"

"Guard this tent like it was your last hope. All the injured mages are here."

Paling, he nodded. "Yes, Stardancer."

The moment Syrelle set Devon down, he said, "Forget about bandages. Just belt my damned leg and give me something that'll dull pain, but not wits.

And Allyn, find my grimoire. I might be stuck in this damned tent, but I can still cast."

Her stardancer's duty made Kyrian want to stay, but the urge to be with Azhani was stronger—so much so that she only waited until she was certain Allyn and Syrelle were handling things before darting out of the tent, baton in hand.

The Ecarthan priest's robes stank of blood and smoke. Assuming the dead man was one of those Arris' former soldiers had hunted down, Azhani had shied away from the body, but refused to quit the ridge she had just fought to ascend, for it offered a vantage point where she could observe the actions of the soldiers below her. Lost in thought, she looked down at the mixed banners of four kingdoms and tried to understand what was happening. Arris the Kinslayer was dead. She was in command of the armies. Her name was cleared. She was again the bearer of her family's honor.

And the world was going mad.

She snarled in frustration and started pacing as she tried to figure out what to do. Vashyra was nowhere to be found. Finally, one of the junior starseekers had been able to tell Azhani that she'd stayed behind in Barton after exhausting herself to the point of collapse. Guilt-ridden, Azhani had made for the nearest hill, wanting a place of quiet where she could think uninterrupted.

Partly, she knew she felt cheated. Arris, the man she'd come to hate like poison, had died a hero. No matter how much she despised him, she would always remember he'd been the man who had taken what mattered most from her—and the man who had saved the woman she loved above any other. It left a sour ball of dissatisfaction roiling in her stomach.

She was empty now. The focus of her driving rage died when Arris did. There was so much to do, though. The rimerbeasts, Kasyrin Darkchilde, this strange darkness—the introduction of Ecarthus—it all felt like the result of one of those grand curses the bards romanticized in tale and song.

Magick. She sneered. By the Twain, how she hated dark magick. If there were one thing she could devote her life to, it would be rooting out and destroying every manifestation of it's presence in Y'Myran.

"Damn you, Darkchilde," she muttered under her breath. Suddenly, her thoughts coalesced: What if all this was Darkchilde's fault? What if every single horrible thing she'd faced since losing Ylera—and even before!—what if that all led back to Kasyrin Darkchilde and his machinations?

But how? How would a sorcerer who was barely powerful enough to live through a fight with her father gather the strength he would almost certainly have to possess to make rimerbeasts rise out of season—not to mention every thing else going on right now?

The answer was practically staring at her. "Ecarthus, of course," she said as she turned to look at the priest's body. "All right, why would a demon help a two-bit sorcerer?" Again, she was able to answer her own question. "Power. Politics. Arris. That's why he subverted him. Damn, this isn't over—it hasn't even begun."

Looking up at the sky, she shouted, "What will you do next, you bastard?"

Gormerath erupted in song.

Immediately, Azhani looked back at camp. In shock, she watched as rimerbeasts appeared, almost seeming to come to life from the air itself. Fear prickled in her veins.

Drawing the sword, she looked up once more and felt something ring through her. Memory, swift as eagle's wings, poured sound into her ears.

"The breaking is at hand. The Blade, the Heart, and the Pawn shall meet, and on that day, the sun will stand still and the stars will no longer spin with time."

"Oh Goddess," she whispered, and started to run toward camp—only to be jerked off her feet by Gormerath's pull. It wanted her to climb, now. She tried to fight it, but no matter how many times she turned around, her feet always put her back on a goat path leading up the side of the mountain.

On and on she went, breaking through the scrub trees and bushes to a spot where she could see the very top of a nearby mesa. There, a black-robed figure stood, outlined by a nimbus of glittering magickal energy. Behind him was a fat, black obelisk, it's eerie red glow flickering like a guttering torch.

Spurred into a run, she raced onward, knowing now that the prophecy was all true. The breaking was at hand. There was time, just barely, for her to turn and spare a glance at the embattled army below. *I love you, Kyrian. Remember that forever.*

And then she tipped her head back and let the Banshee scream.

Goaded by Azhani's war cry, Kyrian charged through camp, dodging the combatants. Her robes were already thick with the gore of those she had stopped to help. Above her, outlined by Gormerath's flame, Azhani glowed like a miniature sun. The light acted as a star for Kyrian to follow.

"I'm coming, my love," she cried, hurrying up the mountain.

Bodies of the slain barred her way, but she shoved them aside. Her fear rose and fell like the prow of a ship in the midst of a hurricane, but she refused to let it stop her. She would not flee from this fight! Onward she ran, cursing when her boots slipped on the wet rocks, sending her to her knees more than once.

Ahead, the sound of combat made her resolve waver, but she pressed on, fighting past the lump in her throat. Rounding a curve, she skidded to a stop at the sight of Azhani facing six rimerbeasts. A fierce grin made her lover look more beautiful than ever and the bright joy filling her laugh told Kyrian that this—this killing machine was truly the Banshee of song and legend.

Behind Azhani, a mage and a soldier huddled against each other, the soldier's hands pressed tight against a massive wound in the mage's chest.

In an instant, Kyrian saw the problem. Azhani needed to protect her soldiers, but to do so, she would have to expose her back to some of the rimerbeasts. If she was going to help, Kyrian either needed to jump into the fight right now or find some way to get to the injured mage so the soldier could take up arms once again.

One of the creatures roared and charged Azhani, grabbing her and pulling her into a bear hug that could squeeze the life from a horse in less time than it would take Kyrian to drink a flagon of ale.

In the end, the decision was easy.

Without a second thought, she burst into a run and leaped for them. As if it were as simple as breathing, she tucked herself into a ball and flipped over the heads of the gathered beasts, landing behind the one that had grabbed onto Azhani. Anger rolled through her as she struck it, crushing its skull. No monster was going to harm the woman she loved!

The rimerbeast fell, but Kyrian was already moving on, following the ingrained patterns of the dance, kicking and punching another rimerbeast so many times that it died before it could so much as twitch in her direction.

And then the Banshee's cry echoed around them as Azhani raised Gormerath once more. The sword blazed and burned and together, they destroyed the remaining rimerbeasts.

When it was over, Azhani kissed her, hard, and pointed at the mesa and the glowing obelisk that crowned it. "I need to be there. I love you."

Kyrian nodded. "I know. I'm going with you." She tossed her haversack at the soldier. "There's bandages and medicine inside." Cleaning her baton, she sheathed it and offered Azhani a simple smile. "Let's go."

Lowering her blade, Azhani extended her hand to her. "Together, then."

And they continued climbing, ready to face whatever came next.

CHAPTER TWENTY-ONE

The sounds of battle faded, distance stripping even the mournful howls of the dying from the wind. All that remained was their breathing, the scuff of their boots on stone, and the occasional whispered comment or popped cork as Azhani or Kyrian took brief sips from their waterskins.

"Feels like it's taking forever," Kyrian said as they stopped to catch their breath.

"Doesn't matter. Have to get there," Azhani replied, continuing on the moment Kyrian indicated she was ready.

Side by side, they went, helping each other climb even the narrowest of rocky prominences and natural bridges until, finally, they reached the edge of the mesa.

"Wait here," Azhani murmured.

By now, fear had become such a tightly wound coil around Kyrian's heart that she merely nodded. "J-Just yell, w-when you need me," she said as Azhani pulled herself up over the top.

Glancing back, Azhani smiled. "I need you. I'll yell when I need help."

"I love you," Kyrian whispered, touching her Astariun token and praying for Azhani's safety.

Standing on a shallow ledge, she peeked up over the rocky edge of the mesa and watched as Azhani used every bit of shadow and cover she could find to creep toward the two figures. Behind them, thrust up from the ground like a terrible spearhead was an obelisk of darkest obsidian. Faintly glowing runic script covered its surface and a slow pulse of ruddy light rolled through the sigils like some kind of magickal heartbeat.

One of the figures was a black-robed man. He stood before the artifact, arms upraised, hands coated in fresh blood. At his feet, bodies lay strewn, their recent, brutal deaths the source of the blood streaming down his arms. His face was upturned to the sky and even in the gloom, Kyrian knew him to be Kasyrin Darkchilde, the sorcerer who had attacked them in Y'Syria.

His lips shaped a chant, the words of which were snatched away by the wind before she could hear them.

She did not know the other man who lurked near the sorcerer, but he wore richly appointed scholar's robes and she assumed he was a servant of Darkchilde's. Thankfully, neither man had noticed them, though she feared that would not last long.

Suddenly, Darkchilde screamed, the sound so loud that it made Kyrian's ears ring. Ugly, dark energy wrapped around his hands and he thrust them into the obelisk, unleashing a torrent of arcane fire that quickly enshrouded him. The entire mountain shook.

"Oh Goddess," Kyrian hissed, willing her arms to grip the nearest stone until the quake ended.

When it was over, she looked up again and watched in shock as Darkchilde was pitched away from the obelisk like he was the pip in a nobleman's cherry.

Stepping out from behind a cluster of boulders, Azhani drew Gormerath. "How's it feel to be tossed aside like yesterday's garbage, Darkchilde?"

"You!" he spat as the other man spun to face her.

Kyrian prayed she was too far away to be seen. As long as they didn't know she was there, she was free to act.

"Were you expecting someone else?" Azhani asked bemusedly.

"You're supposed to be dead!" Darkchilde rounded on the other man and grabbed him by the collar. Shaking him violently, he yelled, "Arris was supposed to kill her! He was mine, by Ecarthus' will!"

Kyrian couldn't hear what the other man said, but by expression of abject terror on his face, she suspected he was begging for his life.

"The pawn learned a new move, Darkchilde. He sacrificed himself to save another." Wolfishly, Azhani grinned. "Someone obviously taught him how to play very well."

"Then I shall deal with you myself!" Darkchilde spat, spinning in place and flinging his hands out toward the obelisk. "Ecarthus!" It was a word of dark, ugly power and the hair on the nape of Kyrian's neck began to prickle.

The glow emanating from the obelisk shifted, pulsing faster and faster, creating a deep, rumbling hum that made the ground shudder.

A terrible groan filled the air and Kyrian had to cover her head as rocks and pebbles began to bounce over the edge of the mesa. Torn between fear of the sorcerer and the terrifying sense that she was going to fall, she scrambled over the ledge, darting behind a nearby clump of stubby bushes, praying her red robes wouldn't give her away.

The ground before the obelisk split. Plumes of noxious smoke and ash swirled up from the rupture in the earth, forcing them all to shield their faces.

"Circus tricks, Darkchilde?" Azhani waved away the smoke. "They'll not stand against my blade." With casual ease, she swept Gormerath in front of her.

Amazingly, the air began to clear as music swelled around them. Kyrian gasped. *This must be the song Azhani has so often spoken of!* It was loud, painfully so, but beautiful as well. Awestruck, she could only watch as Darkchilde threw both hands outward, his fingers twisting as he chanted.

"Lord Ecarthus is no circus trick, Oathbreaker!" Silvery glyphs danced in the air. "Behold, he who comes to devour your soul!" He threw his arms wide as power shot out of the obelisk and through his body, pouring into the rift. The ground shook again and then, slowly, horribly, something began to appear.

Rising from the rupture came first the head, then the shoulders of a truly monstrous being. At first, Gormerath's song rose in pitch, but began to wane as the beast opened his eyes and smiled. Possessed of an inhuman face that was equally beautiful and terrifying, skin as red as a river of blood, yet smooth as polished stone, and fangs that dripped with the ochre of a rimerbeast's venom, Ecarthus was the most hideous thing Kyrian had ever seen. Coal black horns twisted from his skull, a necklace of bones and skulls hung from his neck, and thick ropes of slime clung to his chest and shoulders.

Ripping his hands from the earth, Ecarthus flexed his fingers, shaking goo from his poisonous-looking claws.

Almost comically, he was still stuck in the earth from the waist down. To Kyrian, this was a blessing in disguise. She began to pray.

::Darkchilde!:: the demon roared, his horns taking on an eerie greenish glow.

Kyrian winced at the pain his "voice" poured through her skull. It seemed to echo both in her head and her ears, making them ring. Azhani cringed and stumbled back a step. Even the scrawny lackey seemed affected, for he clapped his hands to his head, though Kyrian was sure it wouldn't help.

"I have brought you your enemy, master," Darkchilde said triumphantly.

Chains of glowing metal were wound about Ecarthus' belly, reaching deep into the earth. Grabbing a link, the demon screamed, **::I care little for the mortal flea, slave. Finish the spell! Free me!::**

Azhani backed away, fear masking her face even as Kyrian continued to pray, begging the Twain to give them strength. Gormerath's song had faded to a mere whisper.

Evil rolled off Ecarthus in thick, dark waves. Kyrian's guts were twisted into so many knots that half her prayers were lost as she fought the urge to vomit. Though she longed to get up and stand at Azhani's side, the aura of pain and death permeating the mesa had shattered her resolve. It was all she could do not to flee, gibbering in fear.

Memory spun and tumbled in her mind's eye. Over and over, she saw the bandit's blood creeping down the length of her baton as his dying groans grew louder and louder.

Frozen in place, she watched as Ecarthus continued to rise from his earthen prison. Above them, the sky was pure black. No sun, no moon, not even a single star was out to cast light upon them. Only the ruddy glow of the obelisk offered any relief from the oppressive darkness crushing into them.

::**Yes, my slave,**:: Ecarthus crooned as Darkchilde chanted, taking power from the obelisk and shaping it into sigils he threw at the chains, breaking them a link at a time. ::**Success is ours! I will be free!**::

Capering about like a madman, Porthryos watched as Ecarthus began to step out of the earth. *I will be rich, rich, rich! Gold, jewels—they'll be mine, all mine!* Gleefully, he rubbed his hands together and laughed. *There will be feasting and women—so many women, and they will all obey me! Not like that damnable whore of Arris'!* Batizha had figured out what he was doing. Had come to him with his sack of krile and flung it at him. Had accused him of treason. *Hah! Without me, she wouldn't have had her precious "King Arris."* Well, he couldn't have her ruining everything. Not when they'd been so close to success.

So he'd dealt with it, and the first moment he could, he'd snuck away to join his master in his preparations for Ecarthus' rising. Now it was happening, it was really happening and there was nothing, nothing at all to stop them... except that bitch, Azhani Rhu'len.

Curiously, he watched her, realizing all of a sudden that she was terrified. *By Ecarthus' glory, I could...I could kill her right now and she couldn't stop me!*

It was such a stunning revelation that he very nearly wept.

Master will shower me in gold coins for weeks! Drawing his dagger, he charged.

The mesa was aglow with an eerie red light. Visibility was poor, but when a glint of metal appeared in the hand of Darkchilde's lackey, Kyrian almost couldn't believe what she was seeing. In shock, she watched as he raised a wickedly curved dagger and charged right for Azhani.

In that moment, all her fear vanished. Training took over. As she assessed the situation, she drew her baton and straightened. She knew there was no way she could stop the man's attack. No, what she needed now was a distraction so incredible, he stopped himself.

"Fly true," she whispered, launching her baton high into the air.

End over end the enchanted weapon tumbled, arcing across the mesa. Impossibly, it sped up, spinning so quickly that it seemed to flicker like lightning.

With a sickening thunk, it crashed into its target, shattering bone and sending a spray of blood splashing over the obelisk. A man screamed in agony.

The sorcerer's servant stumbled, then spun around, his dagger falling from his hand as he stared at Darkchilde. Blood sheathed Kasyrin's face. His skull was split and broken, bits of bone sticking up whitely in the mess.

"Master?" the servant whimpered.

Kyrian cursed softly. She'd aimed to kill.

Darkchilde tried to reach for his head, but couldn't seem to tear his hands away from the stream of energy pouring through him.

::Ignore thy pain, slave. It is but a temporary sting. Finish thy spell and we will find your assailant and rip them apart,:: Ecarthus rumbled, lifting his hand and extending his finger. A ripple of greenish energy oozed out of him and coiled around Darkchilde's legs, slid up his body and covered the wound in his head.

"Yes, master," Darkchilde said, continuing to chant as his servant retrieved his blade then scurried to his side.

Quickly, Kyrian ducked behind the bushes to avoid being seen. She'd failed. The one chance she'd had to prove herself and she'd utterly failed!

Terror was an insidious monster. So many times in her life, Azhani had fought the beast and won, but today, every battle was a complete rout. She could not look at Ecarthus, could not focus on the demon or his servants. Not when doing so filled her mind with visions of the most terrifying experience of her life. Ecarthus wasn't just frightening, he was the physical incarnation of everything Azhani loathed and feared. He used magick like a toy, he killed without thought, and each time she even tried to glance in his direction, she wanted to run screaming or throw herself at his feet and beg for mercy.

Instead, she retreated within herself, closing her eyes and cringing behind a boulder, sobbing softly and praying that somehow, some way, she could dredge up the courage to act. Darkchilde had to be stopped, but…how?

::*Hear me, my daughter. The time of testing has come.*::

Azhani shivered as the soft caress of sound-that-wasn't-sound silkily echoed through her thoughts. The voice—Her voice—it was so familiar, so strong, so beautiful, so peerless and Azhani wanted to weep for it. Memory, shaped and hammered into perfect blades, slipped into her thoughts and cut through the hazy fog of spells she never knew had been laid to reveal what she had so joyfully experienced in a forest grove not very far from where she now crouched. A year's passage of time felt too little.

"Astariu?" she whispered, awestruck. "You came to me, you…blessed me when all that I was had been destroyed."

::*Yes.*::

Warmth flowed over her, and she looked up to see the faint outline of a woman standing beside her, her hand resting on Azhani's shoulder. The face belonged to no earthly woman, for no person of flesh could be so beautiful and so terrible at once.

Tears flooded Azhani's eyes. "Have I failed you, then?"

::*No, never!*:: Her grip tightened. ::*I have come again, as promised,*:: She said gently.

"Why?"

Astariu glanced over at the demon struggling to free himself from its arcane prison. ::*Dost thou trust in me, my warrior?*::

There had been a time when Azhani wasn't even sure she could trust herself, much less a goddess who had seemingly abandoned her. But time, love, and an unexpected sacrifice by someone she had sworn was her enemy had taught her that no one was ever truly forsaken.

Calmly, she replied, "Yes."

Without warning, the world went black. A far off chime of bells reverberated through her and…

...She burned. A suffusion of fire hotter than the forges of Y'Dror consumed her being. Pain crushed her bones, tore her muscles, destroyed her body. She was pushed, pulled, twisted, and drawn toward an unknown goal. Sightless, she could only suffer a pounding, quenching, raging, clanging, grinding, merciless shift of perspective.

And then it was over. A cool sensation spread over her. In fascinated detachment, Azhani watched as her entire body became awash in the azure aura of the goddess Astariu. "Well, that's not what I was expecting," she tried to say, but her mouth didn't move. No sound rolled in her throat, no breath slipped through her lungs. She was stiff, cold, and felt almost nothing.

She tried to scowl, but could not; tried to will her right arm to move, but instead, she scratched her nose with the left—only the perspective was completely wrong. Instead of seeing her hand come for her face, she watched her arm rise, her hand turn, her fingers curl toward her nose, and then, oddly, she saw her hand scratch her face, but she was not actually *in* the body doing the scratching. It wasn't even like looking into a mirror, for when she did that she was aware of her body and her surroundings. Right now, her "surroundings" were everything. The rocks, the sky, the mesa, the tableau of sorcerer, scholar, and demon. She could even see Kyrian hiding in the scrubby bushes.

And then it all moved far too fast. Her body rushed through the air and she opened her mouth to give voice to song.

Gormerath's shrill tone warbled from her throat.

I'm a sword? Perplexed, Azhani tried to understand how it was possible, but it couldn't be, because that felt all wrong. *No, no, no.* She was moved again, swung low and fast. *Goddess, I'm the Blade!*

With a bright, beautiful laugh, Astariu said, **::Yes, my child, thou art. So it was written and so it has become.::**

There was no reason to doubt Astariu's words. Already, her mind was filling with the knowledge of what she was to do, how she was to use Gormerath's power when she was called upon to act. Still, there was one last thing she needed to know, one last thought that belonged to her mortal self. Understanding that she had just surrendered her life in order to fight Ecarthus, Azhani asked, "What of Kyrian?"

::My stardancer loves thee deeply, warrior,:: Astariu said, smiling sadly. **::I fear she will not lightly accept thy loss.::**

Azhani found no comfort in Astariu's reply, but she had expected none. Life, it seemed, had always conspired against her. *Forgive me, Kyrian.*

Abandoning herself to Gormerath's song, Azhani said, "I am ready. Strike now, my lady, while you still have the element of surprise."

::*Always the tactician, my warrior. Thou hast pleased me yet again!*:: Astariu's joy wrapped around Azhani like a living cloak of love.

Resolutely, Astariu gripped the weapon's hilt and stepped out from behind the rock, fearlessly striding toward Ecarthus. Halfway there, an invisible wall stopped her in her tracks.

"Darkchilde's work, no doubt," Azhani said.

::*'Tis less than it could have been, had Kyrian's aim not been so true,*:: Astariu sent privately. Then, focusing her will on all present, she shouted, ::*I defy thee, Soul-Eater! Thou shalt not enter this world unchallenged!*::

Startled, Kyrian stared at Azhani. Though she had spoken, it was not her voice that emanated from her body. She recognized it, though, for she had heard it most of her life, during the holiest of ceremonies an Astariun priest could perform. All fear vanished and she calmly strode to Azhani's side, looking up at her in wonder.

"Astariu?" she whispered, almost but not quite reaching out to touch her, just to see if she was real.

If Kyrian had been surprised, Ecarthus was even more shocked.

::**Nay!**:: he shouted, the force of his voice causing rocks to crack and split, sending shards of stone flying everywhere. ::**No more shalt thou bar me from what is rightfully mine, meddling child!**:: Grabbing Darkchilde's shoulder, he laughed as power surged down his arm and into the man's body, jerking him like a puppet and forcing his chant to stop.

Blinking dumbly, Darkchilde looked up, squinted at Astariu-Azhani, and then flung his fingers at her, snarling, "Hold." Twisting, thorn-ridden vines sprouted from his hands and slammed into her. Blood spurted from dozens of wounds as the thorns penetrated Azhani's body.

Kyrian gasped, "No," as Azhani screamed in agony.

Ecarthus laughed and pointed to the man in scholar's robes. ::**Kill her.**::

Grinning wildly, the sorcerer's servant leaped to do the demon's bidding, raising his blade and charging Azhani once more.

No, no, no, this isn't happening. I have to do something! Kyrian's weapon lay beyond her reach, forgotten on the ground behind Darkchilde's feet.

Stardancers, however, do not need weapons. Breaking into a run, she tackled the servant, driving him to the ground and punching him in the throat hard enough to make him gag. He was up quickly, slashing at her with his blade, carving burning lines into her forearms as she desperately tried to block him. The backs of her hands became wrapped in ribbons of blood. Once, the blade got through and left a score along her ribs, cutting through the hardened leather of her robes as if they weren't even there.

Can't keep letting him bleed me. I'll die by inches. Her baton was so close, yet so damnably far away it was as if she didn't have it at all. If she tried to go for it, Astariu-Azhani would be left vulnerable to attack. *I can't leave her unprotected—she's fighting the spell, I can feel it!* And she could—somehow, she just knew that Azhani and Astariu were putting the strength of their combined wills together in an attempt to shatter Darkchilde's magickal binding. Right now, Kyrian really needed to have a weapon in hand. It would make her so much more effective at defending them! Frustration poured through her every thought. *If only the damned thing would come here!* Angrily, she blocked a strike and kicked her opponent in the groin. He dropped like a sack of rocks. Behind him, the baton quivered and then rose, hovering in the air.

"Bitch," he rasped.

The baton spun, then flew straight to her hand.

Without thinking, she rapped him on the back of the head, rendering him unconscious.

Goddess, Devon, I owe you such a big hug if we survive this. "Your turn," she muttered, glaring at Darkchilde. Taking a firm grip on the enchanted baton, she strode across the mesa, death boiling in her veins. She was beyond fear, beyond care, all she wanted was to end this, end him, and take care of Azhani's wounds.

Part of her mind was gibbering insanely. This day, she knew, would give her nightmares for years. If she lived, if Azhani lived, then she would gladly face them.

Astariu-Azhani cursed again and again. The demon was too clever by half. By forcing her to focus all her energies on controlling the pain and keeping Azhani's body alive, she had nothing left to break the spell binding her in place.

"You need to forget the pain," Azhani said.

::*Easy for you to say, you are a sword blade!*::

"I have not always been. Pain is fleeting. Let my body remember how to be what I am."

Astariu was plagued by doubt. How could simple surrender to a mortal offer relief? Yet Azhani sounded so sure and there was no denying that she was a consummate warrior. In that moment, Astariu understood something truly profound, for just as Azhani was fated to do as she had done, so to was she, Astariu, fated to accept her own role in it. She stopped fighting and was overwhelmed by the hot flood of agony. ::**I cannot do this,**:: she said, tempted to try and block it once more.

"Yes. You can," Azhani said. "*We* can. We must."

::*I—*::

"We," Azhani said firmly, surrendering the last bit of herself to her beloved goddess.

Astariu exhaled as the pain slid away, lost in a flood of rage and determination that made her feel like she had been carved of the sun itself. ::*We!*:: she sang, gathering her power once again, focusing it now on the bindings and ignoring the thorns.

::**Thou wilt fail, Astariu,**:: Ecarthus taunted.

::**So you hope,**:: she retorted, the bonds weakening enough that she could take a step forward.

::**Thou art prideful and mean,**:: he said bitingly. ::**You claim the adulation of mortals while forcing me to pick from the leavings of their nightmares. I shall suffer this indignity no longer! The breaking has come! Thy days of drinking the sweet wine of faith hath ended, for now I have risen. A new era dawns! Fear and hatred will slaughter your pathetic ideals of love and tolerance.**:: His laughter echoed across the mesa. ::**I shall sup from the table of mortal misery and leave only the dregs of my hellish prison for you to lick whilst your mad brother capers and dances for me upon a bed of burning bones!**::

Looking into the eyes of her ancient enemy, Astariu said, ::*Hate and fear cannot last in the mortal heart, Ecarthus. The blessings of love and faith will always win through the harshest of lies. No matter what comes of this day, know that thy nightmares shall never reach the infinite glories of love.*::

With a derisive snort, Ecarthus threw open his arms and snarled, ::**Then stop me, little godling. Strike me down where I stand!**::

Raising her arm, Kyrian took a breath as she looked at the back of Kasyrin Darkchilde's head and plotted the exact spot her baton would land. It had to be fast, hard, and merciless. His survival was not an option.

It's now or never. Every lesson she'd ever had, every practice bout she'd ever fought put her right here, in this moment, giving her the strength and knowledge of how and where to strike. Muscles tightened; she found her balance and swung. The baton descended. Time became broken into heartbeats. She froze as visions of the past assaulted her, filling her mind with juddering, gore-soaked pictures of blood and death.

Her thoughts spun in never-ending circles. Sharp tears cut streaks into her cheeks.

Murderer. The whisper was insidious, pricking tiny thorns in her ears. *You're a killer, Kyrian. A destroyer. Evil. Fit only to serve Ecarthus' will. Darkness will forever stain you.*

"No," she moaned.

Yes.

Through tears, she watched as Astariu-Azhani broke band after band of the spell-woven tentacles that bound her. Even in her agony, she kept fighting. Their eyes met and in them, Kyrian saw the infinite love both had for her. New memories slipped around her. Laughter, joy, love—endless, beautiful candlemarks where they held each other no matter what pain or ills troubled them. It was all hers, it would always be hers. Azhani's love, Astariu's love was made of stronger stuff than any darkness Ecarthus could weave.

"Fear will not rule me," Kyrian growled, snapping the demon's spell and driving the baton into Darkchilde's head.

"Ecarthus unbound…Ecarthus unbound…Ecarthu—" The chant was abruptly ended as Kyrian shattered his skull like an overripe pumpkin.

Astariu-Azhani grinned. ::*As thou hast requested, so thou hast received,*:: she said as Ecarthus screamed in frustration. The last of her bonds disintegrated. Raising her sword, she saluted Kyrian, who returned it with her blood-soaked baton.

::**No!**:: Ecarthus wailed as he shot bolts of energy at Darkchilde's lifeless body. ::**Rise, slave! Thou wilt not fail me now! Rise and say the words to free me from this prison!**::

Darkchilde did not move.

Kyrian looked up at the demon, raised her fist in a rude gesture, and said, "Guess we're all having a terrible day."

Ecarthus' gaze landed on her like a load of iron bars. ::**You! You have breathed your last, creature of Astariu! You'll trouble me no more!**:: He slapped her halfway across the mesa with one negligent flip of his hand. ::**Now die!**:: he snarled as a bolt of pure energy formed over his hand.

With a wild scream, Astariu leaped, deflecting the demon's spell with her sword. ::*Hast thou forgotten me, spawn of slime?*:: she yelled, smashing the blade into his knuckles, cutting deeply into his flesh.

Roaring, he batted at her, but could not avoid her blows. Chains still bound him to the earth, forcing him to take the punishing cuts.

::*Thou wilt pass from this place and return nevermore, Ecarthus. It is thy destiny,*:: she said calmly, driving her sword straight into his heart.

Azhani felt herself slide into the demon's half-solid flesh. Pain once again shattered her thoughts as all that she was—every day's breath, every heartbeat's memory, every piece and parcel that made her—filled the demon's soul. Her mortality blazed into Ecarthus, shattering the last link in the chain binding him to his hellish prison.

He laughed as he surged upward, only to collapse on the bare rock as black blood burbled over his lips and dripped onto his chest.

In that moment, when she and he were one being, when her darkness and his entwined, when the Banshee and the demon knew nothing but oneness, Azhani learned a host of terrible truths. Much of what she saw made little sense, but something in the morass stood out—the rimerbeasts that had been such a burden on the people of Y'Myran were creatures of his will. He was why they had come to torment and terrorize Y'Myran, their purpose to gather the power that was needed to free their demonic master from the prison in which had been sealed.

Kasyrin Darkchilde had been his creature, too. Everything the sorcerer had done was to further Ecarthus' aims.

All that death. Centuries upon centuries of careless destruction, and all for this? Hatred seethed within her, for here was the being ultimately responsible for the deaths of all those she had loved. Her father, her king, her beloved Ylera—all lives snuffed so that he might escape his prison.

"*You wanted to be here so badly that you destroyed everything I ever loved!*" she screamed. "*So be it. Welcome to Y'Myran, Ecarthus. May the earth that covers your grave be warning to any who dares follow your path!*"

Coughing as he struggled to rise, Ecarthus looked down at the blade lodged in his chest and gaped, for it had begun to glow. Golden light poured from the sword, spreading over him. Everywhere it touched, his perfect, unblemished skin withered and turned to ash.

"No," he whispered, his power lost.

"Yes," she replied heartlessly. "*You are mortal now, beast. For you, time has become unbound. This is my gift to you for all the bitter tears you have given me.*"

"N—" he gasped, then was no more. The sword clattered to the ground and lay shrouded by dust until an errant breeze came and swept it away, leaving the blade to remain alone and lifeless.

Silence swallowed the top of the mesa. Every heartbeat was like thunder in Kyrian's ears as she sheathed her baton, stepped over Darkchilde's body and wearily made her way to Astariu-Azhani's side. *Astariu-Azhani.* She could think of her no other way, for though the woman before her wore her beloved's face, nothing about her felt like Azhani. This woman, this stranger with a lover's face, wore power like it was a raiment of common cloth. Kneeling, Kyrian looked up at her and softly asked, "Is it over?"

Astariu-Azhani touched Kyrian's shoulder, then motioned for her to stand. *::Yes.::*

With a long sigh of relief, Kyrian murmured, "All praise to the Twain. You saved us."

She smiled, though she was crying. *::I had help.::*

Sadness, now? But why? The reason for Astariu-Azhani's gentleness slowly crept into Kyrian's thoughts. *No, oh no.* Shaking her head, she whispered, "Azhani?"

Astariu-Azhani's voice was braided through with ringing pride and infinite sorrow. *::She was the instrument of prophecy, as was written.::*

"Prophecy?" Kyrian rasped as she fought tears. "No. No. Please, no," she whimpered, scrubbing her eyes. They'd all been over that damnable thing a thousand times. Nothing about them had made sense.

"*The breaking is at hand. The Blade, the Heart, and the Pawn shall meet, and on that day the sun will stand still and the stars will no longer spin with time. The

Beast will rise to seek his place among mortals. Stand well against the storm, and sages shall sing of thy glory into the mists of Eternity. Fall, and all shall blacken and fade."

"No!" Kyrian screamed as the words raced through her thoughts. "No, no, no," she sobbed, falling into Astariu-Azhani's arms. The goddess held her as she wept. "Azhi…she was the Blade."

::**Yes,**:: Astariu replied solemnly.

They both looked at the weapon that had been Gormerath, that had housed Azhani's spirit. The sword, once bright, was now charred and dull. Fine cracks chased the metal and crystalline structure. It seemed so brittle that a single touch might cause it to shatter.

"Damn you." Kyrian pushed away from Astariu-Azhani and knelt beside the sword. Tenderly, she caressed the hilt. "Damn you!" she wailed, grief consuming her. "She was everything to me, do you understand? Everything!" Hatred filled her as she looked up at the goddess. "I loved her enough to kill. To *kill*."

::**I'm sorry,**:: Astariu-Azhani whispered, reaching for her.

"Don't you even," Kyrian snapped, pulling away. "Don't you even think to offer me comfort. You are a cold, cruel witch to wear her face and offer me tenderness!" Pointing at the sword, she snarled, "This is my love's corpse. You wear a lie, Astariu. Begone, before I see if another god can die on this damned mountain."

The words, she saw, hurt.

::**You will always be my stardancer, Kyrian,**:: Astariu whispered as she turned away from her. ::**You will always have my Fire. And my love.**::

"I don't want it," Kyrian said dully. "Just go." She shed her armor and took the sword into her arms, cradling it delicately. The edge pressed into her cheek, cutting her to the bone.

She didn't care.

::**Brother,**:: Astariu cried. ::**It's thy turn.**:: There was a flash of light, the sound of something hitting the ground, and then, nothing.

Kyrian opened her eyes. Not two feet away, Azhani's body lay. She dragged herself to her lover's side and knelt beside Azhani, placing Gormerath atop her chest. This was all she had strength for. "Oh, Azhi," she whispered, grabbing Azhani's blood-smeared hand and holding it against her face. More tears welled in her eyes as she rocked back and forth. "Oh, my love."

There was only one answer now. One thing she could do. Her belt pouch had everything she would need. A little pinch of this, a little drop of that, and Kyrian would join her in The Great Fields. It would be so, so very easy.

"'Ere now, lass," a man said softly.

Kyrian jerked in shock and looked up as a kindly-faced man put his hand on her shoulder.

"Put up yer tears and join me for a wee drop." He held out a battered flask, which she took.

A strange lassitude washed over her as soon as she touched it. Uncapping it, she drank deep, then gasped at the sudden burn of the raw liquor it held.

"That's the spirit, lass!" he said, smiling warmly.

"W-Who are you?" She frowned as she studied the man's odd face. He was plain, homely, even, and yet so beautiful she wanted to touch the laugh lines that crinkled the edges of his eyes with the reverence of a lover.

"Never ye mind about that, lass. Think of me only as a bearer of gifts and good tidings, if ye'd but ask for them."

Confused, she got to her feet. "What could you have that I would want?" Nothing about the man spoke of wealth or power—neither of which she craved, anyway.

He shrugged and danced a comical little jig, laughed gleefully. Spreading his arms wide, he said, "Ye'll ne'er know 'til ye ask." Taking her hand, he spun her into his arms, swaying her around in the steps of an ancient pavane. "Tell me, lass—if there were but one thing you could have, what would it be?"

Gaping at him as if he were daft, she said, "I want my life back. I want to wake up tomorrow and be in Azhani's arms. I want…I want every day of the life we dreamed of and more! I want to remember what it was like to love the gods, not hate everything they are."

"Oh, lass," he said, cupping her face and stroking her cheek lightly. "Such powerful love ye bear." He sighed. Then, with a mischievous wink, he said, "I can do that!" and sprinted away, dancing around and around, giggling like a child and clucking like a chicken.

Kyrian was sure she'd lost her mind. The air seemed to thicken; her body felt too tight. Her head throbbed and pounded and ached fiercely. Then, the strange little jester came to a complete stop, clapped his hand over his mouth and then flung it toward her like a child blowing kisses—only his lips came flying at her, slammed into hers and vanished, reappearing on his face.

"There ye go, lass—pass it on and all will be well," he said amiably.

"Are you completely insane?" she blurted.

"Perhaps I am, perhaps I am merely privy to that which you are not." He touched his finger to the side of his nose. "The question is, lass—how much do you want your wish to be true?"

She had nothing—not one thing—to lose. Racing to Azhani's side, she knelt, pushing away the sword as she pressed herself against her. "Oh, my love, my very sweet and precious love. You must come back to me. You must live," she whispered, blinking back tears once more.

Her lips began to tingle.

"You can't leave me. I need you, Azhani. Do you hear that? I need you! You promised me a future, you promised me forever! I won't let you leave me, I won't let fate steal what we earned!" She kissed her fiercely.

The tingling vanished. The lips under hers warmed and opened as a tiny gasp of air escaped.

"Azhi?" she sobbed. Clutching her close, she reached for the Fire that Astariu promised would still be there. It came racing to her call, suffusing every part of her with the gentle warmth of her goddess' love. Azhani's life force was dim and Kyrian wasted no time, throwing herself into the healing with unfettered joy. Every wound, every cut, bruise, and break in her lover's body was hers to feel and she mercilessly wiped them out, healing her from head to toe.

She took risks, drawing raw energy straight from the earth. There was a massive, untapped source right below her feet and she used every drop of it to close wounds, mend cracked and broken ribs, and return her beloved Azhani to health.

Kyrian worked until she was drained, until there was nothing left of the well of power beneath her feet, until exhaustion threatened to send her reeling into unconsciousness. Tenaciously, she hung on, for Azhani would not rouse. She was in perfect health on the outside, but deeper, gouged into her soul, were wounds so gaping, so terrible, that Kyrian's magick could not touch them. Injuries taken on the battlefield where Azhani had fought the demon that Astariu's Fire could not reach.

There would be no giving up, though, not now. If Kyrian's magickal arsenal had failed, then she would do the one thing she could do—she would love her. Pulling Azhani into her arms, she kissed her, opening her heart and letting every last ounce of her emotion spill through the healing link. Without reservation or fear, she gave freely, letting Azhani feel it all.

"Come home, my love," she whispered, closing her eyes and singing her chants over and over until her throat was raw.

It was only when a hand cupped her cheek that she stopped. Fearfully, she opened her eyes and swallowed a sob of joy, for Azhani was looking up at her, a strange, peaceful smile blossoming on her face.

"Hello, my love," she rasped. "I missed your eyes."

"Oh, Azhi," Kyrian cried as she rained kisses on her face.

Laughing brightly, Azhani laced her fingers in Kyrian's hair and claimed her lips in a lengthy, loving kiss.

An eternity later, they parted and Kyrian stood. Filled with profound gratitude, she made her way to the man's side. "I don't know how to thank you." Impulsively, she kissed his cheek.

Blushing, he replied, "'Twas my honor to help, lass."

"Still, I owe you everything," she said softly as she looked around them. Destruction had left its mark on the mesa. The massive obelisk was no more. All that remained was a pile of cracked and pitted rubble where Darkchilde's body had lain. Several large pieces of the obelisk had landed on the servant, crushing him. Kneeling, she touched the man's throat, but there was no pulse. "He's dead. Who was he?"

"Porthyros Omal, the scholar. One of Arris' toadies," Azhani said as she joined her. "Thodan hired him to be a tutor for the boy years ago." She shook her head. "He's the bastard who poisoned him. Where's the demon?"

Kyrian pointed to a scattering of ashes caught in the snow. "That's what's left."

Slowly, Azhani got to her feet, then looked up. Overhead, the sun glared brightly. Whatever magick had darkened it was now gone.

The strange little man began picking around in the ruins while Kyrian just stared at the bodies. She'd killed them—it didn't matter that Porthryos' death had come as a result of the obelisk falling, she'd left him there and consequently, he had died.

"Goddess," Azhani said suddenly and Kyrian looked over at her. She'd retrieved Gormerath and was examining the ruined blade. "It's…she's gone." Grief made her face look drawn and lost.

Sadly, Kyrian nodded. "She seems so fragile now."

Out of habit, Azhani sheathed the blade. "Vashyra should have her. She's…important."

Everything felt very strange right now. With all that had happened, all they had experienced, and yet, the aftermath of this battle was so much like any other, that she found herself falling into similar habits—she was already thinking about the herbs she'd need to grind for healing poultices once they returned to camp! With a sigh, Kyrian made her way back to Azhani. Wrapping her arms around her, she clung tightly. "Those men…I-I killed them."

"I know." Azhani's tone was soft, almost tentative, as if she were afraid of speaking too loud lest she shatter something precious and fragile.

Kyrian looked up at her. She was numb, now. Too many emotions had caught her up in a hurricane of fear and grief. Exhaustion made her reach for the comfort of love, of relief, of the pleasure of her lover's embrace. Still, disquiet lingered. "It was easy—too easy. Killing shouldn't be that easy."

"Sometimes it is," Azhani replied, brushing a kiss over her forehead. "It doesn't mean anything."

"I-no." Kyrian shook her head quickly. "I can't believe that. No. It means something, it means…" She knuckled her eyes. "Am I a murderer?"

"No," Azhani said fiercely. "No, love. You took no pleasure in the dealing of death. You killed because you had to, to survive, to save us."

Chewing her lip, Kyrian said, "I-I don't regret it. They had to die, there was no other choice. But I hate with all I am that…that I had to be the one. I had to, to kill them." Grief—true, pain-heavy sorrow—washed over her and she cried, burying her face against Azhani's chest. The words to the pathsong felt rusty and wrong on her lips, but she could not—would not—condemn the men, no matter how evil they had been, to wander lost and alone.

Surprisingly, Azhani joined her, as did the strange man who was now standing beside them.

When it was over, Kyrian dried her tears and whispered, "Thank you."

"Peh," the man said with a wave of his hand. "Ye should nae fash yerself o'erlong for these scoundrels. 'Twas the hand of fate that reached through ye to deliver their ultimate destiny. Ye were but a tool, young stardancer, voiceless and choiceless in this play of gods."

Frowning, Azhani said, "It matters not whose choice it was, stranger. From her hand came death's cold touch, and it's memory will linger long past your next mug of ale."

"Aye. Ye've the right of it, and I regret this were the only way."

Pulling away from Azhani, Kyrian stared at him intently. "Who are you, that you speak of our fate with such familiarity? Where did you come from? And where did you get the power to revive the dead?"

Chuckling, he replied, "Full of questions, aren't ye?"

She crossed her arms and waited.

"Hmph. Well then, p'raps ye'd better recall me thusly." He clapped his hands. There was a puff of smoke and suddenly, a black-robed stranger stood before them. Upon his cheek was branded a death's head tattoo, and in his hand he held a wickedly curved dagger. "Do you know me now?" he whispered ominously.

Recoiling, Kyrian shivered. Evil radiated from him in a way that made her want to grab Azhani's hand and run far, far away. "I-I can't place you," she stammered.

"I know you," Azhani snarled, her hand dropping to the hilt of her dagger. "I killed you."

"Aye," he said, his body shimmering, shifting, and changing to that of a tall, handsome scholar whose noble mien immediately put them at ease. He smiled warmly, then reached up to rub his shoulder, saying, "You're a better than fair shot, warrior. The wound ached for many days."

Mouth agape, Kyrian whispered, "I know you now." In disbelief, she staggered forward, then dropped to her knees. "You're Astarus!"

Clapping his hands in delight, he began to shimmer as a brilliant blue aura surrounded him. ::*Splendid guess, my dear!*:: The breeze ruffled his hair and he lifted his hand. ::*Time for me to go.*:: He turned and walked away.

"Wait!" Kyrian yelled racing after him, Azhani at her side. Grabbing his arm, she looked up at him. "Why? Why did you kidnap me?"

He smiled and tenderly caressed their faces, saying, ::*Someone had to make certain you two met.*:: With a sigh, he gathered them to him, holding them both close as he said, ::*Good work, my children. You have Our everlasting gratitude.*::

And then he was gone.

Lost in the moment, Kyrian could only stand there, her face tingling with the warmth of the god's touch, and wonder how she was ever going to apologize for the terrible things she'd said to Astariu.

"Kyr?" Azhani said as she looked around the mesa wearily.

"Yes, love?"

"I'm tired. Let's go home."

The journey down the mountain felt twice as arduous as the trek up. Halfway down, they had to stop and find a boulder upon which to rest. As Kyrian massaged her legs, Azhani shaded her eyes and tried to see where the army was camped, but they were still on the wrong side of the mountain's face.

"Azhi, do you have anything to drink? My waterskin is empty."

"No, but I think I hear a waterfall over there." She took Kyrian's flask and hiked around a rocky outcrop. Sure enough, a thin stream of water ran down the side, spilling into several shallow pools. She filled both skins and returned. "Here, drink," she said, offering one to Kyrian.

"Thank you."

Nodding, she settled on the ground between Kyrian's legs and rested her head against her knee. Icy wind buffeted them. Night was coming soon, but for the first time in weeks Azhani felt little fear of the darkness. "We can't rest long, love. It's going to get much, much colder," she said as she stroked Kyrian's calf gently.

"I know, but it's nice just to sit a moment," Kyrian said with a heavy sigh. "I'm so tired." She pulled Azhani's thick braids away from her face and dampened a corner of her robe. "You're a mess," she said with a chuckle.

"Am I?" Azhani smiled as Kyrian washed her face.

"Yes, but you're my mess," she replied, bending down to kiss her. "Now hold still."

"All right," Azhani mumbled, closing her eyes while Kyrian worked.

Moments later, Kyrian gasped, "Twain's grace!"

"What is it?" she murmured sleepily. Despite the surprised utterance, Kyrian seemed as relaxed as she felt, so she didn't bother moving just yet.

Kyrian said nothing.

Concerned now, Azhani opened her eyes. "Did you see something? Is there a rimerbeast?" She started to rise. "Loan me your baton and I'll take care of it!"

"No, love." Kyrian put her hand on Azhani's shoulder. "We're safe, I swear."

"What is it, then?" Azhani replied, resuming her seat.

Sheepishly, she said, "I, well, ah…" Plucking Azhani's dagger from her belt, she cleaned the blade until it shone and held it up so that it reflected Azhani's face. "Look."

Bewildered, Azhani took the blade and examined her face. Here and there, bits of dried blood and dirt still clung, making her skin seem even darker than usual. "I need a bath," she grumbled as she tried to pull some of the unraveled braids away from her face. It was that motion that revealed the miracle, for there on her right cheek, where the scar of her greatest shame and loss had been, now sat a silvery, sword-shaped mark that was the exact duplicate of her original tattoo.

In disbelief, she touched it, gaping in wonder as she felt the faintly raised edges of the new scar.

"How?" she whispered, unable to stop a flood of tears.

Kyrian took the dagger from her and then kissed her. "Does it matter? I think…I think we must accept that what was taken from you has now been returned. Astariu has reclaimed her warrior, my love." They kissed again. "Come. As you said, we should not linger. Let's get back to camp. I'm sure they still need us."

CHAPTER TWENTY-TWO

The rimerbeast attack was over, but devastation had been left in its wake. The once orderly army encampment was in shambles. Soldiers already exhausted from battle were forced to work night and day to remove the bodies of the dead. Not one man or woman spent the day dry-eyed, and the priests stood at the fires, chanting the pathsong from sun up 'til sundown.

Rimerbeast carcases were tossed into a giant pit, covered with pitch, and unceremoniously burned. Those who died, however, were spoken of, their names inscribed on a scroll Azhani swore to give over to Queen Lyssera's hand herself. From the lowest camp follower to the most decorated of soldiers, no one who had died on the day of the Breaking would be forgotten.

Their one saving grace was that with Ecarthus' defeat, the rimerbeast attacks appeared to have halted. Whether they had vanished with their creator for good or if this was just the end of this season's hatching remained to be seen. Vashyra and the starseekers were looking for answers in their scrolls. The seers of Astarus were consulting their tomes and scrying crystals, all looking for some sign that had yet to present itself. Azhani and Kyrian both did their best to provide what answers they could, but even with the strange and terrifying things Azhani had learned while she had been one with Ecarthus, they still could not be completely sure the cycle was broken for good.

Both Azhani and Kyrian had been stunned to learn that the battle they'd waged upon the mesa had been witnessed by all present. Already, stories were spreading, racing through camp as fast as eager tongues could tell them. Though they'd been reluctant to speak of the events they'd survived, both had told their tale to Vashyra, who had used magick to inscribe their words into the Astariun annals. Along with what remained of Gormerath, the story would be kept in the great archive in Y'Len.

Though many others pestered them to speak, neither woman took the time. If Kyrian wasn't with the chirurgeons tending the wounded and dying, she was at Azhani's side, working tirelessly to restore what equipment could be mended and dispose of what was ruined beyond repair. When Azhani wasn't in camp, she was in the hills and mountains, ranging from cave to cave with the patrols, trying to find some clue to the fate of the rimerbeasts.

Since Azhani and Kyrian were so reluctant to wear the mantle of feted heroes, it fell upon others to rise. Padreg, Elisira, Allyndev, Syrelle, and Devon found themselves surrounded by soldiers constantly wanting to thank them for their efforts to stave off the rimerbeast attack. This might have led to overweening pride but for one thing—Allyndev, Syrelle, and Devon were barely speaking beyond what was utterly necessary.

This deeply worried Elisira, who spent many a night huddled against Padreg, plotting ways she might get the three talking to each other again.

"I tell you, Paddy, they're writ as three, just as Ytragon, Virasha, and Komar," she said while pulling another blanket over them to stave off the winter chill. "I can feel it as surely as I hear my soul sing your name."

He chuckled softly and shook his head. Three in love wasn't absolutely unheard of, but most members of the high royal family tried not to complicate matters when it came to affairs of the heart. "Nah, nah. 'Tis only the burnt leavings of supper souring your stomach, my love. Syrelle and Allyndev will marry, you'll see. Young Devon knows his place."

Scowling fiercely, she said, "You are the one souring my stomach, my lord, with your ill-considered words. I know you not to be a fool nor blighted with a narrow and craven heart. Why bait me with airs that are better suited to the rotted tongues of my father's cronies?"

Padreg shifted and looked into her eyes for a long time. "Do ye truly think them struck by the whims of *korethka*, my love?"

She nodded. "Aye, and if your eyes are as clear as always, you know it too. They will be as Ytragon and his loves. High King Ysradan is no cruel man—he would not deny his daughter her happiness, no matter that it might cause gnashing of teeth and flailing of hands among the more hidebound of his court."

Growing silent again, he gently sifted his fingers through her hair as she warmed her hand against his belly, stroking him lightly, teasing him with promises of more than simple caresses. Still, most of his thoughts were devoted to reviewing what he knew of Allyndev, Syrelle, and Devon. Understanding grew and blossomed. Finally, he said, "Three is rare, love, but I've no argument against it. In truth, I simply did not see what you did. Yet now that you've spoken of it, I must consider it."

"And?"

"And having done so, I begin to see that their troubles lie not in love and place, but pride and fear. Three is strange, my love. Even in Ytragon's time, many were wary of the implications of a king whose heart was seemingly split in two. Syrelle could be a queen, should Ysradan choose to circumvent convention. I fear that if this is their road, then it will be a rocky path to follow."

"Then it is upon us to see that they have friends on that road," she said firmly.

"Aye. I will seek out young Devon and learn his mind."

"And I will speak to Syrelle—but who will beard Allyndev?"

He grinned wolfishly. "Azhani. I doubt he'll speak to any other."

True to his word, Padreg went to Devon while he was still in the care of the chirurgeons. At first, he said nothing of Allyndev or Syrelle.

"You fare well, I see." Wincing in pain, he took a seat beside Devon's cot.

"As well as you, I'd wager, my lord," Devon replied with a grin as he nodded to the bandages encircling Padreg's ribs.

"Aye, they still sting some." In the heat of battle, he'd been struck and torn from hip to armpit by a rimerbeast's claws. Among the first to be treated by a stardancer, the wounds were little more than raw cuts now, but the skin still burned and ached when he moved wrong.

"And Lady Elisira? How is her arm?" Devon asked.

"Healing." Elisira had been grabbed and flung hard, slamming into the ground with enough force to snap the bones. "And complaining of a powerful itching."

Devon laughed. "I've heard similar in here—and my own absent foot itches quite fiercely at times. The chirurgeons tell me that it is because my spirit still has two feet, even if my body does not."

"You know the starseekers are working hard to secure a carved leg for you, lad."

"Yes, I know," he said dully.

Coughing softly, Padreg opened his mouth to ask about Syrelle and Allyn only to be interrupted by a chirurgeon bringing Devon some medicine. The moment the man was gone, Devon swallowed the tea and hesitantly said, "My lord, I-I've been meaning to ask you something."

"Of course, lad. Speak your mind."

"I-Is there still a place for me, in your court in Y'Nor?"

Taken aback, Padreg replied, "Of course! You're a fine mage in your own right, a good man, and I happen to know Gwytian is looking forward to having both you and Jasyn to teach just as soon as we return home, but what about your friends?" *Eli will be so saddened—she was so sure of their feelings, and I was coming to believe in them as well. Could it be that he doesn't know? Has it been that long since King Ytragon and his consorts ruled?* Casting his thoughts through his history lessons, he almost grimaced when he realized it had been nearly two hundred years since a king had claimed the right to have two spouses. *Ah, lad, and I bet you've not heard of good old Ytragon, may his randy majesty forever romp to his heart's content.*

"Good, excellent, good," Devon said quickly, then yawned. "Oh, the medicine must be making me sleepy."

Padreg was too kindly to push an obviously weary man to speak on things of such a delicate nature. Standing, he placed his hand on Devon's shoulder. "Rest, lad. You'll need your strength."

Three days later, Devon was released from the chirurgeon's care. Allyndev and Syrelle were waiting to take him back to the tent they shared. Devon found the reunion oddly comforting, then shocking when, supported between them, he entered the tent and found their three beds had been replaced by a single nest of thick cushions in the center of a heavy rug. Avisha was already there, claiming a spot closest to the brazier.

"W-Where's our beds?" he asked softly.

Allyn helped him to settle on a warm cushion. "Destroyed. I like this better anyway. Three will sleep far warmer than two, right, Sy?"

Syrelle smiled as she examined the bandages on Devon's thigh. "Yes. And maybe between you little bears, I'll finally stop shivering at night." She reached up to tug on Devon's bearded chin playfully. His breath caught in his throat. *Goddess, she's so very beautiful. And Allyn, so handsome—they deserve each other so much.* His ability to think, however, quickly became derailed when she kissed him.

"Sy?" he whispered against her lips.

"Sh," she murmured, kissing him again, harder this time.

"Oh Goddess," he moaned, nearly passing out when she stepped away and Allyndev slid his hand into his hair and pulled him into another searing kiss. "I must be dreaming."

"If you were dreaming, Devvy, I'd be a good deal warmer, I'd hope," Syrelle said dryly. "Because right now, I'm freezing!"

Allyn laughed. "Come on, let's get under the covers—we've got a candlemark or so before someone will come looking for us."

"Bu…but, wh-what's going on?"

Syrelle patted his cheek. "We, dear Devon, are making sure you aren't thinking of doing something stupid."

"But…I'm just a commoner. An apprentice mage!" he replied weakly. "H-How can you…" He looked at her, then at Allyndev. "Or you…even th-think about w-wanting me?"

Allyndev smirked. "Oh, Dev, trust me, it's very, very easy to think about."

"Mmhm," Syrelle murmured. "It's a favorite subject of my daydreams, actually."

"Oh Goddess," he said, gasping when she put her hand on his chest and pushed, causing him to collapse into the cushions. "I-I never, I mean…" He closed his eyes, then opened them, finding both Allyn and Syrelle lying beside him. Sy's hand was on his belly, Allyn's drifting distractingly lower. "A-Allyn, I-I wouldn't. Injured, still, oh!" he blurted against Syrelle's lips when she kissed him again.

"We are not going to do anything that would hurt you, Devvy," she said gently. "But we want you to understand how serious we are about what we want, and what we hope you want, as well."

"Oh," he said feeling as though his tongue were suddenly as thick as they no doubt thought his skull was. With a jerky nod, he mumbled, "I-I want it. Goddess, I love you, both of you." The corners of his eyes stung.

"And we love you," Allyndev said as he kissed him tenderly. "And we're going to take care of you and make sure you remember that every day of your life."

Smiling crookedly, Devon said, "I am way too damned lucky."

They laughed.

"No, we're lucky." Syrelle snuggled against him. "And you're warm. Goddess, I think I can feel my toes!"

"Here, let me snuggle up and find out." Allyn moved around to slide in behind her. "Mm, yes, nice and toasty. But wait," he added as he covered her breast with his hand. "I think you might be cold somewhere else. Dev, we should make sure she's warm all over, don't you think?"

Hardly believing what was happening, Devon nodded slowly. "I think we should definitely take care of our princess. We wouldn't want her turning into an icicle."

Syrelle stretched out between them and sighed. "Just remember, my loves, Devon's leg still has several dozen stitches in it. If we pop them, he has to go back to the chirurgeon's tent."

"Oh, yes, right," Allyn said wryly. "Well, let's just snuggle up then. That's safe, isn't it?"

"Should be," Devon said as he got himself up onto his uninjured hip. He winced as pain shot up his back. "Damn."

"Here, brace your legs against mine." Syrelle reached over, took hold of Devon's wounded leg, and moved him so that his bandaged thigh was resting against her backside. "There. Try not to move too much."

Despite the intimacy of their position, Devon merely nuzzled her hair. "What, me, move? Nuh-uh. This is perfect."

Chuckling, she took his hand and pulled his arm around her, kissing his knuckles gently before turning to kiss Allyn. "Good. Nap. Lots of work to do later."

"All right," he said, closing his eyes.

With a soft, rumbling meow, Avisha crawled over, stretched out behind Devon, sighed contentedly, and began to purr.

The army healed. Order was restored. Upon learning of the shift in circumstances between Allyndev, Syrelle, and Devon, Azhani's only reaction was to pile responsibility upon responsibility on Allyn's shoulders. She then told him to ask them for help whenever he floundered.

"That was well done," Padreg said after Allyndev had left with yet another list of tasks to somehow accomplish by morning.

Azhani grinned. "Well, as your lady has quite honestly pointed out, nothing is going to change their hearts. We might as well take best advantage of the Twain's blessing and let them continue to work together—three competent minds working on a problem are far better than one."

"Indeed, my friend, in-very-deed!" he said with a hearty laugh.

There was plenty to do. As the titular head of two armies, Azhani's back was bowed double with a massive burden. Twain willing, though, she would see them all home and safe.

Only after all the injured were able to travel did she order the army to strike camp and march south, toward Y'Dan. Arris had left the kingdom in shambles and she was intent on driving out any remaining Ecarthan priests before they could commit further atrocities.

Their journey southward brought welcome news. Messengers came bearing missives telling of great victories against the black ships that had terrorized Banner Lake, against the ogres plaguing Y'Nor, against the dragon that had been a scourge to both dwarven and human citizens of Y'Dror, and against the giant scorpions that had threatened the people of Y'Skan. Bottles of wine from King Naral came with the last messenger, and with them was a long letter filled with his grand relief that the grape crop had been saved from the infestations of burrowing beetles.

And finally, they heard from High King Ysradan.

It was a concise note, but one bearing the welcome news that he and the queen were alive. In it, he expressed his regret at not being able to stop the terrible things that had taken place in Y'Dan. He repudiated Arris, added his own support to Azhani's claims of innocence, and vowed to meet her in Y'Dannyv so that they could jointly repair the wrongs that had been done to the kingdom and assure the people of Y'Dan a better future.

It felt to Azhani like something from a minstrel's tale. The battles were won, the heroes were now returning home to claim their victory. Deep down, though, she wondered what she was going to find—and if it was even anything she desired to have anymore.

Snow blew around Kyrian as she leaned over to pat Arun's neck before dismounting. A waiting soldier handed her a dry towel and she softly thanked him.

"'Tis no trouble, Stardancer," he said respectfully. "This be a tough march, with all the snow."

She nodded and carefully wiped Arun's legs down while the young man held up a dish of hot mash for the horse to eat. They'd been traveling for most of the day and this was just another stop to care for their mounts and burden beasts. Azhani's orders. Kyrian had to hide a smile at her stern-faced, tender-hearted lover's insistence that everyone, including their horses, get the best possible treatment on the march to Y'Dannyv.

Without the rimerbeasts, their greatest enemies were now the fevers and colds that spread from person to person like wildfire. All of Kyrian's free candlemarks were spent treating the ill in what she hoped wasn't a futile effort to prevent an epidemic.

Sadly, no one was immune, not even Azhani. Two days into their journey, she'd been struck down by a coughing sickness after forgetting to change her cloak following a brief storm.

Proving to be a better patient than anticipated, Azhani now meekly rode in the back of a nearby wagon with Allyndev, Syrelle, and Devon at her beck and call while Padreg and Elisira kept to the head of the column. In truth, the "tireless trio," as Kyrian called Azhani's three helpers, were everywhere. If Syrelle wasn't with the chirurgeons helping the sick and wounded, she was out with the hunters, trying to add meat to their dwindling supplies. Allyndev's face and battered Y'Syran armor was such a familiar sight among the men, most no longer bothered with titles and greeted him like he was an old friend. And Devon, sweet, sunny-smiled Devon, did his best to entertain the wagon-bound wounded with small illusions and tricks—or by scribing for Azhani when the mood struck her to dictate reports.

In fact, Kyrian could see him now, causing ghostly flowers to fall over the face of a sickly soldier.

Wandering over, she smiled and said, "How do you fare this day, Jadrielle?"

Jadrielle coughed. "Well enough, I s'pose, Stardancer, with Twinklefingers to entertain me."

With a snort, Devon snapped his fingers and showered her in an illusion of leaves, making her laugh and bat them away. "Twinklefingers? Hmph. That's Sir Twinklefingers to you, soldier," he said, winking at Kyrian.

"All right, Sir Twinklefingers." Kyrian kissed his cheek fondly. "Make sure you get something to eat. You're still healing and I'd hate for you to end up back on the sick list."

He nodded. "Trust me, I have no intention of being your patient anytime soon." He held up a mug full of steaming tea. "I'm keeping warm and dry, I promise."

"Good man." She turned to head back to Arun, who, having eaten, was more than ready to get going again. Two more days on the road would bring them to Kellerdon and after thirteen days of cold and wet travel, she was looking forward to a peaceful rest in the farming community. Most of the Y'Dani soldiers were hoping the guard's outpost on the outskirts of the town would be large enough for everyone to have a comfortable bed. Kyrian wasn't so sure they'd be that lucky, but flat, cleared land would be more than good enough. Add the possibility of reaching out to Lyssera for fresh supplies, and the stop would be more than worth the trials of their travels.

"I don't get it," Allyndev said as he wrapped himself around Syrelle and waited for Devon to snuff the candle. It was freezing and the faster they got under the covers, the sooner they'd get to enjoy one of the best perks of their new relationship—Avisha's extremely warm body draped over the three of them. "Why am I suddenly the one everyone thinks is in charge?"

"Maybe because Azhani's making it clear you're part of her retinue?" Devon said thoughtfully.

"And because you know what to do," Syrelle said, helping Devon get settled under the blankets.

"But it's mostly common sense!"

Devon laughed. "Listen, there's Twain knows how many of us. We're tired, we're sick, we're freezing, and here's this handsome prince walking around like he's gotten his hands on something that looks like a plan—why wouldn't they listen? Blood and bones, half the army's used to listening to Arris—you've got to be a damned sight better leader than him."

"But why not Padreg? He's a king. Or Elisira? She's from Y'Dan. Or even Syrelle? She's the High King's daughter, by Astarus' balls!" Allyn said as Syrelle elbowed him in the gut.

"Because I'm trying very hard not to be thought of as Ysradan's daughter," she said darkly. "Ysradan's daughter does not fight like a she-beast in heat. Ysradan's daughter does not hold vomit basins and wipe blood and pus from wounds or help big, burly, screaming, crying soldiers to pee or pray or any of the thousand other embarrassing things wounded men and women have to do in very public ways. I want to be just Sy, not some crown-wearing princess who's too pretty to love her people more than she loves her dresses."

Flummoxed, Allyn buried his head against her shoulder. "You humble me."

"Why?" she asked, half turning to look at him curiously. "It's nothing greater or nobler than you, love. You and Devvy each give tirelessly of yourselves. That's why people look to you."

Devon nodded. "Face it, Prince—you're a leader now."

With a heavy sigh, Allyn replied, "Goddess. I hope I'm strong enough for that."

"Of course you are," Syrelle said promptly. "You've got Devon and me to help you."

"I'm glad," he said quietly. "But…why is Padreg letting me do this? The fiction of being too wounded to play hero is going to wear thin when those bandages come off."

"Padreg's got his own concerns," said Devon. "As you said, he's a king, and his kingdom is his focus—or didn't you notice Aden and Syrah leaving the other day with a string of relief mounts so they could make all haste to Y'Nym?"

"No, I missed that."

"Well, even though I'm not a part of his court anymore, he still talks to me as if I were," he said bemusedly. "And he told me that they lost a great many of their best brood stock, both cattle and horses. He's having to call upon the southern clans to help and that's a tricky situation, one that requires him to carefully word every message he sends to avoid looking weak or demanding. It's a fine, fine balance, but if he doesn't maintain it, the northern clans could stand to lose a great deal come next spring."

"I didn't know that," Allyndev replied solemnly. "I guess it makes sense that he would be more concerned about that than latrines and garbage dumps. But still, why me?"

"Because you're royalty, Allyn," Syrelle said. "Even if the elves were too blind to see it—you were born to the crown and people can easily recognize that."

Allyn made a face. "I'll never wear a crown. No matter what shape peace between the kingdoms takes, I'll always be Alynna's Y'Dani bastard."

"Maybe so," Syrelle replied. "But a soldier doesn't care if a man is a bastard or a blue blood so long as he can give orders that make sense."

"Keep reminding me of that, Sy. I have a feeling I'll need to remember it every day for a while."

Devon chuckled. "When have we ever let you forget something, Allyn?"

"Never, I hope," he whispered, taking the time to tenderly kiss them both. "Thank you. I couldn't do this without you."

Syrelle smiled. "And, Twain willing, you won't have to."

"Ah, about that...what are you going to tell your parents?" Nervously, Devon chewed his lip. "I mean, I'll...I'll be happy to just stay in the background. I can be your gimpy mage friend who keeps you up late talking about Twain only knows what and—"

Syrelle silenced him with a kiss. "No. You are both my beloveds, Dev. I'll not lie to my parents—or anyone else—about how I feel."

Since Allyndev had similar concerns, hearing her say that was heartening. "I...I feel the same, Dev. I don't care what they say. Anyone who tries to tell me who I can and can't give my heart to...well, they can just go...go eat a rimerbeast pie!"

Devon grimaced. "Yuck. I don't think there's enough spices in all Y'Myran to make that sound at all appetizing, love."

"Oh, well, such cowardly beggars wouldn't be kings in the city of hearts, then," Allyndev replied affably. "For 'tis the bravery of fools and dreamers that sends me all filled with the pureness of joy to the glorious haven of your love."

Syrelle snorted. "I think you've been reading too many old sonnets."

"Maybe," he said as he ran his fingers through her hair. "But that's only because I've run out of ways to describe your beauty in my thoughts."

"Charmer," she murmured, blushing.

"Hey, I think you're pretty, uh, pretty," Devon said as he kissed her shoulder.

She laughed fondly. "You're charming too, my Devon. Just in a different and completely adorable way."

Kyrian did not expect to find her tent occupied, so she was quite surprised to see her lover curled up on the bed playing "chase-the-string" with Zhadosh. Looking up, Azhani offered her an inviting smile, the effect of which was ruined by a sudden bout of coughing.

With a sigh, Kyrian dropped her mittens on a nearby trunk. "You know, I'm surprised you escaped the chirurgeons alone rather than orchestrating a full invalid rebellion."

Azhani scowled. "Well, hello, I'm happy to see you, too."

"Oh, Azhi," she said, going to her and touching her face. "Why are you here? Your fever still hasn't broken."

Ruefully, Azhani grabbed Kyrian's hand and kissed it. "I know where I should be, love, but where I need to be is here, with you." As Zhadosh bounced down to the foot of the bed, Azhani pulled Kyrian down with her and held her close, adding, "Tomorrow, we reach Kellerdon."

"Yes, I know all this." Kyrian hummed softly as she gently petted Azhani's head, threading faint fibers of Astariu's Fire through her lover's body to chase off as much of the sickness as she could.

"And I need to present a strong front to any remaining supporters of Ecarthus," Azhani said as she slowly relaxed.

"Not to mention give everyone the hero they need to cheer for after everything that's happened." She chuckled as Azhani scowled darkly. "It'll be interesting to watch you, love. I've seen you with hard men and women, like the people of Barton, with the soldiers and nobles of the army, and even royalty, but I don't know that I've ever seen how you react to simple folk like the farmers of Kellerdon."

Sourly, Azhani snapped, "I don't treat farmers any differently than I do kings, Kyrian."

Hearing the hurt in her tone, Kyrian quickly shook her head. "No, no, I said that wrong. What I meant was that it will be interesting to see how they treat you—to them you were once a hero, then a murderer, and now, you are a hero again."

Azhani sighed and muttered, "I haven't thought about it. To be honest, I've tried not to."

Standing, Kyrian began peeling off her traveling clothes and reaching for clean, warm robes. "You should. I heard Padreg and Eli talking to Captain Niemeth about it earlier. They're going to need to know if this army is being led by a usurping conqueror or a cadre of returning heroes."

Azhani stretched out on the bed. Taking this as an invitation, Zhadosh bounded up and began roughly kneading her thigh.

With a squawk, Azhani grabbed the kitten by the scruff and pulled him away. "Hey, stop that, you little thorn bush!" Bringing him up to eye level, she growled. "I will not be your personal pincushion, little man. Go poke someone else!" Then, overcome by a fit of coughing, she dropped him.

Kyrian scooped the kitten up and cuddled him even as she began putting together the ingredients for a tea that would ease Azhani's cough. "It's okay, Zhadosh. She doesn't really mean it."

The kitten mewed.

"Yes I do," Azhani mumbled, but when Kyrian turned to give her a look, she sighed and said, "No, I don't."

Fondly, Kyrian said, "You're not going to scare him away, love. He's made us part of his family now."

"I just wish he'd stop trying to turn me into a sieve," Azhani said as Kyrian set a pot of water to warm on their brazier.

Kyrian snorted. "A sieve? Hardly. He just likes to fluff his pillow before sleeping. Reminds me of a certain warleader I know."

Indignantly, Azhani pointed to her thigh. "Fluffing? Kyr, I'm bleeding!"

Turning to glance at the wound, Kyrian held back a laugh. Two tiny pinpricks marred Azhani's soft brown skin. "Azhi, love, you do worse to yourself when you repair your armor."

"But—" Azhani pouted.

"You are entirely too adorable," Kyrian said as she leaned down to kiss her and then set Zhadosh on the bed. A short while later, she held out a cup of tea. "Here, drink this. It will soothe your cough."

"Thank you." Azhani sipped the liquid slowly, then made a face. "At least I know you cherish me enough to make your best bitter brew."

Kyrian rolled her eyes. "It's far from my bitterest, love. There's honey enough in there to fill a hive and you know it!"

Azhani chuckled. Growing contemplative, she sipped the tea and slowly dragged the string toy over the bed. After a while, she looked up. "We will approach Kellerdon as returning friends. Half the army is Y'Dani. This is their home. We'll raise Thodan's flags in concert with Lyssera's. Hopefully, the town's citizens will see that we mean to be peaceful."

"I find I agree with your wisdom," Kyrian replied. "Now, finish your tea. You need rest. The dawn will come soon enough."

Azhani slid under the covers. "I hope I won't need to shout. My throat still feels like I swallowed a sword blade."

"You could always put Allyndev in charge of negotiations."

"Don't tempt me," she said quietly.

"It isn't temptation, love. It's hard not to see that you're grooming him to be a leader," Kyrian said as she snuffed all the lanterns in the tent.

"Noticed that, did you?"

Kyrian joined Azhani in the bed. "Mmhm. I'm not the only one."

"Good. He's earned the right to lead."

"Any reason why you say that?" Kyrian asked curiously as Zhadosh started kneading both of them in preparation of lying down.

"Ouch, stop that!" Azhani hissed, then added, "Perhaps."

"Care to share? Relax, love. He'll settle soon."

"Really? Because I think he's doing it on purpose," she growled as Zhadosh continued poking and prodding her.

"He's just a baby."

"He's about to be a pair of gloves!"

"Azhani…"

With a much put-upon grumble, Azhani shoved Zhadosh onto Kyrian's hip, rolled onto her stomach and went to sleep, leaving Kyrian to lie there with the kitten, petting him and softly telling him that it was okay, that Azhani really did adore him, and that all he had to do was go to sleep now. Zhadosh yawned, licked his paws, and then settled down with his head resting on Azhani's backside.

CHAPTER TWENTY-THREE

Azhani gritted her teeth as Allyndev and Kellerdon's mayor bickered back and forth over camping rights. She had taken Kyrian's advice—partly because it was sound and partly for her own reasons—and put the young Y'Syran prince in charge of negotiations. Sadly, Mayor Graystone appeared to be among those who disliked elves, or perhaps he just didn't like the color of Allyndev's socks. Either way, he seemed determined to be difficult and Azhani was close to intervening.

This problem all stemmed from the fact that the outpost they had expected to find, a sturdy fort garrisoned and granted lands enough to house an army, was little more than a shack big enough for half a dozen soldiers. Scouts had returned bearing rumors that there were Ecarthans in the area, and Azhani had no intention of moving the army anywhere until they were destroyed.

The mayor, however, was unwilling to offer the lands necessary for an army of any size to set up an encampment near his town. Natives were welcome, but he insisted that everyone else had to keep going south, or west, or east—or even back north, just so long as they weren't his problem.

"We are not here to invade, Mayor Graystone," Allyndev said calmly. "We simply require a place to camp so we can help your people rid the land of the foul Ecarthan priests and their hideous temples. Surely you can see the sense to restoring the Twain to their rightful place here in Y'Dan." His tone was reasonable. Frustration, though, was writ in every line of his body.

Huffily, the mayor drew his bulky body up in some approximation of the soldier he might have once been. "Prince Allyndev, we of Kellerdon are of course most grateful for the offer of aid from Y'Syria—but we are, I assure you, quite capable of restoring order ourselves."

By this point, Azhani had endured his imperious attitude enough. "Apologies, Prince Allyndev," she murmured as she moved past him and glowered at the mayor. In a stern, commanding tone, she growled, "As acting warleader of Y'Dan, I am no longer inclined to listen to your mincy blathering, Mayor Graystone. By law, you are required to quarter and provision my men. Now, if you insist on refusing, I fear I shall have to remove you from office and find someone who will cooperate."

Blanching, he quickly said, "Warleader, please, we cannot—our homes aren't large enough for an army!"

"I know. We will take the fallow fields and avoid despoiling those areas your farmers seek to till this spring." She crossed her arms as she waited for his reply.

Mayor Graystone stared at her for a moment, then sank into himself. Bowing his head, he nodded. "Yes, Warleader. It shall be as you command." With a gesture, he indicated a wide swath of snow-covered ground. "The south fields are fallow this year. Please, try not to trample the westward ones."

"Of course," she said, then turned to Allyndev. "Take ten men and rope off the western fields. Post warn-off markers and assign soldiers to guard them. Make it known that any who enters that area will be subject to my discipline if their reasons aren't sound."

"Yes, Warleader," Allyn said, quickly striding away.

"Devon, ask my squad to join us. We'll be off to investigate that temple." She pointed to a black building located at the center of town. The area around it was desolate, devoid of even stray dogs. Ugly, squat, and stinking of charnel, it was clear why the people of Kellerdon preferred to avoid it. "I'd like to make sure it's no longer a threat."

"Of course, Warleader." Devon hobbled off.

Entering the temple, Azhani was struck by the aura of hopelessness that clung to it like greasy cobwebs. Bloodstains and discarded bodies were all that was left of the horrors that once took place, but she and her men searched it top to bottom, just to be sure. Vashyra's starseekers then moved in and began cleansing it with the same rituals and prayers they would use to bless a cave that had once held rimerbeast eggs.

Three candlemarks later, it was done. The southern fields had transformed into a hive of activity as the army's encampment spread outward and the town folk, now assured that Azhani's people were there to help, willingly came to trade foodstuffs and aid for tales of the beast season and the occasional handful of Y'Syran gold.

Azhani was pleased to know that Allyndev and his men had finished roping off the western fields and though things might be a little cramped for the army, there was still plenty of ground for them to occupy. As she explored the area, she began making plans to send patrols out in the morning. All surrounding lands would be scoured until no trace of Ecarthus' poison remained.

For a brief moment, she regretted the loss of Gormerath, but she still had her father's sword, and the good steel was more than enough to finish the demon's lingering menace.

Y'Dan would be safe once more, she would see to it.

To an outsider's view, the farmhouse looked innocuous enough. Yet both the starseeker and the stardancer in Allyndev's patrol had reported feeling ill at ease just standing on the land. Though he had not been born with the magick-blessed blood of one of his homeland's famed gardeners, Allyn agreed. There was a palpable aura of "wrongness" that clung to the cluster of buildings. Some of it, he was sure, was due to the scent of burnt flesh that permeated the air. However, that wasn't all of it, for the place was utterly silent—no sign of life anywhere, not even a disgruntled chicken. Since all the buildings were in good repair and the land had been well-tended, it left Allyn feeling that this place needed investigation, now.

A surge of emotion welled up within him. Some called it battle frenzy, others, fear. For him, it was merely a warning that he needed to keep a clear head. Taking a quick breath, he said, "All right, I'm convinced. We're breaching." He turned to the man in an Y'Dani tabard. "Larrig, you're with me."

Larrig nodded and grimly unsheathed his blade, motioning to the other soldiers who were assigned to his command.

Allyn waited until they'd all moved up to the farmhouse perimeter before addressing the remaining soldiers. "Teague, take to the trees and cover us. Norgood, hang back with your men."

"Aye, sir," Teague said quietly, waving to his archers. The cluster of elven soldiers immediately faded into the trees, seeking high ground.

"Ye sure, lad? We can have those walls down in a blink," Norgood said as he nodded to the dwarves who waited nearby. Of all those who'd taken to following Allyndev around, Norgood was one of the few to question his orders, and though Allyn knew he meant no disrespect, it rankled slightly.

Allyndev nodded. "Aye. I want to give them," he indicated the Y'Dani soldiers, "every opportunity to get a little payback on the bastards who tormented them over the last year."

Norgood grinned. "I'd hoped it might be thusly, lad. I look forward to the show. We'll hang back, then, and trap any strays for ye."

"Thank you." Allyn ran to join Larrig and the others. "On three, ready?"

They breached the door to the farmhouse and rushed inside, only to find it empty.

"Damn me," Larrig grumbled, beginning to sheathe his sword.

"Hold steady," Allyndev hissed, and with a quick motion indicated they should listen.

Everyone held their breath and grew still. Slowly, something filtered through the creaking of armor and shifting of feet. Someone was whimpering.

Nervously, Allyn looked around, trying to make the house talk to him and tell him what it was that he needed to know. It appeared completely empty, but that was a lie. Placing his hand on a wall, he began looking for something hidden from view. The others copied him. Shortly, their starseeker grabbed his arm and dragged him into a bedroom. Here an ornamental carving on the wall proved to be a doorknob. Allyndev nodded and signaled for the soldiers to join him. With Larrig standing opposite, he reached for the handle and gave it a turn, shoving the door open and raising his sword.

Packed tightly within a tiny, foul-smelling chamber were a cluster of men, women, and children. All were in various stages of ill health. Some had terrible, festering sores that oozed blood and pus, while others had been beaten so badly Allyn couldn't determine if they were alive or dead. In the far corner sat an emaciated woman holding a feebly crying infant to her breast. Her tuneless lullaby nearly broke his heart.

Every one of them gazed up at Allyndev and his soldiers in abject fear.

Feeling sick to his stomach, Allyn took a shallow breath and offered them the most gentle smile he could muster. Quickly, he sheathed his sword. "Peace be with you, citizens," he said warmly, stepping into the filthy room and reaching for the first person he could touch. "I am Allyndev Kelani of Y'Syr and we are here to free you."

An elderly man looked up at him with rheumy eyes as he rasped, "Be ye a ghost, then?"

"Nay, granther, I'm as alive as you." He reached down to help him stand. "Let me take you to safety."

As he slowly grasped Allyndev's hand, the old man broke into tears, sobbing, "By the Twain, ye do be real!"

As Allyndev led him away, Larrig and the other soldiers filed in, each reaching for one of the waiting people. Once they were outside, the chirurgeons immediately took over, quickly treating the injured. For most, this merely meant giving them cups of warmed broth and all the water they could stomach.

"All right, we're not done here," Allyn said as the last of the prisoners left the farmhouse. "Norgood, send in two men to make sure the house is completely clear. Larrig, you're with me. We're for the barn."

They moved across a fallow field toward a hay barn while the elven archers ran parallel to them. Dread closed its claws around him as he ran, for out here in the open, they were vulnerable. Hopefully, the archers would see trouble and warn him, but by the time they reached the barn door, his heart was firmly lodged in his throat.

Here the smell of death was strongest. One of the men gagged, another actually vomited because the odor was so horrible. Allyn waited until they signaled readiness, then sent men around to the sides and back of the building to cover any exits. After giving them the count of thirty heartbeats, he whispered, "For the peace of Y'Dan!"

They threw themselves at the barn doors, smashing them open.

Daylight revealed the sight their noses had already discovered. Blood and death made what was once a simple hay barn into a temple of horrors. Two dozen men and boys knelt before an altar of Ecarthus, their voices raised in a droning chant. Amazingly, none of them seemed to notice the warriors' presence, which stunned Allyndev to the core. *Are they deaf?* In dismay, he stared at the scene before him and softly cursed, for upon the altar lay the still-twitching body of a woman. Above her stood a priest, his arms upraised, her heart held in his hands. Blood streamed down his arms and dripped onto his face as he cried, "For the glory of our beloved lord! May he reign forever!"

Allyndev and his soldiers watched in shock as the heart was flung into a brazier. As it began to pop and sizzle, the kneeling priests intoned, "Ecarthus lives."

Suddenly, an arrow appeared in the throat of the standing priest. As he toppled over, one of the others seemed to snap out of his trance. Leaping up, he spun round, spotted Allyndev, and shouted, "Destroy them. Feed our lord the blood of the nonbelievers!"

"Crush them!" Allyndev snarled. "Offer no quarter or mercy to these butchers."

They met in the middle of the barn. Swords clanged against daggers and cudgels.

On his own, Allyn faced two men head on, shield-bashing one and gutting the second. Knives seemed to be everywhere. Twice, he was stabbed in the back and leg. Both times, his armor held. Someone picked up a torch and swung it at him, forcing him to duck the flames as he drove his sword into another man's chest.

There was no chance to think, only to react. At times, he found himself back to back with Larrig or one of the others, and they worked in concert, killing efficiently. There seemed to be an endless number of priests. Even the young ones fought viciously, their teeth bared, their eyes alight with fanatical fervor. One threw himself at Allyn, knocked him down and bit him in the cheek, ripping away a chunk of flesh even as he brained him with the hilt of his sword.

Face aching, he got to his feet only to have to avoid being set afire by another priest. This one had torches in both hands and was weaving them about himself like a shield of flame.

"Ecarthus guides me!"

"Then tell him to show you the way to Hell!" Allyn yelled, twisting aside and striking the man's head off.

All around them, the hay was burning. Dropped torches had rolled and set several fires.

"My prince, we need to get out of here," Larrig screamed. "The roof's not stable."

Allyndev looked up and gasped at the sight of three columns of flame that were chewing through the beams. "Retreat!" he yelled, grabbing a downed Y'Dani soldier and racing for the doors. As they staggered outside, they were followed. The fighting continued. Allyn felt something sharp drive itself into his side and he spun, crying out as the blade was ripped free.

A black-robed priest held up his blood-coated dagger and purred, "Ecarthus shall feast upon your soul!"

"Not today!" he retorted, raising his sword.

Arrows filled the air, cutting down the remaining priests.

"Thanks, Teague." Allyn reached back to feel the wound. It was shallow, thankfully, but it hurt.

Teague saluted him. "You should seek the chirurgeons, my prince. We'll see to this."

He shook his head. "I'll stay. I want to make sure there's nothing left of them."

"Were there any survivors?"

"No, only victims. This is their pyre," he said sadly. "Someone ask one of the stardancers to come sing the pathsong. These bastards don't deserve it," he added, kicking the body of the priest. "But the innocent ones do."

"Aye, my prince," Teague replied, saluting him. "It shall be done."

For ten days, the army remained in Kellerdon. Six more Ecarthan temples were discovered and sacked, the priests put to death and their prisoners freed. Allyndev led three of the patrols that found them. He and his men traveled all the way to the shores of the Western Sea, restoring peace and order.

Farmers who had fled into the forest slowly returned to Kellerdon, welcoming Azhani and her army with open arms, calling them heroes to any who would listen. More and more, Allyndev found himself thrust into the spotlight, usually by Azhani herself. Confused and yet strangely honored to be drawn into the rough, joyful embrace of Y'Dan's people, he made it a point to learn their names, to taste homemade pies, to play with their children and generally become familiar with these warm, joyful people.

They were his father's people, whoever he'd been—or was and from time to time, he found himself looking at the men's faces, searching for some hint of recognition, but not once did he feel anything but the moment's joy and relief. There was no happy reunion between father and son to be found among the survivors of the Ecarthan terrors.

Every night, a bonfire was lit in the center of Kellerdon and the day's discoveries of Ecarthan artifacts were thrown in. The flames consumed robes, wall hangings, daggers—anything bearing the crimson obelisk was destroyed while the priests of the Twain chanted blessings.

One night, while pitching a handful of bloodied robes into the fire, Allyn turned to Devon and Syrelle and said, "You know, I could live here. In Kellerdon, I mean. Or even Y'Dan, I guess."

Devon looked over at him with interest. "Really? Why's that?" Carefully, he tore apart a book, tossing each page into the fire and watching to be sure it burned.

Allyndev took a swig from a mug of ale. "The people. I've never met anyone who looks at me like they do. I'm not the halfbreed prince or Alynna's shame to them. I'm just Allyndev, the man who's freed their friends."

Syrelle touched his shoulder lightly. "You're more than that, Allyn. You're a hero."

With a snort, he said, "I'm no hero. Not like Padreg and Eli—chasing those priests all the way into the sea! I'll not forget that sight anytime soon."

As he pitched the last page into the fire, Devon shrugged. "Why not? Just because your deeds aren't spectacles that draw a crowd doesn't make them any less amazing. I've watched you make sure that the people you've rescued eat well and get plenty of warm blankets. Not to mention the way you see that those whose families were decimated aren't forgotten by their communities in the rush of joy for the ones who did return."

"I…it just seems wrong to forget them," Allyn murmured. "They're the ones who suffered, not me."

"And that's why Azhani chose rightly when she put you in charge of your own patrol." Syrelle kissed his cheek tenderly.

Devon nodded. "Aye. I've never known Azhani to be wrong about that sort of thing. Father always said she'd not let able hands stand idle."

"What I'm quite proud of is how you're always choosing Y'Dani soldiers to join you." Syrelle hurled a tapestry into the fire.

Allyn smiled as he looked over at Kyrian and Azhani. They were sitting with the mayor, laughing as he played chase-the-string with Zhadosh. "Azhani's idea, I suppose. She and I talked about what could be done to help these people reclaim their pride and I suggested letting them kill the priests. It was meant to be a jest, but she agreed with me."

"And I promise you, each soldier who has the chance to get a little back from those bastards will thank you for the rest of their days," Devon said with a solemn smile. "I know Father would have sung your praises all the way to Y'Dannyv for that. You'd be his hero."

"I'm no hero," Allyn muttered as he tossed the last robe into the fire.

Devon and Syrelle wrapped their arms around his waist and pressed in close, kissing him affectionately.

"Maybe not," Syrelle murmured as she rested her head on his shoulder.

"But I'd say you're doing a fine imitation of one." Devon winked at him playfully. "So why ruin a good act?"

Allyndev laughed. "So, you're saying I should just…go along with it, even though I don't feel very heroic?"

"Ah, and so he begins to understand the role of a leader at last," Syrelle said with a delighted chuckle.

"I knew he'd get it eventually," Devon said affably. Growing serious, he added, "Allyn, you've got a chance to do something great for Y'Dan. The Y'Noran's say that there's no sweeter wine than the affection of one's peers, so drink up, my friend, for the love is flowing!"

It was on Allyn's tongue to retort that he didn't wish to become a drunkard, but in truth, he did enjoy it. Finally, he was able to be proud of himself without having someone come along and poke holes in him just because he wasn't what they wanted. Here in Y'Dan, he'd come to learn that he was absolutely capable of standing next to people like Padreg, Elisira, Azhani, and Kyrian. He knew, without a doubt, that he deserved to be in their company.

I've learned how to fall, I've learned how to walk—maybe what I'm supposed to learn now is how to run.

Smiling now, he turned and kissed each of them warmly. "I'd rather have some more ale. Come on, let's get some food and go find a comfortable place to sit. I hear there's supposed to be juggling later!"

CHAPTER TWENTY-FOUR

On a clear winter morning, Azhani Rhu'len, the Banshee of Banner Lake, returned to the city of Y'Dannyv. Though an army marched behind her, she was no conqueror, but simply a warrior fulfilling the oaths she had sworn to uphold. Beside her rode her closest friends and allies. Though the lake sparkled brilliantly, its clear waters only filled her with sharply painful memories of a time when it ran red with the spilled blood of Arris' soldiers. This moment was not one of triumph for her, only uneasy relief.

In the time since that fateful day had come and gone, her beloved city had changed dramatically. Buildings that had once been draped in colorful swags of cloth now seemed sober and plain, their bright hues traded for unrelenting black. Inns and taverns seemed almost abandoned and the few townspeople she saw cringed away from the army's procession, their faces haunted by the kind of terror that filled her with impotent rage.

Y'Dannyv was a city of broken spirits.

No children played in its streets. No beggars pleaded for alms. No minstrels made merry and no prostitutes called down to invite the soldiers in for a little recreation after their long march.

Azhani shivered. Y'Dannyv was haunted, cold, closed, and smudged by a darkness she feared might never wane.

Ahead of them, a line of men dressed in the green and black livery of Arris' personal guard stood beside a small cluster of angry, black-robed Ecarthan priests.

Carefully, Azhani marked where each of the priests stood. If they could end this peaceably, she would, for she was heartily sick of war and death, but she wanted to be sure that all those who had tied their fate to that of Kasyrin Darkchilde and his demonic god felt the full wrath of those they had harmed.

Beside her, Kyrian clutched her reins tightly and Azhani offered her a quick, reassuring smile. "Be at ease, my love."

"It's hard to relax. I can't see how this is going to end in anything but bloodshed," she replied softly.

"I know. But you'll be safe."

Kyrian looked up at her, a sad, almost wistful look on her face. "I'm not worried about me, Azhi. I don't want to lose you, again."

Grimly, Azhani smiled. "You will not." She glanced over at Allyndev, who rode to the other side of her, scratching fitfully at his newly-grown beard. For as long as she'd known him, he'd gone clean-shaven, but a week ago, she'd asked him to put his razor aside. Though he clearly hadn't understood her strange request, he'd honored it. *Goddess, it's like seeing a ghost.* As Padreg joined them, she said, "I've got plenty of protection."

"Aye," Padreg said quietly. "And we'll not suffer the bastards to lay hands upon ye, Warleader."

"I agree." Allyndev looked around. "Goddess, I can't believe how much of this city is made of stone. It's like the earth itself spawned the buildings."

"Thodan's ancestors wanted to be sure their houses were sturdy, my prince," Azhani said quietly. "And unlike the elves, they lacked the magick to coax the trees to become their homes. They did, however, understand the cutting and shaping of rock, and the alchemy of concrete."

"So I can see," he said with a sigh, scratching his face again.

Half turning, Padreg looked back at the other riders. "And what think you, Devon, of Y'Dannyv's new face?"

Wiping tears from his cheeks, Devon shook his head. "I hate it. It's…dead. Places I remember are gone or so terribly changed they'll never be the same."

Syrelle took his hand and squeezed it. "Maybe not, but we're here to put it to right."

Azhani nodded. "Yes, Princess, that we are."

Zhadosh suddenly hissed and they all looked to the center of the city, where the king's council marched up to stand with the men of Arris' guard and the priests of Ecarthus. Unlike the priests, these men greeted Azhani with looks of veiled relief.

Dismounting, Azhani approached a man she recognized. Valdyss Cathemon was the leader of the High Council and had been one of the first to speak out against her when Arris had called her a betrayer.

Stepping forward, he smiled cheerfully. "Welcome to Y'Dannyv, Azhani Rhu'len. In the name of the High Council, I greet you as the rightful warleader of Y'Dan."

The irony was almost too much to bear. As Azhani stared at him, the Ecarthan priests began to look around, scowling when Azhani's soldiers flooded in, their weapons drawn.

"A strange greeting, coming from you, Valdyss." Azhani's voice rang through the square.

Windows and doors opened and curious faces appeared, looking out to see what was happening. Within moments, stunned people spilled onto the streets, their muttered whisperings rising to a crescendo of questions.

"The warleader?"

"She's back?"

"Wasn't she exiled?"

"Has she come to save us?"

The priests snarled at them, but, much to Azhani's surprise, Valdyss turned and said, "Take them, now!" Acting in concert, the soldiers garbed in Arris' livery turned and slew the priests to a man. Though many tried to resist, those who did manage to escape the blades of Arris' guard were quickly struck down by Azhani's soldiers.

As their bodies hit the cobblestones, he looked back at Azhani. "I am a man of circumstance, Warleader. Today I have been allowed to act in a way that pleases me. A year ago, I was not so lucky. I hope you will at least allow this to be the act I am remembered by." And then he knelt and bowed his head as if waiting for the executioner's sword to fall upon his neck.

The other councilors did the same.

"By your actions, you acknowledge that I was wrongfully cast out; that my guilt is made to innocence, and that my word is now law!" Azhani said. "What you do not know," she continued, raising her voice until it filled the square, "is that Arris himself pardoned me! By his hand, I was absolved of the shame of oathbreaking, and by his word I am, as I have always been, warleader of Y'Dan!"

The square erupted in cheers.

"Yes, Warleader," Valdyss replied quietly. "We serve at your command."

"Furthermore, I have proof that one man was guilty of treason of the most heinous and terrifying kind," she said as Padreg joined her. In his hands, he carried three bound and locked books that had been discovered among the personal effects of Porthyros Omal. In them, he had arrogantly detailed every stage of Kasyrin Darkchilde's plans, including the assassination of King Thodan, the murder of Ylera Kelani, and the destruction of Azhani's honor.

"Let these be placed into the royal archives and copied to be shared with any and all who request them, for they are evidence that evil was done to the people of Y'Dan."

"Yes, Warleader," he replied quietly. "And what of us, Warleader? How shall we serve our kingdom?"

"That is for High King Ysradan to decide. For now, you are to remain here under house arrest," Azhani said stiffly. Turning away from him, she called, "Let it be known that, for the safety of Y'Dan, I declare martial law! Let those who would fear the righteous wrath of the Twain flee before the swords of our vengeance!"

There was a mad scramble as the citizens quickly dispersed to their homes. She let them go. If any of them were harboring Ecarthans, their neighbors would likely turn them in before long.

"Allyndev, Padreg, let's go!" Azhani said grimly, signaling for the soldiers to follow.

The battle for Y'Dannyv was short, brutal, and ultimately, very satisfying, for by sun's lowering, not one Ecarthan priest was left alive.

As he watched the proceedings in the council chamber, Derkus Glinholt seethed with impotent rage. While Valdyss and the others bowed and scraped before Azhani and the others like they were sent by the gods themselves, Derkus could only stare at his daughter, his precious, perfect Elisira, and see how she'd been utterly defiled by that hulking brute Padreg. Imagine, his lovely flower wilted into some horse-loving plainswoman! It was enough to make him want to drink. So he did. Copiously.

Elisira eventually approached him. He had to admit to being proud that she didn't cow before him, while at the same time being deeply irritated for the same reason. *She's my daughter! I deserve more respect!*

"Hello, Father." Her tone was fraught with an emotion he couldn't recognize.

"Hello, Daughter," he said disdainfully. "Have you come to demand a dowry for your barbarian? He'll not have one from my coffers."

She sighed. "Nay, Father. Padreg requires nothing but your blessing."

With a sneer, he replied, "He'll never have it. You were mine to give, Daughter. He is no better than a common thief! You should be happy I do not seek redress from the High King."

"Then you should also be happy he will not accuse you of an attempt at regicide," she said angrily. "Go home, Father. Stay there. That is the only favor I can offer you. If you do not…" She looked over at Azhani, whose face was set in lines of unflinching determination. "I cannot guarantee you'll be spared the noose."

"The noose!" he snapped. "I am part of the king's council! I do not get a commoner's death!"

"Fine, the headsman's axe," she growled. "Just go. I do not want your death, Father. Neither does Padreg. Enough blood has been spilled. It's time to heal now."

Deflated, Derkus looked down at his hands. "You were mine, Eli. I was supposed to be the father of a queen."

Softly, she replied, "You are—and one day, you might see that for yourself." With that, she turned and went to join Padreg and the others.

Derkus sighed and got up, his bones suddenly aching. Two of Azhani's soldiers were there to walk him out. One sported a bandage on his arm and wore the arms of Y'Syr on his tabard. Curious, Derkus looked up and nearly stumbled back at the face he saw. Blinking owlishly, he rubbed his eyes and realized it had been a mistake. This man was merely the halfbreed prince, Allyndev.

"Too much to drink," he muttered, stumbling down the hall to his room, the two men trailing after him.

"And we were able to free over a hundred men, women, and children from the cells beneath the temple," Azhani said as Allyndev returned to the council chamber. His quick nod was all she needed to know that Councilor Glinholt was secured. Tomorrow, he would be escorted back to his estate on the western coast, where he would hopefully live out the remainder of his life in quiet exile. Smiling, Azhani added, "Prince Allyndev here should be commended, for he risked considerable injury in retrieving the key that opened the prisons."

Valdyss Cathemon turned to look at Allyn. "Truly?"

He shrugged. "I can't say what might have happened. The key had fallen—or more likely had been thrown by the fleeing priests—under the heavy braziers. They were still lit. It would have taken candlemarks to saw through the bars. It seemed easiest to attempt to fetch it."

"I see," Valdyss replied as he stared at the bandage covering the prince's right forearm. "Were you burned?"

Allyndev nodded. "It's minor, my lord. 'Twill heal and leave a small mark."

"Y'Dannyv owes you a debt, Prince Allyndev," Valdyss replied solemnly. "And even more gratitude."

"Y'Dannyv doesn't owe me anything, Counselor." He turned to Azhani. "Do you have further need of me, Warleader?"

"No, that will be all for now, my prince. You should get some rest," she said quietly.

Bowing respectfully, Allyndev exited the council chamber.

"There's something about him…" Valdyss said thoughtfully. "Is he Ylera's boy?"

Azhani glared at him. "Alynna's. Ylera had no children."

"My apologies," Valdyss said quickly. "I meant no offense."

She sighed. "I know, Councilor. But it's…painful. Especially here." She looked at the spot where her beloved's body had once lain.

He bowed deeply. "Again, my humblest apologies. I hope you will believe me when I say that neither I nor anyone now present had anything to do with that heinous act."

"I know, Councilor. I have been made fully aware of who was responsible and why," she said sadly. "But that comes to another point—Ylera Kelani was a true friend to Y'Dan, and she deserves to be honored as such."

"I agree. What did you have in mind?"

Azhani glanced at Kyrian, who took her hand and squeezed it gently. "Ylera loved gardens, Councilor. Big, beautiful gardens. And music. Always, she loved her music."

"Then there will be gardens and minstrels aplenty to fill them," he said with a gentle smile. "And whatever else you require. The kingdom, as I believe Thodan wanted, is yours."

Azhani shook her head. "I don't want the kingdom, Valdyss, but I do have some plans."

Valdyss studied her a moment. "Going to cause a disturbance, are you?"

She merely grinned. "That seems to be my gift."

Elisira saw her father off the next morning. They did not speak, but as he rode away, escorted by ten hand-picked soldiers, Derkus turned and looked back at them, half lifting his hand as if to wave.

Softly, Padreg said, "He may yet remember that his pride and his heart are not one, my love."

"Perhaps." Elisira sighed. "My only hope is that he avoids trouble."

A dozen other nobles of Arris' court were also making their way toward the gates, the clatter of their wagons and carriages loud against the cobbles.

"The rats flee before the cats are unleashed, I see," Padreg said dryly.

Elisira snorted. "Truly spoken, my lord. Y'Dannyv will not miss them."

Across the city in Ydannoch castle, the members of Arris' personal guard were gathering every piece of their former king's livery and sending it off to be donated to the poor. To a man, they took joy in donning original arms of Y'Dan, proudly bearing the wheat sheaf on their chests.

From the balcony in her office, Azhani watched as they set to drilling for the day. Aside from the aches and pains in her leg, she almost felt as though time had reversed itself.

"Azhi?" Kyrian said as she entered the room. "Allyndev sent me to tell you the mayor is here."

"Is he?" She turned away from the window. "What does he want now?"

"To ask if he has our permission to tell people they can raise the pennants and banners of their family arms again."

"Oh, for pity's sake," she grumbled. "Yes, yes, of course!"

Kyrian chuckled. "That's what Allyn said, but the mayor insisted he hear it from you—I gather there were some fairly dire penalties for it just a week ago."

Making a face, Azhani snapped, "There appear to have been dire penalties for farting, as well, but no one is asking my permission to break wind, are they?"

"Azhi," Kyrian said reproachfully. "You're a hero—you saved them from Ecarthus' priests."

"It wasn't just me." Azhani shook her head ruefully. "But I do understand what you're saying. They need structure and order they recognize and respect. Come on, let's go tell the mayor he can have his pretty city back."

For Kyrian, the most rewarding aspect of restoring Y'Dannyv to rights was seeing an Astariun temple raise its banners once again. Now the doors stood open wide, revealing an altar covered in wreaths of dried flowers and letting the sweetly fragrant smell of incense spill out to welcome an ever-grown line of worshipers, and Kyrian found peace in the utter joy in their smiles. Children rushed in to hug red-and-blue robed priests. When she walked through the streets, strangers stopped and bowed to her, their faces wet with tears as they begged her blessings. She gave them freely.

The day the market reopened, she was among the first to browse the hastily assembled stalls, looking for fresh treats to share with Azhani. She even bought a nice fish for Zhadosh from the docks.

"Morning, Stardancer," a man said, doffing his cap to her. Portly and balding, the faint points on his ears told her all she needed to know about how life must have been for this fruit seller just a few weeks ago.

"Good morrow…?" She stopped to study his wares, which looked to be some dried fruits, jams, jellies, and other preserves.

He smiled, his gap-toothed grin wonderfully pleasant. "Hardag, Stardancer. Never thought I'd come home, but—we heard the warleader's come back, and so here we are. Ain't got much, but a man's got to start somewhere."

"Indeed, good Hardag, they certainly do. Let me see if I can't give you a good push on that road, hm? I happen to know someone who'll enjoy all the honeyed preserves you can sell me," she said cheerfully.

Who would wear the crown of Y'Dan?

It was the question bandied about the city and the castle. Azhani couldn't walk ten feet without overhearing someone ask it, and always the answer was, "I don't know, but maybe…" And then, inevitably, a favorite candidate was filled in.

For some, the choice seemed clear—Azhani herself. Much to her chagrin, Azhani had been told repeatedly by Padreg and others that most of the army would support her taking the crown. Others filled in the names of councilors, distant relatives of Thodan's, even the Princess Syrelle, since she at least was royalty and would likely never sit the throne in Y'Mar.

There was even a rumor that Arris had gotten a bastard on one of the chambermaids, but none of the babes in arms looked at all like the prior king, and to a one, their mothers claimed the fathers to be the men to which they were wed.

"Azhani," Valdyss said as he paced around her office. "Surely you must see that you are the right choice! Thodan himself wished you to take the throne."

"I don't want it," she said tiredly. "I don't even want to be warleader right now, Valdyss. I'm only here because I need to be." She peered down at the slowly growing garden that would one day be her final tribute to her lost Ylera. "This place, this city, this castle—it's all pain for me," she said quietly. "And I loathe it." She walked over to him, staring him deep in the eyes. "You do not want a queen like me, Valdyss Cathemon. I will never love this kingdom—not like a queen should."

"Then tell me, Warleader, what are we to do? You have all the power right now," he said weakly.

"I know," she said with a sigh. "And that's why we're waiting for someone else to take it from me. Ysradan should be here soon enough. He'll set things right."

"I pray the people are as patient as I," he replied.

Princess Syrelle was alternately excited and terrified. The bright green and purple sails of the Y'Maran royal fleet had been spotted approaching Y'Dannyv at dawn. Soon she would be reunited with her family. She longed to see them so badly that she could barely sit still, yet at the same time she knew she had many hurdles to leap with them, not the least of which were the two men who were currently standing beside her on the docks.

"Are you sure you want me here, Sy?" Devon asked softly. "I don't need them to know me."

She glared at him. "Devon, we talked about this. You and Allyn are both my beloveds. I'll not have either of you thought of as anything but equal partners in my life."

"I know what you said, but you're the daughter of the high king, not a farmer who needs all the strong arms he can marry," he said with a sigh. "The rules are different."

"No, they aren't. And if they are, then we'll change them, won't we, Allyn?"

Allyndev smiled affably. "I'm terrified, too, Devvy, but one thing I've learned from Azhani is that facing my fears is so much better than running from them. If that means the three of us stand here and let the high king see how much we love each other, then so be it."

Devon took a deep breath. "All right. Together then."

The ships docked. Ropes were thrown and secured to moorings. Gangplanks were lowered, and finally, Ysradan descended.

Syrelle's breath caught, for her father walked with a limp that bespoke of the pain of a healing wound. "Papa!" she called, racing across the docks and throwing herself into his arms. "You're hurt!" she whispered, crying into his chest.

"Only a little, my sweet lass." He held her tightly. "'Twill heal soon enough."

"It had better," she said. "Is my demon spawn brother with you?"

Before Ysradan could reply, a child's voice chirped, "I'm right here, fish breath!" Ysrallan appeared out from behind a pair of soldiers, his face already smudged with dirt.

"Ysrallan!" she said, licking her thumb and reaching for him as he squirmed away from her. "I swear, Rallie, you attract dirt like flowers collect bees!"

He stuck his tongue out at her. "Bees sting. I bite." He clacked his teeth together playfully. Then he threw his arms around her waist and hugged her, mumbling, "You've been gone forever and ever, Rellie."

She sighed. "I know, little brother, but I had to go."

Ysrallan murmured, "Mama and Papa got hurt." Fear laced every syllable.

Syrelle inhaled sharply. "Is it bad, Rallie?"

"I don't know," he whispered. "No one will tell me anything."

Swallowing heavily, Syrelle looked for her mother and finally spotted her walking toward them, taking slow, measured steps. A bandage encircled her head, covering her eyes. "Oh Goddess," Syrelle whimpered as Ysrallan snuggled against her.

"Ysradan?" Queen Dasia called.

"Here, my love," he replied, reaching for her. "With Syrelle and Ysrallan."

Unerringly, Dasia made her way over to them. She was smiling. "My family is whole again."

Letting go of Ysrallan, Syrelle moved to embrace her mother. "What happened?"

"A rather unfortunate encounter with a kraken's breath," Dasia replied blandly. "But I have been assured the blindness is temporary."

"Are you certain?" Syrelle asked.

"Nothing is sure, sweetling, but the stardancers caring for me tell me that it is so," Dasia said. "Now, Warleader Azhani has made mention of a pair of young men we might want to meet? Tell me all about them," she added with a warm smile. "After all, if I'm to have two new sons, I need to know all I can."

"Mother, we're not getting married," Syrelle said exasperatedly.

"No? Don't tell your father. He's been driving himself mad trying to decide what to give you as dowry. Do you have any idea how long it's been since a child of the high king had two spouses?"

"Oh Goddess," Syrelle groaned, not wanting to consider the wild, convoluted history surrounding her royal ancestor. "Two centuries."

"Exactly. We really can't wait to get to know your young men."

Syrelle felt decidedly dizzy about that.

"Rellie's in love," Ysrallan sing-songed cheerfully. "So where are they? I wanna see how ugly they are."

"Rallie!" Syrelle yelped as Ysrallan giggled mischievously.

"As you can see, you were missed, my lass." Ysradan draped his arm around her. "And if those two young men I see trading nervous smiles down on the docks aren't intending to do the honorable thing, I might just have to get testy with them."

"Father, please…we, it's…" She sighed as her family strode right past her and to where Devon and Allyndev were standing. Ysrallan acted as his mother's eyes and led her right to Allyndev's side. By the looks that soon appeared on their faces, they were getting quite the earful, and as much as she wanted to eavesdrop, Syrelle knew that this moment had to be theirs.

Besides, she was just a little concerned about whether they'd be scared off by talk of marriage.

Outwardly calm, Azhani watched as Syrelle and her family shared in the joy of seeing each other again. Only when it appeared that they were heading her way did she begin to feel her control slip, for beneath her placid exterior, she was a mess of nerves. It had been at least five years since she and Ysradan had last spoke, and she had no idea what he would think of her, once called oathbreaker, now sung as hero of Y'Dan. Would he accept the word of king and council or would he strip her of all she had regained and send her once again into exile?

As soon as the high king and queen came into earshot, she bowed deeply. "Y'Dan offers its thanks to the Twain that you both are safe, my king, and welcomes you to the fair city of Y'Dannyv with all joy."

"Thank you, Warleader Rhu'len," he said affably. Taking her hands in his, he touched his head to hers. "We have come, as you requested, to set right the pain felt so keenly by this benighted land."

And with that one greeting, Azhani's restoration was complete. No one in all the kingdoms would dare gainsay the high king. If he called her warleader, then warleader she was.

Releasing her, Ysradan moved on to Padreg, embracing him warmly. "Good gods, lad, you've grown like one of your plains weeds!"

Padreg laughed and bowed deeply. "It has been a few seasons, my king."

"So it has, so it has." Next, he went to Elisira, smiling as he considered her. "And you, lass—you were but a wee child the last time I beheld your face. Glinholt's daughter, right?"

"Aye," she said with a warm smile. "Thank you for remembering."

"Ah, I never forget a beautiful face." He kissed her cheek fondly. "You look just like your mother," he added softly. "May she rest well."

"Thank you, my king."

Kyrian stepped up to receive the king and he frowned a little. "Pardon me, stardancer, but I know you not. Yet your face, I assure you, will haunt my dreams with its loveliness until the day I set eyes upon our beloved goddess."

Blushing, she said, "I'm Stardancer Kyrian, Your Majesty."

"Well then, I am most pleased to be making your acquaintance, Kyrian." He kissed her hand.

She managed a smile. "You're quite the charmer, aren't you, my king?"

"I like to think so," he said cheerfully. "I understand the kingdoms owe you quite the debt, Stardancer Kyrian, for without your gentle care for our beloved warleader we might be arse deep in rimerbeasts. You've earned a boon of me and I intend to honor it whenever you ask."

"I, ah, thank you, Your Majesty."

"Think on it a while, Stardancer. Whatever's in my power to grant is yours to ask," he said, then went on to greet Valdyss Cathemon.

Azhani stepped up to take her hand.

"Don't let him rattle you, love."

Kyrian gave her a look. "I'm not rattled at all, merely trying to decide if I should collect on that boon as soon as I can."

Bemusedly, Azhani said, "Oh? And what would you ask for?"

Kyrian merely smiled. "Wait and see, my love."

Queen Dasia greeted them next. As Azhani knew she would, within moments of being introduced Kyrian offered to aid the queen's stardancers in her healing. It wasn't long before everyone was climbing into the carriages waiting to take them to Ydannoch castle.

Azhani shared hers with Ysradan, of course.

"I still can't believe Thodan's gone," he said quietly. "I always thought of him as like boot hide—tough as nails and impossible to ruin."

"I miss him too," Azhani said sadly.

"It just pains me so much to know how hard he fought for peace, only to see it ruined in such a short time," Ysradan growled. "And now, his dreams are gone—his legacy, demolished!"

"Not entirely, Your Majesty. We have much to discuss."

For a full day, High King Ysradan made himself available to the nobility of Y'Dan, starting first with a proclamation in open court formally absolving Azhani of any wrongdoing. His words were little more than ceremony, but by night's fall there was such an air of celebration that it seemed as if the city was caught up in a party that might never end.

From pub to inn, great house to simple farmer's croft, the story of the Battle of Shield Mountain spread. The conflict between Azhani and Ecarthus grew more and more incredible with each retelling until Azhani herself couldn't recognize the events.

For a full week, Y'Dan celebrated. The last of the Ecarthan temples were razed, its priests defrocked and hanged, and the worship of the Twain was restored.

History was made when Queen Lyssera arrived from Y'Syr. For the first time in centuries, an elven ruler stepped onto Y'Dani soil with peaceful intent and was welcomed with opened arms.

High King Ysradan's solution to the problem of who would rule Y'Dan was to call a conclave, inviting all the kingdoms to participate. Though it would be the Y'Dani council that proffered candidates, Ysradan vowed to heed the words of Y'Dan's closest neighbors regarding any decisions he might make.

Representing Y'Nor was Padreg, of course. Kuwell Longhorn stood for the Y'Drorans, Iften Windstorm for the Y'Skani, and an affable older woman named Ladethya Corrinder came on behalf of the Y'Tolians. As she was someone who had survived the Ecarthan occupation, Lady Ladethya's counsel was one that Ysradan chose to seek the most often, closing himself up in his chambers with her and his queen, Dasia, at his side.

Impasse had been reached. Azhani flat out refused the crown every time it was offered, and no one could come to any consensus on another candidate.

Some showed too much favoritism for one family or other, others had a history of bigotry toward the elves, and still others were so unknown that no one felt they could truly win the hearts of the kingdom.

It was, for all concerned, a time of great frustration.

Midwinter approached with all the timidity of a bull on a rampage. Y'Dannyv was blanketed under several feet of snow and many were suffering from the cold, but the council chamber was stuffy and overcrowded. Stifling a yawn, Azhani glanced at the day candle and counted the lines. Too few remained before it would mark midnight.

Solstice was but three days away. Deathly tired of the interminable meetings, arguments, and bickering, she just wanted the holiday to consume them so she could lose herself in marriage to Kyrian.

It wasn't that she didn't care who sat upon the Granite Throne—there was no one present who cared more—it was just that she felt bled dry by the kingdom. She'd given them so much, lost pieces of her heart that would never return, and now they all clung to the hope that she could put aside that pain, take up their crown, and wear it, thorns and all.

At one time, she might have. Once, with Ylera as her queen, she might have been able to summon the regal presence everyone claimed she bore and do as Thodan had asked. Now all she wanted was to be as far away from Y'Dan as she could get.

Nervously, she drew silly little curlicues on the borders of her parchment. Kyrian looked over at her, smiled, and then gave her knee a gentle squeeze. With a soft sigh, she put the pen aside, forcing herself to concentrate on the latest effort by Lord Zolicar to get his candidate—a potato farmer with three drops of royal blood in his family line—nominated to the throne. That Zolicar's youngest daughter was married to the man surely had nothing to do with his zeal in promoting him.

Kyrian's presence made listening to him drone on about this "Lord" Kinevan bearable, but only just.

"Will he go on much more, do you think? I'm beginning to suspect that he is the one who married the man, not his daughter," Kyrian said dryly.

Azhani hid a laugh behind a fit of coughing, then winked at her. "I just might have an idea."

"Oh?" Kyrian replied, her eyebrows quirking upward. "Care to share?"

"Soon. I just need to take advantage of the right moment," she murmured, casting a glance in Lyssera's direction. The queen of the elves appeared to be as disdainful as they were of Lord Zolicar's candidate.

Finally, Lord Zolicar finished by saying, "My lords and ladies, I therefor humbly submit that we elevate Kinevan to the Granite Throne. Let this nightmare come to an end, and let us once more raise our voices in gleeful praise. Long live the king!"

"Thank you, Lord Zolicar." Valdyss stood and looked around the chamber. "Now, if there's no further business to present today, might I suggest—"

"I'd like to speak." Azhani stood and made her way to the center of the room.

"Of course, Warleader," he replied, immediately ceding control to her.

She gave him a knowing grin. "My lords and ladies, I have waited, watched, and listened as you debated what to do with Thodan's crown. Some of you offered it to me—some of you argued against it. Most of you know I do not want it." There were a few whispers of surprise from the assembled council, but most everyone nodded along with what she said.

Deliberately, she paced from one side of the chamber to the other, saying, "We have nearly turned this kingdom inside out looking for someone fit to rule it, someone whose blood bears all the right connections, whose integrity is above reproach, and whose bravery is felt to be second to none. Frankly, I have to say, you shall not find someone in this kingdom to match those qualifications to your satisfaction."

Several people gaped at her in shock.

Others snapped, "Blood and bones, Warleader, what do you mean by that?"

She grinned. "Exactly what it sounds like—Thodan's heir will not be taken from the men and women of Y'Dan."

"I'm afraid you have us at a loss, Warleader," Valdyss said quietly.

"I know. But I think it's time we ended this little debate." She moved to stand in front of Queen Lyssera. "Don't you agree, my queen?"

After looking up at her with an expression of dismay and horror flickering across her lovely features, Queen Lyssera closed her eyes briefly and said, "Azhani, please—don't do this."

"I'm sorry, Lyss," Azhani murmured. "I must. Forgive me."

Lyssera bowed her head. "I hope you know what you're doing. If anything happens—"

"I'll submit myself to your judgment without reservation," Azhani replied solemnly. "My oath on it."

That seemed to satisfy her. Nodding once, Lyssera sat back and gestured quickly. "Go on, then."

Azhani returned to the center of the room. "If you will all bear with me, I believe it's time to share a story whose telling has been long in the coming."

"We are here at your pleasure, Warleader," Valdyss replied calmly.

"I'll try to be brief," she said, looking at her friends and loved ones. Kyrian, resplendent in crimson robes of silk and velvet, offered her a smile loaded with love and joy. Next to her were Padreg and Elisira, curiosity making them both seem far younger than their actual ages. High King Ysradan and his queen, Dasia, both sat with the weary posture of those whose bottoms have grown numb. All the ambassadors stared, with their retinues and scribes milling about anxiously. The gallery was filled with curious observers. Devon sat with his crutches rested next to Avisha, whose loud purr seemed to penetrate even the most grating of voices. Beside him, Princess Syrelle's simple clothes had been replaced by courtly finery that made her radiant beauty almost overwhelmingly stunning, and of course, on her other side was Prince Allyndev.

Oh, Allyn. Azhani beheld him, seeing only the ghost of the gawky boy she had taken under her wing the previous spring. He had grown, had erupted into manhood just as she had known he would. To her mind he was everything she had hoped he would become.

"I'm going to ask you to go on a journey with me," she said finally, beginning to pace around the room once more. "We'll venture back twenty years, to a time when I was but a lass living here in Ydannoch castle, where my father was warleader and my king was a man driven by one deep desire—peace. For centuries, the elves of Y'Syr and the humans of Y'Dan had warred. In all that time, the reasons for our warfare had been lost. We did it because it was habit, and Thodan was tired of it. So tired that he was willing to trust that the elven queen felt the same way, and thus he sent my father to sue for peace." She smiled. "To everyone's great surprise, Queen Lyssera was more than willing to sit at the treaty table. However, it would take time, and hard work, and so the first of many secret journeys was undertaken. In my father's company, Thodan made the trek to Y'Syria."

Ysradan coughed softly. "I was never more proud of a man than I was when Thodan told me of his plans. Seeking peace is a gods-given quest."

Nodding, Azhani said, "Thodan was driven by a nearly inhuman need to succeed, but he was, beyond a peacemaker, a man. And like many men, Thodan's heart was empty. If you'll recall, he'd yet to marry Queen Siobhan, and no matter how focused he was on his political needs, he was distracted. For you see, he'd met someone—a woman whose astounding wit, beauty, and charisma had left him completely dumbfounded. To his utter and great joy, she returned his affections. Sadly, their love affair could never end well, for he was Y'Dani and she, Y'Syran."

Everyone in the room hung on her words. She could feel them leaning toward her, almost willing her to speak.

"I was there, my lords and ladies, and though I did not then know the importance of the moment, I can still clearly remember the day when King Thodan met Warleader Alynna Kelani." She moved to stand in front of Allyndev. "Your mother."

"Yes, master," he said quietly.

"Master no longer, my friend," she murmured. Raising her voice, she added, "I don't remember what was said, but I do know that in those few weeks we spent in Y'Syria, I'd never seen Thodan smile so much. For you see, Prince Allyndev, your father was so deeply in love with your mother that he almost forgot the purpose that had sent him to parley with the elves."

Shock held Allyndev fast in his seat. "My f-father?" he whispered, staring up at Azhani and unable to see anything but a childhood filled with taunts, half-heard whispers, and shame.

"Yes, my prince." She went to her knees and took his hands in hers. "He loved her very deeply, so much so that he would have surrendered his kingdom to be with her, had he the choice. It was not to be. Neither the humans nor the elves would allow it. Not then, not when peace was a promise for a future yet unwritten."

He was shaking. So many emotions spun through him that he could barely grasp one before another was taking its place. "B-but h-how? W-why did he not fight for her?" he rasped, blinking back a slew of tears. "I thought he loved her?"

She cupped her hand to his bearded cheek and smiled sadly. "He did. But your mother, in her wisdom, knew that their love would tear the kingdoms apart before peace even had a chance to blossom, so she told him a single lie—one that shaped the future for all of us, for you see, she made him believe she did not love him."

"Oh Goddess," he groaned, bowing his head, knowing it to be truth, for his mother had been like that. Noble, self-sacrificing, brave—three words he'd heard ascribed to Alynna Kelani for his entire life.

"Thodan left Y'Syr with a broken heart and a pouch full of promises of peace. Within two years, he had met and married Queen Siobhan and she gave him Arris. They were happy—blissful, even, until Queen Siobhan was killed in a sudden squall on Banner Lake."

Numbly, Allyndev nodded. "I remember," he said quietly. "I sent a letter of condolence to Arris."

Azhani smiled then and rose, coaxing him to stand with her before taking her tale to the rest of the room. "We had an heir in Arris, and so Thodan never remarried. Instead, he threw himself into the ideal of peace. Of course, we had distractions. Rimerbeasts, bandits, barbarians—for a long time, it seemed as though Y'Dan's northern border would never be safe. But we fought them all back, and young Arris grew up, cared for by his mentor, Porthyros Omal."

A soft growl of anger rolled through the room, and Allyndev could barely hold back his own snarl of hatred for the man who had poisoned his cousin. *No, my brother. Arris was my brother. And Thodan was my father. Oh, Gods. Oh, oh Gods.* Realization of what was going to happen crashed down on him and he could barely keep himself from throwing up. *Can it be? Can I really be Thodan's son?* Allyndev was dizzy with the implications.

"But despite it all, we prospered, my lords and ladies," Azhani said quietly.

Almost no one was paying attention, though. All eyes in the room were on Allyndev, making him feel like he'd been stripped naked and sent to caper about before a room full of granthers.

Azhani came back to him. "And you, Prince Allyndev, you grew up in Y'Syr. You learned your letters and numbers, discovered a deep and abiding love for the earth and its growing things, lifted your eyes to the heavens and sought answers in the stars that spin above us. And yet no destiny came to collect you."

"I always thought I wasn't worthy." He reached for Devon and Syrelle's hands and found them there, waiting for him.

"You were always worthy," Azhani said gently. "You just needed time, my prince. Time to grow into your heritage, time to become the son of the man your mother loved with all her heart. Thodan the Peacemaker, were he alive today, would look upon you and know you as his, as I know you as his, as all who truly open their eyes to see will know you as Allyndev Thodan, rightful king of Y'Dan."

"Oh Goddess," he gasped. His stomach turned into a pit of knots.

"Breathe," Devon whispered as Syrelle shoved a flask into his hand.

"Drink," she hissed. "And don't you dare pass out."

Quickly, Allyndev fumbled it open and drank. Raw alcohol burned down his throat, making him cough at its harshness.

Azhani chuckled. "Look at him. This man, this brave, honest, honorable man whose name has been on the lips of every soldier to pass through these halls. How many of you have felt as though you've seen him before, though all know that this is Prince Allyndev's first visit to Y'Dan?"

"You have a strong point, Warleader," Valdyss Cathemon said quietly. "From the moment we met, I have felt a certain familiarity to him. I thought it was merely because he resembled Ylera superficially, but I am beginning to believe it is more than that."

Rising, High King Ysradan approached. Allyndev scrambled to meet him, bowing deeply as the man drew near. "Your Highness," he mumbled respectfully.

Ysradan circled him slowly, then stopped and grabbed his face, tilting it this way and that in the light. "By Astarus' blood." He blinked rapidly as tears spilled down his cheeks. "She's right. This boy is Thodan's—there's no mistaking this face." Suddenly, he grabbed hold of him, crushing Allyndev in his embrace.

The gruff affection undid him and he broke, collapsing into Ysradan's arms and sobbing. After all this time, he finally had a past. He had something more than shame and dishonor, something beyond the daily cruelties heaped upon him by men and women twice his age just for having rounded ears. He was not a bastard, he was not some pervert's get, he had a father! His existence wasn't through some tawdry act, but made of love and joy.

All his life, Allyn had tried to ignore those people and their horrible insinuations, but part of him had been unable to let go completely. Now, finally, he had answers.

"I have a father," he whispered brokenly. "I have a father!" It was a tragedy and a triumph and he hated it as much as he wanted it, for he had finally found the man he had sought among all the Y'Dani faces—and he was already gone.

He would never know Thodan and yet, he felt, from all those around him, that maybe he could finally begin to understand the man who had given him life.

"Ah, Gods," Ysradan said wistfully. "Would that you could see this lad, my old friend, and be proud!" He grasped Allyndev by the shoulders and squeezed roughly. "He would have loved you, boy, and don't you forget it!" Turning, he wrapped his arm around Allyn in a protective, paternal manner. "Fool me not, Queen of Y'Syr. I would hear your warrant on this boy's parentage."

Fear shot through Allyndev then, for with just a few words, his aunt could unmake this entire moment.

Regally, Lyssera inclined her head. "You have not been led astray, Ysradan. By my warrant, I name King Thodan of Y'Dan as father of Allyndev Kelani, prince of my house."

"Thank you, Your Majesty. Your candor is appreciated," Ysradan said solemnly. "We understand what you are surrendering to us, and though we grieve with you, we ask you to share our joy for this most perfect of solutions."

Lyssera smiled. "I am losing a nephew, my king, but gaining an ally. Sorrow will not cloud my eyes overlong, for my heart fills with gladness even now knowing that the land of my greatest friend will lie broken and kingless no longer."

"No, it shall not," Ysradan said. "You are to be thanked as well, Warleader, for without your willingness to face Y'Syr's wrath, we might never have known the truth."

"Truth, Your Highness, has a way of finding the light. I only gave it a push in the right direction," Azhani replied with a bow.

"Indeed." Ysradan led Allyndev to the empty throne that sat in the very center of the chamber. "So, lad, we come to you," he said as he stared Allyndev in the eye. "Your truth has marked us all. We recognize it, we hear it, and we know it. You are Allyndev Kelani-Thodan."

"Yes." Allyndev nerves faded as he took a deep breath.

"Y'Dan's throne sits empty and her people cry out for a king—will you take the crown and accept the legacy of your father?"

The walls of the council chamber were adorned with the portraits of the kings who had come before, images that ran through time all the way back to Ysradaran, the Firstlander prince who founded the kingdom. Allyndev stared at the one of Thodan and tried to imagine, just for a moment, what it would have been like to grow up here in Y'Dan, to have known his younger brother Arris, to have chased him through Ydannoch's halls, tussling as children do.

For a moment, it almost seemed as if he could hear an echo of boyish laughter. Swallowing heavily, he fought back a wave of sudden apprehension.

What right did he have to stand here, a foreigner, a halfbreed unwanted by his own people, and take what he hadn't earned? Who was he to think he could rule better than someone like Azhani, who at least had years and years of experience to guide her judgments? He was nothing—less than nothing, for he was just a tainted bastard who would never bring honor to anyone's house, much less earn the right to rule one.

The muscles in his legs started to bunch as if to propel him from the room at a dead run. He glanced around, and instinctively he looked first at Syrelle and Devon. Both were crying and smiling. The moment they seemed to understand he was focusing on them, both nodded vigorously.

Bolstered, he looked at Azhani, who saluted him, and then, finally, at Lyssera.

She smiled.

And then he asked himself, What do I want?

The answer, of course, was easy once he let himself choose. Kneeling before Ysradan, he said, "I will, my king. With all my heart, I will gladly wear Thodan's crown."

The chamber walls shook with the ferocity of the cheer that thundered through the room.

"Then rise, King Allyndev."

Slowly, Allyndev rose.

Azhani knelt and was quickly followed by Lord Cathemon. One by one, the nobles of the council, the observers, and even Syrelle and Devon went to their knees. Only Ysradan and Allyndev remained standing.

Ysradan smiled warmly and stepped aside.

As the day candle's wax burned into the midnight line, Allyndev Kelani-Thodan, king of Y'Dan, took his throne.

Ydannoch castle seemed overrun by an army of pages. With both a coronation and a wedding in the immediate future, every man, woman, and child with a drop of noble blood came racing to the city to pledge their allegiance and express their well-wishes. Though some had counseled against such a double ceremony, both the king-to-be and his advisers felt that returning Y'Dan to a sense of normalcy was more important than rousing all the pomp and circumstance that could be gleaned from such events.

Kyrian found it stunning that she and Vashyra were the most senior of the priests of the Twain in Y'Dan, but because of the previous regime's policies, it was up to them to perform many of the day to day-tasks that would normally be handled by the castle's clergy. When it came to crowning the king, they would share the honor. Vashyra happily claimed the right to sing the chants that would bind Kyrian and Azhani's lives in marriage. Kyrian was honored by this offer, but it meant more work fell on her shoulders as Vashyra took her task to heart and buried herself in the kingdom's libraries, seeking out every last possible Y'Dani custom associated with each ceremony. She even went so far as to query the ancient kitchen drudge whose only duty for the last twenty years had been to churn butter for the king's table, just to see if the granther's memory held any forgotten traditions the people of Y'Dan would be overjoyed to celebrate.

In a quiet ceremony presided over by Kyrian and one of Vashyra's acolytes, Queen Lyssera released Azhani from her duties as the Y'Syran warleader and installed Captain Evern as commander of the army. Because Allyndev had yet to be formally crowned, immediately following Lyssera's ceremony, Lord Valdyss Cathemon released her from the same service to Y'Dan, making Azhani the master of her own future for the first time since she was fourteen years old.

"Who will take your place?" Kyrian asked as Lord Cathemon ceremonially placed a tattered Y'Dani tabard in a cask that held those of Y'Dan's previous warleaders.

"I don't know," Azhani replied softly. "But may the Twain be merciful to them."

Allyndev, who had attended out of respect for his mentor, smiled. "I've been thinking of offering the position to Captain Niemeth, with the hope that he will take Jadrielle Enias as his second."

"It would be a wise choice," Azhani said with a sigh. "Niemeth was a good man caught in a bad situation. He did what he could to keep his people alive, and that's the mark of a true warleader. And young Jadrielle has enough bravery for ten of us."

Queen Lyssera chuckled. "I've heard it said she can out-shoot any of my rangers."

"She can," Azhani said proudly. "I saw her put an arrow in the eye of a leaping rimerbeast, drop her longbow and tear the throat out of another with a crossbow bolt."

"Twain's grace!" she gasped. "Careful, nephew, I may steal her for myself."

"You may try, Auntie," Allyndev replied cheerfully. "But I happen to know that Jadrielle's quite sweet on one of the noblewomen haunting my halls."

Lyssera sighed. "A queen can try," she said with a teasing wink. "Come, I believe there's a small feast to be had. Let's not disappoint the kitchen staff by refusing to eat it."

While the everyday chaos of castle life raged on around them, Kyrian and Azhani retreated to their rooms as often as possible, finding peace in each others arms and the company of the rapidly growing Zhadosh. Though he had not formed the traditional bond of hunter and companion with Kyrian, he seemed to prefer her company over Azhani's, much to her dismay.

"He hates me," Azhani grumbled as she nursed a fresh set of scratches on her hand.

Kyrian made a face. "He doesn't hate you, Azhi, he just plays rough. I keep telling you to put the gloves on."

"They make my hands sweat," Azhani replied sourly. "And itch."

Sighing heavily, Kyrian treated the scratches on Azhani's hand and then grabbed the gloves. "Let me see what I can do." She took them off to the castle stillroom, returning nearly a candlemark later. "Here," she said, tossing them at Azhani. "Try them now."

Dubiously, Azhani pulled one on, wiggled her fingers. "What'd you do?"

"Dusted them with arrowroot powder and the herbs soldiers sprinkle into their boots for long marches."

Azhani laughed. "Ah, my clever stardancer," she said fondly. "Thank you." She pulled her down onto her lap and kissed her languidly.

Grabbing Azhani's tunic, Kyrian began undoing the laces and growled, "Now will you remember to wear the damned gloves?"

"Yes, love," she whispered, inhaling sharply when Kyrian yanked open her shirt and began painting kisses over her collarbone. "Twain's grace, I love you!"

Kyrian smiled. "And I love you." She trailed her tongue farther down Azhani's chest, curling it over her nipple and then sucking lightly.

Forgotten, the gloves slid to the floor as Azhani buried her hands in Kyrian's hair and lost herself in their joyful loving.

Unlike Zhadosh with Azhani, Avisha had fully bonded with Devon. What this meant, he didn't learn until wandering the streets of Y'Dannyv one afternoon with just the cat as his company. He was searching for a crowning-gift for Allyndev, but had such a limited budget that everything he wanted cost far more than his purse could bear. Frustrated, he wasn't paying attention to the cobbles and caught one of his crutches in a crack, sending him crashing into the ground. His crutches flew across the street, and were so far away they might as well have flown to Y'Syr.

He was utterly alone but for Avisha.

"Twain curse it!" he snapped angrily, not relishing the task of dragging himself across the muck-encrusted street or liking the idea of making himself vulnerable to petty pickpockets by casting a spell to call them to his side. He might not have much coin in his pouch, but they wouldn't know that. They would simply assume that his power meant profit for their taking.

Avisha headbutted him, purring loudly as she licked his face.

"No, no, I'm not mad at you." He pressed his cheek against her flank. "I just can't walk anymore." Staring at his crutches, he sighed. I should charm them to return to my hand at a thought. It would be costly, in terms of magickal energy, but perhaps worth the effort.

She huffed softly, then pulled away from him and loped across the street. There she grabbed one of the crutches and dragged it back to him.

Incredulous, he took hold of it and was using it to lever himself back upright when she brought him the second crutch. "Twain's grace, Avisha," he said wonderingly as she rubbed her head against his knee and purred even louder. "How did you learn to do that?"

Later, when he spoke to some of the hunters, they explained that her breed was very intelligent—so much so that they could easily intuit the needs of their chosen partners. "You beautiful, incredible lady," he said as he petted her and gave her a fish to devour. "You're going to make my life so very interesting, aren't you?"

If Avisha had an answer for him, she was keeping it to herself. She did, however, eat every last morsel of fish.

The bonds between Allyndev, Devon, and Syrelle deepened and grew as strong as braided steel. That Syrelle would one day pledge to them seemed so clear that Ysradan and Dasia started treating both Allyn and Devon as sons, and Ysrallan welcomed having older brothers to tease and torment.

One night, as they enjoyed a private meal in Allyndev's quarters, Dasia raised her wine glass, gestured to the company gathered round the table, and said, "Perhaps we ought to simply marry them all next week. You two won't mind some company on the stage, will you, Azhani?"

Azhani laughed. "I wouldn't mind sharing the honors," she said as Kyrian grinned wickedly.

While Allyndev went pale and Devon blushed, Syrelle merely rolled her eyes. "Are you insane, Mother? Do you know how many people would never forgive us if we had a crowning, a warleader's wedding, and two royal marriages in one afternoon? Some of them would bankrupt themselves trying to send enough gifts!"

"Not to mention the fact that my very beloved mother would toss me over her knee and tan my backside like it was the cheapest of hides!" Padreg said in mock outrage. Beside him, Elisira laughed so hard she nearly fell off her chair.

"'Tis true that Lady Ketri is overly fond of the notion of attending her son's wedding," she said once she'd composed herself.

Dasia sighed. "I suppose I can bear to wait—but you best not take too long!"

"Yes, Mother," Syrelle said dryly. Allyndev breathed a sigh of relief, Devon downed the entire contents of his ale mug, and Padreg softly thanked her.

Azhani turned to Kyrian. "Looks like we're going to be all alone up there." She shook her head. "No, love. We'll have each other, always."

Grinning now, Azhani replied, "So we shall. A toast, then, to joyous hearts!"

"Aye!" Ysradan said as he lifted his glass. "And to a future of peace."

Azhani tried not to fidget. With the burdens of being warleader lifted from her shoulders, she suddenly felt as though every moment spent doing anything that required her to be stuck in one place too long was an irritation to be avoided. Today, however, she could not escape her final duties to Y'Dan. In truth, she was bursting with pride and seething with nerves, which would probably account for her inability to stay still. Not only was she seeing the crowning of a king, but joining herself in marriage to a woman who had done everything possible to turn her once-shadowed life into a world of life and joy.

Patience, she counseled herself, then looked over at Starseeker Vashyra, who was a bastion of absolute calm in the sea of chaos surrounding them.

Standing tall, her long, glorious hair swept back from her angular face, the bright star mark of her station seeming to glow from her forehead, Starseeker Vashyra lifted her arms to begin intoning a prayer. Her acolytes joined her, singing descant. The unearthly beauty of their voices blended in a song glorious enough to still even the most restless of crowds.

Azhani relaxed and let the prayer wash over her. *I come to you, O Blessed Twain, washed in light, my heart open to thy love. I give praise to you, O Blessed Twain, that all within my seeing and knowing shall have joy, prosperity, and peace.*

As the hymn came to an end, Starseeker Vashyra smiled. "Good morning, citizens of Y'Dan."

Her voice seemed soft at first, but Azhani knew she was using magick to make it heard all throughout the square. Even now, part of her wanted to disapprove, but she could not bring herself to speak out against the presence of magick, not when the Twain's gifts were why she was able to stand here on this day, on this morning, and enjoy what was to come.

It was chilly and wet, but still the city teemed with visitors—men, women, and children from all levels of society jammed the streets, packing in around the square to see their new king crowned. The very buildings themselves were platforms, with people crammed onto rooftops, shoved into windows and doorways, and a few enterprising souls hanging from lampposts so they could witness what Azhani knew was an historic event.

Even the docks were full, with ships rocking heavily in their moorings as their masts were hung not with sails, but people, all vying to see what was happening in the center of town.

"Today, we celebrate," Vashyra said with a smile. "You brave and noble people who have suffered much at the hands of darkness are now free to enjoy the light. But let us not forget those who were lost along the way, those whose sacrifices brought us to this beautiful morning. We honor them, cherish them, mark their names into our hearts and histories so that, in the fullness of time, they will be remembered not with sadness, but with pride. Let us guide them with our hearts and prayers, let us show them, one last time, the way home."

Azhani bowed her head and turned as Kyrian led the other stardancers up onto the stage, their voices raised in the pathsong. Azhani shivered, for the eerie harmony was bittersweet, but one that she needed to experience to forget all her cares and finally say the ultimate goodbye to friends and lovers alike.

Walk free, my beloved, she prayed, picturing Ylera's golden smile. And rest easy in the Fields. We'll see each other again.

As the pathsong came to a close, Vashyra began to read a litany of names. Starting with Ylera Kelani and continuing through every man, woman, and child who'd been lost to Ecarthus' terror. It was a harrowing list, one that left many eyes reddened from tears. Azhani wept with them, and it was cleansing.

The sun was setting by the time Vashyra, her voice long having gone dry, took a deep breath and said, "Finally, let us speak of Arris, son of Thodan, whose short life among us was wrought with so much pain. May he, and all those who went before, find peace in the arms of the Twain."

"Peace." The word seemed to live in every breath shared by the crowd. If prayer was the vehicle to send those lost souls home, then Azhani was sure they'd all found The Great Fields.

"We have mourned, Y'Dan. It is time now to celebrate, for you will be kingless no more." Turning, she gestured to Prince Allyndev, motioning for him to come stand before her. Slowly, he made his way across the stage. Clean-shaven now, his youthful face no longer seemed quite so innocent to Azhani, yet it lacked the careworn weariness she remembered from Thodan's wrinkled visage.

Cheers began to roll through the square. Nervously, Allyndev raised his hand to wave, but dropped it when Vashyra began to speak once more.

"Allyndev, prince of the House Kelani, you have been recognized as the son of Y'Dan's beloved King Thodan and rightful heir to the throne," she said. "Thus, by the grace of our beloved Twain, it is your duty to take up the burden of the crown to protect and defend the land from all who would rise against its people, to provide heirs to rule after you, and to guide the kingdom toward peace and prosperity. Do you accept this task, knowing full well that it is one that will consume the entirety of your life?"

"I do," he replied simply.

"Do you promise to promote wisdom, justice, and mercy in law, encourage fairness in commerce, and be swift in the defense of your allies?"

"I do."

"Then, Allyndev, prince of the House Kelani, I grant you the blessings of our beloved Twain and name you king of Y'Dan," Vashyra proclaimed, her voice seeming to thunder through the city. "Kneel, my king."

Allyndev knelt and Azhani thought she might burst with pride at how serene and confident he seemed.

An acolyte approached, bearing the crown upon a velvet pillow. Vashyra took it, holding it so that the setting sun set the jewels aflame. "Your humility is an honor for all to behold," she said as she placed the crown upon his brow. "Rise, King Allyndev. Rise, and greet your people."

King Allyndev stood, a broad, joyful grin making him seem again the innocent boy.

The Y'Dani herald stepped forward, blew a note on his trumpet, and intoned, "All hail King Allyndev Kelani-Thodan. Long live the king! Hip-hip-"

"Huzzah!"

Fists, capes, caps, swords, even children were hoisted into the air as the people saluted their new monarch. Caught up in the fever of their joy, Azhani held her blade high, cheering loudly, not bothering to hide her laughter when Allyndev gaped at the sight before them.

She was not surprised they loved him so readily. The city was full of people who'd come bearing tales of Allyndev's heroism as the army had trekked homeward. Though his face might have been overlooked, his name would have stayed with them as one who had brought peace and healing to a ravaged countryside.

The cheering went on for some time, but eventually Allyndev raised his arms and motioned for quiet. Slowly, the crowd calmed. Shaking his head bemusedly, he said, "My friends, my new countryman, I am—utterly overwhelmed and honored by your welcome. Thank you."

More cheers filled the square.

He smiled. "I also know you've stood for many long candlemarks, and for that I must bow to you, for you have honored so many with your perseverance." He bent toward the gathered throng. "But now I beg your patience and ask that you remain just a while longer, for there is yet one joyful duty to perform." He began to pace along the stage, making eye contact now and then and unknowingly mimicking the man who had sired him.

Azhani remembered Thodan in his heyday, when he could stand before the crowd for candlemarks, speaking passionately, holding them all in the grip of his voice and convictions. Allyndev, it seemed, had inherited some of that charisma.

"Today, as you know, is winter solstice, a day heavy with tradition. Marriage, my people, is our binding joy, for on this day we reach toward the future and ask the gods to bless us, to let us enjoy a union of hearts and bodies that will unite us in unending happiness." He gestured to Azhani then. "Today, I am entrusted with the greatest honor, one I cherish with all I am, for today, I will witness the joining of two of my friends, two women who have given so much of themselves to this great kingdom. I invite you, people of Y'Dan, to stand with me and celebrate while Azhani and Kyrian pledge their vows before the gods. What say you?"

"Huzzah!" The stage shook with the force of their voices.

Azhani had to swallow several times to get the lump in her throat to dissolve. That the people of Y'Dan loved Allyndev was a given, but that they had such depth of feeling for her was more gratifying than she could ever say.

With a boyish grin on his face, Allyndev made a hurrying motion. "Come, come, I can smell the feast from here. Let's finish this so we can go eat!"

Azhani and Kyrian both laughed and joined him in standing before Starseeker Vashyra. Torches started to appear, filling the square with softly flickering light. Azhani's armor, polished to within an inch of its life, caught and reflected their glow, making Kyrian's robes appear to shimmer with a life of their own.

"You look beautiful, my love," Azhani murmured as Kyrian took her hand.

"As do you." Kyrian smiled joyfully. "Though I don't envy Elisira the work that must have gone into all those braids," she added as she playfully tugged on one.

Azhani chuckled. "She had help," she said as Padreg and Elisira joined them.

"Good. I'd hate to have to treat her for a sprained wrist the morning after my wedding night." Kyrian winked at her.

Vashyra cleared her throat. "Are we ready, ladies?"

They both nodded and smiled at her.

Raising her voice, she took a breath, and began. "Long has it been said that the Twain do not spin the tumblers of Fate lightly. Thus, it is incumbent upon us all to cherish the lives we intersect as though we may never unlock that path of destiny again. Today, we have come to bear witness to a crossing that has resulted in a love so profound, one need not question its fortitude, for it has withstood the greatest test any could conceive. Together, you held fast against our most fearsome enemy and emerged victorious. Today, it is our joy and honor to bear witness to your reward. Azhani, daughter of Rhu'len, do you ask a boon of the gods?"

"Aye, Starseeker, I do, with all my heart," she said, turning to look into Kyrian's eyes. "Kyrian, from this moment forward, I crave only to walk the road of life at your side. I want to be your partner, your friend, and the sword at your back should the darkness send its minions across our path once more."

"Your request has been heard," Vashyra said calmly. "And do you, Kyrian, of Y'Len temple, ask a boon of the gods?"

In a clear and strong voice, Kyrian said, "Yes. I crave the right to greet every sun's rise and set at the side of my beloved, Azhani Rhu'len. I ask to be her partner, her friend, and the shield that guards her against the machinations of evil, should darkness again cross our path."

"Your words have not fallen upon deaf ears." Taking their joined hands, Vashyra bound them with a silver cord. "For the Twain have given me a vision. In it, I saw you, always together, a binding of hearts and purpose. This cord is a symbol of that union—as it entwines your hands, so too have your destinies become enmeshed. Azhani and Kyrian, the tapestry of your lives has begun to be woven and the future you face will be one shared. On your honor, do you swear to meet all that it brings with humility, love, and understanding?"

Smiling as she stared deep into Kyrian's eyes, Azhani said, "I do."

"Oh yes," Kyrian said joyfully, smiling so brightly the torches seemed almost unnecessary.

"Then it is my truest and most compelling honor to proclaim you wed!"

Myriad emotions tumbled through Azhani then, and she blinked back a sharp press of tears. This moment was hard won and filled with shapes and shards of regret and loss. Her past would always sing echoes in her heart, but it was only that—a past. With a happy sigh, she said, "Ah, my beloved Kyrian, you are such an incredible gift. Truly, your faith and strength are the keystones of my soul. Because of you, I live. But it is more than just existing, for each day I wake full with the knowledge that I am not alone, that with me stands the most amazing and perfect partner I could ever desire. For that, I will love you long after the stars in our heavens fade into darkness."

Kyrian blinked several times. "I should have brought a bucket for these tears." Louder, she said, "Azhani, my dearest love," and drew their bound hands up so she could kiss Azhani's knuckles lightly. "You are my best and greatest friend. You gave me trust when I had not earned it and taught me courage when I thought I had none. Because of you, I will never again fear the unknown. Now every day is one I greet with eagerness and joy, because you are there beside me. For that, I will love you long after all the mountains in all the lands have worn away to dust and sand."

Heartbeat upon heartbeat passed as Azhani looked into Kyrian's eyes. She could have stayed like that forever, but instead she lowered her head as Kyrian raised hers, and softly they kissed.

It was possible that the crowd was cheering, though Azhani could hear little beyond the thundering echo of her heart.

"Oh love," Kyrian whispered, sinking her hand into Azhani's hair and kissing her with absolute abandon.

Even through her closed eyes, Azhani knew by the incredible feeling of warmth and comfort that wafted through her that Astariu's Fire had crowned them, bathing them in a brief golden glow.

"Clearly, the gods have blessed your union," Vashyra said as they parted. Her hands were extended and on them rested two woven silver bracelets. "These tokens are the symbol of your oaths—let them remind you of this day and how love can make miracles."

Solemnly, Azhani took one of the bracelets and slid it onto Kyrian's wrist, then waited while Kyrian did the same for her.

With a gentle prod from Allyndev, the herald blew a brassy note on his horn and intoned, "To Azhani and Kyrian, may their love blossom anew with each passing day. Hip-hip-"

"Huzzah!"

Kyrian was enchanted by the jugglers. Three scantily clad, incredibly agile men and women moved around the feast hall, tossing forks, knives, turkey legs, even apples back and forth without breaking stride. It was an amazing feat, but better still was their silly, witty banter. And if she tired of humor, there was music at the other end of the hall in the form of a quartet of the finest minstrels she'd ever had the pleasure to hear perform. Put that together with the rich, delicious food, and she felt as though all her senses were being drowned in the happiness flowing through the city and the castle.

It had been this way for a week now, with no sign of diminishing. It wasn't that King Allyndev was being overly lavish—in fact, the opposite was true. The entertainment, the food, even the company was all provided by well-meaning visitors coming to pay their respects and swear oaths of allegiance to their new king.

Snow now coated the rooftops, and soon the lake would be completely frozen over. Just this morning, she had stood on the balcony of the rooms she shared with Azhani and watched as a ship was hoisted out of the water and moved to dry dock.

High King Ysradan would leave with tomorrow's tide. Tonight, he sat close to Allyndev, likely imparting as much wisdom as he could, but also likely taking the measure of one of the men his daughter so obviously loved.

"But surely, Your Highness, you can't think it a good idea for your daughter to be so welcoming of a commoner's advances," Lord Taserlane, a provincial noble from somewhere near the southern coast of Y'Dan, said to Queen Dasia.

Intrigued, Kyrian turned to listen to the queen's reply.

Dasia sighed. "My lord, Devon Imry is a man of irreproachable honor, a highly skilled mage, and from what Padreg of Y'Nor has said, also a fine warrior in his own right. Had my daughter not set her claim to him, I might have considered enjoying his obviously charming company myself!"

Lord Taserlane gaped at her.

"Do close your mouth, my lord. There are no flies to catch here," she said condescendingly, then moved to sit beside Kyrian, who was struggling not to laugh. Patting her shoulder lightly, Dasia said, "Please share your mirth, stardancer. Fools like that aren't satisfied until they've earned their keep in laughter."

Lord Taserlane very quickly found somewhere else to be.

"Your Majesty, may I say that you are more like your daughter than I expected?" Kyrian said delicately.

She chuckled. "Of course you may—and I hope you will call me Dasia, especially given how very kind you've been these last weeks. I do not know that I'd have recovered as quickly as I have without your gentle care."

"It was my honor, my..." Kyrian stopped herself. "Dasia."

"There you go!" Dasia said cheerfully. "Now, where is your blushing bride?"

"Chasing our kitten out of a tree, likely. Or perhaps showing the new warleader the ropes—either seems likely, since Niemeth and Zhadosh have taken an instant dislike to each other," Kyrian replied with a rueful sigh.

"Pity. Niemeth seemed like such a good man, too. I hope Avisha is a kinder judge of character?" Dasia glanced over to where Devon sat with his constant companion.

Kyrian grinned. "From what I hear tell, Niemeth has taken to carrying a pocket full of cooked chicken just for her."

"Ah, a wise man, then," she said, taking a mug of ale from a passing server.

Suddenly, the courtyard door banged open, startling everyone. Prince Ysrallan stumbled in and fell over, covering his face to protect it from the hail of snowballs being tossed his way. Most of the snowballs missed the boy and instead struck several nobles that were in their paths—including Padreg, Elisira, and High King Ysradan.

"Papa!" Ysrallan shouted as another volley of snow flew inside. "Help!"

Ysradan and Dasia traded glances, then laughed and raced outside, bringing half the court with them. Soon, the entire courtyard was filled with laughing men and women all eagerly tossing snowballs at each other.

Y'Dannyv was quiet. Snow fell in thick clouds, blanketing the city and keeping its people mostly indoors. The lake had frozen over, but not before King Ysradan returned to Y'Mar and Queen Lyssera left for Y'Syr. Padreg and Elisira stayed a day longer, but then they too took a ship home, returning to Padreg's beloved Y'Noran plains. Azhani and Kyrian stayed.

In public, Azhani claimed it was because she disliked traveling in winter, but the truth was simply that King Allyndev and Warleader Niemeth needed her. She was the voice of simplicity and reason when the members of the High Council demanded insane defenses be built in the wake of the Ecarthan troubles. For Niemeth, she was a mentor, since she knew many of the secrets to which he had rarely been privy.

It was not an easy time, but neither was it filled with true trouble. Mostly, Azhani found it to be a series of headaches that she allowed Kyrian to soothe in the privacy of their chambers.

The new year came and went, winter ravaged the land, and people began to relax as, with each passing day, neither rimerbeasts nor Ecarthan priests were discovered. There was peace at last.

EPILOGUE

Spring's promise kissed the night air. Clouds heavy with rain instead of snow lowered over the horizon and Kyrian watched as a faint crackle of lightning danced between them. Looking to the southeast, she wondered what living in the plains would be like. Soon she and Azhani would pack their things and take ship to Y'Nor, where Azhani would choose among Padreg's stallions to breed Kushyra. That they would stay on the plains until the promised foals were delivered was a forgone conclusion.

Kyrian had never been to Y'Nor. It would be new and she was looking forward to it, but she couldn't quite bring herself to feel the joy Azhani felt. It seemed Azhani could barely wait for the lake to thaw before escaping Y'Dannyv.

That's what it was, Kyrian knew—escape. This city, this kingdom, had burned scars into her wife's heart that would never properly heal. Kyrian herself felt the weight of some of those scars tighten around her chest. So many had died, all for one man's ill-fated vengeance. Kasyrin Darkchilde had brought misery to thousands, but tonight Kyrian could think only of poor, drug-maddened Arris Thodan, and wonder if his spirit had truly, as he'd cried at the last, been consumed by the demon Ecarthus.

It was a fate she prayed he'd avoided.

Thunder rumbled. A cold, icy wind caressed her naked body. She shivered.

Deep thoughts make poor company. You should be in bed with your wife, not standing out here in the rain.

She didn't move.

Instead, she remained, buffeted by wind and rain, watching as the storm took the city. Was it a message? A sign that somewhere, a young man's soul was rent and torn by a mad demon banished forever from this world? Or was it merely her overactive imagination painting bogeymen where raindrops fell?

"Still looking for owldragons, my love?" Azhani murmured as she slid her arms around Kyrian's waist and pressed her very warm body against her. "They don't fly this far south." Gently, she cupped her breasts and stroked her nipples as she dusted kisses along the side of her throat.

Inhaling sharply, Kyrian chuckled and leaned back against her. "No. I don't need to find owldragons anymore, Azhani. You've already shown me they exist."

"Mm, so I have," she said distractedly.

"I was just thinking about the past…and the future." Kyrian closed her eyes as Azhani's touch grew more insistent.

"And?"

"And I think you need to take me back to bed, love," she said, deciding that it was only a storm and that portents, demons, and lost kings were a concern for sages, not stardancers who were deliriously happy with the life they had.

"Gladly." Azhani scooped her up and carried her to the bed.

The sheets were still warm, and Kyrian smiled as she reached for Azhani. Imperiously, she commanded, "Love me," and pulled her atop her.

"Every day for the rest of my hopefully very long life," Azhani said eagerly, kissing her with absolute abandon.

"*Our* very long lives," Kyrian said when they parted. "We're doing this together, Azhani."

"Of course, love. Just like always." Azhani laughed as Kyrian flipped her onto her back. "Just like always."

ABOUT SHAYLYNN ROSE

Shaylynn Rose has never wanted to do anything other than create. From an early age, she was writing stories and poems, painting pictures, making jewelry, and exercising her imagination in every way she could. A fascination with mythology grew into a full-on love for fantasy and science fiction, and through this, she discovered the world of role-playing games, where she developed and honed her storytelling chops. Eventually these loves merged when she began writing the first of many stories, most of which aren't fit to print but nonetheless allowed her to stretch her muscles little by little.

The late nineties brought the advent of television shows such as Xena: Warrior Princess and Buffy the Vampire Slayer, and through these mediums, she discovered the world of fan fiction, beta readers, and feedback. This was, for her, a perfect storm for nurturing her creativity. Through the Xena fandom, she met Ciegra, who pushed and shoved and generally encouraged her to stretch beyond the comfort zone of fan fiction and back to the place where stories first began—the world of original tales.

With Ciegra (and, once the secret was out, her family and numerous other friends) constantly cheering her on, Shaylynn found the courage to write and eventually publish her first novel, *Banshee's Honor*. Sadly, Ciegra passed away in 2011, but her spirit lives on, always pushing Shaylynn to keep writing, to share the characters that live inside her head, and to stay away from writing laundry lists instead of stories.

OTHER BOOKS FROM YLVA PUBLISHING

www.ylva-publishing.com

BANSHEE'S HONOR

Shaylynn Rose

ISBN: 978-3-95533-103-0
Length: 379 pages (153,000 words)

Warleader—in Y'Dan, this is a title of pride, of honor, and of joy. Oathbreaker—a word branded only on those whose crimes are so heinous, all must know of their crime. Both of these names have been given to Azhani Rhu'len. Only one of them is right.

CAGED BIRD RISING
A GRIM TALE OF WOMEN, WOLVES, AND OTHER BEASTS

Nino Delia

ISBN: 978-3-95533-319-5
Length: 237 pages (62,000 words)

In a world dominated by men, it should be Robyn's greatest fortune that the handsome Hunter Wolfmounter sees her as the perfect fertile wife. But an encounter with a mysterious wolf changes her worldview. She flees into the woods, where she meets Gwen, who helps her to change—into one of the independent beasts she has always been warned about. But the men are hot on her trail.

SIGIL FIRE

Erzabet Bishop

ISBN: 978-3-95533-206-8
Length: 131 pages (30,000 words)

Sonia is a succubus with one goal: stay off Hell's radar. But when succubi start to die she's drawn into battle between good and evil.

Fae is a blood witch turned vampire, running a tattoo parlor and trading her craft for blood. She notices that something isn't right on the streets of her city. The denizens of Hell are restless.

The killer has a target in sight, and Sonia might not survive.

TRUE NATURE

Jae

ISBN: 978-3-95533-034-7
Length: 480 pages (141,000 words)

Successful CEO Rue Harding has no idea that her adoptive son, Danny, is a shape-shifter or that his new tutor, wolf-shifter Kelsey, has been sent to get him away from her.

But when Danny runs away and gets lost in New York City, Kelsey and Rue have to work together to find him before his first transformation sets in and reveals the shape-shifter's secret existence to the world.

COMING FROM YLVA PUBLISHING

www.ylva-publishing.com

HAVE A BITE

R.G. Emanuelle

Delphine Bouchard is a celebrity chef who also happens to be a vampire. A food critic with a grudge? Sabotage in her restaurant, and a vampire hunter? Cryptic messages, human corpses, and a witch coven that's pressuring her to keep her head down? It's all in a day's work for Del, who must protect her business, her loved ones, and herself, before she becomes the hunter's next victim.

CROSSING BRIDGES

Emma Weimann

As a Guardian, Tallulah has devoted her life to protecting her hometown, Edinburgh, and its inhabitants, both living and dead, against ill-natured and dangerous supernatural beings.

When Erin, a human tourist, visits Edinburgh, she makes Tallulah more nervous than the poltergeist on Greyfriars Kirkyard—and not only because Erin seems to be the sidekick of a dark witch who has her own agenda.

While Tallulah works to thwart the dark witch's sinister plan for Edinburgh, she can't help wondering about the mysterious Erin. Is she friend or foe?

Banshee's Vengeance
© 2015 by Shaylynn Rose

ISBN: 978-3-95533-475-8

Also available as e-book.

Published by Ylva Publishing, legal entity of Ylva Verlag, e.Kfr.

Ylva Verlag, e.Kfr.
Owner: Astrid Ohletz
Am Kirschgarten 2
65830 Kriftel
Germany

www.ylva-publishing.com

The first edition was published under the title *Banshee's Honor* (pages 186 ff.) by P.D. Publishing, Inc. (USA, North Carolina) in 2003.

No part of this book may be reproduced, scanned, or distributed in any printed or electronic form without permission. Please do not participate in or encourage piracy of copyrighted materials in violation of the author's rights. Thank you for respecting the hard work of this author.

This is a work of fiction. Names, characters, places, and incidents either are a product of the author's imagination or are used fictitiously, and any resemblance to locales, events, business establishments, or actual persons—living or dead—is entirely coincidental.

Credits
Edited by Therese Arkenberg
Cover Design by Kaitlyn Connolly
Printlayout by Streetlight Graphics

Lightning Source UK Ltd.
Milton Keynes UK
UKOW02f0423121215

264602UK00001B/40/P